THE REPUBLIC
OF WINE

THE REPUBLIC

OF WINE

A NOVEL

Mo Yan

Translated from the Chinese
by Howard Goldblatt

Arcade Publishing • New York

FIRST NORTH AMERICAN EDITION

Originally published under the title *Jiu Guo* in 1992 by the Hung-fan Book Company in Taiwan

The characters and events in this book are fictitious. Any similarity to real persons, living or dead, is coincidental and not intended by the author.

ISBN 1-55970-531-0

Published in the United States by Arcade Publishing, Inc., New York
Distributed by Time Warner Trade Publishing

Visit our Web site at www.arcadepub.com

10 9 8 7 6 5 4 3 2 1

BP

PRINTED IN THE UNITED STATES OF AMERICA

Translator's Note

For the Chinese reader, *The Republic of Wine* packs quite a wallop, much like the colorless liquors distilled in Mo Yan's home province of Shandong and elsewhere in China, Maotai being the most famous. Few contemporary works have exposed and satirized the political structure of post-Mao China, or the enduring obsession of the Chinese about food, with the wit and venom of this explosive novel; none even approaches its structural inventiveness. As with many of Mo Yan's novels, *The Republic of Wine* was considered extremely subversive, and could be published in China only after a Taiwanese edition appeared in 1992. Subsequently included in his multi-volume collected works under the new title *Republic of Drunks* (*Mingding guo*), it continues to thrill some and horrify others.

In the book, letter-writer Mo Yan tells Li Yidou that he has 'long wanted to write a novel on liquor.' Well, here it is, under the terse but revealing title of *Jiu guo*, the literal meaning of which is 'country of alcohol.' (The generic term *jiu* refers to all alcoholic beverages, and must be expanded adjectivally to indicate type.) Most of what is guzzled in *The Republic of Wine* is actually 120-proof and stronger liquor made of sorghum or other grains.

Beyond the characters' preoccupation with food, drink, and sex, the satiric tone and fantastic occurrences, and the imaginative narrative framework, Mo Yan has filled his novel with puns, a variety of stylistic prose, allusions – classical and modern, political and literary, elegant and scatological – and many Shandong localisms. It would serve little purpose to explicate them here, particularly since a non-Chinese reader could not conceivably 'get' them all. It does not take cultural understanding to realize that a crack investigator would be unlikely to go anywhere in a truck, Liberation or not, although few readers could be expected to know the answer to the lady trucker's question, 'Know why this road's in such terrible shape?' (the locals make sure it stays that way so they can pick up lumps of coal that are dislodged from trucks leaving the mine).

I have, as far as possible, remained faithful to Mo Yan's original, not entirely consistent, text. I can only hope that the enjoyment and understanding gained from this translation outstrip the losses.

So, after this brief hors-d'oeuvre: *Bon appetit!* Cheers!

THE REPUBLIC
OF WINE

Chapter One

I

Special Investigator Ding Gou'er of the Higher Procuratorate climbed aboard a Liberation truck and set out for the Mount Luo Coal Mine to undertake a special investigation. He was thinking so hard as he rode along that his head swelled until the size 58 brown duck-billed cap, which was normally quite roomy, seemed to clamp down on his skull. He was not a happy man as he took off the cap, examined the watery beads on the sweatband, and smelled the greasy odor. It was an unfamiliar odor. Slightly nauseating. He reached up to pinch his throat.

The truck slowed as the potholes grew more menacing and made the creaky springs complain eerily. He kept banging his head on the underside of the cab roof. The driver cursed the road, and the people on it; such gutter language spewing from the mouth of a young, and rather pretty, woman created a darkly humorous scene. He couldn't keep from sneaking furtive looks at her. A pink undershirt poking up above the collar of her blue denim work shirt guarded her fair neck; she had dark eyes with an emerald tinge, and hair that was very short, very coarse, very black, and very glossy. Her white-gloved hands strangled the steering wheel as the truck rocked from side to side to avoid the potholes. When she lurched left, her mouth twisted to the left; when she veered right, it twisted to the right. And while her mouth was twisting this way and that, sweat oozed from her crinkled nose. Her narrow forehead and solid chin told him that she was or had been married – a woman to whom sex was no stranger. Someone he wouldn't mind getting to know. For a forty-eight-year-old investigator, and an old hand at that, such feelings were ludicrous at the very least. He shook his large head.

Road conditions continued to deteriorate, and they slowed to a caterpillar crawl, finally settling in behind a column of stationary trucks. She took her foot off the gas, turned off the ignition, removed her gloves, and thumped the steering wheel. She gave him an unfriendly look.

'Good thing there's no kid in my belly,' she remarked.

He froze for a moment, then said, somewhat ingratiatingly:

'If there had been, you'd have shaken it loose by now.'

'I wouldn't let that happen, not at two thousand per,' she replied solemnly.

That said, she stared at him with what might be characterized as a provocative look in her eyes; she appeared to be waiting for a response. Scandalized by this brief and inelegant exchange, Ding Gou'er felt like a budding potato that had rolled into her basket. As the forbidden mysteries of sex were suddenly revealed in her ambiguous and suggestive remark, the distance between them all but vanished. With feelings of annoyance and uncertainty creeping into his heart, he kept a watchful eye on her. Her mouth twisted again, making him very uncomfortable, and he now sensed that she was a guarded, evasive woman, foolish and shallow, certainly no one with whom he had to mince his words.

'So, are you pregnant?' he blurted out.

Now that he'd dispensed with conventional small talk, the question hung out there like half-cooked food. But she forced it down her gullet and said almost brazenly:

'I've got a problem, what they call alkaline soil.'

Your tasks may be important, but no investigator worthy of the name would allow those tasks to be in conflict with women. In fact, women are a part of one's tasks.

Reminded of those lines, which were so popular among his colleagues, he felt a lustful thought begin to gnaw at his heart like an insect. Ding Gou'er took a flask from his pocket, removed the plastic stopper, and helped himself to a big drink. Then he handed the flask to the lady trucker.

'I'm an agronomist who specializes in soil improvement.'

The lady trucker smacked the horn with the palm of her hand, but was able to coax only a weak, gentle bleat out of it. The driver of the Yellow River big-rig in front of them jumped out of his cab

2

and stared daggers at her from the roadside. Ding Gou'er could feel the anger radiating from the man's eyes through the gleaming surface of his mirror-lens sunglasses. She snatched the flask out of his hand, sniffed the mouth as if measuring the quality of the contents, then – down the hatch, every last drop. Ding Gou'er was about to compliment her on her capacity for drink, but quickly changed his mind. Praising someone for drinking skills in a place called Liquorland sounded pretty lame, so he swallowed the words. As he wiped his mouth, he stared openly at her thick, moistened lips and, casting decorum to the wind, said:

'I want to kiss you.'

The lady trucker's face reddened. In a shrill, brassy voice, she roared back:

'I want to fucking kiss you!'

Left speechless by the response, Ding Gou'er scanned the area around the truck. The driver of the Yellow River big-rig had already climbed back into his cab. A long, snaking line of vehicles stretched ahead, while a canopied truck and a donkey cart had fallen in behind them. The donkey's broad forehead was decorated with a red tassel. Squat, misshapen trees and weed-infested ditches with an occasional wildflower lined the roadside. Powdery black smudges disfigured the leaves and weeds. Beyond the ditches lay autumnal dry fields, their withered yellow and gray stalks standing ethereally in the shifting winds, looking neither cheery nor sad. It was already mid-morning. A mountain of waste rock pierced the sky ahead, releasing clouds of yellow smoke. A windlass standing at the mine entrance turned leisurely. He could only see part of it; the Yellow River big-rig blocked out the bottom half.

She kept shouting the same sentence over and over, the one that had given Ding Gou'er such a fright, but she didn't make a move. So Ding Gou'er reached over to touch her breast with the tip of his finger. Without warning she crushed up against him, cupped his chin in the palm of her icy hand, and covered his mouth with hers. Her lips felt cold and mushy, not resilient; freakish, like puffs of cotton waste. That was a turn-off, it killed his desire, and he pushed her away. But, like a plucky fighting cock, she sprang back at him hard, catching him off guard and making resistance all but impossible. He was forced to deal with her the same way he dealt with criminals, try to make her behave.

They sat in the cab gasping for breath, the investigator pinning her arms down to keep her from putting up any resistance. She kept trying to force herself on him, her body twisting like a coil, her back arched like a leaf spring; she grunted from the exertion like an ox caught by the horns. She looked so fetching, Ding Gou'er couldn't help but laugh.

'What are you laughing at?' she demanded.

Ding Gou'er let go of her wrists and removed a business card from his pocket.

'I'll be on my way, young lady. If you miss me, you can find me at this address. Mum's the word.'

She sized him up, studied the card for a moment, then his face, with the keen intensity of a border guard examining a visitor's passport.

Ding Gou'er reached out and flicked the lady trucker's nose with his finger, then tucked his briefcase under his arm and opened the passenger door. 'So long, girl,' he said. 'Remember, I've got the right fertilizer for alkaline soil.' When he was halfway out the door, she grabbed his shirttail.

The look of timidity mixed with curiosity in her eyes now convinced him that she was probably quite young, never married, and unspoiled. Lovable and pitiable at the same time. He rubbed the back of her hand and said with genuine feeling: 'Girl, you can call me uncle.'

'You liar,' she said. 'You told me you worked at a vehicle control station.'

'What's the difference?' He laughed.

'You're a spy!'

'You might say so.'

'If I'd known that, I wouldn't have given you a ride.'

Ding Gou'er took out a pack of cigarettes and tossed it into her lap. 'Temper, temper.'

She flung his liquor flask into the roadside ditch. 'Nobody drinks out of something that tiny,' she remarked.

Ding Gou'er jumped out of the cab, slammed the door shut, and walked off down the road. He heard the lady trucker yell after him:

4

'Hey, spy! Know why this road's in such terrible shape?'

Ding Gou'er turned to see her hanging out the driver's window; he smiled but didn't answer.

The image of the lady trucker's face stuck in the investigator's head for a moment like dried hops, frothing briefly before vanishing like the foam on a glass of beer. The narrow road twisted and turned like an intestinal tract. Trucks, tractors, horse carts, ox carts . . . vehicles of every shape and hue, like a column of bizarre beasts, each linked by the tail of the one in front and all jammed up together. The engines had been turned off in some, others were still idling. Pale blue smoke puffed skyward from the tractors' tin exhaust stacks; the smell of unburned gasoline and diesel oil merged with the stink of ox and horse and donkey breath to form a foul, free-floating miasma. At times he brushed against the vehicles as he shouldered his way past; at other times he had to lean against the squat, misshapen roadside trees. Just about all the drivers were in their cabs drinking. Isn't there a law against drinking and driving? But these drivers were obviously drinking, so the law must not exist, at least not here. The next time he looked up, he could see two-thirds of the towering iron frame of the windlass at the mouth of the coal mine.

A silver gray steel cable turned noisily on the windlass. In the sunlight, the iron frame was a deep, dark red, either because it was painted or maybe just rusty. A dirty color, a mother-fucking dirty dark red. The huge revolving drum was black, the steel cable turning on it gave off a muted yet terrifying glint. As his eyes took in the colors and radiant light, his ears were assailed by the creaking of the windlass, the moans of the cable, and the dull thuds of underground explosions.

An oval clearing bordered by pagoda-shaped pine trees fronted the mine. It was crowded with vehicles waiting to haul away the coal. A mud-spattered donkey had thrust its mouth up into the needles of a pine tree, either for a snack or to work on an itch. A gang of grubby, soot-covered men in tattered clothes, scarves tied around their heads and hemp ropes cinching up their waists, had squeezed into one of the horse carts, and as the horse ate from its feedbag, they drank from a large purple bottle, passing it around with great enjoyment. Ding Gou'er was not much of a drinker, but he liked to drink, and he could tell the good stuff from the bad. The pungent smell in the air made it obvious that the purple bottle was filled with poor-quality liquor, and from the appearance of the men drinking it, he guessed that they were farmers from the Liquorland countryside.

As he passed in front of the horse, one of the farmers shouted hoarsely, 'Hey, comrade, what time does that watch of yours say?'

Ding raised his arm, glanced down, and told the fellow what he wanted to know. The farmer, his eyes bloodshot, looked mean and pretty scary. Ding's heart skipped a beat, he quickened his pace.

From behind him, the farmer cursed, 'Tell that bunch of free-loading pigs to open up.'

Something in the young farmer's unhappy, ill-intentioned shout made Ding Gou'er squirm, even though there was no denying it was a reasonable demand. Already a quarter past ten, and the iron gate was still secured with a big, black, tortoise shell of a cast-iron padlock. The faded red letters of five words – Safety First Celebrate May Day – on round steel plates had been welded to the fence. Early autumn sunlight, beautiful and brilliant, baked the area and made everything shine as if new. A gray-brick wall, which stood head high, followed the rises and hollows of the ground, lending it the curves of an elongated dragon. A small secondary gate was latched but unlocked; a wolfish brown dog sprawled lazily, a dragonfly circling round its head.

Ding Gou'er pushed on the small gate, bringing the dog quickly to its feet. Its damp, sweaty nose was but a fraction of an inch from the back of his hand. In fact, it probably touched his hand, since he felt a coolness that reminded him of a purple cuttlefish or a lychee nut. Barking nervously, the dog bounded off, seeking refuge in the shade of the gate house, among some indigo bushes. There the barking grew frenzied.

He raised the latch, pushed open the gate, and stood there for a moment, leaning against the cold metal as he cast a puzzled look at the dog. Then he looked down at his thin, bony hand, with its dark jutting veins, which carried blood that was slightly diluted with the alcohol he had consumed. There were no sparks, no tricks, so what made you run off when I touched you?

A basinful of scalding bath water fanned out in the air above him. A multi-hued waterfall like a rainbow with a dying arc. Soapsuds and sunlight. Hope. A minute after the water ran down his neck, he felt cool all over. A moment later his eyes began to burn and a salty yet sweet taste filled his mouth like a faceful of grime, the non-corporeal essence of wrinkles. For the moment, the special investigator forgot all about the girl in the cab. Forgot the lips like cotton waste. Some time later, he would tense visibly at the sight of a woman holding his business card, sort of like gazing at mountain scenery through a heavy mist. Son of a bitch!

'Lived long enough, you son of a bitch?' The gatekeeper, basin in hand, stood there cursing and kicking the ground. Ding Gou'er quickly realized that he was the target of the curses. After shaking some of the water out of his hair and mopping off his neck, he spit out a gob of saliva, blinked several times, and tried to focus on the gatekeeper's face. He saw a pair of coal-black, shady-looking, dull eyes of different sizes, plus a bulbous nose, bright red like a hawthorn, and a set of obstinate teeth behind dark, discolored lips. Hot flashes wove in and out of his brain, slithering through its runnels. Flames of anger rose in him, as if an internal match had been struck. White-hot embers singed his brain, like cinders in an oven, like lightning bolts. His skull was transparent; waves of courage crashed onto the beach of his chest.

The gatekeeper's black hair, coarse as a dog's bristly fur, stood up straight. No doubt about it, the sight of Ding Gou'er had scared the living hell out of him. Ding Gou'er could see the man's nose hairs, arching upward like swallowtails. An evil, black swallow must be hiding in his head, where it has built a nest, laid its eggs, and raised its hatchlings. Taking aim at the swallow, he pulled the trigger. Pulled the trigger. The trigger.

Pow – pow – pow –!

Three crisp gunshots shattered the stillness at the gate to the Mount Luo Coal Mine, silenced the big brown dog, and snagged the attention of the farmers. Drivers jumped out of their cabs, needles pricked the donkey's lips; a moment of frozen indecision, then everyone swarmed to the spot. At ten thirty-five in the morning, the Mount Luo Coal Mine gatekeeper crumpled to the ground before the sounds had even died out. He lay there twitching, holding his head in his hands.

Ding Gou'er, chalky white pistol in his hand, a smile on his lips, stood ramrod stiff, sort of like a pagoda pine. Wisps of green smoke from the muzzle of his pistol dissipated after rising above his head.

People crowded round the metal fence, dumbstruck. Time stood still, until someone shouted shrilly:

'Help, murder –! Old Lü the gatekeeper's been shot dead!'

Ding Gou'er. Pagoda pine. Dark green, nearly black.

'The old dog was an evil bastard.'

'See if you can sell him to the Gourmet Section of the Culinary Academy.'

'The old dog's too tough.'

'The Gourmet Section only wants tender little boys, not stale goods like him.'

'Then take him to the zoo to feed to the wolves.'

Ding Gou'er flipped the pistol in the air, where it spun in the sunlight like a silvery mirror. He caught it in his hand and showed it to the people crowding round the gate. It was a splendid little weapon, with the exquisite lines of a fine revolver. He laughed.

'Friends,' he said, 'don't be alarmed. It's a toy gun, it isn't real.'

He pushed the release button and the barrel flipped open; he took out a dark red plastic disk and showed it around. A little paper exploding cap lay between each hole in the disk. 'When you pull the trigger,' he said, 'the disk rotates, the hammer hits the cap, and – *pow*! It's a toy, good enough to be used as a stage prop, but something you can buy at any department store.' He reinserted the disk, snapped the barrel back into place, and pulled the trigger.

Pow –!

'Like so,' he said, a salesman making his pitch. 'If you still don't believe me, look here.' He aimed the pistol at his own sleeve and pulled the trigger.

Pow –!

'It's the traitor Wang Lianju!' shouted a driver who'd seen the revolutionary opera *The Red Lantern*.

'It's not a real gun.' Ding Gou'er lifted his arm to show them.

'You see, if it had been real, my arm would have a hole in it, wouldn't it?' His sleeve had a round charred spot, from which the redolent odor of gunpowder rose into the sunlight.

Ding Gou'er stuffed the pistol back into his pocket, walked up, and kicked the gatekeeper who lay on the ground.

'Get up, you old fake,' he said. 'You can stop acting now.'

The gatekeeper climbed to his feet, still holding his head in his hands. His complexion was sallow, the color of a fine year-end cake.

'I just wanted to scare you,' he said, 'not waste a real bullet on you. You can stop hiding behind that dog of yours. It's after ten o'clock, long past the time you should have opened the gate.'

The gatekeeper lowered his hands and examined them. Then, not sure what to believe, rubbed his head all over and looked at his hands again. No blood. Like a man snatched from the jaws of death, he sighed audibly and, still badly shaken, asked:

'What, what do you want?'

With a treacherous little laugh, Ding Gou'er said:

'I'm the new Mine Director, sent here by municipal authorities.'

The gatekeeper ran over to the gate house and returned with a glistening yellow key, with which he quickly, and noisily, opened the gate. The mob broke for their vehicles, and in no time the clearing rocked with the sound of engines turning over.

A tidal wave of trucks and carts moved slowly, inexorably toward the now open gate, bumping and clanging into each other as they squeezed through. The investigator jumped out of the way, and as he stood there observing the passage of this hideous insect, with its countless twisting, shifting sections, he experienced a strange and powerful rage. The birth of that rage was followed by spasms down around his anus, where irritated blood vessels began to leap painfully, and he knew he was in for a hemorrhoid attack. This time the investigation would go forward, hemorrhoids or no, just like the old days. That thought took the edge off his rage, lessened it considerably, in fact. There's no avoiding the inevitable. Not mass confusion, and not hemorrhoids. Only the sacred key to a riddle is eternal. But what was the key this time?

The gatekeeper's face was scrunched up into a ludicrous, unnatural smile. He bowed and he scraped. 'Won't our new leader follow

9

me into the reception room?' Prepared to go with the flow – that was how he lived his life – he followed the man inside.

It was a large, spacious room with a bed under a black quilt. Plus a couple of vacuum bottles. And a great big stove. A pile of coal, each piece as big as a dog's head. On the wall hung a laughing, pink-skinned, naked toddler with a longevity peach in his hands – a new year's scroll – his darling little pecker poking up like a pink, wriggly silkworm chrysalis. The whole thing was incredibly lifelike. Ding Gou'er's heart skipped a beat, his hemorrhoids twitched painfully.

The room was unbearably hot and stuffy from a fire roaring in the stove. The bottom half of the chimney and the surface of the stove had turned bright red from the furious heat. Hot air swirled around the room, making dusty cobwebs in the corners dance. Suddenly he itched all over, his nose ached dreadfully.

The gatekeeper watched his face with smarmy attentiveness.

'Cold, Director?'

'Freezing!' he replied indignantly.

'No problem, no problem, I'll just add some coal . . .' Muttering anxiously, the gatekeeper reached under the bed and took out a sharp hatchet with a date-red handle. The investigator's hand flew instinctively to his hip as he watched the man shamble over to the coal bin, hunker down, and pick up a chunk of shiny black coal the size and shape of a pillow; steadying it with one hand, he raised the hatchet over his head and – *crack* – the coal broke into two pieces of roughly equal size, shining like quicksilver. *Crack crack crack crack crack* – the pieces kept getting smaller, forming a little pile. He opened the grate and released white-hot flames at least a foot into the air – *whoosh*. The investigator was sweating from head to toe, but the gatekeeper kept feeding coal into the stove. And kept apologizing: 'It'll warm up any minute. The coal here is too soft, burns too fast, got to keep putting in more.'

Ding Gou'er undid his collar button and mopped his sweaty brow with his cap. 'Why do you have a fire in the stove in September?'

'It's cold, Director, cold . . .' The gatekeeper was shivering. 'Cold . . . plenty of coal, a whole mountain of the stuff . . .'

The gatekeeper had a dried-out face, like an overcooked bun.

Deciding he'd frightened the man enough, Ding Gou'er confessed that he was not the new Director, and that the man was free to heat the place up as much as he liked, since Ding Gou'er had work to do. The toddler on the wall was laughing, incredibly lifelike. He squinted to get a better look at the darling little boy. Gripping the hatchet firmly in his hand, the gatekeeper said, 'You impersonated the Mine Director and assaulted me with your pistol. Come along, I'm taking you to the Security Section.' Ding Gou'er smiled and asked, 'What would you have done if I had been the new Director?' The gatekeeper slid the hatchet back under the bed and took out a liquor bottle. After removing the cork with his teeth, he took a hefty swig and handed the bottle to Ding Gou'er. A yellow slice of ginseng hung suspended in the liquid, along with seven black scorpions, fangs bared, claws poised. He shook the bottle, and the scorpions swam in the ginseng-enhanced liquid. A strange odor emanated from the bottle. Ding Gou'er brushed the mouth of the bottle with his lips then handed it back to the gatekeeper.

The man eyed Ding Gou'er suspiciously.

'You don't want any?' he asked.

'I'm not much of a drinker,' Ding Gou'er replied.

'You're not from around here, I take it?' the gatekeeper asked.

'Old-timer, that is one plump, fair-skinned toddler,' Ding Gou'er said.

He studied the gatekeeper's face. It was a look of dejection. The man took another hefty swig and muttered softly, 'What difference does it make if I burn a little coal? A whole ton of the stuff doesn't cost more than . . .'

By now Ding Gou'er was so hot he could no longer stand it. Though he found it hard to take his eyes off the toddler, he opened the door and walked out into the sunshine, which was cool and comforting.

Ding Gou'er was born in 1941 and married in 1965. It was a garden variety marriage, with husband and wife getting along well enough, and producing one child, a darling little boy. He had a mistress, who was sometimes adorable and sometimes downright spooky. Sometimes she was like the sun, at other times the moon.

Sometimes she was a seductive feline, at other times a mad dog. The idea of divorcing his wife appealed to him, but not enough to actually go through with it. Staying with his mistress was tempting, but not enough to actually do it. Anytime he took sick, he fantasized the onset of cancer, yet was terrified by the thought of the disease; he loved life dearly, and was tired to death of it. He had trouble being decisive. He often stuck the muzzle of his pistol against his temple, then brought it back down; another frequent site for this game was his chest, specifically the area over his heart. One thing and one thing only pleased him without exception or diminution: investigating and solving a criminal case. He was a senior investigator, one of the very best, and well known to high-ranking cadres. He stood about five feet eight, was gaunt, swarthy, and slightly cross-eyed. A heavy smoker, he enjoyed drinking, but got drunk too easily. He had uneven teeth, and wasn't bad at hand-to-hand combat. His marksmanship was erratic: in a good mood he was a crack shot; otherwise he couldn't hit the broad side of anything. Somewhat superstitious, he believed in blind luck, and fortune seemed to follow him everywhere.

The Procurator General of the Higher Procuratorate handed him a China-brand cigarette and kept one for himself. Taking out his lighter, Ding lit the Procurator General's cigarette, then his own. The smoke filling his mouth tasted like buttery candy, sweet and delicious. Ding Gou'er noticed how ineptly the Procurator General smoked. He opened a drawer and took out a letter, glanced at it, then handed it over.

Ding Gou'er quickly read the scrawled letter from a whistle-blower. It was signed by someone calling himself Voice of the People. Phony, obviously. The contents shocked him at first; but then came the doubts. He skimmed the letter again, focusing on the marginal notations in the florid script of a senior official who knew him well.

He studied the eyes of the Procurator General, which were fixed on a potted jasmine on the window sill. The dainty white flowers exuded a subtle perfume. 'Do you think it's credible?' he asked. 'Could they really have the guts to braise and eat infants?'

The Procurator General smiled ambiguously. 'Secretary Wang wants you to find out.'

Excitement swelled in his chest, yet all he said was, 'This shouldn't be the business of the Procuratorate. What about the public security bureaus, are they napping?'

'It's not my fault I've got the famous Ding Gou'er on my payroll, is it?'

Slightly embarrassed, Ding Gou'er asked, 'When should I leave?'

'Whenever you like,' the Procurator General replied. 'You divorced yet? Either way it's just a formality. Needless to say, we all hope there isn't a word of truth in this accusation. But you are to say nothing about this to anyone. Use any means necessary to carry out your mission, so long as it's legal.'

'I can go, then?' Ding Gou'er stood up to leave.

The Procurator General also stood up and slid an unopened carton of China-brand cigarettes across the table.

After picking up the cigarettes and leaving the Procurator General's office, Ding rode the elevator to the ground floor and left the building, deciding to go first to his son's school. The renowned Victory Boulevard, with its unending stream of automobiles, blocked his way. So he waited. Across the street to his left a cluster of kindergartners was lined up at the crossing. With the sun in their faces, they looked like a bed of sunflowers. He was drawn to them. Bicycles brushed past, like schooling eels. The riders' faces were little more than white blurs. The children, dressed in their colorful best, had tender, round faces and smiling eyes. They were tied together by a thick red cord, like a string of fish, or fruit on a spit. Puffy clouds of automobile exhaust settling around them glinted like charcoal in the sunlight and filled the air with their aroma; the children were just like a skewer of roast lamb, basted and seasoned. Children are the nation's future, her flowers, her treasure. Who would dare run them over? Cars stopped. What else could they do? Engines revved and sputtered as the children crossed the street, a white-uniformed woman at each end of the line. Faces like full moons, encasing cinnabar lips and sharp white teeth, they might as well have been twins. Stretching the cord taut, they brusquely maintained order:

'Hold on to the cord! Don't let go!'

As Ding Gou'er stood beneath a roadside tree with yellowed leaves, the children crossed to his side, and waves of cars were already whizzing past. The column began to curve and bend; the children chirped and twittered like a flock of sparrows. Red ribbons around their wrists were fastened to the red cord. No longer standing in a straight line, they were still attached to the cord, and the women only had to draw it taut to straighten them out. Thoughts of the earlier shouts of 'Hold on to the cord! Don't let go!' enraged him. What bullshit! How, he wondered, could they let go, when they're tied to it?

He leaned against the tree and asked one of the women coldly: 'Why do you tie them like that?'

She gave him an icy glare.

'Lunatic!' she said.

The children looked over at him.

'Lu–na–tic–!' they echoed in unison.

The way they drew out the syllables, he couldn't tell if it was spontaneous or coached. Their lilting, falsetto voices rose like birds on the wing. Smiling idiotically, he nodded an apology to the woman on the far end, who dismissed him by looking away. He followed the column of children with his eyes until they disappeared down a lane bordered by a pair of high red walls.

It was a struggle, but he finally made it to the other side of the street, where a Xinjiang vendor roasting skewers of lamb hailed him in a heavy accent. He wasn't tempted. But a long-necked girl walked up and bought ten. Reddened lips like chili peppers. Dipping the skewers of sizzling, greasy meat into the pepper jar, she bared her teeth as she ate, to protect her lipstick. His throat burning, he turned and walked off.

A while later he was in front of the elementary school smoking a cigarette and waiting for his son, who didn't see him as he ran out the gate with his backpack. He had blue ink smudges on his face, the marks of a student. He called his son's name. When the boy reluctantly fell in behind him, he told him he was being sent to Liquorland on business. 'So what?' Ding Gou'er asked his son what he meant by So What? 'So what? means So what? What do you expect me to say?'

'So what? That's right. So what?' he said, echoing his son's comment.

Ding Gou'er walked into the mine's Party Committee Security Section, where he was greeted by a crewcut young man who opened a floor-to-ceiling cabinet, poured a glass of liquor, and handed it to him. This room too was furnished with a large stove, which kept the temperature way up there, if not as stifling as the gate house. Ding Gou'er asked for some ice; the young fellow urged him to try the liquor:

'Drink some, it'll warm you up.'

The earnest look made it impossible for Ding Gou'er to refuse, so he accepted the glass and drank slowly.

The office was hermetically sealed by perfectly dovetailed doors and windows. Once again Ding Gou'er started to itch all over, and rivulets of sweat ran down his face. He heard Crewcut say consolingly:

'Don't worry, you'll cool off as you calm down.'

A buzzing filled Ding Gou'er's ears. Bees and honey, he was thinking, and honeyed infants. This mission was too important to be undone by carelessness. The glass in the windows seemed to vibrate. In the space between heaven and earth outside the room, large rigs moved slowly and noiselessly. He felt as if he were in an aquarium, like a pet fish. The mining rigs were painted yellow, a numbing color, an intoxicating color. He strained to hear the noise they made, but no dice.

Ding Gou'er heard himself say:

'I want to see your Mine Director and Party Secretary.'

Crewcut said:

'Drink up, drink up.'

Touched by Crewcut's enthusiasm, Ding Gou'er leaned back and drained the glass.

He no sooner set down his glass than Crewcut filled it up again.

'No more for me,' he said. 'Take me to see the Mine Director and Party Secretary.'

'What's your hurry, Boss? One more glass and we'll go. I'd be guilty of dereliction of duty if you didn't. Happy events call for double. Go on, drink up.'

The sight of the full glass nearly unnerved Ding Gou'er, but he had a job to do, so he picked it up and drank it down.

He put down the glass, and it was immediately refilled.

'It's mine policy,' Crewcut said. 'If you don't drink three, how edgy you will be.'

'I'm not much of a drinker,' Ding Gou'er protested.

Crewcut picked up the glass with both hands and raised it to Ding Gou'er's lips.

'I beg you,' he said tearfully. 'Drink it. You don't want me to be edgy, do you?'

Ding Gou'er saw such genuine feeling in Crewcut's face that his heart skipped a beat, then softened; he took the glass and poured the liquor down his throat.

'Thank you,' Crewcut said gratefully, 'thank you. Now, how about three more?'

Ding Gou'er clamped his hand over the glass. 'No more for me, that's it,' he said. 'Now take me to your leaders.'

Crewcut looked at his wristwatch.

'It's a bit early to be going to see them now,' he said.

Ding Gou'er whipped out his ID card. 'I'm here on important business,' he said truculently, 'so don't try to stop me.'

Crewcut hesitated a moment, then said, 'Let's go.'

Ding followed Crewcut out of the Security Section office and down a corridor lined with doors, beside which wooden name-plaques hung.

'The offices of the Party Secretary and Mine Director aren't in this building, I take it,' he said.

'Just come with me,' Crewcut said. 'You drank three glasses for me, so you don't have to worry that I'll lead you astray. If you hadn't drunk those three glasses, I'd have taken you to the Party Secretary's office and simply handed you over to his appointments secretary.'

As they walked out of the building, he saw his face reflected dimly in the glass door and was shocked by the haggard, unfamiliar expression staring back at him. The hinges creaked when the door was opened, then sprang back and bumped him so hard on his backside that he stumbled forward. Crewcut reached out to steady him. The sunbeams were dizzyingly bright. His legs went wobbly, his hemorrhoids throbbed, his ears buzzed.

16

'Am I drunk?' he asked Crewcut.

'You're not drunk, Boss,' Crewcut replied. 'How could a superior individual like you be drunk? People around here who get drunk are the dregs of society, illiterates, uncouth people. Highbrow folks, those of the "spring snow," cannot get drunk. You're a highbrow, therefore, you cannot be drunk.'

This impeccable logic completely won over Ding Gou'er, who tagged along behind the man as they passed through a clearing strewn with wooden logs. A bit bewildering, given the range of sizes. The thick logs were a couple of meters in diameter, the thin ones no more than two inches. Pine, birch, three kinds of oak, and some he couldn't name. Possessed of scant botanical knowledge, he was happy to have recognized those few. The gouged, scarred logs reeked of alcohol. Weeds that were already beginning to wither had sprouted between and among the logs. A white moth fluttered lazily in the air. Black swallows soared overhead, looking slightly tipsy. He tried to wrap his arms around an old oak log, but it was too thick. When he thumped the dark red growth rings with his fist, liquid oozed out over his hand. He sighed.

'What a magnificent tree this was at one time!' he remarked.

'Last year a self-employed winemaker offered three thousand for it, but we wouldn't sell,' Crewcut volunteered.

'What did he want it for?'

'Wine casks,' Crewcut answered. 'You must use oak for high quality wine.'

'You should have sold it to him. It isn't worth anywhere near three thousand.'

'We do not approve of self-employment. We'd let it rot before we'd support an entrepreneurial economy.'

While Ding Gou'er was secretly applauding the Mount Luo Coal Mine's keen awareness of the public ownership system, a couple of dogs were chasing each other around the logs, slipping and sliding as if slightly mad, or drunk. The larger one looked a little like the gate-house dog, but not too much. They scampered around one stack of logs, then another, as if trying to enter a primeval forest. Fresh mushrooms grew in profusion in the plentiful shade of the huge fallen oak, layers of oak leaves and peeled bark exuded the captivating smell of fermented acorn sap. On one of the logs, a mottled old giant, grew hundreds of fruits shaped like little babies: pink in color, facial features all in the right places, fair, gently wrinkled skin. And all of them boys, surprisingly, with darling little peckers all red and about the size of peanuts. Ding Gou'er shook his head to clear away the cobwebs; mysterious, spooky, devilish shadows flickered inside his head and spread outward. He reproached himself for wasting so much time at a place where he had no business spending any time at all. But then he had second thoughts. It's been less than twenty-four hours since I started this case, he was thinking, and I've already found a path through the maze – that's damned efficient. His patience restored, he fell in behind the crewcut young man. Let's see where he plans to take me.

Passing by a stack of birchwood logs, he saw a forest of sunflowers. All those blossoms gazing up at the sun formed a patch of gold resting atop a dark-green, downy base. As he breathed in the unique, sweet, and intoxicating aroma of birch, his heart was filled with scenes of autumn hills. The snow-white birch bark clung to life, still moist, still fresh. Where the bark had split open, even fresher, even more tender flesh peeked through, as if to prove that the log was still growing. A lavender cricket crouched atop the birch bark, daring someone to come catch it. Unable to contain his excitement, the crewcut young man announced:

'See that row of red-tiled buildings there in the sunflower forest? That's where you'll find our Party Secretary and Mine Director.'

There looked to be about a dozen buildings with red roof tiles nestled amid the contrasting greens and golds in the forest of thick-stemmed, broad-leafed sunflowers, which were nourished by fertile, marshy soil. Under the bright rays of sunlight, the yellow was extraordinarily brilliant. And as Ding Gou'er took in the exquisite scenery, a giddy feeling bordering on intoxication spread throughout his body – gentle, sluggish, heavy. He shook off the giddiness, but by then Crewcut had vanished into thin air. Ding jumped up onto a stack of birchwood logs for a better vantage point, and had the immediate sensation of riding the waves – for the birchwood stack was a ship sailing on a restless ocean. Off in the distance, the mountain of waste rock still smoldered, although the smoke had given up much of the moisture it had carried at dawn.

Undulating black men swarmed over the exposed mounds of coal, beneath which vehicles jostled for position. Human shouts and animal noises were so feeble that he thought something had gone wrong with his hearing; he was cut off from the material world by a transparent barrier. The apricot-colored rigs stretched their long limbs into the opening of the coal pit, their movements excruciatingly slow yet unerringly precise. Suddenly dizzy, he bent over and lay face-down on one of the birchwood logs. It was still being tossed by the waves. Crewcut had indeed vanished into thin air. Ding slid down off the birchwood log and walked toward the sunflower forest.

He could not help thinking about his recent behavior. A special investigator, highly regarded by the country's senior leaders, crouching on a pile of birchwood logs like a puppy too scared of the water to appreciate its surroundings; this behavior had already become a factor in his investigation of a case that would become an international scandal if the accusations proved to be true. So spectacular that if it were made into a movie, people would scoff. He supposed he was a bit drunk, but that didn't alter the fact that Crewcut was a sneak, and not altogether normal, no, decidedly not normal. The investigator's imagination began to soar, wings and feathers carried on gusts of wind. The crewcut young man is probably a member of the gang of people who eat infants, and was already planning his escape while he was leading me through the maze of logs. The path he chose was full of traps and dangers. But he had underestimated the intelligence of Ding Gou'er.

Ding clasped his briefcase to his chest, for in it, heavy and steely hard, was a Chinese six-nine repeater. Pistol in hand, he was bold, he was brave. Reluctantly he took a last look at the birchwood and oak logs, his colorful comrade logs. The cross-sectioned patterns turned them into targets, and as he fantasized hitting a bull's-eye, his legs carried him to the edge of the sunflower forest.

That a quiet, secluded place like this could exist in the midst of seething coal mines reminded him of the power of human endeavor. The sunflowers turned their smiling faces to greet him. He saw hypocrisy and treachery in those emerald green and pale yellow smiles. He heard cold laughter, very soft, as the wind set the broad leaves dancing and rustling. Reaching into his briefcase to feel his cold, hard companion, he strode purposefully toward the red buildings, head held high. With his eyes fixed on the red buildings, he felt a palpable threat from the surrounding sunflowers. It was in their coldness and the white burrs.

Ding Gou'er opened the door and walked in. It had been quite a journey, filled with a range of experiences, but finally he was in the presence of the Party Secretary and the Mine Director. The two dignitaries were about fifty, and had round, puffy faces like wheels of baked bread; their skin was ruddy, about the color of thousand-year eggs; and each had a bit of a general's paunch. They wore gray tunics with razor-sharp seams. Their smiles were kindly, magnanimous, like most men of high rank. And they could have been twins. Grasping Ding Gou'er's hand, they shook it with gusto. They were practiced hand-shakers: not too loose, not too tight; not too soft, not too hard. Ding Gou'er felt a warm current surge through his body with each handshake, as if his hands had closed around nice pulpy yams straight from the oven. His briefcase fell to the floor. A gunshot tore from within.

Pow – !

The briefcase was smoking; a brick in the wall crumbled. Ding Gou'er's shock manifested itself in hemorrhoidal spasms. He actually saw the bullet shatter a glass mosaic painting on the wall; the theme was Natha Raises Havoc at Sea. The artist had fashioned the heavenly Natha as a plump, tender little baby boy, and the investigator's accidental firing had mangled Natha's little pecker.

'A crack shot if I ever saw one!'

'The bird that sticks out its head gets shot!'

Ding Gou'er was mortified. Scooping up his briefcase, he took out the pistol, and flipped on the safety.

'I could have sworn the safety was on,' he said.

'Even a thoroughbred stumbles sometimes.'

'Guns go off all the time.'

The magnanimity and consoling words from the Mine Director and Party Secretary only increased his embarrassment; the high spirits with which he had stormed through the door vanished like misty clouds. Cringing and bowing low, he fumbled with his ID card and letter of introduction.

'You must be Comrade Ding Gou'er!'

'We're delighted you've come to assess our work!'

Too embarrassed to ask how they knew he was coming, Ding Gou'er merely rubbed his nose.

'Comrade Director,' he said, 'and Comrade Party Secretary, I've come on the orders of a certain high-ranking comrade to investigate reports that infants are being braised and eaten at your esteemed mine. This case has far-reaching implications, and strictest secrecy must be maintained.'

The Mine Director and Party Secretary exchanged a long look – ten seconds at least – before clapping their hands and laughing uproariously.

Ding Gou'er frowned and said reproachfully:

'I must ask you to take this seriously. Liquorland's Deputy Head of Propaganda, Diamond Jin, who is a prime suspect, comes from your esteemed mine.'

One of them, either the Mine Director or the Party Secretary, said:

'That's right, Deputy Head Jin was a teacher at the elementary school attached to the mine. But he's a talented and principled comrade, one in a million.'

'I'd like you to fill me in.'

'We can talk while we enjoy some food and drink.'

Before he could open his mouth to protest, he was bundled into the dining room.

II

My Dear, Esteemed Mo Yan

Greetings!
I am a Ph.D. candidate in liquor studies at the Brewer's College here in Liquorland. My name is Li, Li Yidou – One-Pint Li – but of course that's only a nom de plume. You'll forgive me for not revealing my real name. You are a world famous writer (that's not flattery), so you'll have no trouble figuring out why I chose that particular pseudonym. My body may be in Liquorland, but my heart

is in literature, splashing away in the sea of literature. Which is why my academic adviser, who is my wife's father, the husband of my mother-in-law, thus my father-in-law – in elitist terms, lord of the castle, more commonly, 'the man' – Yuan Shuangyu, Professor Yuan, is always criticizing me for ignoring my true career, and why he has even tried to goad his daughter into divorcing me. But I shall not be deterred. For the sake of literature, I would willingly climb a mountain of knives or rush into a sea of flames. 'For thou I shalt waste away, happy that the clothes hang loose on my body.' My retort to him is always the same: What exactly is ignoring one's true career? Tolstoy was a military man, Gorki a baker and a dishwasher, Guo Moruo a medical student, and Wang Meng the Deputy Party Secretary of the Beijing branch of the Youth League in China's new democracy. They all changed careers and became writers, didn't they? When my father-in-law tried to counter my arguments, I just glared at him, like the legendary eccentric, Ruan Ji, except that I lacked the power of my illustrious predecessor and was unable to mask completely the white-hot anger in my black eyes. Lu Xun couldn't do it either, right? But you know all this already, so why am I trying to impress you? This is like reciting the *Three Character Classic* at the door of Confucius, or engaging in swordplay in front of the warrior Guan Yu, or boasting about drinking to Diamond Jin . . . but I stray from my purpose in writing.

My dear, esteemed Mo Yan, I have read with great enjoyment everything you've written, and I bow low in respect for you. One of my souls leaves the mortal world, one flies straight to Nirvana. Your work is on a par with Guo Moruo's 'Phoenix Nirvana' and Gorki's *My Universities*. What I admire most about you is your spirit, like that of the 'Wine God,' who drinks as much as he wants without getting drunk. I read an essay in which you wrote, 'liquor is literature' and 'people who are strangers to liquor are incapable of talking about literature.' Those refreshing words filled my head with the clarified butter of great wisdom, removed all obstacles to understanding. Truly it was a case of: 'Open the gates of the throat and pour down a bucket of Maotai.' There cannot be a hundred people in this world who are more knowledgeable about liquor than I. You, of course, count among them. The history of liquor and the distillation of liquor, the classification of liquor, the chemistry of liquor, and the physical properties of liquor, I know them all like the back of my hand. Which is why I am so captivated by literature, and why I believe I am capable of producing good literature. Your judgment would be my liquor of assurance, serving the same purpose as that glass of liquor the martyred hero Li Yuhe took from Aunt Li just before he was arrested. So, Mo Yan, Sir, now you must know why I am writing this letter. Please accept the prostration of your disciple!

Recently I saw the film adaptation of your novel *Red Sorghum*, which you also worked on, and was so excited I could hardly sleep that night. So I drank, one glass after another. I was so happy for you, Sir, and so proud. Mo Yan, you are the pride of Liquorland! I shall appeal to people from all walks of life to pluck you from Northeast Gaomi township and settle you here in Liquorland. Wait for news from me.

I mustn't carry on too long in this first letter. I include with it a short story for your criticism. I wrote it like a man possessed the night I saw your movie *Red Sorghum*, after tossing and turning, and finally drinking the night away. If you think it has promise, I would be grateful if you would recommend it for publication somewhere. I salute you with enormous respect, and wish you

Continued success,
Your disciple

Li Yidou

PS: Please let me know if you are short of liquor. I will attend to it right away.

III

Dear Doctor of Liquor Studies

Greetings!
Your letter and the story 'Alcohol' both arrived safely.

I am a haphazardly educated person, which is why I
hold college students in such high regard. And a Ph.D.
candidate, well, that is the apex.

During times like this, it is fair to say that literature is
not the choice of the wise, and those of us for whom it is
too late can but sigh at a lack of talent and skills that
leaves us only with literature. A writer by the name of Li
Qi once wrote a novel entitled *Don't Treat Me Like a Dog*,
in which he describes a gang of local punks who are deprived
of opportunities to cheat or mug or steal or rob, so one of
them says: Let's go become goddamned writers! I'd rather not
go into detail regarding the implications. If you're interested,
you can find a copy of the novel for yourself.

You are a doctoral candidate in liquor studies. I envy
you more than is probably good for me. If I were a doctor
of liquor studies, I doubt that I'd waste my time writing
novels. In China, which reeks of liquor, can there be any
endeavor with greater promise or a brighter future than
the study of liquor, any field that bestows more abundant
benefits? In the past, it was said that 'In books there are
castles of gold, in books there are casks of grain, in books
there are beautiful women.' But the almanacs of old had
their shortcomings, and the word 'liquor' would have
worked better than 'books.' Take a look at Diamond Jin,
that is, Deputy Head Jin, the one with the oceanic capacity
for liquor, a man who has earned the undying respect of
everyone in Liquorland. Where will you find a writer
whose name can be uttered in the same breath as his? And
so, little brother (I'm unworthy of being called 'sir'), I
urge you to listen to your father-in-law and avoid taking
the wrong path.

In your letter you said that one of my essays inspired you to become a writer. That is a big mistake. I wrote the asinine words 'liquor is literature' and 'people who are strangers to liquor are incapable of talking about literature' when I was good and drunk, and you must not take them to heart. If you do, this insignificant life of mine will be all but over.

I have read your manuscript carefully. I have no grounding in literary theory and hardly any ability to appreciate art. Any song and dance from me would be pointless. But I have mailed it off to the editors at *Citizens' Literature*, where the finest contemporary editors have gathered. If you are a true 'thousand-li steed,' I am confident there's a master groom out there somewhere for you. I have plenty of liquor, but thanks for asking.

Wishing you
Health and happiness,

Mo Yan

IV

Alcohol, by Li Yidou

Dear friends, dear students, when I learned that I had been engaged as a visiting professor at the Brewer's College, this supreme honor was like a warm spring breeze in midwinter sweeping past my loyal, red-blooded heart, my green lungs and intestines, as well as my purple liver, the seat of acquiescence and accommodation. I can stand behind this sacred podium, made of pine and cypress and decorated with colorful plastic flowers, to lecture to you primarily because of its special qualities. You all know that when alcohol enters the body, most of it is broken down in the liver . . .

Diamond Jin stood at the podium in the General Education Lecture Hall of Liquorland's Brewer's College solemnly discharging his duties. He had chosen a broad and far-reaching topic for this,

his first lecture – Liquor and Society. In the tradition of brilliant, high-ranking leaders, who steer clear of specifics when they speak in public – like God looking down from on high, invoking times ancient and modern, calling forth heaven and earth, a sweeping passage through time and space – he proved his worth as visiting professor by not allowing the details of the topic to monopolize his oration. He permitted himself to soar through the sky like a heavenly steed, yet from time to time knew he must come down to earth. The rhetoric flowed from his mouth, changing course at will, yet every sentence was anchored in his topic, directly or indirectly.

Nine hundred Liquorland college students, male and female, heads swelling, hearts and minds ready to take flight, along with their professors, instructors, teaching assistants, and college administrators, sat as one body, a galaxy of celestial small-fry gazing up at a luminous star. It was a sunshiny spring morning, and Diamond Jin stood behind a tall podium gazing out at his audience with diamond-clear eyes. Professor Yuan Shuangyu, who was well past sixty, sat in the audience, looking up at the stage, his white hair seeming to float above his head, the picture of elegance. Each strand of hair was like a silver thread, his cheeks were ruddy, his composure grand; like an enlightened Taoist, he was a man who embodied the spirit of a drifting cloud or a wild crane. His silvery head towering over all those others had the effect of a camel amid a herd of sheep. The elderly gentleman was my academic adviser. I knew him, and I knew his wife, and later on I fell in love with his daughter, and I married her, which meant that he and his wife became my in-laws. I was in the audience that day, a Ph.D. candidate majoring in liquor studies at the Brewer's College, and my academic adviser was my own father-in-law. Alcohol is my spirit, my soul, and it is also the title of this story. Writing fiction is a hobby for me, so I am free of the pressures of a professional writer; I can let my pen go where it wants, I can get drunk while I write. Good liquor! That's right, really really good liquor! Good liquor good liquor, good liquor emerges from my hand. If you drink my good liquor, you can eat like a fat sow, without looking up once. I set my liquor-filled glass down on a lacquered tray with a crisp clink, and when I close my eyes I can see that lecture hall now. The laboratory. All that lovely liquor in the Blending Laboratory, each glass beaker filled with a different red on the scale; the lights singing, the wine surging through my veins, in the flow of time my thoughts travel upstream, and Diamond Jin's small, narrow, yet richly expressive face has a seductive appeal. He is the pride and glory of Liquorland, an object of reverence among the students. They want their future sons to be like Diamond Jin, the women want their future husbands to be like Diamond Jin. A banquet is not a banquet without liquor; Liquorland would not be Liquorland without Diamond Jin. He drank down a large glass of liquor, then dried his moist, silky lips with a silk handkerchief that reeked of gentility. Wan Guohua, the flower of the Distilling Department, dressed in the most beautiful dress the world has ever seen, refilled our visiting professor's glass with liquor, her every motion a study in grace. She blushed under his affectionate gaze; we might even say that red clouds of joy settled on her cheeks. I know that pangs of jealousy struck some of the girls in the audience, while for others it was simple envy, and for yet others tooth-gnashing anger. He had a booming voice that emerged unobstructed from deep down in his throat, which he never had to clear before speaking. His coughs were the minor flaws of which only prominent people can boast, a simple habit that did nothing to lessen his refined image. He said:

Dear comrades and dear students, do not have blind faith in talent, for talent is really nothing but hard work. Of course, materialists do not categorically deny that some people are more lavishly endowed than others. But this is not an absolute determinant. I acknowledge that I possess a superior natural ability to break down alcohol, but were it not for arduous practice, attention to technique, and artistry, the splendid ability to drink as much as I want without getting drunk would have been unattainable.

You are very modest, but then, individuals with true abilities generally are. People who boast of their talents tend not to have natural talents, or have very few of them. With consummate grace you drank down another glass of liquor. The young lady from Distilling gracefully refilled your glass. I refilled my own glass with a tired hand. People exchanged knowing smiles as greetings. Liquor was the Tang poet Li Bai's muse. But Li Bai is no match for me, for he had to pay for his liquor, and I don't. I can drink laboratory brews. Li Bai was a literary master, while I am but an amateur scribbler. The Vice-Chairman of the Metropolitan Writers Association urged me to write about aspects of life with which I am familiar. I frequently take some of the liquor I steal from the laboratory to his house. He wouldn't lie to me. How far have you gotten in your lecture? Let us prick up our ears and concentrate our energy. The college students were like nine hundred feisty little donkeys.

Little donkeys. The expression on the face of Professor Diamond Jin, our Deputy Head, and his gestures, differ hardly at all from the little donkeys'. He looks so lovable up there behind the rostrum, hands flying, body twisting. He was saying, My relationship with liquor goes back forty years. Forty years ago, the founding of our People's Republic, such a joyous month for us all, a time when I was just taking root in my mother's womb. Prior to that, according to my findings, my parents were no different than anyone else – frenzied to the point of folly, and all pleasures that followed sank into a state of wild ecstasy, as exaggerated as if flowers had fallen from heaven. So I am a product, or maybe a byproduct, of ecstasy. Students, we all know the relationship between ecstasy and liquor. It matters not if carnivals coincide with celebrations of the wine god, and it matters not if Nietzsche was born on the festival of the wine god. What matters is that the union of my father's ecstasy sperm and my mother's ecstasy egg predetermined my long association with liquor. He unfolded a slip of paper handed up to him and read it. I am an ideological worker for the party, he announced with tolerance and magnanimity, so how could I be a spokesman for idealism? I am a materialist, through and through. I will always and forever hold high the banner of 'Material goods first, spiritual concerns second,' the words embroidered in golden threads. Even though it is a result of ecstasy, sperm is material; so, using this logic, is not the egg of ecstasy material as well? Or, from a different angle: Is it possible for people in a state of ecstasy to abandon their own flesh and bone and be transformed into purely spiritual beings flying off in all directions? And so, my dear students, time is precious, time is money, time is life itself, and we must not let this simplest of issues have us running around in circles. At noon today I am going to open the first annual Ape Liquor Festival for benefactors, including Chinese-Americans and our brethren from Hong Kong and Macao. They deserve the best.

From where I was standing at the rear of the hall, I saw the deltoid muscles below the neck of my mother-in-law's husband grow taut and turn red when Diamond Jin mentioned the words Ape Liquor. The old fellow had been salivating for most of his adult life over thoughts of the supremely wondrous liquor of this legend. For the two million inhabitants of Liquorland, turning the legend of Ape Liquor into a container of liquid fact would be a dream come true; a task force had been formed, with extraordinary funding from the municipal coffers. The old fellow had headed up the task force, so whose deltoids *would* tense up, if not his? I couldn't see his face. But I believe I know what it looked like at that moment.

Dear students, let the following sacred image take form before our eyes: A school of ecstatic sperm, lithe tails flapping behind them, like an army of bold warriors storming a fortress. Oh, they may be wildly ecstatic, but their movements are sprightly yet gentle. The Fascist ringleader Hitler wanted the youth of Germany to be quick and nimble as ferocious hunting dogs, tough and pliable as leather, and hard and unyielding as Krupp steel. Now even though Hitler's idealized German youth may be somewhat analogous to the school of sperm wriggling before our eyes – one of which is my very own nucleus – no metaphor, no matter how apt, is worthy of being repeated, especially when the creator of that metaphor was among the most evil men who ever walked the face of the earth. Better that we use domestic clichés than the best the foreigners have to offer. It's a matter of principle, nothing to take for granted. Comrade leaders at all levels, take heed, do not be slapdash in this regard, not ever. In medical books sperm cells are described as tadpoles, so let's set those tadpoles a-swimming. A cloud of tadpoles, one carrying my origins with them, swims upstream in my mother's warm currents. It is a race. The winner's trophy is a juicy, tender white grape. Sometimes, of course, there is a dead heat between two of the competitors. In cases like this, if there are two white grapes, each competitor is awarded one; but if there is only one white grape, then they must share the sweet nectar. But what if three, or four, or even more competitors arrive at the finish line at the same time? This is a unique case, a particularly rare occurrence, and scientific principles are abstracted from general conditions, not unique cases, which require special debate. At any rate, in this particular race I reached the finish line ahead of all the others, and was swallowed up by the white grape, becoming part of it and letting it become part of me. That's right, the most vivid metaphor imaginable is still inferior – Lenin said that. Without metaphor there can be no literature – that's Tolstoy. We frequently use liquor as a metaphor for a beautiful woman, and people often use a beautiful woman as a metaphor for liquor; by so doing, we show that liquor and a beautiful woman share common properties, but are individuated by distinctive properties within those common properties, and that the common properties within the distinctive properties are what deindividuate a beautiful woman and liquor. Seldom does one gain true understanding of the tenderness of a beautiful woman by drinking liquor – that is as rare as phoenix feathers and unicorn horns. By the same token, it is difficult for one to gain a true understanding of the qualities of liquor via the tenderness of a beautiful woman – that is as rare as unicorn horns and phoenix feathers.

His oration that day had us dumbstruck, we shallow college students and slightly less shallow graduate students. He had consumed more liquor than we had drunk water. Genuine knowledge comes from practice, my dear students. A marksman feeds on bullets; a drinking star is steeped in alcohol. There are no shortcuts on the road to success, and only those fearless people who have the courage to keep climbing on a rugged mountain path have any hope of reaching the glorious summit!

Truth's glory shone down upon us, and we responded with thunderous applause.

Students, I had a miserable childhood. Great people struggle their way out of the seas of misery, and he was no exception. I yearned for liquor, but there was none. Deputy Head Jin related to us how, under highly adverse circumstances, he substituted industrial alcohol for sorghum liquor in order to toughen his internal organs, and I want to use pure literature to portray this extraordinary experience. I took a drink and clinked my glass down on the lacquer tray. It was getting dark, and Diamond Jin stood somewhere between Deputy Head and ecstatic sperm. He waved to me. He was wearing a tattered lined jacket as he led me to his hometown.

A cold winter night, a crescent moon and a skyful of stars illuminated the streets and the houses, the dry, withered branches and leaves of willow trees, and the plum blossoms of Diamond Jin's village. Not long after a recent heavy snowfall, the sun had come out twice, melting the snow and forming icicles that hung from eaves and gave off a faint glow of their own under the natural light from above; the accumulated snow on rooftops and tips of branches glowed as well. Based upon Deputy Head Jin's description, it was not a particularly windy winter night, as the ice on the river cracked and split under the onslaught of the astonishing cold. The cracks sounded like explosions in the late night air. Then the night grew quieter and quieter. The village was fast asleep, that village in our Liquorland suburbs, and one day we may very well take a ride in Deputy Head Jin's VW Santana to admire the sacred spots and visit the sites of relics; every mountain, every river and lake, every blade of grass, and every tree can only increase our reverence for Deputy Head Jin; and what intimate feelings they will be! Just think, born in an impoverished, ramshackle village, he climbed slowly into the sky until he shone down over all of Liquorland, a resplendent star of liquor, his radiance dazzling our eyes and filling them with tears, causing an upsurge of emotions. A broken-down cradle is still a cradle, nothing can replace it, and every indication points to the likelihood that a limitless future stretches out ahead of Deputy Head Jin. When we follow in the footsteps of Diamond Jin, who has entered the top ranks of leadership, wandering through the streets and byways of his Diamond Village, when we linger on the edges of his murmuring streams, when we stroll along the high, tree-lined banks of the rivers, when we amble past his cattle pens and stables ... when the sorrows and ecstasies of his childhood, his loves and his dreams ... ad nauseam flood his heart like floating clouds and flowing water, how can we gauge his state of mind? How does he walk? What is his expression like? When he walks, does he start with his left foot or his right? What is his left arm doing when he strides forward with his right foot? What about his right arm when he strides with his left foot? How does his breath smell? What's his blood pressure? His heart rate? Do his teeth show when he smiles? Does his nose crinkle when he weeps? So much cries out to be described, and there are so few words in my lexicon. I can only raise my glass. Out in the yard, snow-laden dead branches cracked and splintered; ice on a distant pond was three inches thick; dried-out ice covered clumps of reeds; geese, wild and domestic, roosting for the night were startled out of their dreams and honked crisply, the sound carrying through the clean, chilled air all the way to the eastern room of the home of Diamond Jin's seventh uncle. He says he went to his seventh uncle's house every evening, and stayed till late at night. The walls were jet-black; a kerosene lamp stood atop an old three-drawer table against the east wall. Seventh Aunt and Seventh Uncle sat on the brick bed platform; the little stove repairman, Big Man Liu, Fang Nine, and storekeeper Zhang all sat on the edge of the platform killing time through the long night, just like me. Every night they came; not even stormy weather could keep them away. They reported on what they'd done that day and passed on news they'd picked up in villages and hamlets in rich, vivid detail, full of wit and humor, painting a vast canvas of village life and customs. A life rich with literary appeal. The cold was like a wildcat that crept in through cracks and gnawed at my feet. He was just a child who couldn't afford a pair of socks, and had to curl his blackened, chapped feet in woven-rush sandals, icy drops of sweat coating his soles and the spaces between his toes. The kerosene lamp seemed to blaze in the dark room, making the white paper over the window sparkle, the freezing air streaming in through its rips and tears; sooty smoke from the kerosene flame wisped toward the ceiling in neat coils. Seventh Aunt and Seventh Uncle's two children were asleep in a corner of the brick bed; the girl's breathing was even, the boy's was labored, high one moment, low the next, mingled with nightmare babble that sounded like a dream brawl with a gang of ruffians. Seventh Aunt, a bright-eyed, educated woman with a nervous stomach was hiccuping audibly. Seventh Uncle gave every appearance of being a muddle-headed man whose nondescript face had no distinctive curves or angles, like a slab of gooey rice-cake. His clouded eyes were forever fixed dully on the lighted lamp. Actually, Seventh Uncle was a shrewd man who had schemed and plotted to trick the educated Seventh Aunt, ten years his junior, into marrying him; it was a convoluted campaign that would take far too long to recount here. Seventh Uncle was an amateur veterinarian who could puncture a vein in a sow's ear and inject penicillin intravenously, and who also knew how to castrate hogs, dogs, and donkeys. Like all men in the village, he liked to drink, but now the bottles were empty; all the fermentable grains had been used up, and food had become their biggest concern. He said, We suffered through the long winter nights with growling stomachs, and at the time no one dreamed that I'd ever make it to this day. I don't deny that my nose is keenly sensitive where alcohol is concerned, especially in rural villages where the air is unpolluted. On cold nights in rural villages, threads of a variety of smells come through clear and distinct, and if someone is drinking liquor anywhere within a radius of several hundred meters, I can smell it.

As the night deepened, I detected the aroma of liquor off to the northeast, an intimate, seductive smell, even though there was a wall between it and me, and it had to soar across one snow-covered roof after another, pierce the armor of ice-clad trees, and pass down roads, intoxicating chickens, ducks, geese, and dogs along the way. The barking of those dogs was rounded like liquor bottles, exuberantly drunk; the aroma intoxicated constellations, which winked happily and swayed in the sky, like little urchins on swings; intoxicated fish in the river hid among lithe water weeds and spat out sticky, richly mellow air bubbles. To be sure, birds braving the cold night air drank in the aroma of liquor as they flew overhead, including two densely feathered owls, and even some field voles chomping grass in their underground dens. On this spot of land, full of life in spite of the cold, many sentient beings shared in the enjoyment of man's contribution, and sacred feelings were thus born. 'The popularity of liquor begins with the sage kings, though some say Yi Di, and others Du Kang.' Liquor flows among the gods. Why do we offer it as a sacrifice to our ancestors and to release the imprisoned souls of the dead? That night I understood. It was the moment of my initiation. On that night a spirit sleeping within me awakened, and I was in touch with a mystery of the universe, one that transcends the power of words to describe, beautiful and gentle, tender and kind, moving and sorrowful, moist and redolent . . . do you all understand? He stretched his arms out to the audience, as they craned their necks toward him. We sat there bug-eyed, our mouths open, as if we wanted to go up to see, then eat, a miraculous potion lying in the palm of his hands, which were, in fact, empty.

The colors emanating from your eyes are incredibly moving. Only people who speak to God can create colors like that. You see sights we cannot see, you hear sounds we cannot hear, you smell odors we cannot smell. What grief we feel! When speech streams from that organ called your mouth, it is like a melody, a rounded, flat river, a silken thread from the rear end of a spider waving gossamerlike in the air, the size of a chicken's egg, just as smooth and glossy, and every bit as wholesome. We are intoxicated by that music, we drift in that river, we dance on that silken spider thread, we see God. But before we see Him, we watch our own corpses float down the river . . .

Why were the owls' screeches so gentle that night, like the pillow talk of lovers? Because there was liquor in the air. Why were geese, wild and domestic, coupling in the freezing night, when it wasn't even the mating season? Again, because there was liquor in the air. My nose twitched spiritedly. Fang Nine asked in a soft, muffled voice:

'Why are you scrunching up your nose like that? Going to sneeze?'

'Liquor,' I said. 'I smell liquor!'

They scrunched up their noses too. Seventh Uncle's nose was a mass of wrinkles.

'I don't smell liquor,' he said. 'Where is it?'

My thoughts were galloping. 'Sniff the air,' I said, 'sniff it.'

Their eyes darted all around the room, searching every corner. Seventh Uncle picked up the grass mat covering the brick bed, to which Seventh Aunt reacted angrily:

'What are you looking for? You think there's liquor here in bed? You amaze me!'

Seventh Aunt was an intellectual, as I said earlier, so she was 'amazed.' Back when she was still a newlywed, she criticized my mother for washing the rice so hard she scrubbed away all the 'vitamins.' 'Vitamins' had my mother gaping in stupefaction.

The smell of liquor includes protein, ethers, acids, and phenols, as well as calcium, phosphorus, magnesium, sodium, potassium, chlorine, sulfur, iron, copper, manganese, zinc, iodine, and cobalt, plus vitamins A, B, C, D, E, H, and some other materials – but look at me, listing the ingredients of liquor for you people, when your Professor Yuan Shuangyu knows them better than anyone – my father-in-law's neck deltoids had reddened over being praised by Deputy Head Diamond Jin. I couldn't see the excitement in his face, though basically I could, or nearly so – but there is a pervasive something in the smell of liquor that transcends the material, and that is a spirit, a belief, a sacred belief, one that can be sensed but not articulated – language is so clumsy, metaphors so inferior – it seeps into my heart and makes me shudder. Comrades, students, is it possible that we still need to demonstrate whether liquor is a harmful insect or a beneficial one? No way, no way at all. Liquor is a swallow it's a frog it's a red-eyed wasp it's a seven star ladybug, it's a living pesticide! His spirits soared, and he waved his arms fervently, lost in the exuberance of the moment. The atmosphere in the lecture hall was white-hot; he stood there looking like Hitler. He said:

'Seventh Uncle, just look, the smell of liquor seeps in through the window, settles in through the ceiling, enters wherever there's a hole or a crack . . .'

'The boy is losing his mind,' Fang Nine said as he sniffed the air. 'Do smells have color? Can you see them? This is lunacy . . .'

Doubt clouded their eyes; they looked at me the way they'd look at a child who had truly lost his mind. But to hell with them. On flying feet, I crossed a bridge of colors paved with the smell of liquor, feet flying . . . and a miracle occurred, my dear students, a miracle occurred! His head sagged from the weight of his emotions. Then, as he stood at the podium in the General Education Lecture Hall at the Brewer's College, he intoned in a hoarse but extraordinarily infectious voice:

The picture of a glorious banquet on a snowswept night formed in my mind's eye: A bright gas lamp. An old-fashioned square

35

table. A bowl sits on the table, steam rising from within. Four people sit around the table, each holding a small bowl of liquor, as if cupping a rosy sunset. Their faces are kind of blurred . . . Aiie! They've cleared up, and I know who they are . . . the Branch Secretary, the Brigade Accountant, the Militia Commander, the Head of the Women's League . . . they're holding stewed legs of lamb, dipping them into garlic paste laced with soy sauce and sesame oil . . . pointing my finger, I was talking to Seventh Uncle and the others, like an announcer, but my eyes were blurred, and I couldn't see their faces clearly. Yet I didn't dare strain too hard for fear that the picture would dissolve . . . Seventh Uncle grabbed my hand and shook it hard.

'Little Fish [Yu], Little Fish! What's happened to you?'

As he shook my hand with his left hand, Seventh Uncle smacked the back of my head with his right. The thumping in my head sounded like a chipped brick or a splintered roof tile breaking the placid, mirrorlike surface of a pond; the water splashed in all directions, raising ripples that tumbled upon one another. The picture shattered, and my mind went blank. Angrily I shouted:

'What are you doing? What are all you people doing?'

They gazed at me anxiously. Seventh Uncle said:

'Are you dreaming, boy?'

'I'm not dreaming. I saw the Branch Secretary, the Brigade Accountant, the Head of the Women's League, and the Militia Commander. They were all drinking, and they were dipping legs of lamb into garlic paste, under a gas lamp, around a square table.'

Seventh Aunt yawned grandly.

'Hallucinating,' she said.

'I saw them clear as day!'

Big Man Liu said, 'When I went down to the river to fetch water this afternoon, I did see the Head of the Women's League and two old ladies washing legs of lamb.'

'You're hallucinating, too,' Seventh Aunt said.

'I really did!'

'Really, my ass!' Seventh Aunt said. 'I think you're crazed with hunger.'

The young stove repairman tried to make peace:

'Stop arguing, I'll go take a look. You know, investigate.'

'Are you crazy?' Seventh Aunt said. 'Do you believe in hallucinations?'

The little stove repairman said:

'You folks wait, I'll run out there and run right back.'

'Be careful they don't catch you and beat you up,' Seventh Uncle cautioned him.

The little stove repairman was already out the door. A gust of cold wind blew in, nearly snuffing out the lamp.

The stove repairman came rushing back in, gasping for air. A gust of cold wind nearly snuffed out the lamp. He gazed at me with the look of a simpleton, as if he'd seen a ghost. Seventh Aunt asked with a sarcastic grin:

'What did you see?'

The stove repairman turned and said:

'Fantastic, fantastic, Little Fish is an immortal, he can see everything.'

The stove repairman said that everything was exactly as I had described it. The banquet had taken place at the Branch Secretary's house. He'd climbed the low wall to see.

Seventh Aunt said:

'I don't believe it.'

The little stove repairman went outside to get a frozen sheep's head, which he held up to show Seventh Aunt. One look stopped Seventh Aunt's hiccups.

That night we busied ourselves with cleaning the sheep's head before tossing it into the pot. Our thoughts were on liquor as the sheep's head stewed. Seventh Aunt was the one who came up with the idea: Drink ethyl alcohol.

Seventh Uncle, a veterinarian, had a bottle of alcohol he used as a disinfectant. Needless to say, we diluted it with water.

Thus began an arduous tempering process.

People who grow up on industrial alcohol will shy away from no alcoholic drinks.

Sad to say, the little stove repairman and Seventh Uncle went blind.

He raised his arm to look at his wristwatch. Dear students, he said, that's the end of today's lecture.

Chapter Two

I

The Mine Director and Party Secretary stood facing him; they were holding their left arms bent across their chests, their right arms thrust out, palms straight, like a pair of professional traffic policemen. Their faces were so alarmingly alike they seemed to serve as one another's mirror. Between them lay a path, about a meter wide and covered with a scarlet carpet, which intersected with a floodlit corridor. Ding Gou'er's heroic mettle vanished in the face of this genuine show of courtesy, and as he cowered near the two dignitaries, he did not know if he should step forward. Their cordial looks were like redolent grease assailing his nostrils, getting thicker by the moment and not lessened or diluted by Ding Gou'er's hesitancy. The gods never speak – how true that is. But while the men didn't speak, their bearing was more infectious and more powerful than the sweetest, most honeyed words ever spoken, and they left you powerless to resist. Partly because he felt he had to, and partly because he was so grateful, Ding Gou'er stepped in front of the Mine Director and Party Secretary, who immediately fell in behind him, the three men forming a triangle. The corridor seemed endless. This baffled Ding Gou'er, for he clearly recalled the layout of the place: Only a dozen or so rooms occupied the space enclosed by sunflowers, too few to accommodate a corridor this long. Every three paces a pair of red lamps shaped like torches hung on facing walls covered with milky white wallpaper. The brass hands holding the torches were shiny bright and remarkably lifelike, as if protruding through the walls themselves. With growing trepidation he imagined two lines of bronze men standing on the other side; walking down the red-carpeted corridor was like marching between a phalanx of armed guards.

I've become a prisoner, and the Party Secretary and Mine Director are my military escort. Ding Gou'er's heart skipped a beat as cracks opened in his brain to let in a few threads of cool reason. He reminded himself of the importance of his mission, his sacred duty. Playing house with a young female hadn't prevented him from carrying out this sacred duty, but drinking might. He stopped, turned, and said:

'I'm here to conduct an investigation, not drink your liquor.'

There was more than a hint of inhospitability in his voice. The Mine Director and Party Secretary exchanged looks that were exactly alike; without a trace of irritation, they said with the same warmth and friendliness they had displayed from the beginning:

'We know, we know, we're not asking you to drink.'

Poor Ding Gou'er still couldn't tell which of the two men was the Party Secretary and which was the Mine Director; but, afraid he might offend them by asking, he decided to keep muddling along, particularly since the two men were the spitting image of each other, as were the official positions of Party Secretary and Mine Director.

'After you, please. Whether you drink or not doesn't alter the fact that you have to eat.'

So Ding Gou'er kept walking, thoroughly annoyed with the triangular formation of one in front and two in the rear, as if the corridor led not to a banquet but to a courtroom. He tried slowing down so they could walk in a straight line. Fat chance! Every time he hung back, they kept pace, maintaining the integrity of the triangle and leaving him always in the position of the one under escort.

The corridor veered abruptly and the red carpet began sloping downward; the torches were brighter than ever, the hands holding them more menacing, as if they were truly alive. A flurry of alarming thoughts flickered in his head, like golden flies, to which he reacted by instinctively clasping his briefcase even more tightly under his arm, until that lump of cold, hard steel rubbed against his ribs to calm him a bit. Two seconds was all it would take to point the black muzzle at the men's chests, even if that sent him straight to Hell or right to his grave.

By now, he knew, they were well underground; even though

the torches and red carpet were as bright and colorful as ever, still, he felt chilled, chilled but not actually cold.

An attendant with bright eyes and sparkling teeth, in a scarlet uniform and a fore-and-aft cap, was waiting for them at the end of the corridor. Her welcoming smile, mastered through long experience, and the heavy aroma of her hair had the desired calming effect on Ding Gou'er's nerves. Fighting back the urge to kiss her hair, he conducted a silent self-criticism and self-exoneration. The girl opened a door with a shiny stainless-steel doorknob. At last the triangle disintegrated, and Ding Gou'er breathed a sigh of relief.

A luxurious dining room appeared before them. The colors and lights were soft enough to evoke thoughts of love and happiness, or would have if not for the faint wisps of a very strange odor. Ding Gou'er's eyes lit up as he drank in the room's decor: from cream-colored sofas to beige curtains, from a spotless white ceiling with floral etchings to a spotless white tablecloth. The light fixtures were exquisite and delicate, like a string of fine pearls; the floor had a mirrorlike finish, obviously recently waxed. As he was sizing up the room, the Party Secretary and Mine Director were sizing him up, unaware that he was trying to locate the source of that strange odor.

The circular table had three tiers. The first was devoted to squat glasses of beer, long-stemmed glasses of grape wine, and even longer-stemmed glasses of strong colorless liquor, plus ceramic teacups with lids, sheathed imitation-ivory chopsticks, a variety of white ceramic plates, stainless-steel utensils, China-brand cigarettes, wooden matches with bright red heads in specially designed boxes, and fake crystal ashtrays in the shape of peacock tails. Eight plates of cold cuts adorned the second tier: shredded eggs and rice noodles with dried shrimp, hot and spicy beef strips, curried cauliflower, sliced cucumbers, ducks' feet, sugared lotus root, celery hearts, and deep-fried scorpions. As a man of the world, Ding Gou'er saw nothing special in them. The third tier was occupied only by a potted cactus covered with thorns. Just the sight of it made Ding Gou'er squirm. Why not a vase of fresh flowers? he wondered.

There was the usual polite deferring all around before they sat

40

down, and it seemed to Ding Gou'er that, given the circular shape, there was no seat of honor to worry about. But he was put right on that score when the Party Secretary and Mine Director insisted that he sit nearest the window, which was in fact the seat of honor. He acquiesced, and was immediately sandwiched between the Party Secretary and Mine Director.

A bevy of attendants fluttered around the room like so many red flags, sending drafts of cool air his way and spreading that strange odor to every corner of the room; it was, to be sure, mixed with the fragrance of their face powder and the sour smell of sweat from their armpits, plus smells from other parts of their bodies. The more the odor merged with the other smells, the less poignant it became, and Ding Gou'er's attention was diverted.

A steaming apricot-colored hand towel dangling from a pair of stainless-steel tongs appeared in front of Ding Gou'er, catching him by surprise. As he reached for the towel, instead of cleaning his hands, he allowed his eyes to trace the tongs up to a snowy white hand and beyond that a moon face with dark eyes beneath a veil of long lashes. The folds of the girl's eyes made it seem as if she had scarred eyelids, but that was not the case. Now that he'd had a good look, he wiped his face with the towel, then his hands; the towel was scented with something that smelled a bit like rotten apples. He'd no sooner finished his ablutions than the tongs whisked the towel away from him.

As for the Party Secretary and Mine Director, one handed him a cigarette, the other lit it.

The strong colorless liquor was genuine Maotai, the grape wine was from Mount Tonghua, and the beer was Tsingtao. Either the Party Secretary or the Mine Director, one or the other, said:

'As patriots we boycott foreign liquor.'

Ding Gou'er replied:

'I said I wasn't drinking.'

'Comrade Ding, old fellow, you've come a long way to be with us. How does it make us look if you don't drink? We've dispensed with the formalities, since this is just a simple meal. We can't show the intimate relationship between official ranks if you won't drink with us, can we? Have a little, just a little, to let us save face.'

With that the two men raised their liquor glasses and held them out to Ding Gou'er, the colorless liquid sloshing around ever so gently, its distinctive bouquet very tempting. His throat began to itch and his salivary glands kicked in, sending spittle pressing down on his tongue and wetting his palate. He stammered:

'So sumptuous . . . more than I deserve . . .'

'What do you mean, sumptuous, Comrade Ding, old fellow? Are you being sarcastic? We have a small mine here, with little money and few frills, and a mediocre chef. While you, old Ding, come from the big city, have traveled widely, and have seen and done everything. I imagine there isn't a fine beverage anywhere you haven't sampled, or a game animal you haven't tasted. Don't embarrass us, please,' said either the Party Secretary or the Mine Director. 'Try to put up with this meager fare the best you can. As ranking cadres, we must all respond to the call of the Municipal Party Committee to cinch up our belts and make do. I hope you'll be understanding and make allowances.'

A torrent of words flowed from the two men as they eased their glasses ever closer to Ding Gou'er's lips. With difficulty he swallowed a mouthful of sticky saliva, reached for his own glass, and held it out, feeling the exceptional heft of the glass and the quantity of liquid it held. The Party Secretary and Mine Director clinked glasses with Ding Gou'er, whose hand shook for a moment, spilling a few drops of liquor between his thumb and forefinger, where the skin turned joyously cool. As that joyous coolness sank in, he heard voices on either side of him say: 'A toast to our honored guest! A toast!'

The Party Secretary and Mine Director drained their glasses, then turned them upside down to show that not a drop remained. Ding Gou'er was well aware of the three-glass penalty for leaving a single drop in one's glass. He first drank down half the contents, and his mouth was suddenly awash with ambrosia. Not a word of criticism emerged from the two men, who merely held up their empty glasses to show him. Succumbing to the awful power of peer pressure, Ding Gou'er drained his glass.

The three empty glasses were quickly refilled.

'No more for me,' Ding Gou'er demurred. 'Too much liquor makes work impossible.'

'Happy events call for double! Happy events call for double!'

Ding Gou'er quickly covered his glass with his hand.

'I said, no more,' he said, 'that's it for me.'

'Three glasses to begin the meal. It's a local custom.' With three glasses of liquor now under his belt, Ding Gou'er was getting light-headed, so he picked up his chopsticks and reached out for some rice noodles, which, with their mixed-in eggs, were slippery. Either the Party Secretary or the Mine Director, helpful as always, anchored the two thin noodles with his own chopsticks and helped carry them to his mouth.

'Suck!' he directed loudly.

Ding Gou'er sucked with all his might, and with a loud slurp, the quivering noodles slipped into his mouth. One of the attendants covered her mouth and giggled. A woman laughing for all to see raises a man's sense of glee. Suddenly, the atmosphere around the table had turned lively.

The glasses were refilled; the Party Secretary or Mine Director raised his and said, 'A visit by Special Investigator Ding Gou'er to our humble mine is a great honor, and on behalf of all the cadres and miners, let me offer three toasts. Refusing to drink them will show your disdain for members of the working class, to the black-faced miners who dig the coal.'

Noting the blush of excitement on the man's pale face, Ding Gou'er contemplated the eloquent toast, so pregnant with significance that he could not refuse. It was as if the eyes of thousands of coal miners, in their hard-hats and tightly cinched belts, sooty from head to toe, white teeth glistening, were trained on him, raising a tumult in his heart. With a show of bravado, he tossed down three glassfuls, one after the other.

The other man wasted no time in raising his glass to wish Special Investigator Ding Gou'er good health and happiness on behalf of his own eighty-three-year-old mother. Now Ding Gou'er was a filial son whose white-haired old mother still lived in the countryside, so how could he refuse to drink, son to mother?

After nine cups of liquor had sloshed into his stomach, the investigator felt his consciousness being stripped from his body. No, stripped is the wrong image. He was sure that his consciousness had turned into a butterfly whose wings were curled inward for the moment, but was destined to emerge with exquisite beauty from the central meridian of his scalp, stretching its neck as it worked its way out. The empty shell abandoned by the butterfly of his consciousness would be its cocoon, devoid of heft, light as a feather.

At his hosts' urging, he had no choice but to drink, one cup after another, as if trying to fill a bottomless pit, yet leaving not even a tiny echo in its wake. As they drank and drank, an unending succession of steaming, mouth-watering dishes was trundled into the room by three red serving girls, like three tongues of flame, like three balls rolling here and there, lightning-fast. He vaguely recalled eating a red crab the size of his hand; thick juicy prawns covered in red oil; a green-shelled turtle steeped in celery broth; a stewed chicken, golden yellow in color, its eyes reduced to tiny slits, like a new variety of camouflaged tank; a red carp, slick with oil, its gaping mouth still moving; steamed scallops stacked in the shape of a little pagoda; as well as red-skinned turnips, so fresh they could have just been plucked from the garden. His taste buds were alive with aromatic tastes: oily, sweet, sour, bitter, spicy, salty; his mind visited by a welter of thoughts, he gazed around the room through the aromatic haze. A pair of eyes suspended in the air saw molecules of colors and odors of every conceivable shape moving with infinite freedom in the finite space to form a three-dimensional body in the shape and size of the dining hall. To be sure, there were also molecules stuck to the wallpaper, stuck to the window curtains, stuck to the sofa covers, stuck to lamps, stuck to red girls' eyelashes, stuck to the greasy foreheads of the Party Secretary and Mine Director, stuck to all those shimmering beams of light, once shapeless, now possessing bending, twisting shapes . . .

After a while, he sensed that a hand with many fingers was offering him a glass of red wine. The last remaining dregs of consciousness in the shell that was his body pulled together for one final Herculean effort to help his fragmented self follow the spinning movements of that hand, like the spreading petals of a pink lotus. The glass of wine also grew out in layers, like a doctored photograph, forming a pink mist in those relatively stable, relatively scarlet surroundings. It was not a glass of wine, it was the sun rising in the morning, a fireball of cold beauty, a lover's heart. He

44

would soon sense that it had taken on the appearance of a murky brown full moon that had once hung in the sky, before boring its way into the dining hall, or a swollen grapefruit, or a yellow ball covered with fuzz, or a hairy fox spirit. His consciousness sneered as it hung from the ceiling, and cool air from the air conditioner broke through the barriers that kept it from reaching the top, where it gradually cooled and formed butterfly wings of incomparable beauty. Having broken free of the body housing it, his consciousness spread its wings and soared around the dining hall. Sometimes it rubbed against the silken window curtains – of course, its wings were thinner, softer, and brighter than the curtain material; sometimes it rubbed against the chandelier, with its refracted light; sometimes it rubbed against the cherry-red lips and peach-red nipples of the red girls, or other, even more private, more cunning parts. Traces of it were everywhere: on teacups, on liquor bottles, in floorboard cracks, between strands of hair, in the microscopic holes of China-brand cigarette filters . . . Like a rapacious, territorial wild animal, it left its mark on everything. For a winged consciousness, there were no barriers; it was shapeless, yet had shape; it threaded its way happily and freely through and among the beaded rings on the chandelier, from ring A to ring B and from ring B to ring C. It went wherever it wanted, circulating round, back and forth, weaving in and out without hindrance. But at last it tired of its game and made its way under the skirt of a voluptuous red girl, where it caressed her legs like a gentle breeze, raising goosebumps, until a moist, oily feeling was replaced by a dull, heavy one. It rose at high speed, closed its eyes as it flew through the forest, the tips of green shrubs rubbing the wings with a scratchy sound. Its ability to fly and change shape allowed it to leap tall mountains and ford wide rivers. It teased a little red mole in the valley between the two arched breasts and had some fun with a dozen or so beads of sweat. Its final move took it up into a nostril, where it tickled her nose hairs with its antennae.

The red girl sneezed loudly, spitting the thing out like a projectile, which struck the cactus on the dining table's third tier. It bounced off as if it had been slapped by a thorny hand. Ding Gou'er had a splitting headache, his stomach was churning like a powerful whirlpool, and his skin itched painfully, as if covered by prickly nettles. It stopped on his scalp to rest, to gasp for breath, and to sob. Ding Gou'er's eyes were working again, and he saw the Party Secretary and Mine Director raise their glasses in a toast. Their voices bounced off the walls, like waves crashing on a rocky shore before being dragged back out to sea, or a shepherd boy on a mountain peak calling out to his flock: Wa – wa – wa – Hey-ya – hey-ya – hey-ya –

Here we go again, thirty cups . . . on behalf of Deputy Head Jin . . . thirty cups . . . drink up drink up drink up, anybody who doesn't drink doesn't deserve to be called a man . . . Diamond Diamond Diamond Jin knows how to drink . . . the old fellow can drink an ocean of liquor, vast and boundless . . .

Diamond Jin! The name bored into Ding Gou'er's heart like a diamond drill, and as the wrenching pain seemed to tear it apart, he opened his mouth and spewed a small river of filthy liquid along with a frightening verbal assault:

'That wolf – urp – who eats braised baby boys – urp – wolf –!'

Like a frightened bird, his consciousness returned; his intestines were in knots, causing unspeakable agony. A pair of fists thumped him on the back. Urp – urp – liquor – sticky liquid, tears and snot pouring down: Autumn rains turn the earth and sky gray, a green sheet of water fills the eyes.

'Feeling better, Comrade Ding Gou'er?'

'Comrade Ding Gou'er, are you feeling any better?'

'Go on, throw up, get rid of it. You'll feel better when all that bitter juice is out of your stomach.'

'All people need to throw up, good hygiene requires it.'

He was propped up by the Party Secretary on one side and the Mine Director on the other, each thumping him on the back as they fed encouraging remarks into his waiting ears, like country doctors trying to save a drowned child or teachers trying to educate a wayward youth.

After Ding Gou'er had brought up a stomachful of green liquid, a red serving girl coaxed a cup of green dragon-well tea past his lips, then another red serving girl tried to do the same with a glass of yellow, aged Shanxi vinegar, and either the Party Secretary or the Mine Director forced a piece of candied lotus root into his mouth, while the other held a piece of honeyed snow pear under his nose, and a red serving girl wiped his face with a cool towel treated with peppermint oil, and another red serving girl swept up the mess on the floor, and another red serving girl followed behind her, cleaning the last traces of the mess with a mop treated with disinfectant, and another red serving girl removed the dishes and glasses from the table, and another red serving girl laid out new settings.

Deeply moved by this lightning-quick series of ministrations, Ding Gou'er wished he hadn't blurted out his accusation as he was retching a moment ago; he was about to apologize for any offense when either the Party Secretary or the Mine Director said:

'Ding, old fellow, what do you think of our serving girls?'

Embarrassed by the question, Ding Gou'er looked into those tender flower-bud faces and said approvingly:

'Good! Great! Wonderful!'

Obviously well trained, the red serving girls rushed up to the table like a litter of hungry puppies or a troop of Young Pioneers presenting bouquets to honored guests. Empty glasses all but covered the three levels of the dining table, so the girls picked up the nearest glass, big or small, filled it with red wine, yellow beer, or colorless liquor, and raised it raucously to toast Ding Gou'er.

Ding Gou'er's skin was sticky with sweat, his lips seemed frozen, and his tongue had grown stiff – unable to spit out a word, he clenched his teeth and poured the magic elixir down his throat. As they say, even valiant generals wilt before a pretty face.

At this moment, he wasn't feeling very good, because the trouble-making little demon in his brain was wriggling around and once again poking its head out through his scalp. Now he knew what was meant when people said the body cannot contain the soul. The agonizing thought of his soul hanging upside down from the rafters scared the wits out of him, and he could barely keep from covering his head with his hands to block the escape route of his consciousness. Aware that that would show a lack of decorum, he was reminded of the beaked cap he had worn when he was making his move on the lady trucker. The cap, in turn, reminded him of his briefcase, and the dark pistol it contained, a thought that opened up the sweat glands under his arms. His darting glances caught the attention of one of the smarter red girls, who fetched his briefcase from somewhere. After taking it from her and assuring himself that his metal friend, that 'hard' bargainer, was still inside, he stopped sweating. His beaked cap, however, was not there, and he thought back to the watchdog and the gatekeeper, to the young man in the Security Section, to the wooden logs, and to the sunflower forest; these scenes and the people in them seemed so remote at this moment that he wondered if he'd actually seen them, or if they were all part of a dream. As he carefully placed the briefcase between his knees, the wavering, disorderly spirit, with its mutinous tendencies, created a flashing light before his eyes, alternating between extreme clarity and blurred edges; he saw that his knees were covered by oily stains that appeared to be an illuminated map of China one moment and a darkened map of Java the next, and though they were sometimes a bit out of placement, he worked hard to straighten them out, hoping that the map of China would always be illuminated and that the map of Java would always be dark and blurry.

A moment before Diamond Jin, Deputy Head of the Liquorland Municipal Party Committee Propaganda Department, walked in the door, Ding Gou'er experienced sharp abdominal pains. A tangle of venomous snakes was writhing and twisting inside his guts: pungent, oh so pungent, sticky, ah so sticky, tangled, entwined, illicit, sneaky, pulling and dragging and hauling and hissing, a real tangle of venomous snakes, and he knew that his intestines were making mischief. The feeling moved upward, a burning flame, a balding bamboo broom sweeping the walls of his stomach – *scrape scrape* – as if it were a painted chamber pot with a buildup of filth. Oh, dear mother, the investigator groaned inwardly, this is more than I can bear! I've fallen on evil times. I've fallen into the sinister trap of the Mount Luo Coal Mine. Fallen into the trap of food-and-liquor! Fallen into the trap of pretty faces!

Ding Gou'er got to his feet, bent over at the waist, and found he couldn't feel his legs, which was why he never knew who or what guided him back into his seat. Was it his own legs or his brain? Was it the keen, sparkling eyes of the red girls? Or was it the Party Secretary and Mine Director who pushed down on his shoulders?

Once his hind quarters were resettled in the chair, he heard a rumbling noise escape from down below. The red girls covered their mouths and giggled. He didn't have the strength to react angrily; his body and his consciousness were filing for divorce, either that or – the same old trick – his turncoat consciousness was about to flee. At this painful, awkward moment, Deputy Head Diamond Jin, his body sparkling like diamonds, emitting a golden aroma, pushed open the red naugahyde-covered, soundproof door of the dining room, like a breath of spring, a ray of sunlight, the embodiment of ideals, the promise of hope.

He was an urbane, middle-aged man with a swarthy complexion, a high-bridged nose on a long face, and eyes shielded by tea-colored, silver-rimmed crystal-mirror spectacles. In the lamplight his eyes were like bottomless black wells. Of medium height, he was wearing a freshly pressed dark blue suit over a snowy white dress shirt and a blue-and-white striped tie. His black leather shoes shone like glass. He had a full head of loosely coifed hair, neither rumpled nor thinning. The man had one additional unique feature: a bronze (maybe gold) inlaid tooth. That, in a nutshell, was Diamond Jin.

Ding Gou'er got clearheaded in a big hurry, sensing, almost as if it were fate, that he was now face-to-face with his true adversary.

The Party Secretary and Mine Director jumped to their feet, unconcerned that they banged their knees on the edge of the table on their way up. Someone's sleeve knocked over a glass of beer, the yellow liquid quickly soaking the tablecloth and dripping onto their knees. They didn't care. Pushing their chairs back, they rushed from both sides of the table to greet the new arrival. Happy shouts of Deputy Head Jin, you're here! erupted even before the beer glass hit the table.

The man's booming laugh squeezed the air in the room in waves and pressed down on the beautiful butterfly atop Ding Gou'er's head. He stood up in spite of his desire not to. He smiled despite his wish to keep a straight face. A smiling Ding Gou'er rose to greet the man.

In unison, the Party Secretary and Mine Director said:

'This is Deputy Head Diamond Jin of the Municipal Party Committee Propaganda Department, and this is Investigator Ding Gou'er of the Higher Procuratorate.'

Clasping his hands in front, Diamond Jin smiled and said:

'My apologies for being so late.'

He thrust his hand toward Ding Gou'er, who shook it in spite of his desire not to. This child-eating devil's hand should be cold as ice, he thought. So why is it so warm and soft? And comfortably moist. He heard Diamond Jin say politely:

'Welcome! I've heard wonderful things about you.'

Once everyone was seated, Ding Gou'er clenched his teeth in his determination not to take another drink, so as to remain in complete control of his faculties. It's time to go to work! he silently commanded himself.

He was now sitting shoulder to shoulder with Diamond Jin, and was prepared for anything. Diamond Jin, ah, Diamond Jin. You may be an impregnable fortress, you may be on intimate terms with the rulers, your roots may grow strong and deep, your network may be wide and far-reaching, but once you are in my grasp, your days are numbered. If bad times are in store for me, no one can look forward to good ones.

Diamond Jin spoke up:

'Since I came late, I'll pay a penalty of thirty cups!'

Ding Gou'er certainly never expected to hear those words. Turning to look at the Party Secretary or Mine Director, he saw that the man was smiling knowingly. A red serving girl entered with a fresh liquor service on a tray. The cups sparkled as they were placed in front of Diamond Jin. Another red serving girl walked up with a decanter and filled them, bobbing like a phoenix nodding its head. Calling upon years of training, she filled them expertly, confidently, and purposefully, without spilling a drop. The pearl-like bubbles atop the first cup had not yet popped by the time the last cup was filled. They were a bed of unusual flowers that had bloomed in front of Diamond Jin; a sigh of awe escaped from Ding Gou'er. Awed first by the red serving girl's extraordinary skill and grace, and second by Diamond Jin's machismo. This proved the saying that 'Without a diamond, one cannot create porcelain beauty.'

Diamond Jin removed his suit coat, which was taken away by a red serving girl.

'Comrade Ding, old fellow,' he said, 'would you say these thirty cups are filled with mineral water or colorless liquor?'

Ding Gou'er sniffed the air, but his sense of smell was anesthetized.

'If you want to know the flavor of a pear, you must eat one. If you want to determine whether this is real liquor or not, you'll have to taste it for yourself. Please select any three of these cups.'

Now Ding Gou'er knew from the investigative materials he'd read that Diamond Jin was renowned for his drinking abilities, but he still had doubts. With the urging of the others, he picked out three of the cups and tasted their contents with the tip of his tongue. The liquid had a sweet, fermented taste. It was the real thing.

'Comrade Ding, old fellow,' Diamond Jin said, 'those three are for you.'

'It's the custom,' one of the others said. 'You've already sampled them.'

Then they said, 'We don't miss it if you drink it, but we do if you spill it, for wastefulness is the greatest sin.'

Ding Gou'er had no choice but to drink down the three cups.

'Thank you,' Diamond Jin said, 'thank you very much. Now it's my turn.'

He picked up a cup of liquor and drank it down, noiselessly and without spilling a drop; his simple yet elegant style showed that he was no ordinary drinker. His pace quickened with each succeeding cup, but with no effect on accuracy or results – cadenced and rhythmic. He held out the last of the thirty cups and described an arc, like a bow moving across violin strings; the soft, elegant strains of a violin swirled in the air of the dining hall and flowed through Ding Gou'er's veins. His caution began to crumble, as warm feelings toward Diamond Jin surfaced slowly, like water grasses budding atop a stream during a spring thaw. He watched Diamond Jin bring the last cup of liquor to his lips and saw a look of melancholy flash in the man's bright black eyes; he was transformed into a good and generous man, one who emanated an aura of sentimentality, lyrical and beautiful. The strains of the violin were long and drawn-out, a light autumn breeze rustled fallen golden leaves, a small white blossom appeared in front of a grave marker; Ding Gou'er's eyes grew moist, gazing at the cup as if it were a stream of water bubbling up past a rock and emptying into a deep green lake. There was love in his heart for this man.

The Party Secretary and Mine Director clapped and shouted their approval. Ding Gou'er, immersed in richly poetic emotions, kept still. A silence settled over the scene. The four red serving girls stood without moving, like canna indigos, each in a different pose, as if listening intently or deep in thought. A strange sound emerged from the air conditioner in the corner, shattering the stillness. The Party Secretary and Mine Director clamored for Deputy Head Jin to drain thirty more cups of liquor, but he shook his head.

'No more for me,' he said. 'That would be wasteful. But since this is my first meeting with Comrade Ding, I must toast him three cups thrice.'

Ding Gou'er gazed in stupefaction at this man who could down thirty cups of liquor without showing it, and was so intoxicated by the man's decorum, by his honeyed voice, and by the gentle glitter of his bronze or gold tooth inlay that he lost sight of the mathematical logic that three times three equals nine.

Nine cups were arrayed in front of Ding Gou'er, and nine more in front of Diamond Jin. Ding Gou'er was powerless to resist the man's appeal; his consciousness and his body were moving in opposite directions. His consciousness screamed: You mustn't drink! while his hand picked up the cup and emptied the contents into his mouth.

Nine cups of the strong liquor made the trip down to his stomach, and his tear ducts were working overtime. Why the tears were flowing he didn't know, especially at a banqueting table. No one hit you, no one gave you an earful, so why are you crying? I'm not crying. Just because there are tears doesn't mean I'm crying. More and more tears flowed, until his face looked like a puddle of rain-soaked lotus leaves.

'Bring on the rice,' he heard Diamond Jin say. 'Let Comrade Ding eat something before he takes a rest.'

'There's still one more important dish!'

'Oh,' Diamond Jin said thoughtfully. 'Then bring it in.'

A red serving girl removed the cactus plant in the middle of the table. Then two red serving girls entered carrying a large round gilded platter in which sat a golden, incredibly fragrant little boy.

II

Dear Mo Yan

I received your letter. Thanks for taking the time to write and for recommending my story to *Citizens' Literature*. It's not drunken arrogance – that would never do – when I say that my story opens new creative and artistic horizons and is filled with the spirit of the wine god. If *Citizens' Literature* decides not to publish it, the editors must be blind.

I read the novel you recommended, *Don't Treat Me Like a Dog*. It infuriated me, if you want the truth. Li Qi, the author, trampled all over the sublime, sacred endeavor we call literature, and if that's tolerated, nothing is safe. If I ever meet him, I tell you, he's in for the verbal fight of his life.

You were absolutely right when you said that if I applied myself diligently to the study of the craft I'd have a brilliant future in Liquorland, never having to worry about where my next meal or next suit of clothes came from; I'd have a house, status, money, and a bevy of beautiful women. But I am a young man with ideals, not content to steep in alcohol for the rest of my life. I want to be like the young Lu Xun, who gave up the study of medicine for a writing career; I want to give up alcohol for a writing career, to use literature to transform society, to transform the Chinese sense of nationhood. In pursuit of this lofty goal, I would gladly lose my head or spill my hot blood; and since I'm willing to do that, how could I concern myself with worldly possessions?

Mo Yan, Sir, my heart is set on literature, so firmly that ten mighty horses could not turn me from my goal. My mind is made up, so you needn't try to change it. And if you do, I'm afraid that my feelings for you will turn to loathing. Literature belongs to the people. Why then should you be permitted to write, and not me? One of the tenets of the communism envisioned by Marx was the integration of art with the working people and of the working people with art. So when communism has been realized, everyone will be a novelist. Of course we are now only in the initial stage, but nowhere do the laws of the initial stage state that a doctor of liquor cannot write novels, do they? Please, Sir, never pattern yourself after those lousy bastards who make a bit of a name for themselves, then try to monopolize the literary arena; seeing anyone else write something gets their dander up. The proverb says it best: Yangtze waves push others ahead of them, whitecaps on a river give way to those that follow; new leaves replace the old in a lovely forest, and the young eventually triumph over their aging predecessors. Any reactionary who thinks he can suppress a rising force is the same as 'the mantis that tried to stop the oncoming wagon, a tragic overrating of one's abilities.'

In our research institute, we have a woman who deals with reference materials. Her name is Liu Yan, and she fashions herself as your student. Back when you were a political instructor at the Baoding Officer Candidate School, she was in your class. She's shared with me plenty of interesting stories, which have helped me gain an even clearer understanding of you. She said you once had very unflattering things to say in class about the famous writer Wang Meng. You said he published a piece in the weekly supplement to *China Youth News* exhorting young writers to back off from the crowded, narrow path of literature. She said you raged: 'Is Wang Meng in a position to monopolize the literary establishment? If there's food, everybody eats, if there's clothing, all are clothed. You want me to back off? Well, I'm going full-bore ahead!'

When I heard that anecdote, Sir, I ran out and polished off half a liter of wine. I was so worked up that all ten fingers were trembling, the blood surged through my veins, and my ears were as red as peony blossoms. Your comment was like a clarion, a solemn wake-up call for our fighting spirit. I want to be just like you were then:

sleeping on brushwood and eating gall, sparks leaping from your eyes, using your pen as a weapon, preferring death over dishonor.

When I listen to Liu Yan tell stories about you, then reread the letter you sent, I'm both saddened and disappointed. What you urged me to do is nigh unto the same thing as Wang Meng urged young writers (including you) to do back then! What agony this has caused me. Sir, Sir, please don't pattern yourself after such shameless, petty individuals! After throwing away the beggar's staff, do not turn and beat other beggars. Please don't forget the pain as soon as the scab falls off. If you do, you'll lose the love and esteem not just of me, but of tens of thousands of young writers just like me.

Last night I wrote another story, this one called 'Meat Boy.' In this story, I think I have shown more maturity in adopting Lu Xun's style of writing, turning my pen into a sharp dagger to flay the resplendent veneer of spiritual civilization and expose the barbaric core of our wretched morality. This story of mine can be considered an example of 'grim realism.' I purposefully threw down the gauntlet before those who use literature as a 'plaything' and are part of the 'punk movement,' that is, I use literature to awaken the populace. It was my intention to launch a violent attack against all the corrupt, venal officials here in Liquorland, and the story must be considered a 'ray of sunlight in our dark kingdom,' a latter-day 'Madman's Diary' [by Lu Xun]. I include it with this letter and await your critical comments. 'A true materialist fears nothing.' So please, don't feel you need to pussy-foot around it. Just say what's on your mind and don't beat around the bush. Laying all your cards on the table is one of our party's great traditions.

After you've read 'Meat Boy,' if you think it's of publishable quality, I'd be grateful if you found a home for it. Naturally, I know you need connections even to deliver a body to the crematorium these days, and getting fiction published must be worse. So take the battle to them. If you have to host a meal, go ahead. If a gift is required, you have my blessing. I'll take care of expenses (please remember to get receipts).

'Meat Boy' took a lot of effort to complete, so *Citizens' Literature* is my first choice. I have my reasons: First, *Citizens' Literature* is China's 'official' literary magazine, in the forefront of new literary trends. Publishing a story there is better than publishing two in a provincial or municipal magazine. Second, I want to adopt the tactic of 'pound away at one spot and forget the rest.' That's the only way to break into that mighty fortress, *Citizens' Literature*!

With respectful best wishes,
Your disciple

Li Yidou

PS: A friend of mine is off to Beijing on business, and I've asked him to deliver a case of twelve bottles of Liquorland's finest, Overlapping Green Ants, which I helped develop in the lab. I hope you enjoy it.

Li Yidou

III

Dear Doctor of Liquor Studies

How are you?
Thanks for the Overlapping Green Ants. The color, bouquet, and taste are all first-rate, though I get the feeling there's a lack of harmony somehow, sort of like a girl with lovely features who lacks that indefinable appeal to make her a true beauty. The liquor from my hometown is known for its high quality, too, though it doesn't compare with what you make in Liquorland. According to my father, before Liberation [1949], in that little,

underpopulated village of ours, there were two distilleries producing sorghum liquor, and both had recognizable names. One was Zongji, the other was Juyuan. They employed dozens of hired hands, not to mention mules and horses and all the noise that went along with it. As for making liquor out of millet, well, just about every family in the village did it, and it was pretty much a case of wine-scented air above every house. One of my father's uncles once gave me a detailed explanation of how the distilleries operated, including the distilling art, the technology, management, things like that. He'd worked at Zongji for over a decade. His descriptions produced a wealth of material for the chapter 'Sorghum Wine' in my novel *Red Sorghum*. The pervasive smell of liquor in and around my hometown was also a constant inspiration.

Liquor interests me very much; I've thought long and hard about the relationship between it and culture. The chapter 'Sorghum Wine' in my novel gives a pretty good picture of my thoughts on the subject. I've long wanted to write a novel on liquor, and making the acquaintance of a true-to-life doctor of liquor studies like you is the great good fortune of three lifetimes. I'll probably be bombarding you with questions from now on, so please stop referring to me as 'Sir.'

I've read both your letter and the story 'Meat Boy,' and have many thoughts to share with you, in no particular order of importance. I'll start with your letter:
1. In my view, the human traits of arrogance and humility are contradictory and interdependent at the same time. It's impossible to say which is good and which is bad. The truth is, people who appear to be arrogant are in fact humble, and people who seem to be humble, deep down are quite arrogant. There are people who are arrogant at certain times and under certain circumstances, but extremely humble at other times and under different circumstances. Absolute arrogance and life-long humility probably do not exist. Your 'drunken arrogance' is, to a large extent, a chemical reaction, and no fault can be

found in that. So your feeling of self-satisfaction after you've been drinking is fine with me, and a couple of well-placed curses toward *Citizens' Literature* don't break any laws I'm aware of, especially since you didn't include any slurs against their mothers or anything. All you said was. 'If they decide not to publish it, they must be blind.'

2. Mr Li Qi had reasons for writing his novel the way he did, and if you don't like it, just toss it aside and forget it. If you run into him someday, give him a couple of bottles of Overlapping Green Ants, then make yourself scarce. Do not – repeat, do not – make the mistake of adopting the revolutionary-romantic tactic of giving him 'the verbal fight of his life.' This fellow is closely connected to the criminal underground. His meanness is matched only by his brutality, and he'll stop at nothing. There's a story going round about a Beijing literary critic who wrote an article critical of Li Qi's literary offerings one night, after putting away a fine meal, and published it in some newspaper. Before three days had passed, this literary critic's old lady was kidnapped by Li Qi's men and taken to Thailand, where she was sold into prostitution. So take my advice and stay clear of this individual. There are plenty of people in this world God himself wouldn't offend. Li Qi is one of them.

3. Since you say your mind is made up to devote yourself to literature, I'll never again advise you to play the prodigal son, if for no other reason than to keep you from loathing me. If a person inadvertently provokes someone into loathing him, there's nothing he can do. But if he does it intentionally, it's like 'rolling your eyes up to look in a mirror – a search for ugliness.' I'm ugly enough already, so why would I roll up my eyes?

You saved your strongest language for those 'lousy bastards' who want to 'monopolize the literary establishment.' I couldn't be happier. If there are lousy bastards out there trying to monopolize the literary establishment, I'll curse and yell right alongside you.

I was an instructor at the Baoding Officer Candidate

School more than ten years ago, and several hundred students took my classes. I seem to recall two named Liu Yan. One was fair-skinned and always glowering; the other was dark-skinned, short and fat. Which one works with you?

Where having harsh words for Wang Meng is concerned, I really can't recall, but I think I did read his essay urging young writers to engage in a little cold self-evaluation, you know, size up the situation. It's possible I felt it was an attack on me, which likely made me very uncomfortable. But it's unlikely I'd launch an attack on Wang Meng in a class in which I was promoting communism.

If you want to know the truth, I've never tossed away my beggar's staff, and if I were to toss it away someday, I'd surely not go out and 'beat up a beggar,' would I? But there are no guarantees, since people can't dictate the changes they'll undergo throughout their lifetime.

Now for your story:
1. You call it 'grim realism.' Can you tell me what that means? I can't say for sure, although I have an idea. The contents of your story make me shudder, and all I can say is, I'm glad it's fiction. There'd be big trouble if you'd written a journalistic essay with the same contents.
2. As for publishability, normally there are two standards that apply: ideological and artistic. I can never figure either of them out. And I mean just that. I'm not pussy-footing. Fortunately, *Citizens' Literature* has a fine crop of editors, so let them decide.

I've already sent your story to the editorial department of *Citizens' Literature*, and as far as hosting a dinner or sending gifts is concerned, I'm afraid I don't know enough about either to even try. Whether that stuff works with big publications like *Citizens' Literature* or not, that you'll have to find out for yourself.

Wishing you
Good luck,

Mo Yan

IV

Meat Boy, by Li Yidou

A late autumn night; the moon was out, hanging in the western sky, the edges of its visible half blurred like a melting ice cube. Cold rays of light danced in the sleepy village of Liquor Scent. Someone's rooster crowed from a chicken coop. The sound was muffled, as if emerging from a deep cellar.

Muted though the sound was, it still roused the wife of Jin Yuanbao from her sleep. She wrapped a quilt around her shoulders and sat up, feeling disoriented in the surrounding mist. Pale moonbeams slanted in through the window, stamping white designs on the black quilt. Her husband's feet stuck out from under the covers to her right, icy cold. She covered them with a corner of the quilt. Little Treasure slept curled up on her left, his breathing deep and even. The muffled crows of roosters from even farther away came on the air. She shivered and climbed down off the bed, throwing a jacket over her shoulders as she walked into the yard, where she gazed up into the sky. Three stars hung in the west and the Seven Daughters rose in the east. It would soon be dawn.

The woman went inside and nudged her husband.

'Time to get up,' she said. 'The Seven Daughters are up already.'

The man stopped snoring and smacked his lips a time or two before sitting up.

'Is it dawn already?' he asked, with a hint of confusion.

'Just about,' the woman said. 'Get there a little earlier this time, so it won't be a wasted trip like the last time.'

Slowly the man draped his lined coat over his shoulders, reached out for a tobacco pouch at the head of the bed, filled his pipe, and stuck it between his lips. Then he picked up a flint, a stone, and some tinder to make a fire. Angular sparks flew, one landing on the tinder, which caught fire when he blew on it. The deep red flame glowed in the dark room. He lit his pipe and took a couple of quick puffs. He was about to snuff out the tinder when his wife said:

'Light the lantern.'

'Are you sure you want to?' he asked.

'Go ahead and light it,' she said. 'A tiny bit of lantern oil can't make us any poorer than we are now.'

He took a deep breath and blew again on the tinder in his hand, watching it grow brighter and brighter and finally turning into a real flame. The woman brought the lantern over and lit it, then hung it on the wall, where it cast its feeble light throughout the room. Husband and wife exchanged hurried glances, then looked away. One of the many children sleeping next to the man was talking in his sleep, loudly, like shouting slogans. One of the others reached out and rubbed the greasy wall. Yet another was weeping. The man tucked the one child's arm back under the covers and nudged the weeping child.

'What are you crying about?' he said impatiently. 'Little family wrecker!'

The woman took a deep breath. 'Shall I boil some water?'

'Go ahead,' the man replied. 'A couple of gourdfuls will be enough.'

The woman thought for a moment, then said, 'Maybe three this time. The cleaner he is, the better our chances.'

The man raised his pipe without replying, then peeked over at the corner of the bed, where the little brat was sleeping soundly.

The woman moved the lantern over to the door, so the light would shine into both rooms. After washing out the wok, she dumped in the three gourdfuls of water, put the lid on, and picked up a handful of straw, which she lit from the lantern and carefully inserted into the stove. The fire blazed as she fed it more straw, golden tongues of flame licking up to the surface and bringing color to the woman's face. The man sat on a stool beside the bed and stared blankly at the woman, who seemed younger somehow.

The water gurgled to a boil and the woman added more kindling to the stove. The man knocked the bowl of his pipe against the bed, cleared his throat, and said hesitantly:

'Big-Tooth Sun's wife, over at East Village, is pregnant again, and she's still got one at the tit.'

'Everybody's different,' the woman said agreeably. 'Who wouldn't like to have a baby every year? And triplets each time?'

'Big-Tooth's got it made, the son of a bitch, just because his brother-in-law's an inspector. He had poor-quality goods, but that didn't stop him. When he'd have been lucky to reach second-grade, he came out of it with special grade.'

'Becoming an official's easy if you've got connections at court. That's the way it's always been,' the woman said.

'But Little Treasure is a cinch to be first-grade. No other family can match our investment,' the man said. 'You ate a hundred catties of beancakes, ten carp, four hundred catties of turnips . . .'

'I ate? That food may have gone into my stomach, but it stayed there just long enough to turn into milk for him to suck out of me!'

Steam from the boiling water seeped out from under the lid of the wok, causing the lamplight to flicker weakly, like a little red bean, in the misty air.

The woman stopped feeding the stove and turned to the man.

'Bring me the wash basin,' she demanded.

He grunted a reply and went into the yard, quickly returning with a chipped black ceramic basin. The bottom was covered by a thin layer of frost.

The woman removed the lid from the wok, releasing a cloud of steam that nearly extinguished the lantern. Slowly the light returned to the room. She picked up the gourd and scooped hot water into the basin.

'Aren't you going to add cool water?' the man asked.

She tested the water with her hand. 'No,' she said, 'it's just right. Go get him.'

The man went into the next room, bent down, and lifted up the boy, who was still snoring. When he started crying, Jin Yuanbao patted him on the bottom and made cooing sounds.

'Treasure, Little Treasure, don't cry. Daddy's going to give you a bath.'

The woman took the child from him. Little Treasure crooked his neck and nestled against her bosom, groping with his hands.

'Want Mama . . . milk . . .'

She had no choice but to sit in the doorway and open her blouse. Little Treasure took a nipple into his mouth and immediately began gurgling contentedly. The woman was hunched over, as if the child were weighing her down.

The man stirred the water in the basin with his hand.

'He's had enough,' he said to hurry her along. 'The water's getting cold.'

The woman patted Little Treasure's bottom.

'Treasure,' she said, 'my Treasure, stop sucking. You've already sucked me dry. Time for a bath. When you're all clean, we'll take you to town for an outing.'

She pushed the child away, but Treasure refused to give up the nipple, stretching it as far as it would go, like a worn-out piece of rubber.

The man reached out and jerked the child away. The woman moaned, Treasure shrieked tearfully. Jin Yuanbao patted his bottom, harder this time, and said angrily:

'What are you screeching about?'

'Not so hard,' the woman complained. 'Bruises will lower the grade.'

After stripping Treasure's clothes off and tossing them aside, the man tested the water again. 'It's pretty hot,' he mumbled, 'but that'll put a little color in him.' He laid the naked boy down in the basin, drawing yelps of pain louder than the screeches of a moment earlier. As if elevated from a rolling hill to a towering mountain peak. The boy's legs curled inward as he fought to climb out of the basin. But Jin Yuanbao kept pushing him back. Beads of hot water splashed the woman. Quickly covering her face with her hands, she complained softly:

'Treasure's daddy, the water's too hot. Burning his skin will lower the grade.'

'This little family wrecker, his water's got to be just right, not too cold, not too hot. All right, add half a gourdful of cool water.'

The woman scrambled to her feet without covering her droopy breasts; the hem of her blouse hung limply between her legs, like a soggy old flag. After scooping out half a gourdful of water, she dumped it into the basin and stirred it rapidly with her hand.

'It isn't hot,' she said, 'it really isn't. Stop crying, Treasure, stop crying.'

Little Treasure's crying died down a bit, but he continued to struggle. A bath was the last thing he wanted, and Jin Yuanbao had to keep forcing him down into the basin. The woman stood to the side, gourd in hand, as if in a trance. 'Are you dead, or what?' Jin Yuanbao barked. 'Give me a hand here!'

As if waking from a dream, she put down the gourd and knelt beside the basin, where she began washing the boy's back and his bottom. Their eldest daughter – a girl of seven or eight clad only in baggy red knee-length shorts, her shoulders hunched, hair a mess, barefoot – walked into the room rubbing her eyes.

'Die [father], Niang [mother], how come you're washing him? You going to cook him and feed him to us?'

'Get back to bed, damn it!' Jin Yuanbao snapped viciously.

At the sight of his elder sister, Little Treasure cried out to her. But the girl, not daring to say another word, turned and slinked back into the other room, stopping in the doorway to watch her parents at work.

Having cried himself hoarse, Little Treasure could only sob, a hollow, listless sound. The grime on his body turned to greasy mudballs in the murky water.

'Bring me a washing gourd and a piece of soap,' the man said.

The woman fetched the items from behind the stove. 'You hold him,' Jin Yuanbao said, 'while I scrub.'

The woman and Yuanbao changed places.

Yuanbao dipped the washing gourd first in the water, then in the soap dish, and began scrubbing the boy, his neck and his bottom, and everything in between, including even the spaces between his fingers. Covered with soap bubbles, Treasure cried out in pain; the room was suffused with a strange, offensive odor.

'Treasure's daddy, not so rough. Don't break the skin.'

'He's not made of paper,' Yuanbao said. 'His skin's tougher than that! You don't know how cunning those inspectors are. They even probe the assholes, and if they find any grime, they lower their appraisal by one grade. Each grade is worth more than ten yuan.'

Finally, the bath was finished, and Yuanbao held Little Treasure while the woman dried him off. His skin glowed red in the lamplight and gave off a pleasant, meaty smell. The woman fetched a new suit of clothes and took the boy from his father. Little

Treasure began a new search for the breast, which his mother gave him.

Yuanbao dried his hands and filled his pipe with tobacco. After lighting it with the lantern and blowing out a mouthful of smoke, he said:

'I'm soaked with sweat, thanks to this little brat.'

Little Treasure fell asleep, holding the nipple in his mouth. His mother held on to him, reluctant to let go.

'Give him to me,' Yuanbao said. 'I've got a long way to go this morning.'

The woman slipped the nipple out of the boy's mouth, which twitched as if the nipple were still in it.

Jin Yuanbao picked up the paper lantern with one hand, his sleeping son with the other, and went out into the lane, which led to the village's main street. While walking down the lane, he could feel a pair of eyes on his back from the door, and that caused him much emotional distress; but once he was out on the street, the feeling disappeared without a trace.

The moon was still out, turning the blacktop gray. Roadside poplars, their branches bare, looked like gaunt standing men, the tips pale and ghostly. He shivered. The lantern cast a warm, yellow glow, its flickering shadow looming large on the surface of the road. He sniffled as he looked at the waxen tear running down the wick. A dog alongside someone's wall barked languidly; he looked down at the dog's shadow, sharing the sense of languor as he heard it scurry noisily into a haystack. When he left the village, he heard crying children, and looked up to see lights burning in the windows of peasant huts; he knew they were doing what he and his wife had done a while earlier. Knowing he'd gotten the jump on them lightened his mood a bit.

As he neared the Earth God Temple on the village outskirts, he took a packet of spirit money out of his pocket, lit it with the lantern, and laid it in a cauldron by the temple door. The flames licked up through the paper like coiling snakes. He looked inside the temple, where the Earth God himself sat for all time, a spirit-wife seated on either side; all three had icy smiles on their faces. The Earth God and his wives had been fashioned by Stonemason Wang, black stone for him, white for his wives. The Earth God was larger than both his wives put together, like an adult between two children. Thanks to the inadequate skills of Stonemason Wang, all three were ugly as could be. In the summer, owing to a leaky roof, moss grew on the statues, leaving a green, oily sheen. As the spirit money burned, the charred paper curled inward like white butterflies, and scarlet-tipped flames shimmered around the edges before dying out. He heard the paper crackle.

Having thus written off his son's residence registration to the local deity, Jin Yuanbao put the lantern and the little boy on the ground and knelt down to kowtow to the Earth God and his wives. Then he picked up his son and lantern and hurried off.

He reached Salty River by the time the sun rose above the mountain. Salt trees lining the riverbank seemed made of glass; the water was bright red. He blew out the lantern and hid it among the salt trees, then walked to the landing to wait for the ferry to ply its way across the river.

As soon as the boy was awake, he started bawling. Afraid that the energy used for crying might melt off pounds, Yuanbao knew he needed to pacify the child. At his age, he had already begun walking, so Yuanbao took him over to the sandy bank and snapped a branch off a nearby salt tree as a makeshift toy. Taking out his pipe and tobacco, he felt a soreness in his arms when he lifted it to his mouth. By then the boy was smashing black ants in the sand with his toy, which was so heavy it nearly tipped him over when he raised it above his head. The red sun climbing into the sky lit up not only the surface of the river, but the boy's face as well. Yuanbao was content to let his son play by himself. The river was half a li or so in width, its serene water muddy and turgid. When the sun made its appearance in the sky, it lay reflected in the river like a fallen post on a sheet of yellow satin. No sane person would consider building a bridge over a river like this.

The ferry was still tied up on the opposite bank, bobbing up and down in the shallows and looking very small at this distance. Not a big boat to begin with – he'd ridden it before – it was run by a deaf old man who lived in a rammed-earth hut by the river. Yuanbao saw a thread of greenish smoke rising from the hut, and knew that the deaf ferryman was cooking his breakfast. All he could do was wait.

As time passed, other passengers walked up, including two old-timers and a teenage boy, plus a middle-aged woman carrying an infant. The old couple, apparently husband and wife, sat quietly, staring at the muddy water with eyes blank as marbles. The boy, stripped to the waist and barefoot, wore only a pair of blue shorts; his face, like his nearly naked body, was pale and scaly. After running over to the river's edge to release a stream of urine into the water, he walked up next to Jin Yuanbao's son to watch the black ants being pounded into mush by the salt-tree branch. He said something unintelligible to the boy, who, astonishingly, seemed to understand him, since he laughed and flashed his baby teeth. The unkempt hair of the sallow-faced woman was tied up by a white string. She was wearing a blue jacket over black pants, both recently washed. Jin Yuanbao watched with alarm as she held the baby up to pee. A boy! A competitor. But a closer examination showed him to be much thinner than his own son; his skin was dark, his hair a dull brown. Confident that the boy was not in Little Treasure's league, he felt generous.

'Sister-in-law,' he said casually, 'is that where you're headed too?'

She looked at him suspiciously and hugged her child closer. Her lips trembled, but she said nothing.

Rebuffed, Jin Yuanbao walked off to gaze at the scenery across the river.

The sun had leaped a good ten feet above the river, which had turned from a dirty yellow to a glassy gold. The ferry remained quietly tethered on the opposite bank, as smoke continued curling up from the ceiling of the hut; no sign of the deaf ferryman.

Little Treasure and the scaly boy had walked, hand in hand, down the riverbank; anxiously, Yuanbao ran after them and scooped Little Treasure into his arms, leaving the scaly boy to look up at him with an uncomprehending stare. Little Treasure started to bawl and struggled to get down out of his father's arms.

'Don't cry,' his father said to pacify him, 'don't cry, now. Let's watch the old ferryman pole his boat over.'

He glanced again at the opposite bank; as if he had willed it, a man who seemed to glow limped toward the ferry, where several prospective passengers fell in behind him.

Jin Yuanbao held tight to Little Treasure, who soon calmed down and stopped crying. Haltingly, he complained that he was hungry, so his father took a handful of fried soybeans from his pocket, chewed them up, and transferred the pasty mixture to Little Treasure's mouth. Again the boy started crying, as if to protest the food, which he swallowed nonetheless.

The ferry was about halfway across the river when a tall, bearded man burst from the salt-tree thicket. Carrying a child who was at least two feet in length, he joined the crowd of waiting passengers.

Jin Yuanbao, his mouth smelling like burned nuts, tensed fearfully for some reason as he looked at the bearded man, who was sizing up the people on the riverbank. His eyes were big and very dark, his nose pointed and slightly hooked. The child in his arms – a boy – was dressed in a brand-new red outfit with gold stitching here and there, which made him stand out, even though he curled inward. His hair was thick and bristly, his face soft and white, but his slender eyes looked exceptionally old as they surveyed the scene. Definitely not the eyes of a child. And those ears, so big and fleshy. It would have been impossible not to take note of him, even though he was cradled in the bearded man's arms.

The bow of the ferry turned upstream as it drew up to the bank. The waiting passengers clustered together, eyes glued to the boat as it reached the shallows. Exchanging his scull for a bamboo pole, the deaf old man maneuvered the boat toward the bank, the bow raising dirty red waves until it was parallel with the land. A motley group of seven people jumped down off the boat after placing small bills or shiny coins in a gourd hanging beside the cabin; the deaf old man stood there, bamboo pole in hand, watching the river as it flowed east.

Once the incoming passengers had disembarked, the people waiting on the bank scurried aboard. Jin Yuanbao should have been first to board, but he lingered a moment to let the bearded man go ahead of him. The middle-aged woman carrying the child was right behind, followed by the old couple, who were aided by the scaly teenager: first he helped the old lady aboard, then the old man, before spryly leaping onto the bow himself.

Jin Yuanbao, seated directly across from the bearded man, was frightened by the man's deep, dark eyes, and even more so by the sinister gaze of the boy in red cradled in his arms. That was no child, it was a little demon, pure and simple. The penetrating look so unsettled Yuanbao that he couldn't sit still, and he fidgeted so much he made the boat rock. The old boatman may have been deaf, but he decidedly was not dumb.

'You, there,' he said loudly, 'sit still.'

To avoid the little demon's gaze, Yuanbao turned to look at the water, at the sun, at a solitary gray gull skimming the surface of the river. And still he was uneasy, as a series of chills swept over him, until he was forced to stare at the bare back of the boatman as he poled them across the river. Though the back was bent, the old man was quite muscular; years of living on the water had turned his skin the color of polished bronze. The sight of his body brought Jin Yuanbao a measure of comfort and revitalization, which is why he was reluctant to avert his eyes from it. The old man worked at a steady rhythm, gently moving his paddle-shaped scull from the stern, churning the water like a long brown fish chasing after them. The creaks and groans of the rope that lashed the scull down, the crashing of waves against the bow, and the old man's labored breathing all merged into a song of tranquillity; but Jin Yuanbao was anything but tranquil. Little Treasure began to howl, and he felt the child's head press painfully into his chest, as if frightened; he looked up and found himself pinned down by the awl-like gaze of the little demon. A spasm wracked Yuanbao's heart, his hair stood on end. Turning away from the gaze, he hugged his son close, as a cold sweat soaked through his clothes.

They made it to the other bank – finally. As soon as the ferry was tied up, Yuanbao took a sweat-soaked bill out of his pocket and stuffed it into the deaf old man's gourd, then hopped off the boat and onto the damp sand of the riverbank. Without so much as a glance behind him, he scurried across the sandy beach with his son in his arms. After climbing over the embankment, he found the road to town, and took off like a meteor, his feet moving like pistons. He was in a hurry to get to town, and in an even bigger hurry to put as much distance between the little demon in red and himself as possible.

The road was broad and level, and seemingly endless. Only a few yellow leaves remained on the dense yet well-spaced branches of roadside poplars; here and there a sparrow or a crow chirped or cawed. The late-autumn sky was high, the air clean; not a cloud anywhere, but Yuanbao had no time to enjoy the passing scenery as he hurried along like a rabbit trying to outrun a wolf.

It was noon by the time he reached town, tired and thirsty; Little Treasure was hot as a cinder in his arms. He reached into his pocket, found he still had a few coins, and headed for a little wineshop, where he sat at a corner table and ordered a bowlful of bottom liquor, most of which he poured down Little Treasure's throat, saving a mouthful for himself. When he raised his hand to drive off some flies buzzing around Little Treasure's head, his hand froze in mid-air, as if struck by lightning.

There, in another corner, sat the bearded man, the little demon who had thrown such fear into Jin Yuanbao's heart perched atop the table and drinking a glass of liquor as if it were water, his practiced, easy movements showing he knew his way around such an establishment. His body did not fit his movements or his manner, creating an absurd sight for everyone in the room, waiter and customer alike, their eyes glued to the little demon. But the bearded man seemed oblivious to the stares around him, too busy drinking his Penetrating Fragrance to notice. Yuanbao quickly finished his drink, tossed four coins onto the table, picked up Little Treasure, and ran out of the shop, his head so low his chin nearly touched his chest. Materialistic by nature, he was known in his village for his courage; but today was different – he had become a man terrified of his own suspicions.

It was afternoon nap time when Yuanbao found himself standing in front of the Special Purchasing Section of the Culinary Academy, which was housed in a spotless white building with a domed roof and ringed by a high brick wall with a moon gate. A garden of exotic plants and flowers, evergreens, and lush hedges surrounded an oval pond with a man-made hill that spewed water like a volcano, but in the shape of a chrysanthemum, an unending geyser of blooming and falling. The water splashed noisily when it hit the surface of the pond, which was home to turtles with intricate shell patterns. Even though this was Jin Yuanbao's second visit, he was still on pins and needles, like a man about to enter a fairy grotto, every pore of his body tremulous with the prospect of blessings.

Thirty or more people were lined up beside the steel railing; Yuanbao went to the end of the line, behind the bearded man and the little demon in red, whose head emerged above the bearded man's shoulder, the same sinister gaze in his malevolent eyes.

Yuanbao opened his mouth to scream. But he didn't dare, not there.

Two excruciatingly long hours later, the sound of a bell came from inside the building, breathing life into the dispirited, tired people in line, who stood up and began cleaning the faces or wiping the noses or straightening the clothes of the little boys in their arms. A few of them even powdered their sons' faces with cotton and added saliva-moistened dabs of rouge to their cheeks. Yuanbao wiped Little Treasure's sweaty face with his jacket sleeve and ran his fingers through the boy's hair. Only the bearded man kept his composure, as the little demon lay curled in his arms, taking in the scene with his cold eyes – calm, cool, collected.

The steel door up front swung open on groaning hinges to reveal a bright, spacious room. The business of purchasing was about to begin, and the only notable sounds were children's sobs. Purchasing agents spoke to their clients in hushed tones, lending the scene a peaceful, harmonious air. Yuanbao dropped back a bit in line, fearful of the little demon's gaze. It couldn't hurt, since the space inside the railing was wide enough to accommodate only one child-laden adult at a time. No one could squeeze past him from behind. The sound of splashing water in the fountain rose and fell, but never stopped completely; birds chirped in the trees.

After a woman came out of the room empty-handed, the bearded man and the little demon went in to be interviewed. Yuanbao and Little Treasure were a good ten feet away, too far to hear what was said. Putting his fears aside, Yuanbao observed them carefully. He watched a man in a white uniform and a red-bordered chef's hat take the little demon from the bearded man. The normally somber look on the little demon's face was replaced by a smile that terrified Yuanbao; the staff worker, on the other hand, seemed unaffected, since the smile was intended to give him a warm, fuzzy feeling. After removing the little demon's clothes, the man prodded his chest with a glass rod, which made him giggle. A moment later, Yuanbao heard the big man bellow:

'Second-grade? You're trying to cheat me, damn you!'

The staff worker raised his voice slightly:

'I know my business, friend, and how to judge quality. This boy of yours has heft, that I'll admit. But his skin is leathery and his flesh is tough. If he hadn't smiled so sweetly, he'd be no better than third-grade!'

The bearded man grumbled angrily before snatching the proffered bills. After a cursory count, he stuffed them into his pocket and walked out of the room with his head down. Yuanbao heard the little fellow inside, who'd had a second-grade tag stuck to his skin, curse the retreating back of the bearded man:

'You fucking murderer! I hope you get hit by a truck as soon as you walk outside, you bitch-fucking bastard, you!'

His voice was shrill and hoarse, and no one alive could possibly have mistaken the vile language as having come from the mouth of a child not even three feet tall. Yuanbao looked into that face, which had been smiling only a moment ago and was now scowling angrily, his brow creased, and he was reminded of a pint-sized butcher. All five staff workers leaped to their feet in astonishment, faces clouded with fear; for a moment they didn't know what to do. The little demon, hands on his hips, spat a mouthful of saliva at them, then swaggered over to a crowd of huddled children with tags on their bodies.

The staff workers stood dumbfounded for a moment, then exchanged glances, as if comforting one another: No big deal, right? No big deal.

The work recommenced. A ruddy-faced, middle-aged man in a chef's cap sitting behind a desk motioned genially to Jin Yuanbao, who rushed up to him. His heart was in his mouth. Little Treasure started crying again, and Yuanbao tried his best to calm him. He recalled what had happened on the previous occasion: He had arrived late that time, and the quota was already filled. He might have been able to beg his way in the door, but Little Treasure had cried so hard he'd nearly gone crazy. Now it was happening all over again.

'Good little boy, don't cry,' he said imploringly. 'People don't like children who cry all the time.'

The worker asked softly:

'Was this child born specifically for the Special Purchasing Section?'

Yuanbao's throat was so painfully dry that his affirmative answer sounded forced and strange.

'So, he's not a person, right?' the worker continued.

'Right, he's not a person.'

'What you're selling is a special product and not a child, right?'

'Right.'

'You give us the merchandise, we pay you. You're a willing seller, we're willing buyers, a fair business transaction. Once the exchange is made, there'll be no quibbling, is that right?'

'Right.'

'OK, put your thumbprint here.' The worker slid a prepared document across the desk along with an ink pad.

'I don't know how to read, comrade,' Yuanbao said. 'What does this say?'

'It's a written version of the transaction we just completed,' the worker replied.

Yuanbao left a big red thumbprint in the spot pointed out to him by the worker. He felt relieved, as if he'd finished what he came to do.

A staff member walked up and took Little Treasure from him. He was still bawling, which the woman brought to a halt by squeezing his neck. Yuanbao bent down to watch as she removed Little Treasure's clothes and quickly but efficiently examined him from head to toe, including a look up his little asshole and a tug at his foreskin to check the head of his little pecker.

She clapped her hands and announced to the man behind the desk:

'Top grade!'

Yuanbao nearly burst with excitement; he damn near cried.

Another staff member picked up Little Treasure and put him on a scale.

'Twenty-one catties, four ounces,' he announced softly.

A staff member punched a little machine, from which a slip of paper emerged with a whirr. He motioned Yuanbao over.

'Top grade goes for a hundred yuan a cattie,' he said to Yuanbao as he walked up to the machine. 'Twenty-one catties, four ounces works out to be two thousand one hundred forty yuan in People's Currency.'

He handed Yuanbao a stack of bills and the slip of paper.

'Count it,' he said.

Yuanbao was trembling so badly he could barely make his way through the stack of bills. His mind was like mush. Holding on to the money for dear life, he asked with a catch in his voice:

'Is this all mine?'

The man nodded.

'Can I go now?'

The man nodded.

Chapter Three

The boy sat cross-legged in the middle of the gilded platter, golden brown and oozing sweet-smelling oil, a giddy smile frozen on his face. Lovely, naive. Around him was spread a garland of green vegetable leaves and bright red radish blossoms. The stupefied investigator swallowed back the juices that rumbled up from his stomach as he gawked at the boy. A pair of limpid eyes gazed back at him, steam puffed out of the boy's nostrils, and the lips quivered as if he were about to speak. His smile, his naive loveliness, filled the investigator's mind with many thoughts; somewhere, he sensed vaguely, he'd seen this boy. Somewhere, and not so long ago. Crisp laughter rang in the investigator's ears. The aroma of fresh strawberries surged from the boy's tiny mouth. Tell me a story, Papa. Leave Papa alone. The pink-faced child was cradled by the sweet-smiling wife. All of a sudden, her smile turned strange, spooky. Her cheeks twitched noticeably with feigned mystery. Bastards! He banged his fist on the table and stood up angrily.

A meaningful smile showed on Diamond Jin's face, the Mine Director and Party Secretary grinned craftily. The investigator thought he must be dreaming. He opened his eyes to survey the scene; the boy was still sitting cross-legged on the platter.

'After you, Comrade Ding, old fellow,' Diamond Jin said.

'This is a famous dish in these parts,' the Party Secretary and Mine Director said. 'It's called Stork Delivering a Son. We serve it only to visiting dignitaries. It's a dish they won't forget for as long as they live, one that has drawn nothing but praise. We've earned a lot of convertible currency for the nation by serving it to our most honored guests. Such as yourself, sir.'

'After you, Comrade Ding! Special Investigator Ding Gou'er of the Higher Procuratorate, please sample our Stork Delivering a Son.' The Party Secretary and Mine Director waved their chopsticks in the air, urging their guest to dig in.

The boy exuded a powerful, irresistible fragrance. His mouth watering, Ding Gou'er reached into his briefcase to feel the cold muzzle and star-inlaid carved handle of his pistol. The muzzle was round, the sight atop it triangular; it was cool to the touch. Everything felt just right, his senses were in good working order. I'm not drunk, I'm Investigator Ding Gou'er, on assignment in the city of Liquorland to investigate a group of cadres, led by Diamond Jin, who are reputed to be feasting on little boys, a serious charge, a major charge, a damning accusation, a cruelty virtually unknown anywhere in the world, a corruption unprecedented in the history of man. I am not drunk, I am not hallucinating. They're mistaken if they think they can get away with this. A braised child has been placed on the table in front of me, in their words, a platter of Stork Delivering a Son. My mind is clear, but I'll test my faculties, just in case: eighty-five times eighty-five is seven thousand two hundred twenty-five. There, that should prove it. They killed a little boy for my dining pleasure. These conspirators want to make me an accessory by stuffing his flesh into my mouth. He whipped out his pistol.

'Don't move!' he commanded. 'Put your hands up, you monsters!'

The three men sat there stunned, but the red girls shrieked and huddled together, like a flock of startled chicks. Pistol in hand, Ding Gou'er pushed back from the table and retreated a couple of steps, until he was standing with his back to the window. If they had any battle experience, he thought, they'd have little trouble wresting the pistol out of my hand. But they didn't, and now all three were staring down the barrel of his gun. They'd better not move, if they knew what was good for them. His briefcase had fallen to the floor when he stood up. The skin between his thumb and index finger felt the cold steel of the pistol resting against it; he tested the gentle give of the trigger. He had released the safety when he pulled the pistol from his briefcase, so the bullet and firing pin were ready for the next move; one twitch is all it would take.

'You bastards,' he said coldly. 'You lousy Fascists! Get your hands up, I said!'

Diamond Jin raised his hands slowly; the Party Secretary and Mine Director followed suit.

'Comrade Ding, old fellow, aren't you carrying this joke a little too far?' Diamond Jin asked with a smile.

'Joke?' Ding Gou'er gnashed his teeth in anger. 'Who do you think is joking? You child-eating monsters!'

Diamond Jin threw his head back and roared with laughter. The Party Secretary and Mine Director laughed too, but foolishly.

'Old Ding, good old Ding, you're a fine comrade with a strong humanistic bent, for which I respect you,' Diamond Jin said. 'But you're wrong. You've made a subjective error. Look closely. Is that a little boy?'

His words had the desired effect on Ding Gou'er, who turned to look at the boy on the platter. He was still smiling, his lips parted slightly, as if he were about to speak.

'He's incredibly lifelike!' Ding Gou'er said loudly.

'Right, *lifelike*,' Diamond Jin repeated. 'And why is this fake child so lifelike? Because the chefs here in Liquorland are extraordinarily talented, uncanny masters.'

The Party Secretary and Mine Director echoed his praise:

'And this isn't the best we have to offer! A professor at the Culinary Academy can make them so that even the eyelashes flutter. No one dares let his chopsticks touch one of hers.'

'Comrade Ding, old fellow, put down your gun and pick up your chopsticks. Join us in sampling this unique taste-treat!' Diamond Jin lowered his hands and made a welcoming gesture to Ding Gou'er.

'No!' Ding Gou'er replied sternly. 'I hereby proclaim that I will not participate in this feast of yours!'

A look of irritation appeared on Diamond Jin's face as he said in measured tones:

'You sure are stubborn, Comrade Ding, old fellow. We are all men who raised their fists and took an oath before the Party flag. The people's pursuit of happiness may be your responsibility, but it is also mine. Don't delude yourself into thinking that you're the only decent person in the world. People who have partaken of

Liquorland's child feast include senior leaders in the Party and the government, highly respected friends from the five great continents, plus renowned artists and celebrities from China and the rest of the world. They have praised us effusively. You alone, Investigator Ding Gou'er, have responded to our lavish treatment by drawing a weapon on us!'

The Party Secretary or Mine Director echoed the sentiment:

'Comrade Ding Gou'er, what evil wind has clouded your vision? Are you aware that your pistol is aimed not at class enemies, but at your very own class brothers?'

Ding Gou'er's wrist faltered, the barrel of his gun sagged. His eyes blurred and the lovely butterfly that had returned to its cocoon began to squirm again. Feelings of dread pressed down on him like a boulder, weighing heavily on his shoulders until he felt that his position was untenable, and that his skeleton could crumble at any moment. He was face-to-face with a bottomless, foul-smelling cesspool that would pull him down into its obliterating muck and keep him there forever. But that cunning little fellow, the boy gushing perfume, a tiny son joining ranks with his mother, sitting amid a fairy mist the shape and color of a lotus flower, raised his hand, actually raised his hand toward me! His fingers were stubby, pudgy, meaty and so very lovely. Wrinkles on his fingers, three circular seams; the back of his hand sporting four prominent dimples. The sweet sound of his laughter wound round the fragrance hanging in the air. The lotus began to levitate, carrying the child along with it. His round little belly button, so childish and innocent, like a dimple on a cheek. You sweet-talking brigands! Don't think you can lie and cheat your way out of this! The cooked little boy smiled at me. You say this child is actually a famous dish. Whoever heard such nonsense? During the Warring States period, Yi Ya cooked and fed his son to Duke Huan of Qi, and the taste was superb, like tender lamb, but better. You bunch of Yi Yas, where do you think you're going? Get your hands up, and take what's coming to you! Yi Ya had it all over you. At least he cooked his own son. You cook other people's sons. Yi Ya was a member of the feudal landlord class, and devotion to his king was a noble calling. You are ranking Party cadres who kill the sons of common folk to fill your own bellies. Heaven will not tolerate such sins! I hear the piteous wails of little boys in the steamers. I hear them wailing in crackling woks, on chopping blocks, in oil, salt, soy sauce, vinegar, sugar, anise powder, peppercorns, cinnamon, ginger, and cooking liquor. They are wailing in your intestines, in the toilets, and in the sewers. They are wailing in the rivers and in the septic tanks. They are wailing in the bellies of fish and in the soil of farmlands. In the bellies of whales, sharks, eels, and hairtail fish. In tassels of wheat, in kernels of corn, in tender peapods, in the vines of sweet potatoes, in the stalks of sorghum, and in pollens of millet. Why are they wailing? They cry and they cry, they howl, breaking the heart of anyone who hears the sound emerging from apples, from pears, from grapes, from peaches and apricots, and from walnuts. Fruit stalls carry the sound of children crying. Vegetable stalls carry the sound of children crying. Slaughterhouses carry the sound of children crying. From the banquet tables of Liquorland come the chilling, skin-crawling wails of one murdered little boy after another. Who should I shoot if not you three?

He saw greasy faces floating in the mist surrounding the braised boy, appearing and disappearing like the glitter of broken glass. Greasy, cynical, disdainful smiles were draped across their transient faces. The fires of anger filled his chest. Righteous, vengeful flames blazed, turning the room the dazzling bright red of lotus blossoms. You bastards! he roared. Your day of judgment has arrived! He heard a roar erupt from the top of his head, and it sounded strange to him. It bounced against the ceiling and silently shattered into shards like fallen petals, the fragmented sounds dragging behind them smoky red tails that settled like dust over the banquet table. He squeezed the trigger in the direction of the kaleidoscopic faces, those faces with their glass inlays, those sinister smiles. With a *crack*, the trigger drove the firing pin into the green rump of that lovely, shiny copper casing, igniting the gunpowder, faster than the eye can see, compressing the gas and sending the bullet forward, ever forward ever forward ever forward forward forward. With a deafening explosion and a puff of smoke, the bullet burst from the mouth of the barrel. The explosion rolled like waves, ear-splitting crescendos, causing all the unrighteous, all the inhumane to tremble before it. Causing all the decent and honest, all the good and beautiful, all the sweet-smelling to clap their hands and laugh joyously. Long live righteousness, long live truth, long live the people, long live the Republic. Long live my magnificent son. Long live boys. Long live girls. Long live the mothers of boys and girls. Long live me, too. To all, long life, long life, long long life.

Beginning to froth at the mouth, the special investigator mumbled incoherently, slowly, like a dilapidated wall crumbling to dust. Drinking glasses swept off the table by his hand and the pistol it held were sent crashing into his body, soaking his clothes and his face with beer, strong colorless liquor, and grape wine. He lay on the floor, face down, like a corpse fished out of a fermentation vat.

Many minutes passed before Diamond Jin, the Party Secretary, the Mine Director, and the huddled group of red serving girls recovered and crawled out from under the table, rose from the floor, or stuck their heads out from under someone's skirt. The overpowering smell of gunpowder permeated the dining room. Ding Gou'er's bullet had struck the braised boy right between the eyes, shattering the head and sending brain matter splattering against the wall, a mixture of reds and whites, steaming and redolent, releasing an abundance of emotions. The braised boy was now a headless boy. The unsmashed parts of his skull had tumbled to the edge of the table's second tier, between a platter of sea cucumbers and another of braised shrimp, pieces of head like shattered watermelon rind, or pieces of watermelon rind like shattered head, watermelon juices dripping like blood, or blood dripping like watermelon juices, soiling the tablecloth and soiling the people's eyes. A pair of eyes like purple grapes or purple grapes like a pair of eyes rolled around on the floor, one skittering behind the liquor cabinet, the other rolling up to a red serving girl, who squashed it with her foot. She rocked back and forth briefly, a shrill 'Waa!' emerging from between her lips.

In the wake of that 'Waa!' Party spirit, principle, and morality – all those qualities that combine to make a leader – returned to their minds and coordinated their actions. The Party Secretary or Mine Director stuck out his tongue and tasted pieces of the boy's brains that had bespattered the back of his hand. It must have been delicious, because he smacked his lips and said:

'He's ruined a perfectly good plate of food!'

Diamond Jin gave the fellow tasting the splattered brain a dirty look, bringing embarrassment to his face.

'Help Comrade Ding to his feet,' Deputy Head Jin said, 'and be quick about it! Clean off his face and feed him a bowl of sobering-up soup.'

The red serving girls sprang into action. After helping Ding Gou'er to his feet, they wiped his mouth and face, but didn't dare clean his hands. He was still holding the pistol, which could go off again at any time. They swept up the broken glass and mopped the floor, then propped up his head and pried open his mouth with a sterilized stainless-steel tongue-depressor to insert a hard plastic funnel, through which they fed him sobering-up soup, one spoonful after another.

'What grade soup is that?' Diamond Jin asked.

'First,' the red serving girl in charge replied.

'Use second grade,' Diamond Jin said. 'It'll sober him up faster.'

The serving girl went into the kitchen and returned with a bottle of gold-colored liquid. As the wooden stopper was removed, a cool, refreshing odor went straight from the bottle into the hearts of the people in the room. They poured more than half of the golden liquid into the funnel. Ding Gou'er coughed, he choked, the liquid shot up out of the funnel like a geyser.

He felt a cool stream of liquid enter his digestive tract, where it extinguished the fires and reawakened his mental faculties. Now that his body had come back to life, he recaptured the beautiful butterfly of consciousness that was trying to climb out of his skull. When he opened his eyes, the first thing he saw was the headless little boy sitting in the gilded platter; that sent stabbing pains straight to his heart. Dear mother! he blurted out involuntarily. Oh the agony! He raised his pistol.

Diamond Jin raised his chopsticks.

'Comrade Ding Gou'er,' he said, 'if we really are monsters who eat little boys, you have every right to shoot us dead. But what if we aren't? The Party gave you that pistol to punish evil-doers, not to indiscriminately snuff out the lives of the innocent.'

'If you have something to say, out with it,' Ding Gou'er said.

Diamond Jin took one of his chopsticks and thrust it into the headless little boy's darling little erect penis. The boy crumbled in the platter and turned into a pile of body parts. Using his chopstick as a pointer, Diamond Jin launched into his clarification:

'This is one of the boy's arms, it's made of rich lotus root from Moon Lake, melon, and sixteen herbs and spices, fashioned with extraordinary artistry. This leg is actually a special ham sausage. The boy's torso is made from a processed suckling sow. The head, to which your bullet put an end, was fashioned out of a silver melon. His hair was nothing more than strings of the hirsute vegetable. Now it's impossible for me to give you a detailed and accurate description of all the materials or the meticulous and complex workmanship that went into the preparation of this famous dish, since it's patented here in Liquorland. Besides, I have only a rough idea myself. Otherwise, I'd be a chef too. But I am authorized to inform you that this dish is legal and humane, and that it should be the target of chopsticks, not a bullet.'

Having said his piece, Diamond Jin picked up one of the boy's hands and began eating it hungrily. The Party Secretary or Mine Director stabbed an arm with a silver fork and placed it on Ding Gou'er's plate.

'Go ahead, Comrade Ding, old fellow,' he said respectfully, 'dig in.'

Still agitated, Ding Gou'er subjected the arm to a careful examination. It had the appearance of rich lotus root, yet looked like a real arm. The aroma was certainly seductive, sweet, like that of lotus root, yet uniquely unfamiliar. Sheepishly he put the pistol back into his briefcase. Just because I'm here on special assignment doesn't mean I can go around shooting anyone and anything I please! I must be more careful. Diamond Jin picked up a sharp knife and – one-two-three – chopped the other arm into ten pieces. He picked up one and held it out to Ding Gou'er.

'Five-eyed lotus root,' he said. 'How about an arm, does it have eyes?'

As he listened to Diamond Jin gnaw on the arm, he could tell it was lotus root. He looked down at the piece in front of him, and couldn't decide if he should try it or not. The Party Secretary and Mine Director were chewing on the boy's legs. Diamond Jin handed him the knife and smiled his encouragement. Taking the knife, he tentatively laid the blade against the arm. As if drawn by a magnet, it sank into the armlike lotus root with a slurp and sliced it in two.

He picked up a piece of the arm with his chopsticks, closed his eyes, and crammed it into his mouth. Waaa, my god! His taste buds cheered in unison, his jaw muscles twitched, and a hand reached up from his throat to pull the thing down.

'That's the ticket,' Diamond Jin said cheerfully. 'Now Comrade Ding Gou'er is wallowing in the muck with the rest of us. You've eaten a little boy's arm.'

Ding Gou'er froze. 'You told me it wasn't real,' he said as his suspicions returned.

'Oh, my dear comrade,' Diamond Jin said, 'don't be silly. I was just having fun with you! Use your head. Liquorland's a civilized city, not some savage, backwater nation. Who could bear to actually eat children? That the Higher Procuratorate believed such a fantastic tale and actually sent someone to investigate makes quite a case for its standards. Those of a novelist with an overactive imagination, if you ask me.'

The two mine dignitaries held out their glasses.

'Comrade Ding,' they said, 'you had no reason to fire your pistol. Your punishment is three glasses!'

Ding Gou'er accepted this well-deserved punishment with equanimity.

'Comrade Ding, you see everything in black and white,' Diamond Jin said. 'You either love or you hate. Here's to you, three glasses!'

As a man who thrived on flattery, Ding Gou'er happily complied.

Now with six glassfuls in his stomach, the blur returned. When the Mine Director or Party Secretary passed half of the other arm to him, he threw down his chopsticks, snatched it up in both hands, grease and all, and attacked it with his teeth.

Everyone laughed as Ding Gou'er gobbled up the arm. The Mine Director and Party Secretary urged the red serving girls to toast their guest. The coquettish red girls managed to coax Ding Gou'er into downing another twenty-one glassfuls. He was stuck to the ceiling when he heard Diamond Jin say his good-byes.

*

From his vantage point on the ceiling he watched Diamond Jin walk tranquilly out of the dining hall and heard him tell the Mine Director and Party Secretary to attend to something on his way out. The spring-hung naugahyde-covered doors were opened by two red girls, one on either side, respectful and attentive. He noticed how their hair was coifed atop their heads, he noticed their necks, and he also noticed the swellings on their chests. He immediately castigated himself for being such a degenerate voyeur. He saw the Party Secretary and Mine Director say something to the leader of the red serving girls on their way out. Now that all the men had left the room, the red serving girls crowded around the table and dug in, stuffing food into their mouths with both hands. They ate like barbarians, a far cry from their demeanor of a moment before. He saw the shell of his body, slouched in a chair like a hunk of dead meat, his neck pressing against the chair back, his head flopping to one side, liquor dribbling out of his mouth like an overturned gourd. From his vantage point on the ceiling, he wept over the half-dead body he had left behind.

Once they finished eating, the girls wiped their mouths with the tablecloth. One of them picked up a pack of China cigarettes when no one was looking and stuffed it into her bra. He sighed in commiseration for her breast, which had to share its cup with cigarettes. He heard the girl in charge say:

'Come on, girls, carry this drunken kitty over to the guest house.'

Two girls tried lifting him up by the arms, but had trouble holding him, as if he were a rag doll. He heard a girl with a mole behind one ear grumble, The damned dog! That angered him. He watched as one of the girls picked up his briefcase, unzipped it, and took out the pistol, turning it over in her hand to get a good look at it. He cried out in alarm from the ceiling: Put that down! It could go off. But they might as well have been deaf. God help me! She shoved the pistol back into the briefcase, then unzipped an inner pocket and removed his mistress's photograph. Come look at this! she said. The red girls crowded round and happily voiced their opinions. His anger reached its peak, as a stream of filthy language spewed from his mouth. The girls were oblivious to it all.

At long last, the red serving girls managed to hoist up my body

84

enough to drag me out of the dining room and onto the hallway carpet, as if they were disposing of a corpse. One of them kicked me in the calf – intentionally. Slut. My flesh may be insensate, but my spirit isn't. Hovering three feet above their heads, I flapped my wings and began to glide through the air, following behind my useless corporeal body and gazing at it with deep sadness. It was, it seemed, a very long hallway. I watched the liquor seep out of my mouth and run down my neck. It stank to high heaven, and the red girls plugged their noses to avoid it. One had an attack of the dry heaves. With my head slumped on my chest, my neck looked like a wilted stalk of garlic. No wonder my head lolled back and forth. I couldn't see my face, but had a bird's-eye view of both my pale ears. One of the red girls followed along carrying my briefcase.

At long last we made it to the end of the seemingly endless hallway, where I saw a familiar large hall. They dumped my body on the carpet, face up. The sight of that face shocked me: eyes squeezed shut, skin the color of old, torn window paper. My parted lips revealed a motley mouthful of teeth, some white, some black. A foul, boozy breath spilled out, and it was all I could do to keep from throwing up. Shivers wracked my flesh, and my pants were soaked. What a pity, I'd wet myself.

After resting to catch their breath, the red girls carried me out of the hall. A sea of sunflowers lay beneath a blood-red sun, the golden yellow blossoms exuding warmth against the scarlet background. A gleaming silver sedan was parked on a smooth cement road that cut through the sunflower forest. Diamond Jin climbed into the back seat of the car, which drove off slowly, the twin gentlemen waving as it passed by and picked up speed. The red girls dragged me down the road to the accompaniment of a barking dog beneath a sunflower plant whose stem was as thick as a tree trunk. Its glossy black body, topped by white ears, lurched back and forth each time it barked, accordion-fashion. Where were they taking me? Lights all around shone like shifty eyes. All the machinery was just as it had been that morning, including the windlass at the mouth of the mine. A gang of black-faced men in hard-hats came walking up. For some unknown reason, I was afraid to meet up with these men. If they had friendly intentions, well and good, but if not, I was in for it. The men quickly lined up on both sides of the road, forming a gauntlet past which the red serving girls carried me. My nostrils picked up the smell of sweat and damp mine-shaft stench. The men's eyes bored through my body like drills. Some hurled curses as I passed by, but the red serving girls held their heads high and thrust out their chests proudly, ignoring the men. Then I realized that the curses, filled with sexual innuendo, were directed at them, not at me.

They carried me into a remote little building, where two women in white sat across from each other at a writing desk, their knees touching; some words had been carved on the desk. Their knees moved away slightly when we entered the shack; one of the women pressed a button on the wall, causing a door to open slowly. An elevator, apparently. After they carried me inside and closed the door, I saw I'd guessed correctly. The descent was meteoric, and I followed my body down the shaft, like a kite being tugged by its string. Down and down we went. A coal mine, I thought admiringly, which meant that all the activity would be underground. I was convinced they could have built an entire Great Wall underground if they had wanted to. The elevator shuddered noisily three times – we had reached the bottom. A blinding white light filled my eyes as I was carried into a sumptuous grand hall on whose watery smooth marble walls human shadows danced; the relief patterns on the ceiling were illuminated by hundreds of exquisite little lamps. Flowers and potted plants were arrayed around four enormous angular columns with marble facing. The sight of scabby goldfish swimming in an ultra-modern aquarium made my skin crawl. The girls placed my body in room 401. I had no idea how the number 401 was arrived at, and wondered what kind of place this was. Manhattan's high-rises stretch up to Heaven; Liquorland's reach down to Hell. The girls stripped the shoes off my feet before laying me on a bed; my briefcase wound up on a tea table. They left. Five minutes later, a cream-colored serving girl opened the door and walked in to put a cup of tea on the table. Some tea for your honor, I heard her say to my body.

My body did not reply.

The cream-colored girl wore heavy makeup; her lashes were as thick as hog bristles. Just then the telephone at the head of the bed rang. She reached out and picked up the receiver with tapered fingers. The room was so quiet I could hear a man's voice on the other end.

'Is he awake?'

'He hasn't moved. He's scary.'

'See if he's got a heartbeat.'

She laid her palm on my chest; a palpable look of disgust on her face.

'He's got one,' she said.

'Give him some sobering-up tonic.'

'OK.'

The cream-colored girl left the room. I knew she'd be right back. She returned with a metal syringe, the kind veterinarians use. Since the tip was made of soft plastic, I didn't have to worry about an injection. After inserting the tip between my lips, she forced some medicinal liquid through the syringe.

Before long, I heard the sounds of my body coming to and saw its arms move. It said something. It emitted a powerful force that tried to snag me. I struggled, turning myself into a sort of suction cup on the ceiling to resist being drawn downward; but I sensed that a part of me had already fallen prey to the force.

With difficulty, it sat up and opened its eyes, staring blankly at the wall for a long time. It picked up the teacup and drained it thirstily before falling backwards on the bed.

Quite a while later, the door opened softly and a barefoot, bare-chested boy wearing only a pair of blue shorts walked in; about fourteen or fifteen years old, he had scaly skin. He was light on his feet, making no sound at all as he approached me, like a black cat. I watched him with considerable interest. He looked familiar; I'd seen that boy somewhere before. A knife shaped like a willow leaf clenched between his teeth gave him the appearance of a black cat with a fish in its mouth.

I was scared, believe me, scared for that half-dead body of mine. At the same time I was puzzled over how a demon like that could have found his way into this hidden underground spot. The door closed by itself, creating a silence that pounded against my eardrums. As the scaly boy drew up next to me, I smelled a fishy odor, that of a scaly anteater that has just crawled out from under a rock. What was he going to do? His hair, matted and filled with burrs, smelled like little snakes, which slithered into my nostrils and headed straight for my brain. My body sneezed, sending the little demon crashing to the carpeted floor. He scrambled to his feet and touched my throat with his claws. The knife in his mouth emitted a cold blue glint. Oh, how I wanted to warn my body, but I couldn't. I wracked my brains – squeezed them dry is more like it – to recall how, when, and where I'd done anything to offend this little demon. He reached out again, this time to pinch that area called the neck, like a master chef preparing to slaughter a chicken. I could feel his terrifying, hard claw, and still my body lay there helpless, snoring away, oblivious to the knowledge that the Grim Reaper hovered mere inches away. I found myself wishing he'd take the knife from his mouth and plunge it into my body's throat to bring an end to my suffering there in my ceiling perch. But he didn't. Now that he'd had his fill of pinching my throat, his claw moved down to touch my clothing and go through my pockets. He removed a Hero-brand gold fountain pen, took off the cap, and drew some lines on the back of his hand. There were scales there too. After drawing a line, he pulled his hand back, and his lips parted in what might have been a grin and might have been a pained look. I guess the nib made his skin itch, a sensation that either brought him pleasure or rekindled a fond memory. Over and over he drew lines; over and over his lips parted. Each line produced a scratchy sound, and I knew that my top-of-the-line Hero 800 gold fountain pen was a goner. It had been awarded to me as a model worker. This idiotic game went on for half an hour at least, until finally he laid the pen on the floor and recommenced his search of my pockets. He removed a handkerchief, a pack of cigarettes, an electronic cigarette lighter, my ID card, a remarkably lifelike toy pistol, my wallet, and a couple of coins. By the looks of it, this treasure trove had a dizzying effect on him. Like a greedy little boy, he laid it all out on the floor between his legs and began playing with each item as if he were the only person in the world. The fountain pen, of course, no longer interested him. Naturally, instinctively, he picked up the toy pistol and held it in front of him. The chrome barrel glinted in the artificial light. It was a perfectly crafted imitation of the real thing, the kind American military officers wear on their hips. It was beautiful. I knew there were still some caps in the chamber, ready to explode as soon as the trigger was pulled. Joy and excitement made his eyes sparkle enticingly. I was worried he'd give himself away if he pulled the trigger. How much difference was there between the boy's arm and the fresh lotus root? Was my body being tricked? But it was too late to do anything. *Pow!* He pulled the trigger. I saw blue smoke and heard the explosion in the same instant. I held my breath, waiting for the sound of hurried footsteps outside the door and for the cream-colored girls and their guards to come bursting into the room. What could a gunshot in the middle of the night mean but murder or suicide? I began to worry about the plight of my scaly visitor, not wanting him to be caught. I must be honest – I was intrigued by the little fellow, but not because of his scales. There are plenty of scaly creatures – fish, snakes, anteaters – and all but the anteaters, those clumsy, somewhat affected, animals, give me the creeps; I don't care for cold, smelly fish, and dreary serpents disgust me. But my conjectures proved groundless. The gunshot changed nothing: no one came barging into the room, nothing. My visitor fired another round; in truth, this second explosion was unspectacular, commonplace, at least in that sound-proof room, with its thick carpet, protected ceiling, and papered walls. He sat there undisturbed – no fear, no shock; either he was deaf or was a seasoned veteran, unfazed by such things. Having tired of the pistol, he tossed it aside and picked up my wallet, removing its contents – money, grain rations, cafeteria coupons, and expenditure receipts I hadn't yet turned in for reimbursement. He fiddled with the cigarette lighter, from which a bright tongue of flame erupted. He smoked a cigarette. He coughed. He flicked the cigarette onto the carpet. My god! The carpet caught fire, and the stench of burning material rose in the air. Then it hit me: If my body was reduced to ashes, I'd be nothing but a puff of smoke. Its extinguishing would herald mine as well. Wake up, my body!

I hate you, you scaly demon!

No, I don't hate you, I want only to laugh. But I can't, as a matter of fact. He noticed the fire on the carpet and stood up slowly. Lifting one leg of his shorts, he reached in with two fingers, grabbed hold of his water hose, which was pretty big for his size, hard but not erect, and as scaly as the rest of his body, and took aim at the burning carpet. A loud spray of water produced an equally loud sizzle. It was a gusher, powerful enough to put out two such fires. I relaxed as I breathed in the mixed odor of urine and a drenched fire.

He began stripping the clothes from my body, determined to remove my jacket, one way or the other. I heard him panting. Once his task was accomplished, he put the jacket on. The hem came down to his knees. After picking up his new toys, he stuffed them into the jacket pockets. Now what was he going to do?

He spit the knife out and, gripping it in his hand, took a look around the room. He then carved the character for ten [+] into the wall four times, put the knife back between his teeth, as if clenching a willow leaf, flicked his floppy sleeves, and swaggered out of the room.

My body, having been dumped back onto the bed, snored on.

II

Dear Mo Yan, Sir

Please permit me to use that address. It's the only way I can avoid feeling unhappy, awkward, or uncomfortable.

Sir, you are indeed my true, my genuine, mentor, for not only are you a master novelist, but you know your way around a liquor bottle. Your novels are as finely crafted as the foot wrappings of a practiced grandmother. With liquor your accomplishments are, if anything, even greater. It is no great achievement in this day and age to locate a fine novelist, nor, for that matter, a master disciple of the bottle. But to find them both in a single individual is extraordinarily difficult. And you, Sir, are that unique individual.

Your analysis of Overlapping Green Ants was both incisive and accurate, the mark of a true connoisseur. The basic ingredients of this liquor are sorghum and mung

beans, fermented in an old cellar. The culture for our
distiller's yeast is a mixture of wheat, bran, and peas, with
a touch of chaff. The distilled liquor that emerges is a
graceful, muted light green in color with a heavy fragrance,
rich and full bodied, with a real kick. During the blending
process, everything possible has been done to suppress its
fiery nature, but with limited success so far. In order to get
it to a liquor fair, we marketed the not-yet-perfected brew
as Overlapping Green Ants. It is, as you say, high-quality
liquor whose imperfection is a lack of harmony.

Using beautiful women as a metaphor for liquor is the
best, most vivid means of characterizing its qualities. Your
intuition in this regard was right on the mark. My
father-in-law, Professor Yuan Shuangyu, and I have been
trying to come up with ways of improving Overlapping
Green Ants for a long time, and our contemplations have
nearly reached maturity; unfortunately, I have, of late,
become so intoxicated with literature that I can think of
nothing else.

Sir, in this vast world, with its teeming multitudes,
liquor swells like the seas and spirits flow like rivers, yet
the number of true devotees, those who enjoy fine liquor
as they marvel over beautiful women, are rare as morning
stars, as the feathers of a phoenix or the horn of a unicorn,
as a tiger's penis and a dinosaur egg. You, Sir, are one of
them, as am I, your disciple. So, too, is my father-in-law,
Yuan Shuangyu; Deputy Head Diamond Jin counts as half
of one. The great Tang poet, Li Bai, is one. 'I raise my
glass to the moon / With my shadow, we make three.'
How can that be, you ask? Li is one, the moon is another,
the third is the liquor. For the moon is Chang'e, the
heavenly beauty! The liquor is 'Qinglian,' the green lotus,
an earthly marvel. Li Bai and his liquor are fused into one,
becoming what he styled himself – Li Qinglian. That is
why he was able to produce such exquisite visions as he
roamed freely between Heaven and earth. His fellow Tang
poet, Du Fu, counts as half. His intake of liquor was, in
the main, limited to village brews, poor in quality,

overaged and bitter, coarse and lacking polish, like an old widow; no wonder he was unable to write poetry that was vigorous and lively. Cao Mengde [Cao Cao] was one; singing a song when drinking is the same as serenading a beautiful woman. Life is short, beautiful women are like the morning dew. Beauty is constantly aflow and easily lost, so one must enjoy it while one can. From ancient times till today, a span of five thousand years, the number of individuals who have understood that drinking fine spirits is like adoring a beautiful woman does not exceed a few dozen. All the rest are foul leather sacks that can be filled with any brackish liquid. Why waste a drop of Overlapping Green Ants or Eighteen-Li Red on the likes of them?

The mere mention of Eighteen-Li Red makes your disciple's heart flutter. Sir, believe me when I say that it is a masterpiece of earth-shaking proportions. Pissing into a vat of liquor as a blending maneuver was an astonishing touch that only a creative master could have dreamed up. It constitutes a landmark in the history of distilling liquor. The most glorious events invariably incorporate elements of the most despicable nature. People everywhere know that honey is sweet, but how many know what goes into its making? They say that the primary ingredient of honey is nectar from flowers! Yes it is, no one can say differently. Saying that the primary ingredient of honey is nectar is as accurate as saying that the primary ingredient of liquor is alcohol, but that tells us nothing. There are dozens of minerals in liquor, did you know that? There are also dozens of micro-organisms in liquor, did you know that? And there are many more things, most of which even I cannot name, in liquor. Did you know *that*? If my father-in-law does not know and I do not know, it is a cinch that you do not know. There is ocean water in honey, did you know that? And there is manure in honey, did you know that? Honey cannot be produced without fresh excrement, did you or did you not know that?

I have been reading in periodicals recently that certain

benighted individuals, who don't know the first thing about making liquor, have taken offense at your surpassingly uncanny pioneering work, saying that pissing in a vat of liquor is a blasphemy against civilized society. They are ignorant of the fact that the pH factor and water quality play a decisive role in the character of liquor. If the water tends toward alkalinity, the result will be a sour liquor, not fit to drink; but if you add the urine of a healthy boy, you wind up with Eighteen-Li Red (the name itself has a better ring than Scholar Red or Daughter Red), an 'aromatic, full-bodied liquor that leaves a honey-sweet aftertaste.' There is nothing absurd in this, so why must they display their ignorance? As a doctoral candidate in liquor studies, I proclaim: this is science! Science is a solemn endeavor that allows for no hypocrisy. If you don't know something, you must study; there is no call for histrionics, and certainly no room for ad hominem attacks! Besides, what's so dirty about urine? For those individuals who sleep with prostitutes and come away with syphilis, gonorrhea, or AIDS, of course their urine is dirty. But, Sir, what your granddad released into the vat of liquor was a little boy's urine, pure as spring water. The classical masterwork *Materia Medica*, by Mr Li Shizhen, China's famed pharmaceutical master, is absolutely clear on this point: the urine of a little boy as an added ingredient in medicinal herbs is effective in the treatment of high blood pressure, coronary heart disease, arteriosclerosis, glaucoma, breast calcification, and other chronic diseases. Don't tell me they're willing to launch ad hominem attacks on Mr Li Shizhen! The urine of a little boy is the most sacred and mysterious fluid on the face of the earth, and even the Devil himself isn't sure just how many precious elements it contains. The Japanese Prime Minister drinks a glass of urine every day to stay healthy and vigorous. Liquorland's Party Secretary Jiang mixed the urine of a little boy into lotus-root congee to attack the cause of his long-term insomnia. Urine is a true marvel, the finest symbol of human existence. Sir, let's ignore that bunch of ignoramuses. The People's Commissar, Comrade Stalin, said: 'We shall ignore them!' They deserve nothing but horse piss.

In your letter you said you're going to write a novel about liquor. Only you can shoulder up such a heavy burden. My mentor, your soul is the soul of liquor, through and through; your body is the body of liquor, inside and out. Your liquor body is in perfect harmony: red flowers and green leaves, blue mountains and emerald waters, limbs that are hale and hearty, harmonious movements, graceful bearing, elegant motion, true flesh and blood, the picture of life; take anything away and it is too short, add anything and it is too long. My mentor, you are a living, breathing bottle of Eighteen-Li Red! To help in your research on liquor, I have prepared ten bottles of Overlapping Green Ants, ten bottles of Red-Maned Stallion, and ten bottles of Oriental Beauty. I'll send them all with the next school bus for Beijing. From this day on, Sir, stride forward boldly, a bottle forever at your side, pen always at hand, and let those idiots blather away.

The story I sent you last time, 'Meat Boy,' is not a piece of reportage, but it reads like one. It is absolutely true that some of Liquorland's totally corrupt and inhuman Party cadres feast on little boys. I hear that someone has been sent down to investigate, and if someday all this comes to light, it will rock the world. In the future, who but your disciple could write a piece of reportage about this major story? With the explosive material I have at hand, tell me, who has a claim to arrogance, if not me?

I have heard nothing from *Citizens' Literature*. I'd be grateful if you'd lean on them for me.

Our Liu Yan is a 'freckle-faced, glowering' woman, and could be the 'pale-faced glowering' woman you recall. Her freckles might be the byproduct of several illicit pregnancies. She told me once that she is the most fertile of soils, and gets pregnant by any man who comes in contact with her. She also said that the unborn fetuses she leaves behind are invariably snatched away to be consumed by hospital personnel. I've heard that the nutritional value of a six- or seven-month-old fetus is very high, and that makes sense. The fetus of a deer is widely known to be a high-potency tonic, isn't it? An embryonic egg has high nourishment value, hasn't it?

I'm including my most recent work, 'Child Prodigy,' with this letter. It is written in the style of 'demonic realism.' After you've given it a critical reading, please forward it to *Citizens' Literature*. I'll not rest until I've broken through this 'Gate of Hell'!

Wishing you
Happy writing,
Your disciple

Li Yidou

III

Child Prodigy, by Li Yidou

Gentle reader, not long ago I wrote a story for you about a meat child. In it I took pains to paint a picture of a little boy wrapped in red cloth. Perhaps you can recall his extraordinary eyes: mere slits through which a cold but mature glare emanated. They were the typical eyes of a conspirator. Yet they grew not in the face of a conspirator, but were inlaid in the face of a boy not quite three feet tall, which is why they are so unforgettable, and why they had such a shocking effect on a decent farmer in the Liquorland suburbs, Jin Yuanbao. Within the confines of that medium-length story it was impossible to delve deeply into the child's background, so he appears as a full-blown stock image: the body of a not-quite three-foot-tall boy with a shock of bristly hair, the eyes of a conspirator, a pair of large, fleshy ears, and a gravelly voice. He is a little boy, nothing more, nothing less.

This story unfolds in the Special Purchasing Section of a Culinary Academy, beginning at dusk. Gentle reader, 'our story, in fact, is already well underway.'

The moon was out that night, because we needed it to be. A big red moon rose slowly from behind the artificial hill at the Culinary Academy, its rosy beams slanting in through the double-paned windows like a pink waterfall and turning their faces soft and gentle. They were all little boys, and if you have read my 'Meat Boy,' you know who I'm talking about. The little demon was one of them, and would soon be in the position of their leader, or their despot. We shall see.

The boys had cried themselves out before the sun went down behind the mountain. Their faces were tear-streaked, their voices hoarse, all but the little demon, of course. You'd never catch him crying! Back while the other boys were crying their eyes out, he paced the floor like an overgrown goose, hands clasped behind his back as he circled the large room with its lovely scenery. Every once in a while he landed a well-placed kick on the backside of a bawling child. That invariably produced a high-pitched squeal, followed by muted sobs. His foot was transformed into a cure for the weeps. Eventually, he kicked all thirty-one children. And in the midst of sobs from the smallest boy among them, they saw the lovely moon leaping about on the artificial hill like a proud red steed.

Crowding up to the window, they grasped the sill and gazed outside. Those stuck behind the front row held on to the shoulders ahead of them. A fat little boy with a snotty nose raised a chubby finger and pointed skyward.

'Mama Moon,' he whimpered, 'Mama Moon . . .'

One of the other boys smacked his lips and said:

'It's Auntie Moon, not Mama Moon. Auntie Moon.'

A sneer worked its way down the face of the little demon, who screeched like an owl, sending shivers down the boys' spines as they turned to see what was wrong. What they saw was the little demon squatting atop the artificial hill, irradiated by red moonbeams. His red clothes looked like a fireball. The man-made waterfall on the hillside shimmered like red satin as it cascaded beautifully and continuously into the pool at the foot of the hill. Water splashed noisily like strings of cherries.

The children were no longer looking at the moon; instead, they huddled together and gaped at him in stupefaction.

'Children,' he said in a low voice, 'prick up your ears and listen to what your sire has to say. That gizmo, that thing that looks like a proud red steed, is not a mama and it's not an auntie. It's a ball, a celestial being, one that revolves around us, and its name is simply "moon"!'

The children looked at him uncomprehendingly.

He jumped down off the artificial hill, and as he did, his baggy red clothes billowed in the wind, transformed into a pair of grotesque wings.

Clasping his hands behind him, he paced back and forth in front of the children. From time to time he wiped his mouth with his sleeve or spit on the glossy stone floor. Suddenly he stopped, raised an arm that was thin as a goat's leg, and waved it in the air.

'Listen to me, children,' he said sternly. 'You have never been human beings, not since the day you were born. Your parents sold you, like pigs or goats! So from now on, I'll stomp anyone who cries for his mommy or daddy!'

He shook his clawlike hand and roared at the top of his lungs. The moon lit up his pale little face, from which two green lights emerged. Two of the boys burst into tears.

'No crying!' he screamed.

Reaching into the cluster of children, he dragged out the two crying boys and drove his fist into each of their little bellies, sending them thudding to the floor, where they rolled around like basketballs.

He laid down the law: 'I'll do the same to anybody I catch crying!'

The huddle of children grew tighter. None dared to cry.

'Just wait,' he said. 'Leave the search for brightness up to me.'

He immediately commenced a search of the strange and very large room, hugging the walls like a prowling cat. Near the door he stopped and looked up at four lamp cords hanging in a row from the ceiling. He reached up, but the cords were a good three feet from the tip of his middle finger. He jumped a couple of times, but even with plenty of spring in his legs, he barely halved the distance. So, moving away from the wall, he dragged over a willow tree welded out of iron, climbed to the top, then grabbed the lamp cords and gave them a hard tug. With a crackle, all the lights in the room snapped on. There were neon lights, incandescent lamps, tungsten lamps, white lights, blue lights, red lights, green lights, and yellow lights. There were lights on the walls, lights in the ceiling, lights on the artificial hill, and lights on the artificial trees. The lights were blinding and multi-hued, like heaven and earth in a fairy-tale world. Forgetting their miseries and their worries, the children clapped and shouted joyously.

The little demon curled his lip derisively as he marveled over the masterpiece he had created. Then he went to the corner, where he picked up a ring of brass bells and shook them vigorously. Peals rang out, drawing the boys' rapt attention. He wrapped the bells, which seemed to have been put there just for him, around his waist, spit out a mouthful of phlegm, and said:

'Children, do you know where all this light comes from? No, you don't. You're from remote, backward villages where you smash rocks to make fire, so of course you don't know where it comes from. I'll tell you. The source of this light is called electricity.'

The children listened without making a peep. The red moon had receded from the room, leaving behind a row of gleaming eyes. The two boys who had been knocked to the ground climbed to their feet.

'Is electricity good?' he asked.

'Yes, it is!' the boys replied in unison.

'Am I talented or aren't I?'

'Yes, you are!'

'Are you going to do as I say?'

'Yes, we are!'

'All right, children, do you want a daddy?'

'Yes, we do!'

'Starting today, I'll be your daddy. I'll protect you, I'll teach you and I'll supervise you. Anyone who disobeys me will be drowned in the pool. Do you understand?'

'Yes, we do!'

'Call me Daddy three times. All together now.'

'Daddy – Daddy – Daddy!'

'Down on your knees and kowtow to me, all of you. Three times!'

Some of the boys, those with weak minds, did not understand everything the little demon said, but their ability to follow came to their aid. Thirty-one little boys fell to their knees in ragtag fashion, laughing and giggling, to kowtow to the little demon, who jumped onto the artificial hill and sat in the lotus position to receive his sons' kneeling salute.

Once the ritual was ended, he selected four of the glibbest, most agile youngsters as team leaders and divided the thirty-one boys into four teams. With that done, he said:

'Children, from this moment on, you are warriors. Warriors are bold youngsters who dare to fight and dare to conquer. I will train you to struggle against all people who want to eat us.'

Team One's leader asked out of curiosity:

'Daddy, who wants to eat us?'

'Bastard!' The little demon shook his bells. 'Don't ever interrupt me when I'm speaking.'

Team One's leader said:

'I made a mistake, Daddy. I won't interrupt again.'

The little demon said:

'Comrades, children, now I'll tell you who it is who wants to eat us! They have red eyes, green fingernails, and gold-capped teeth!'

'Are they wolves? Or tigers?' asked a chubby, dimpled boy.

Team One's leader gave little fatty a slap.

'Don't interrupt when Daddy's speaking!' he reprimanded him.

The fat kid bit his lip and stifled his sobs.

'Comrades, children, they aren't wolves, but they're meaner than wolves. And they're not tigers, but they're scarier than tigers.'

'Why do they eat children?'

The little demon frowned.

'That makes me really, really mad! I said, no interruptions. Team leaders, take that boy out and make him stand alone as punishment.'

The four team leaders dragged the loose-lipped little boy out of the group; he bawled and fought so hard, you'd have thought they were dragging him to his execution. The moment they loosened their grip, his legs started churning and he hightailed it back to the group. When the team leaders ran back to drag him out again, they were stopped by the little demon:

'Forget it, let him off this time! But let me repeat myself: You children are not permitted to interrupt when Daddy's talking. Why do they want to eat children? Simple, they've grown tired of eating beef, lamb, pork, dog, donkey, rabbit, chicken, duck, pigeon, mule, camel, horse, hedgehog, sparrow, swallow, wild goose, common goose, cat, rat, weasel, and lynx, so they want to eat children. It's because our meat is more tender than beef, fresher than lamb, more fragrant than pork, fattier than dog, softer than mule, harder than rabbit, silkier than chicken, more dynamic than duck, more straightforward than pigeon, livelier than donkey, more pampered than camel, springier than horse, finer than hedge-hog, more dignified than sparrow, fairer than swallow, more mature than wild goose, not as chaffy as common goose, more sedate than cat, more nutritious than rat, less demonic than weasel, and more common than lynx. Our meat tops the charts.'

Having exhausted his list and his wind, the little demon spit on the floor, looking a bit more tired than when he started.

'Daddy,' Team Two's leader spoke up timidly, 'I've got something to say. Is it all right?'

'Go ahead. I've talked myself out. Daddy would love to smoke some hemp right about now. Too bad there isn't any.' The little demon yawned.

'How do they eat us, Daddy? Raw?'

'They have many ways: fried, steamed, braised, cold sliced, fried with vinegar, dry fried, many many ways, but usually not raw. I said usually. They say a certain vice-mayor named Shen once ate a child raw, dipped in imported Japanese vinegar.'

The children huddled tightly, the timid ones sobbing softly.

That invigorated the little demon, who said, 'Children, com-rades, that is why you must do as I say. At this critical juncture, you must show your maturity and transform yourselves overnight into indomitable heroes. No more boo-hoos, no more sniveling. The only way to keep them from eating us is to unite as one, become an impregnable wall of iron and steel. We must become a hedgehog, a porcupine. They've eaten all the porcupine they want, and our meat is a lot milder than a porcupine's. We must become a steel hedgehog, an iron porcupine, so we can make mush out of those man-eating monsters' lips and tongues! They might eat well, but we'll mess up their digestion!'

'But, but, these lights . . .' Team Four's leader was stammering.

The little demon waved him off. 'I know what's on your mind, you don't have to say it. What you want to know is, if they plan to eat us, why give us such beautiful surroundings. Am I right?'

Team Four leader nodded.

'All right, I'll tell you,' the little demon said. 'Fourteen years ago, when I was still a child, I heard people say that the dignitaries of Liquorland ate little boys, and there were enough details in the rumor to make it frightening and mysterious at the same time. After that, my mother started delivering one baby boy after another. But every one of them reached the age of two, then suddenly disappeared. All I could think was, my kid brothers were eaten. At the time, I was ready to expose this monstrous crime, but was thwarted by a mysterious skin disease – scales all over my body that oozed pus when you touched them. It made people sick just to look at me, and no one saw me as an edible commodity. That kept me out of the tiger's lair. Eventually, I turned to thievery. One day, I broke into an official's home and drank a bottle of liquor with paintings of apes on the label. Lo and behold, the scales began to fall off. With each layer, I got smaller, which is why I look like this today. So even though I have the appearance of a child, my mental capacity is as broad as the ocean. Their secret of eating children must be revealed, and I shall be your savior!'

The children's attention was fixed on the little demon and his revelations.

'Now why have they put us in such a big, beautiful room?' he continued. 'Because they want us to be content. If we're not, our meat will turn sour and chewy. Children, comrades, this is what I want you to do. Turn this place into a shambles!'

The little demon picked up a rock from the artificial hill, took aim at a bright red lamp on the wall, and flung it. With his strength, the rock raised a draft as it cut through the air. But his aim was off – the rock thudded against the wall and bounced straight back, nearly taking the head off one of the boys. The little demon picked it up, took aim again and threw it. Another miss. This time followed by curses. He picked it up again, mustered up the tenacious strength of a baby at the nipple – Fuck your mother! – and heaved it with all his might. This time he was right on target. The lamp shattered, sending shards raining down on the floor; the forked filament blazed red for an instant, then went dark.

The children stood stock-still, watching him like marionettes.

'Smash, start smashing! What are you waiting for?'

Some of the little boys yawned.

'Daddy, I'm sleepy, I want to go to bed . . .'

The little demon rushed up and started punching and kicking the yawning boys, eliciting yelps and screeches; one of the bolder, stronger boys actually hit back, drawing blood on the little demon's face. Seeing his own blood, he stepped up and sank his teeth into the boy's ear with such ferocity that he bit off half of it.

That was when the door opened.

An elderly serving woman in a spotless white uniform opened the door and rushed into the room. It wasn't easy, but she finally managed to separate the little demon and the little boy, who was crying so hard he nearly passed out. The little demon was spitting blood, green light streamed from his eyes. But he didn't say a word. His victim's severed ear was twitching on the floor. When the serving woman spotted the ear, then the little demon's face, she paled, let out a fearful yelp, and ran out of the room, her rear end wrenching from side to side, the heels of her shoes raising a mad tattoo on the floor.

The little demon climbed the iron willow tree and pulled the plug on all the lights; a soft threat filled the enclosing darkness:

'I'll bite the ear off anybody who squeals!'

He then walked over to the artificial hill, where he washed the blood off his mouth at the waterfall.

A clatter of footsteps sounded outside the door. Most likely a horde of people about to enter the room. So the little demon picked up the rock with which he'd smashed the wall lamp and hid behind the iron willow tree to wait.

The door was pushed open and a white figure entered, hugging the wall as it groped along in the dark. The little demon took aim at the upper half of the figure and let fly. The figure cried out in pain and started to wobble; the people on the other side of the door ran off in panic. The little demon went over, picked up the rock, took aim on the white figure again, and heaved it with all his might. The figure crumpled to the floor.

A while later, beams of bright light streamed in the door, followed by people with flashlights. The little demon scooted nimbly into the corner, where he lay on the floor, face down, and pretended to be asleep.

Then the lights snapped on above seven or eight husky men, who picked up the unconscious serving woman in white. They also picked up the injured boy, along with his severed ear, and carried them out of the room. Then it was time to find out who was responsible for all this evil.

The little demon was flopped out on the floor snoring loudly. When a man in white picked him up by the nape of his neck, his arms and legs flailed in the air as a series of wails erupted from his mouth, like a pitiful little cat.

The ferreting-out process produced no results. The children were exhausted from a very tiring day, and unbelievably hungry. And after being harassed by the little demon, they could barely hold their heads up and couldn't think straight. And so the investigation ended amid the rumble of snores.

The men in white turned off the lights, locked the door, and left. In the darkness, the little demon smirked.

Early the next morning, before the sun was even up, the little demon got to his feet in the misty room, took the brass bells out from under his shirt, and rang them as hard as he could. The frantic pealing startled the children out of their sleep. After squatting on the floor to relieve themselves, they rolled over and went back to sleep under the glaring eyes of the little demon.

Once the sun was up, a red light flooded the room; by then the children were up and sitting around weeping. They were famished. Hardly a trace of the previous night's excitement remained in their heads. All that energy, all that time spent trying to nurture a sense of power in them, totally wasted. The frustrated little demon wondered how he was going to make anything out of this bunch.

Just so I won't screw things up as a storyteller, I'll narrate my tale objectively, avoiding, as much as possible, any descriptions of what was going on inside the heads of the little demon and the children. I'll stick to their behavior and their speech, and leave it to you readers to interpret what sparked their behavior and lay behind their speech. This is not an easy story to tell, because the little demon keeps coming up with ways to smash it to pieces. He is not a good little boy, that's for sure. (In truth, my story is just about wrapped up.)

Breakfast was sumptuous: egg-drop soup, steamed rolls made of fine flour, milk, bread, jam, salted bean sprouts, and sweet-and-sour radish slices.

The old man who delivered their breakfast took his job seriously, carefully filling each plate or bowl and handing it to one of the children. The little demon got a portion, which he received with his head lowered deferentially, so as not to upset the old fellow, who nonetheless watched him out of the corner of his eye.

After the old fellow left, the little demon looked up, eyes shining, and said:

'Comrades, children, don't eat a bite of this! They want to fatten us up before they eat us. We'll go on a hunger strike. Children, the skinnier you are, the later they'll get around to eating you, and maybe never.'

But the children paid no heed to his impassioned plea; maybe they had no idea what he was talking about. The sight and smell of all that food was all they could think about, so they dug in, stuffing their faces and raising quite a din. The little demon's first impulse was to get rough with them, but he put that foolish thought out of his mind just in time to see a tall man walk into the room. With a furtive look at the man's big feet, he picked up his glass of warm milk and took a long, loud drink.

Sensing the contemptuous look on the man's face, he went back to his milk, with a vengeance, and attacked a steamed bun, making a point of getting his face as dirty as possible and gurgling loudly. In other words, he turned himself into a gluttonous fool.

'Little pig!' he heard the man say.

The man's legs, both the thickness of stone pillars, ambulated toward the front, so the little demon looked up to stare at his back. He noticed that the man had a long, oval head beneath a cap from which several curls of brown hair peeked out. When the man turned around, the little demon saw a ruddy face, with a long, greasy, beaklike nose that resembled a deformed water chestnut smeared with lard.

'Children,' the man said with a devious smile, 'did you have a good breakfast?'

Most replied that they had, but some said no.

'Dear children,' the man said, 'you mustn't eat too much at one sitting, or your digestion will suffer. Now let's go play a game, all right?'

No response from the children, who blinked in disbelief.

The man smacked himself on the head and admitted that he had foolishly forgotten that they were only children and hadn't yet learned what games were all about. 'Let's go out and play the hawk and the chicks, what do you say?'

Shouting their approval, the children followed the man out into the yard. With apparent reluctance, the little demon tagged along.

As the game began, the hawk-nosed man chose the little demon to be the mother hen – maybe because his red clothes made him so conspicuous – with all the other children lined up behind him as the brood. The man was to be the hawk. Flapping his arms, he stared at them and bared his teeth as he began to screech.

Suddenly the hawk swooped down, scrunching up its beak until it nearly touched its thin upper lip, a menacing glare radiating from its eyes. This was indeed a savage, carnivorous raptor. Its dark shadow fell upon the children from above. Nervously, the little demon eyed its deadly twitching talons, as it settled onto the carpet of green grass, then rose into the air, unhurriedly toying with the children, waiting for the right moment. A hawk is a very patient hunter. And since the initiative always rests with the attacker, the defender must never let down its guard, not for a minute.

Suddenly the hawk swooped down like lightning, and the little demon reacted by rushing valiantly to the tail-end of his troops to butt and bite and scratch until the targeted child was wrenched free of the hawk's grasp. The other children whooped and hollered, excited and frightened at the same time, as they fled from the hawk. The little demon nimbly threw himself between hunter and prey. The glare in his eyes conquered that of the stunned hawk.

The second attack commenced, drawing the little demon back into the fray, as he broke free from the brood of children. His movements were too nimble and focused for a mere child. Before the hawk had time to react, the little demon was at its neck, and it suddenly feared for its life. It felt as if an enormous black spider had attached itself to its neck, or a vampire bat with bright red membranes flaring beneath its limbs. It wrenched its head violently to shake the child free, but in vain, for by then the little demon's claws were buried in its eyes. The excruciating pain took all the fight out of it, and with a tortured howl, it stumbled forward and thudded to the ground like a felled tree.

The little demon jumped off the man's head, a smirk on his face that can only be described as evil and brutal. Walking up to the children, he said:

'Children, comrades, I scooped out the hawk's eyes. It can't see us. Now it's time to play!'

The eyeless hawk writhed on the ground, sometimes arching like a footbridge and sometimes slithering like a dragon. Black blood oozed out from between its fingers, which covered its face, like squirming black worms. It wailed pitifully, a sad, shrill, chilling sound. Instinctively, the children huddled together. The little demon took a vigilant look all around; the compound was deserted, except for a few white butterflies flitting over the grass. Black smoke belched from a chimney on the other side of the wall, sending a cloud of heavy fragrance straight to the little demon's nostrils. Meanwhile, the wails of the hawk grew increasingly pitiful and shrill. So after a couple of frenetic spins, he jumped back onto the hawk's back, quickly burying all ten claws into its throat. The look on his face was too horrifying for words as his fingers dug deep in the man's thick neck. Did that give him the same feeling as thrusting his fingers into hot sand or a bucket of lard? Hard to say. Was he enjoying the satisfaction of revenge? Again, hard to say. You, my readers, are more intelligent than the author, something the narrator believes without question. Well, by the time the little demon withdrew his fingers, the hawk's wails were barely audible; blood spurted from the holes in its neck, rising and falling, as if home to crabs that were foaming at the mouth. Holding up ten bloody fingers, the little demon announced calmly:

'The hawk is in its death throes.'

The bolder children crowded around, with the others falling in timidly behind, all gazing down at the hawk's expiring body. It was still twitching, writhing on the ground, though the intensity of movement was weakening. Suddenly the hawk's mouth opened, as if to release a screech; but instead of sound, only blood emerged, making a pattering sound as it hit the grass, sticky and hot. The little demon picked up a handful of mud and stuffed it into the hawk's mouth. Sounds rumbled up from the throat, followed by an explosion of mud and blood.

'Children,' the little demon demanded, 'suffocate him, stuff up the hawk's mouth, so he can't eat us.'

The children sprang into action, as ordered. In unity there is strength. Dozens of hands scrambled to dig up mud, grass, and sand, and cram it into the hawk's mouth; then, like a downpour of rain, they covered its eyes and pinched its nostrils shut. As the children's enthusiasm mounted, they were in the grip of euphoria, enjoying the game of life as they buried the hawk's head in mud. That is how children are: they will gang up on a poor frog, or a snake crossing the road, or a wounded cat. And after beating it half to death, they'll crowd around to enjoy the spectacle.

'Is he dead?'

A pop of air escaped from the hawk's bottom.

'He isn't dead, he just farted. Keep stuffing.'

Another deluge of mud ensued, nearly burying the hawk – yes, it was all but buried under the mud.

When the person in charge of the Special Purchasing Section of the Culinary Academy heard a series of demonic wails in the yard outside the Meat Child Room, her neck and bladder constricted, and the demon of doom bored insect-like into her mind.

She stood up and walked over to the telephone, but when her right hand touched the handset, what felt like an electric shock shot up her arm from her fingertip, numbing half her body.

Dragging her paralyzed body back over to the desk, she sat down, feeling as if she'd been cloven in two, one side cold, the other feverishly hot. Hastily, she opened a drawer and took out a mirror to look at herself. One half of her face was dark and ruddy, the other a ghostly white. Her nerves shot, she somehow made it back to the telephone, but her hand recoiled as if lightning had struck again as soon as she reached out. She seemed on the verge of crumpling to the floor, just as a divine light emerged from her brain to illuminate a road ahead. A lightning-struck tree stood beside the road, half of it a lush green, covered with leaves and luscious fruit, the other half with bronze limbs and an iron trunk, completely denuded, emitting a magical glow in a sea of sunlight. She knew at once: That tree is me. That thought filled her heart with intense warmth, and tears of joy wetted her cheeks. As if mesmerized or infatuated, she gazed at the half of that big tree that had been petrified by lightning, turning away from the green half in disgust. She called out for lightning, summoned it to turn the green half of the tree into bronze limbs and an iron trunk, to transform the tree into one glorious whole. She then reached out to the telephone with her left hand, and her body was as if on fire. Feeling ten years younger, she ran out into the yard and from there to the lawn in front of the Meat Child Room. When she saw the buried hawk, she burst out laughing. Clapping her hands, she said:

'You've killed him well, children, killed him well! Now you must flee, get as far away from this den of murderous monsters as you can!'

With her in the lead, the children passed through a series of iron gates and wound their way through the labyrinthine grounds of the Culinary Academy. But her attempt was doomed to failure. With the exception of the little demon, who made good his escape, every one of the children was caught and dragged back, and the woman was discharged from her post. Why, gentle readers, do you think I've wasted so much ink on this woman? Because she is my mother-in-law. That is to say, she is the wife of Professor Yuan Shuangyu of the Brewer's College. Everyone says she went crazy, and that's how I see it. She spends her time these days at home writing letters of accusation, ream upon ream of them, all mailed off, some to the Chairman of the Central Committee, some to the provincial Party Secretary, one even to the legendary magistrate of Kaifeng Prefecture, Magistrate Bao. Now, I ask you, if she's not crazy, who is? At this rate, she'll go broke just buying stamps.

When two flowers bloom at once, take care of them one at a time. A gang of white-uniformed men dragged the fleeing boys back to the Meat Child Room. It nearly wore them out, since the boys had undergone the baptism of their mortal battle with the now-dead hawk, and had turned savage and crafty; they had run into a wooded area or into hidden spots in walls, or they had climbed trees, or they had jumped into latrines. If there was a hiding place, they found it. The fact of the matter is, after my mother-in-law opened the iron gate of the Meat Child Room, the children went absolutely wild. Though she felt she was leading a group of children out of a den of monsters, it was pure fantasy, since the only thing following her was her own shadow. As she stood by the rear gate of the academy, loudly urging the children to flee, her shouts were heard only by old men and old women who lay hidden beside the waterway leading from the Culinary Academy to the nearby river, awaiting the passage of delectable scraps from the kitchen. My mother-in-law could not see them in their hiding spots amid the astonishingly dense foliage. So why did my mother-in-law, who held such an important position, go crazy? Whether or not it was a result of the electric shocks will require another story.

After the children's escape was discovered, the Culinary Academy's Security Section called an urgent meeting to map out emergency measures, including sealing off the academy. Once the gates were closed, detachments of crack troops began combing the grounds. During the search, ten of the troopers were bitten savagely by the meat children, and one, a woman, was blinded in one eye by a gouging finger. The academy leadership showered the wounded troops with sympathy and consoling words, and even distributed lavish bonuses based upon the severity of their injuries. The recaptured meat children were placed under strict surveillance in a secure room, where a roll call turned up one missing child. According to the white-uniformed serving woman, who had regained her senses after some emergency therapy, the escaped meat child was none other than the boy who had wounded her. He must have also been the one who murdered the hawk. She vaguely recalled that he was dressed all in red, and had a pair of gloomy, snakelike eyes.

A few days later, a janitor out cleaning the waterway discovered a set of red clothing, filthy beyond description; but there was no trace of the little demon, the murderer, the leader of the meat children.

Gentle readers, would you like to know what happened to the little demon?

IV

Dear Doctor of Liquor Studies Yidou

Thanks for the letter. I've read your story 'Child Prodigy.' The little demon, wrapped in his red flag, had my heart pounding and my skin crawling. I couldn't sleep for days. The language in this story is highly polished, my friend, and the ingenuity of the plot never seems to end; it puts me to shame. If you insist that I air specific views, I suppose I can offer a perfunctory criticism or two: the absence of any background on the little demon, which flies in the face of conventional realism, for instance, or the overly loose organization and relative lack of authorial restraint. Not worth worrying about. In the face of your 'demonic realism,' I shy away from any real criticism. I've already forwarded 'Child Prodigy' to *Citizens' Literature*. Since this is an official publication, it's flooded with manuscripts, most of which wind up at the bottom of towering stacks. So don't be surprised that you've heard nothing about the two earlier stories. I wrote to a couple of renowned editors of *Citizens' Literature*, Zhou Bao and Li Xiaobao, and asked them to check into it for me. The two 'treasures' [bao] are friends of mine, and I'm sure they'll help out.

In your letter you mention writing about liquor –
witticisms abound, serious yet humorous, inspirations
from all sides, depth and breadth united – just what I'd
expect from a doctor of liquor. You have my undying
respect. I look forward to more discussions of liquor with
you, since it's a favorite topic of mine.

I don't know whether to laugh or cry over your claim
that pissing in a liquor vat, as I wrote in *Red Sorghum*, is a
technological marvel. I don't know a thing about
chemistry, and even less about the distiller's craft. I wrote
that episode as a practical joke, wanting to poke a little fun
at all those esthetes, them with their eyes bloodshot from
envy. Imagine my surprise when you proved, through
scientific theory, the logic and lofty nature of this episode,
and now, to my admiration for you I must add gratitude.
This is what's known as 'The professional asks How? The
amateur says Wow!' or what we call 'Plant a flower, and
no blooms will show; drop a willow seed, and a shade tree
will grow.'

Regarding Eighteen-Li Red, a serious lawsuit is in the
works. After *Red Sorghum* won its prize at the Berlin Film
Festival, the head of a distillery in my hometown came
running over to the warehouse where I'd set up my study
to tell me he wanted to make a batch of Eighteen-Li Red.
Unfortunately, he couldn't come up with the financial
backing. A year later, on an inspection trip to our county,
members of the provincial leadership asked to try some
Eighteen-Li Red. It was an awkward moment, and after the
dignitaries left, the county revenue office came up with the
money for a task group responsible for a trial production
of Eighteen-Li Red. By trial production, I thought that
meant they were going to mix up a batch or two, design a
new bottle, slap on a label, and that would be that. I don't
know if they added the piss of young boys or not. But
when the distillery excitedly sent their new product to the
county government office to report their success, *Movies
for the Masses* published a notice about a press conference
in Shenzhen, where the Eighteen-Li Red distillery in

Henan's Shangcai county announced to the film community that their brew was the bona fide Eighteen-Li Red from *Red Sorghum*. The cases of their liquor were stamped with the following (or words to this effect): The heroine of *Red Sorghum*, Dai Jiu'er, was originally from Shangcai county in Henan province, and only fled to Northeast Gaomi township in Shandong with her father during a famine. She had taken the recipe for Eighteen-Li Red from Shangcai county to Shandong's Gaomi, which is why Shangcai county must be considered the real hometown of Eighteen-Li Red.

The head of the distillery in my hometown immediately attacked Henan's Shangcai county for their deviousness, and sent someone with authentic Eighteen-Li Red to Beijing to ask me, as the author of the novel, to help him bring Eighteen-Li Red back to Gaomi township, where it belongs. But the clever people in Henan's Shangcai county had already registered their Eighteen-Li Red with the trademark office, and since the law is dispassionate, our Eighteen-Li Red no longer had any legal standing. When the Gaomi people asked me to help them initiate a lawsuit, I said it was a suit without merit, that Dai Jiu'er is only a fictional character, not my real grandmother, and that it's not illegal for the Shangcai county people to insist that she was originally from Henan. There was no way the Gaomi side could win. They'd just have to take their lumps this time. Later on, I heard that the Henan people rode their Eighteen-Li Red into the international market and earned quite a bit of foreign currency. I hope that's true. For literature and liquor to be integrated like that is pretty terrific. And because of newly promulgated copyright laws, I'm going to go to Shangcai county with the film director Zhang Yimou to get a little of what I've got coming to me.

All the wonderful liquors you mentioned are renowned for their quality, but I don't need any of them. What I do need – and badly – is material about liquor, and I hope you'll send me some of the more important items. Naturally, I'll pay the postage.

Please give my best to Liu Yan the next time you see her. Warmest regards,

Mo Yan

Chapter Four

Investigator Ding Gou'er opened his eyes. His eyeballs felt dull and heavy, he had a splitting headache, his breath was foul, and his gums, his tongue, the walls of his mouth, and his throat were coated with a sticky substance. In the murky yellow light of a chandelier he couldn't tell if it was day or night, if it was dawn or dusk. His wristwatch was missing, his biological clock was out of whack, his stomach was growling, and his hemorrhoids were throbbing in rhythm with his heartbeats. Lightbulb filaments that shimmered as hot current passed through them set up a hum that was translated into a ringing in Ding Gou'er's ears. He heard his heart beating against the background hum. When he struggled to get out of bed, his arms and legs refused to do his bidding. A long night of drinking drifted into his consciousness like a distant dream, when all of a sudden that golden-hued, perfumed little boy seated in a gilded platter smiled at him. A strange cry escaped from the investigator as his consciousness broke from its confinement, sending currents of ideas racing through his brain and burning their way into his bones and muscles. He flew out of bed like a carp leaping out of the water, forming a beautiful arc through the air and changing the room's spatial makeup and magnetic field, shattering the light into its prismatic components as the investigator struck a pose not unlike that of a dog fighting over shit just before landing headfirst on the synthetic carpet.

Lying there stripped to the waist, he studied with amazement the four +s [tens] on the wall, as a chill ran down his spine. The vivid image of a scaly youngster and the willow-leaf knife he held in his mouth materialized out of the alcohol. He discovered that he was naked from the waist up; his ribs were nearly poking through his skin, his belly protruded slightly, a shock of tangled brown hair lay limply on his chest, and his belly button was filled with lint. After the investigator splashed cold water over his head and looked in the mirror – puffy face, lifeless eyes, and all – he couldn't shake the feeling that he might as well commit suicide right there in the bathroom. He located his briefcase, took out his pistol, and cocked it. Holding it in his hand, he felt the cold but gentle heft of the handle, and as he stood at the mirror, he was struck by a thought that he was staring into the eyes of an enemy, someone he'd never seen before. He put the muzzle up to his nose, the tip boring its way in, highlighting two rows of parasitic-looking blackheads. He then moved the muzzle up to his temple, causing the skin to quiver joyously. Finally he shoved the muzzle into his mouth and clamped his lips tightly, hermetically, around the cold steel – a needle couldn't have been wedged in – producing such a funny sight that even he felt like laughing. And when he did, so did the reflection in the mirror. The barrel, smelling and tasting of gunpowder, nearly gagged him. When had it been fired? *Pow!* The little boy's head had splattered like a watermelon, sending colorful debris sailing in all directions, the fragrant brain matter staining everything in the area, and he had a picture of someone lapping up the gore like a greedy cat. Pangs of conscience rose in his heart, dark clouds of suspicion descended onto his head. Who could guarantee it wasn't a hoax? That the arms weren't actually made of fresh lotus root and melon? Or that the boy's arms had been prepared in such a way as to look like sections of lotus root and melon?

A knock at the door. Ding Gou'er took the muzzle out of his mouth.

The Mine Director and Party Secretary walked in, all smiles.

Deputy Head Diamond Jin entered behind them, handsome and dignified.

'Did you sleep well, Comrade Ding Gou'er?'

'Did you sleep well, Comrade Ding Gou'er?'

'Did you sleep well, Comrade Ding Gou'er?'

Feeling extremely awkward, Ding Gou'er threw a blanket around his shoulders and said, 'Somebody stole my clothes.'

Instead of replying, Deputy Head Jin fixed his gaze on the four

+s carved into the wall, a grave look frozen on his face. A long silence was finally broken by his muttered comment, 'Him again.'

'Him who?' Ding Gou'er asked anxiously.

'An expert, a shadowy cat burglar.' Diamond Jin rapped the bent middle finger of his left hand on the symbols carved into the wall. 'This is the mark he always leaves after one of his capers.'

Ding Gou'er walked up to get a better look at the carvings. When he did, occupational instincts quickly brought his fuzzy thoughts into focus, and he was feeling pretty good about himself again. Fresh fluids flowed from his aching eyes, his hawklike vision returned in a flash. The four +s had been carved in a straight line, about a third of the way into the wall, the plastic wallpaper curling outward on the edges to reveal the plaster behind it.

Turning to study the expression on Diamond Jin's face, he discovered that the man's handsome eyes were fixed on him, as if he were under scrutiny, as if he had run into a cunning adversary, as if he had fallen into an enemy's trap. But the friendliness that exuded from Diamond Jin's handsome, smiling eyes chipped away at the wariness in the investigator's mind. 'Comrade Ding Gou'er,' he said in the intoxicating voice of fine liquor, 'you're the expert in this area. What do these four tens mean to you?'

The words wouldn't come, for the butterfly of consciousness that had been washed out of his head by alcohol hadn't yet returned in all its gracefulness. And so he could only stare in terror at Diamond Jin's mouth and the light glinting off his gold or bronze tooth.

'I think,' Diamond Jin said, 'that it's a gang symbol, a gang with forty members, or four times ten, in other words, forty thieves, which means an Ali Baba could show up at any time. Maybe you, Comrade Ding Gou'er, will assume the role of Ali Baba without knowing it. That would be a blessing to the two million citizens of Liquorland.' He saluted Ding Gou'er with his hands clasped in front, making Ding feel more awkward than ever.

Ding Gou'er said, 'My papers, my wallet, my cigarettes, lighter, electric shaver, toy pistol, and telephone book were all stolen by those forty thieves.'

'How dare they touch a single hair on the head of the mighty Jupiter!' Diamond Jin said with a raucous laugh.

'Lucky for me they didn't take my real pal here!' Ding Gou'er said as he flashed his pistol.

'Old Ding, I've come to say good-bye. I was going to ask you to join me in a farewell drink, but in consideration of how wrapped up in your official duties you are, I won't disturb you. Come see me at the Municipal Party Committee office if there's anything I can do for you.' Diamond Jin stuck out his hand.

Still in a daze, Ding Gou'er took the other man's hand and, still in a daze, released it; then, still in a daze, he watched Diamond Jin vanish from the room under the escort of the Party Secretary and Mine Director. A dry heave came charging up from his stomach, creating shooting pains in his chest on the way. His hangover hung on. The situation was anything but clear. After sticking his head under the faucet and running cold water over it for a good ten minutes, he drank the glass of cold tea. He took several deep breaths and closed his eyes, settling his diaphragm and clearing his mind of all selfish ideas and personal consider-ations; then his eyes snapped open, and his thoughts were acute and focused again, like an ax sharpened to a razor's edge, ready to hack away at the vines and grasses covering his eyes and clouding his vision; a new thought came to him at that moment, as if splashed brightly on the picture screen of his mind: Liquorland is home to a gang of cannibalistic monsters, and everything that happened at the banquet was part of an elaborate hoax!

After drying his head and face, putting on his shoes and socks, and fastening his belt, he put away his pistol, clapped his hat on his head, wrapped his blue checked shirt around his shoulders – the one the scaly youngster had tossed onto the carpet, where it had soaked up his vomit – and strode boldly to the door; jerk-ing open the dark-brown door, he strode down the corridor in search of an elevator or flight of stairs. A friendly, cream-colored attendant at the service desk told him how to find his way out of the maze.

Outside he was greeted by mixed weather conditions: rolling rain clouds in a sun-splashed sky. It was past noon already, and gigantic cloud-shadows skittered across the ground, as golden sunlight shimmered on yellow leaves. Ding Gou'er's nose began to itch, and seven sneezes followed in rapid succession; he was bent over like a dried shrimp, tears welled up in his eyes. After straightening up, through the misty veil covering his eyes, he saw the enormous black drum atop the dark red windlass at the entrance to the mine, which was still pulling silver gray cable up and down. Everything was just as it had been when he entered: golden sunflowers covered the ground; stacks of lumber gave off a delicate fragrance, spreading the aura of a primeval forest. A rail car carrying lumps of coal shuttled back and forth on narrow tracks between towering mounds of coal. The car was equipped with a small motor attached to a long rubber-wrapped cord. It was manned by a coal-black girl with rows of white teeth that sparkled like pearls. She stood on a ledge at the rear of the car, her bearing proud and majestic as a warrior in full combat readiness. Each time the car reached the end of the line, she slammed on the brake to bring it to a halt, then tipped it to send glistening coal over the side like a waterfall with a loud *whoosh*. What appeared to be the old wolfhound from the gate house came bounding toward Ding Gou'er and barked frantically for a moment, as if pouring out its deep hatred for him.

The dog ran off, leaving Ding Gou'er standing there in disappointment. If I thought things out objectively, he was thinking, I'd have to say I'm a pretty sorry case. Where did I come from? I came from the county seat. What did I come to do? Investigate a major case. On a tiny speck of dust somewhere in the vast universe, amid a vast sea of people stands an investigator named Ding Gou'er; his mind is a welter of confusion, he lacks the desire for self-improvement, his morale is low, he is disheartened and lonely, and he has lost sight of his goal. Bereft of that, with nothing to gain and nothing to lose, he headed toward the noisy vehicles at the coal-loading area.

Without coincidence there can be no novel – a crisp shout rent the air: Ding Gou'er! Ding Gou'er! You son of a gun, what are you doing hanging around here?

Ding Gou'er turned to see where the shouts were coming from. A shock of black, bristly hair greeted his eyes, and beneath that a lively, animated face.

She was standing next to her truck holding a pair of grimy white gloves, looking like a little donkey in the bright sunlight. 'Get over here, you son of a gun!' She waved her gloves in the air as if they were a magic soul-snatching wand, drawing the investigator toward her, drawing Ding Gou'er, who was mired in a 'depression syndrome,' inexorably toward her.

'So, it's you, Miss Alkaline!' Ding Gou'er said, like a common hooligan. As he stood there facing her, he experienced the uplifting feeling of a ship that has finally reached port or of a child when it sees its mother.

'Mr Fertilizer!' she said with a wide grin. 'You're still here, I see, you son of a gun!'

'I was just thinking of leaving.'

'Want to hitch another ride in my truck?'

'Sure.'

'Well, it's not that easy.'

'A carton of Marlboros.'

'Two cartons.'

'Okay, two cartons.'

'Wait here.'

The truck in front drove off with a spurt of black smoke, its tires sending a shower of coal dust into the air. 'Stand aside,' she shouted as she jumped into the cab, grabbed the steering wheel and jerked it this way and that until she stopped directly beneath the spot where the trolley tracks ended. 'Hey, girl, you're really something!' sang out a young man in dark shades in heartfelt praise. 'You can't make a cow big with a genital blow, you can't push a train and make it go, you can't build Mount Tai with just rocks and some snow.' She hopped out of the cab. Ding Gou'er was grinning from ear to ear. 'What are you laughing at?' she demanded.

The trolley rumbled and began to float forward like a big black turtle. From time to time, sparks flew as iron wheels scraped along the iron tracks. The black rubber cord coiled and stretched in the trolley's wake, lively as a snake. Steely determination filled the eyes of the girl on the back of the trolley and her jaw was set, instilling in the observer a sense of respect bordering on fear. The trolley rushed headlong, like a wild tiger coming down the mountain. Ding Gou'er was afraid it would crash into the truck and turn it into a pile of twisted metal. But events proved his fears groundless, for the girl's powers of assessment were infallible, her reactions lightning quick, her mental functions as unerring as a computer. At the very last second, she threw on the brakes, tipping the loaded trolley over and, with a *whoosh*, sending shiny black coal cascading into the bed of the truck – no spillage, none left behind in the trolley. With the smell of coal rising to fill his nostrils, Ding Gou'er's mood lightened even more.

'Got a smoke, pal?' He reached his hand out to Miss Alkaline. 'How about bestowing one on me?'

She handed him a cigarette and stuck one into her own mouth.

Through the misty veil of smoke, she asked, 'What happened to you? Get mugged?'

He was too busy watching a pair of mules to answer.

Both of them watched as a wagon drawn by the mules came their way on the mine road, which was strewn with waste rock, coal dust, broken stone slabs, and rotting lumber; as it drew near, they watched the driver, in an arrogant display of power, grip the reins in his left hand and drive the mules forward with a flick of the whip he held in his right. They were beautiful black mules. The larger of the two, seemingly blind, was strapped to the shafts; the smaller mule, not only sighted, but in possession of a pair of fiery eyes the size of bronze bells, pulled at the harness. Ao-ao-ao – wu-la-la – pull pull pull – The snaking whip snapped and crackled in the air, forcing the doughty little black mule to lurch ahead. And as the creaky wagon bounded forward, disaster struck: The little black mule lost its footing and crashed to the weedy, seedy, unforgiving ground, like a collapsed greasy black wall. The tip of the driver's whip landed on the animal's rump; it struggled mightily to its feet, shaking uncontrollably and rocking from side to side, piteous brays tearing at the heart of all within earshot. The driver, momentarily petrified with fear, threw down his whip, jumped off the wagon, and fell to his knees in front of the mule. He reached down and lifted out a discolored hoof – green and red and white and black all mixed together – that was wedged between two stone slabs. Ding Gou'er grabbed the female trucker's hand and took several steps toward the scene.

Cradling the mule's hoof in his hands, the sallow-faced driver was wailing loudly.

In the traces the older mule hung its head in silence, like a participant in a wake.

The little black mule stood on three legs; its fourth, the maimed rear leg, was thumping against a piece of rotten wood on the ground, like a mallet beating a drum, but with the difference that dark flowing blood stained the wood and the ground around it red.

Ding Gou'er, whose heart was beating wildly, turned to walk away, but Miss Alkaline had a vicelike grip on his wrist; he wasn't going anywhere.

Everyone in the vicinity had an opinion: Some felt sorry for the little mule, others felt sorry for the driver; some blamed the driver, others blamed the rough, pitted road. A flock of quarreling ravens.

'Make way, make way!'

Stunned by the interruption, the bemused crowd parted to let two tiny, skinny people tumble in among them out of nowhere. A close look revealed that it was two women with ghostly white faces like winter cabbages. They wore spotless white uniforms and matching caps. One carried a waxed bamboo hamper, the other a wicker basket. A pair of angels, it seemed.

'The veterinarians are here!'

The veterinarians are here, the vets are here, stop crying, little friend, the vets are here. Hand them the mule's hoof, hurry. They'll reattach it for you.

The women in white hastened to explain: 'We're not veterinarians! We're chefs at the guest house.'

'Municipal officials are coming to tour the mine tomorrow, and the Mine Director has ordered us to treat them like royalty. Chicken and fish, nothing special there. And just as we were worrying ourselves sick, we heard that a mule had lost one of its hooves.'

'Braised mule's hoof, mule's hoof in chicken broth.'

'Driver, go on, sell them the mule's hoof.'

'No, I can't sell it . . .' The driver hugged the hoof tightly, a look of affectionate longing on his face, as if he were embracing the severed hand of his beloved.

'Have you taken leave of your senses, you moron?' one of the women in white demanded angrily. 'Do you plan to reattach that somehow? Where are you going to get the money? I doubt if anyone could manage that on a person these days, let alone a beast of burden.'

'We'll pay top dollar.'

'You won't find a shop like this in the next village.'

'How, um, how much will you give me?'

'Thirty yuan apiece. A good price, wouldn't you say?'

'You only want the hooves?'

'Only the hooves. You can keep the rest.'

'All four of them?'

'All four.'

'He's still alive, you know.'

'What good is he with one missing hoof?'

'But he's still alive . . .'

'Talk talk talk. Do we have a deal or don't we?'

'Yes . . .'

'Here's the money! Count it.'

'Take him out of the traces, quickly!'

Holding the money for the four hooves in his hand, the driver handed the severed hoof to one of the women in white, trembling perceptibly. She placed it gingerly in her bamboo hamper. The other woman took a knife, hatchet, and bone saw out of her wicker basket, jumped to her feet, and, in a loud voice, pressed the young driver to free the little black mule from the traces. He squatted down bow-legged, bent over at the waist, and, with trembling fingers, freed the little black mule from the harness. Slow as it sounds in the retelling, in real life what happened next was over in a flash. The woman in white raised her hatchet, took aim on the mule's broad forehead, and swung with all her might, burying the ax blade so deeply in its head, she couldn't pull it out, no matter how she tried. And while she was trying to remove her ax, the little black mule's front legs buckled, carrying the rest of the animal slowly to the ground, where it spread out flat on the bumpy, pitted roadway.

Ding Gou'er breathed a long sigh.

There was still a bit of life in the little mule, as the shallow, raspy sounds of breathing proved; weak trickles of blood slid down its forehead on either side of the buried hatchet, soaking its eyelashes, nose, and lips.

Once again it was the woman who had buried the hatchet in the mule's forehead who picked up a blue-handled knife, leaped onto the mule's body, grabbed a hoof – a jet-black hoof in a lily-white hand – and described a brisk circle right in the curve where the hoof joined the leg; then another circle, and with a little pressure from the lily-white hand, the mule hoof and mule leg moved away from one another, attached only by a single white tendon. A final flick of the knife, and the hoof and leg parted company once and for all. The lily-white hand rose into the air, and the mule hoof flew into the hand of the other woman in white.

It took only a moment to amputate the three hooves, during which time the onlookers were mesmerized by the woman's incredible skill; no one spoke, no one coughed, no one farted. Who'd have dared take such liberties in the presence of this woman warrior?

Ding Gou'er's palms were sweating. All he could think of was the Taoist tale of the marvelous skills of the ox-butcher Chef Ding.

The woman in white worked the hatchet until she was finally able to remove it from the forehead of the little black mule, which finally breathed its last: belly up, its legs sticking up stiffly in four directions, like machine-gun barrels.

The truck had left the winding, bumpy road of the coal mine behind; the towering mounds of waste rock and the spectral mine machinery had all but disappeared in the heavy mist behind them; the barking of the watchdog, the rumbling of trolleys, and the thumping of underground explosions could no longer be heard. But the four machine-gun legs of the mule kept floating before Ding Gou'er's eyes, keeping him on edge. The lady trucker's mood was also affected by the image of the little black mule, for she greeted every mile of bumpy road with crude curses; then, once she was on the highway to town, she threw the truck into high gear, opened the ventilation window, and put the pedal to the metal, keeping it there as the engine groaned under the strain. Like a Fascist bullet. Roadside trees bent in their wake as if felled by a giant ax; the ground was a whirling chess board, as the arrow on the speedometer pointed to eighty kilometers. Wind whistled, wheels spun dizzily. Every few minutes, the exhaust pipe belched out a cloud of smoke. Ding Gou'er watched her out of the corner of his eye with such admiration he gradually forgot the mule legs stretching skyward.

Not long before they reached the city, steam from the overheated radiator fogged up the windshield. Miss Alkaline had turned the radiator into a boiler. With an outburst of foul curses, she pulled to the side of the road. Ding Gou'er followed her out of the cab and, with a momentary sense of 'I told you so,' watched as she raised the hood to let the engine cool off in the breezes. The heat nearly bowled him over; what water remained in the radiator hissed and gurgled. As she unscrewed the radiator cap using her glove, he noticed that her face was radiant as a sunset.

She removed a tin bucket from under the truck. 'Go!' she commanded angrily. 'Get me some water!'

Neither daring nor willing to disobey, Ding Gou'er took the bucket and, playing the fool, said, 'You won't drive off while I'm out getting water, will you? When rescuing someone, go all the way. When taking someone home, see him to the door.'

'Do you understand science?' she demanded angrily. 'If I could drive off, why stop? Besides, you've got my bucket.'

Ding Gou'er made a face, knowing that this little bit of humor might make a little girl giggle, but had no effect on this shrew. Yet he made the face, anyway, in spite of himself.

'Don't make a fool of yourself,' she growled, 'wrinkling your nose and giving me the evil eye like that. Now go get some water.'

'Out here in the middle of nowhere? Where am I supposed to find it?'

'If I knew, would I be sending you?'

Reluctantly, Ding Gou'er picked up the bucket, parted the yielding roadside shrubbery, stepped across the shallow, bone-dry roadside ditch, and found himself standing in the middle of a harvested field. It was not one of those fields to which he was accustomed, where you can see for miles in every direction, like a vast wilderness. Having made it to the outskirts of the urban center, he could see signs of where the city's arms, or at least its fingers, had reached: here a lonely little multi-storied building, there a smokestack belching smoke, dissecting the field in crazy quilt fashion. Ding Gou'er stood there feeling unavoidably, if not overwhelmingly, sad. After a reflective moment, he looked up into the setting sun and its layers of red clouds on the western horizon, which effectively drove away his melancholy; he turned and strode in the direction of the nearest, and strangest-looking, building he saw.

'Head for the mountains, and kill the horse.' No statement was ever truer. Bathed in the blood red sunset, the building seemed so very near, but for the man on foot it was so very far. Cropland kept popping up between him and the building as if falling from the sky, keeping him from walking toward where his happiness lay. A major surprise awaited him in a harvested cornfield where only dry stalks remained.

By then dusk had nearly fallen, turning the sky the color of red wine. Cornstalks stood like silent sentries. Even though Ding Gou'er turned sideways to walk down a plowed row, he unavoidably brushed against silken corn tassels, making rustling sounds. All of a sudden, a hulking shadow appeared in his path, as if it had sprung up out of the ground, throwing such a fright into the investigator, a man of renowned courage, that he shivered from head to toe and his hair stood on end; instinctively brandishing the tin bucket, he was ready to strike. But the monster stepped back and said in a muffled voice:

'What's the big idea, trying to hit me?'

Once he had regained his composure, the investigator discovered that it was a very tall and very old man standing in his way. Starlight shining through the deepening dusk fell on the man's bristly chin and rats' nest of hair; two deep green eyes were circled by the hazy outline of a face. He sensed that the big-boned man, dressed in rags, was probably a hard-working, simple-living, diligent and courageous, decent man. His raspy breath came in thick, short bursts, mingled with metallic coughs.

'What are you doing here?' Ding Gou'er asked.

'Cricket snatching,' the old man replied, lifting a clay pot as proof.

'Cricket catching?'

'Cricket watching,' the old man said.

Crickets were leaping around in his pot, banging loudly into the clay walls – *pi-pi pa-pa* – as the old man stood there quietly, his shifty green eyes looking like a pair of exhausted fireflies.

'Cricket catching?' Ding Gou'er asked. 'Do folks around here enjoy cricket fighting?'

'No. Folks around here enjoy cricket snacking,' the old man drawled, as he turned, took a couple of steps, and knelt on the ground. Cornstalk leaves rustled, then settled on his head and shoulders, transforming him into a grave mound. Starlight kept getting brighter and brighter, cool breezes wafted this way and that, leaving no trace either way and creating an air of deep mystery. Ding Gou'er's shoulders stiffened as a chill coursed through his heart. Fireflies glided through the air like optical illusions. And then the dreary calls of crickets erupted all around him; everywhere, it seemed, nothing but crickets. Ding Gou'er looked on as the old man turned on a tiny flashlight, sending a ray of golden light to the base of a cornstalk, where it wrapped itself around a nice fat cricket: bright red body, square head with protruding eyes, thick legs and a bulging abdomen, breathing heavily and poised to leap away at any second. The old man reached out and caught it in a little net. From there, into the clay pot. And, before long, from there into a pot full of hot oil; and, finally from there into a human stomach.

The investigator was vaguely reminded of an article he'd read in *Haute Cuisine* listing the nutritive value of crickets and the many ways they can be prepared.

The old man crawled forward. Ding Gou'er threaded his way through the cornfield and headed quickly for the light ahead.

It was an extraordinarily appealing, wholesome, lively night in which exploration and discovery went hand in hand, study and work stood shoulder to shoulder, love and revolution were united, starlight above and lamplight below echoed one another from afar to illuminate dark corners. Light from a mercury-vapor lamp lit up a rectangular sign until it dazzled the eyes. With his tin bucket in hand, Ding Gou'er squinted to read the large black characters on the white signboard, fashioned in the Song Dynasty calligraphic style:

SPECIAL FOODS CULTIVATION INSTITUTE

It was a relatively small institute. As a welter of thoughts raced through his mind, Ding Gou'er sized up the handsome little buildings and the large, brightly lit tents. A gateman in a brown uniform and wide-brimmed hat, with a holster on his hip, appeared from behind the gate and shouted breathlessly: 'What do you want? Just what do you think you're doing, poking around like that? You wouldn't have a little thievery in mind, would you?'

Noting the tear-gas pistol in the man's holster and the electric prod he was waving haughtily, Ding Gou'er's anger took hold. 'Mind your tongue, young man,' he said.

'What? What did you say?' the young gateman bellowed as he moved up closer.

'I told you to mind your tongue!' Ding Gou'er was a favorite of the public security and judicial system, and used to getting his way. Being yelled at by a gateman made his palms itch, got his dander up, soured his mood. 'Watchdog!' he hissed.

The 'watchdog' let out a yelp, leaped a good twenty centimeters into the air, and roared, 'You little bastard, who the hell do you think you're talking to? You're dead meat!' He drew his tear-gas pistol and aimed it at Ding Gou'er.

With a deprecatory laugh, Ding said, 'Careful you don't shoot yourself with that. If you're going to subdue someone with tear gas, you'd better be standing upwind.'

'Well, who'd have guessed a little bastard like you could be such an expert?'

'I use tear-gas guns like that to wipe my ass!' Ding Gou'er said.
'Bullshit!'

'Here come your bosses!' Ding Gou'er said, pursing his lips and pointing to a spot behind the gateman.

When the gateman turned to look, Ding Gou'er casually swung his tin bucket and knocked the tear-gas pistol out of the man's hand. Then, with a swift kick, he unburdened him of his electric prod, which also flew out of his hand.

The gateman thought about bending over to pick up his gun, but Ding raised his bucket and said, 'Do that and you'll be flat on the ground like a dog fighting over shit.'

Knowing he'd met his match, the gateman backed off, then turned and ran for the little building. Ding Gou'er strode through the gate with a smile.

A gang of men dressed exactly like the gateman came running out of the building. One of them had a metal whistle in his mouth: *Brrrt – brrt – brrt*, he blew with all his might. That's the guy – beat the shit out of that son of a bitch – a dozen or so electric prods waved in the air. Like a pack of mad dogs, they surrounded Ding Gou'er.

He reached into his waistband. Oops, his pistol was in his briefcase, which was in the truck back on the road.

One of the men, a red armband around his bicep – probably a minor commander or something – pointed at Ding Gou'er with his electric prod and asked truculently:

'What the hell do you want?'

'I'm a truck driver,' Ding Gou'er answered, raising his tin bucket as proof.

'A driver?' the commander asked suspiciously. 'Then what are you doing here?'

'Looking for water. My radiator overheated.'

The tension lessened considerably; several brandished electric prods were lowered.

'He's no driver,' the humiliated gateman shouted. 'This guy knows how to use his fists and feet.'

'All that proves is what a loser you are,' Ding Gou'er said.

'Who do you drive for?' the commander continued the interrogation.

Ding Gou'er recalled the sign on the door of the truck. 'Brewer's College,' he answered without missing a beat.

'Where were you headed?'

'The mine.'

'Your papers?'

'In my jacket pocket.'

'Where's your jacket?'

'In the truck.'

'Where's the truck?'

'On the highway.'

'Who else is in the truck?'

'A good-looking girl.'

The commander giggled. 'You Brewer's College drivers are horny asses.'

'Horny asses, you said it!'

'Well, get a move on!' the commander said. 'We've got water inside, so what're you hanging around out here for?'

As Ding Gou'er followed them into the building, from behind he heard the commander chewing out the gateman: 'You incompetent moron, can't you even handle a run-of-the-mill truck driver? If the forty thieves ever showed up, they'd probably trick you out of your balls.'

The blinding lights inside the building made Ding Gou'er dizzy. His feet sank into the soft folds of a scarlet lamb's-wool carpet; hanging on the walls were colorful photographs, all farm products: corn, rice, millet, sorghum, plus some others he'd never seen before. Ding Gou'er surmised that these were hybrid grains that the institute's agri-scientists had taken pains to develop. The commander, warming up to Ding Gou'er a bit, pointed the way to the toilet, where, he said, he could fill his bucket with water from a tap used for rinsing out rags. Ding Gou'er thanked him, then watched him and his troops file into a little room, from which thick, acrid smoke escaped when the door was opened. Probably playing poker or mahjong, he concluded, although they could just as easily be studying the latest Central Government directive. He smiled, but only for a moment, before picking up his bucket and proceeding cautiously to the toilet, noticing the wooden signs on doors as he passed them: Technical Section, Production Section, Accounting Section, Financial Section, Dossier Room, Reference Room, Laboratory, Video Room. The door to the Video Room was ajar; people were working inside.

Bucket in hand, he peeked inside, where a man and a woman were watching a videotape. The images on the big-screen TV shocked him, for there on the screen, in ancient official script, were the following words:

A Rare Delicacy – Chicken Head Rice.

The soundtrack was of the tantalizing Cantonese tune 'Bright Clouds Chasing the Moon.' At first he wasn't interested in the video, but it quickly exerted a powerful pull on him. The cinematic images were breathtakingly beautiful. A chicken-killing production line. Chicken heads methodically lopped off, one after another, as the music swelled. The announcer says, 'The broad masses of cadres at the Special Foods Cultivation Institute, under the encouragement of . . . have pooled their efforts and the wisdom of the masses, and, in the spirit of "when attacking a stronghold, show no fear," struggling without letup, day and night . . .' A group of emaciated, large-headed individuals in white uniforms were doing something with an array of test tubes. Another group of individuals – lovely young women with their hair tucked under their caps and wearing white full-sized aprons – were picking up kernels of raw rice with tweezers and stuffing them into the decapitated chicken heads. Another group of women, dressed exactly like the previous group, and just as beautiful, buried the rice-stuffed chicken heads in fiery red flower pots. Then the scene changed, and rice sprouts had emerged from the pots. Dozens of sprinklers kept the rice sprouts watered. Another scene change, and the sprouts now have tassels. One final scene change, and they are several bowls of steaming, blood-red, shiny and moist pearl drops of rice laid out on a flower-bedecked banqueting table. Several dignitaries – some handsome, some buxom, some big and tall – sit around the table savoring this rare delicacy, smiles of satisfaction on their faces. With a sigh, Ding Gou'er realized how impoverished his knowledge was, like the proverbial frog at the bottom of a well. The man and woman in the room began talking even before the video ended, and Ding Gou'er, wanting to avoid a scene, picked up his bucket and walked off. A moment later, on his way out the gate, he fell under the withering glare of the gateman; he could feel the man's eyes boring into his back. As he threaded his way back through the cornfield, the dry leaves brushed against his eyes and made them water. The old man catching crickets was nowhere in sight. He was still a long way from the truck when he heard the lady trucker bellow:

'Where in the goddamned hell did you go to get that water, the Yellow River or the Yangtze?'

He set the bucket of water down and flexed his poor, numbed muscles.

'I got it in your mama's goddamned Yarlung Zangbou River.'

'Goddamn it to hell, I thought you fell into the river and drowned.'

'I not only didn't drown, I watched one of your mama's goddamned videos.'

'One of those goddamn-it-to-hell kung-fu films or a porn job?'

'It wasn't one of your mama's goddamn kung-fu films and it wasn't a porn job. It was about that rare delicacy, chicken-head rice.'

'What's so rare about chicken-head rice and what the goddamn hell's the idea of your mama's goddamn this and your mama's goddamn that?'

'If not for those your mama's goddamn this and goddamn thats I'd have to find some other way to shut your mama's goddamn mouth.'

Ding Gou'er grabbed the lady trucker around the waist, wrapped his arms tightly around her, and crushed his multi-flavored mouth onto hers.

II

Dear Mo Yan

Your letter arrived safely.

Still no word from *Citizens' Literature*. I'm getting anxious, and I wish you'd nudge the editors, Zhou Bao and Li Xiaobao, one more time, urging them to get in touch with me.

Last night I wrote another story, which I call 'Donkey Avenue.' For this story I adopted creative techniques from the martial-arts genre, and I ask you to read it with your customary discerning eye. You have my permission to forward it to the magazine of your choice.

I'm sending the research material on liquor you requested. As for the thirty bottles of fine liquor, I'll send them with the next bus to Beijing. For a master to drink his disciple's liquor is in perfect accord with the nature of things. You'll recall how Confucius asked for ten strings of dried meat from each of his disciples as 'tuition' for the instruction he dispensed.

The continued silence from *Citizens' Literature* has sent me into a funk, as if my soul had taken flight. As someone who has had the same experience, you must understand how I feel.

Respectfully wishing you
Happy writing!
Your disciple

Li Yidou

III

My Brother Yidou

I received your letter and the manuscript. The research material on liquor hasn't arrived yet, but printed matter usually takes longer.

I do indeed understand how you feel, since I've been there myself. To be honest, I've done or considered doing just about anything I could think of to see one of my manuscripts get into print. As soon as I received your letter, I placed a phone call to Zhou Bao, who told me he's read all three of your stories, several times each. He said he still can't make up his mind, that he simply doesn't know what to say. He wanted me to tell you he's agonizing over it. He's sent all three to Li Xiaobao, asking him to give them a quick read and let him know what he thinks. The last thing he said was that even though there are parts of all three stories he has some problems with, the author's talent is unquestioned. That should make you feel better. For a writer, talent is everything. Lots of people make a career out of writing, producing many works and knowing exactly what it takes to become a great writer. But they never break into the big time, because they lack one thing: talent, or a sufficient amount of it.

I've already read 'Donkey Avenue' three times, and my overall opinion is that it is unrestrained, bold. It reminds me a bit of a wild donkey rolling on the ground and kicking its legs in the air. In a word: wild. You didn't happen to write it after drinking some Red-Maned Stallion, did you?

There were a few spots where I didn't understand what you were getting at, so here are some hastily formed opinions:

1. Is that scaly boy who rides the little black donkey in the story, the one who can fly on eaves and walk on walls as if his feet were on solid ground, a chivalric hero or a thief? He has already made appearances in 'Meat Boy' and 'Child Prodigy' (he is the same person, isn't he?), and always as a mere mortal, it seems. Now in this story he has become a sort of superman, half genie and half goblin, which may be a bit much, don't you think? Of course, you never said that these stories comprised a series. But there's also the question of his unclear relationship to the little goblin in red. In 'Child Prodigy,' if I'm not mistaken, you said that the little goblin was in fact that little scaly creature, right?

I've never dared to disparage kung-fu novels. Their ability to attract so many readers is enough to make them respectable. I read a stack of them last year over the summer break, and I was so absorbed in them, I nearly forgot to eat and sleep. But when I was finished, even I was baffled. Why, knowing full well there wasn't a truthful word in any of them, was I so mesmerized? Some say kung-fu novels are fairy tales for adults, a theory I find convincing. Of course, after reading dozens of them, I've discovered that they're heavily formulaic and that it wouldn't be hard to cook up one of my own. But it would be no easy feat to reach the artistic level of a Jin Yong or a Gu Long. You attempted some 'cross breeding' in your novel, which is an intriguing idea, whether it succeeds or not. There is, as a matter of fact, a decidedly avant-garde woman writer named Big Sister Hua, whose experimentation with 'cross breeding' has been remarkably successful. You might want to read some of her works. I hear she lives in Seven Stars county (where the county head is famous for selling rat poison), not far from Liquorland. When you find some free time, you should go see this 'ladybug' writer.

2. I once heard Big Mouth Zhao, a student at the Lu Xun Academy of Literature, say that Dragon and Phoenix Lucky Together is a classic Cantonese dish. Its ingredients are poisonous snakes and wild chickens (needless to say, in this age of cutting corners, there's a very good chance that river eels and domestic chickens have taken their place). For your Dragon and Phoenix Lucky Together, however, you use the external genitalia of male and female donkeys. Who would dare dip his chopsticks into that? I'm concerned that this dish, given its blatant bourgeois liberalization potential, might not be accepted by literary critics. Currently, some popular 'heroes' in the literary field are intent upon finding 'smut' in literary works, with their dog-keen noses, eagle-sharp eyes, and a magnifying glass. It's hard to escape them, just as a cracked egg can't be safe from a fly looking for a place to deposit its maggots. Ever since writing 'Ecstasy' and 'Red Locusts,' I've been coated with the stinking saliva they spit on me. Adopting a battle strategy from Gang of Four days, they scrutinize my works by taking them out of context, attacking a single point without taking the whole text into consideration, ignoring the functions of those 'unsavory details' and their particular settings. Instead of focusing on a text's literary value, they employ biological and moral viewpoints to wage a violent assault, and deny me the opportunity to defend myself. Therefore, based on personal experience, I urge you to choose a different dish.

3. Now about Yu Yichi. I'm deeply interested in this character, although you didn't devote much space to describing him. The portrayal of dwarfs is not uncommon in literary works, either in China or abroad, but few could be considered typical. I hope you'll utilize your talent to memorialize this dwarf. Didn't he ask 'you' to write his life story? I believe this would be a fascinating 'biography.' He's a dwarf who, born into a literary family, has read all the classics and is well versed in statecraft, yet has endured decades of humiliation. Then, through some magic intervention, he enjoys a meteoric rise, obtaining wealth, fame, and position; now he vows to 'f— all the beautiful women in Liquorland.' But what sort of psychology motivates this grandiose boasting? What sort of psychological transformation occurs in the process of acting upon this grandiose boast? What sort of mental state is he in after carrying out this grandiose boast? Behind all these questions lie numerous brilliant stories; why not try your hand at one or more of them?

4. As to the opening of your story, please forgive my directness, but it reads like meaningless grandiloquent gibberish. The story would be tighter if you deleted it altogether.

5. In the story, you characterize the father of the twin sister dwarfs as a leader in the Central Government; if you intend this to be viewed positively, the higher his position, the better. But your works frequently reveal derogatory criticism toward those in power, and that's a no-no: society is shaped like a pagoda, getting progressively smaller toward the top; that makes it easier to link the characters in your story with real-life people. If someone from the top of the pagoda were to set his sights on you, it would be a lot worse than a head cold. So I suggest that you give the twin dwarfs a less illustrious background and their father a somewhat diminished official position.

These are just some random jottings, filled with contradictions. Disregard what I've written after you read it, and don't be too conscientious. In this world, one should never be too conscientious about anything; it's a sure path to bad luck.

I think it's best to send your masterpiece 'Donkey Avenue' to *Citizens' Literature*; if they turn it down, I can always recommend another magazine.

I've written several chapters of my long novel *The Republic of Wine* (tentative title). Originally I thought I'd have no trouble writing about liquor, since I've been drunk a time or two. But once I started, I encountered all sorts of difficulties and complications. The relationship between man and liquor embodies virtually all the contradictions involved in the process of human existence and development. Someone with extraordinary talent could write an impressive work on this topic; unfortunately, with my meager talents, I reveal my shortcomings at every turn. I hope you'll expound more on liquor in future letters. That might serve as an inspiration to me.

Wishing you
Good Luck!

Mo Yan

IV

Donkey Avenue, by Li Yidou

Dear friends, not long ago you read my stories 'Alcohol,' 'Meat Boy,' and 'Child Prodigy.' Now please accept my next offering, 'Donkey Avenue.' I ask your indulgence and consideration. The irrelevant comments you have just read, in the view of literary critics, must not be inserted into a fictional work, for they destroy the integrity and unity of the work. But, since I am a doctoral candidate in liquor studies, one who daily views liquor, smells liquor, drinks liquor, who embraces liquor kisses liquor rubs elbows with liquor, for whom every breath of air is an act of fermentation, I embody the character and the temperament of liquor. What does nurture mean? This is what it means. Liquor infatuates me until I am incapable of following rules and regulations. Liquor's character is wild and unrestrained; its temperament is to talk without thinking.

Dear friends, come with me as I pass through the elaborate arched gate on my way out of Liquorland's Brewer's College, leaving the liquor-bottle-shaped classroom building behind, and leaving the liquor-glass-shaped laboratory building behind, and leaving the intoxicating aroma of smoke billowing from the smokestack of the college-run winery behind. 'Put down your bundle and travel light,' as you walk along with me, sharp-eyed and clearheaded, always knowing where we are and where we're going; we cross the beautifully carved China fir footbridge over Sweet Wine stream, putting the gurgling water, the water lilies floating on the water, the butterflies resting on the water lilies, the white ducks playing in the water, the fish swimming in the water, the fishes' feelings, the white ducks' moods, the floating duckweed's ideas, the flowing water's somniloquy . . . all that behind us. Please note: The main gate of the Culinary Academy entices us by sending exquisite aromas toward us! That is where my aging mother-in-law works. Not long ago she went mad and has been at home ever since, hiding day and night behind black curtains, where she does nothing but write letters of exposé and denunciation. So we leave her for the moment and ignore the fragrant aromas drifting over from the Culinary Academy. There is compelling and eternal truth in the saying, 'Birds die in pursuit of food, man dies chasing wealth.' In times of chaos and corruption, men are just like birds, to all appearances free as the wind, but in fact, in constant peril from traps, nets, arrows, and firearms. OK, your noses have been contaminated by the smell, so quickly cover them with your hands and leave the Culinary Academy behind, following me on the slant down to the narrow Deer Avenue, where you can hear the cries of deer, as if they were grazing on wild duckweed. Shops on both sides of the street have hung deer antlers above their doors, their crisscrossing points creating a forest of spears or a grove of swords. We walk on the ancient path paved with slippery, moss-covered flagstones, between which green grass pokes out. Watch your step, don't trip and fall. Carefully, cautiously, we weave in and out, until we turn into Donkey Avenue, where the street beneath our feet is also paved with flagstones that have been worn smooth over time by blowing wind and pouring rain and rolling wheels and galloping hooves, rounding the edges and making them smooth as bronze mirrors. Donkey Avenue is slightly wider than Deer Avenue; its stone slabs are covered with filthy, bloody water and blackened donkey hides. It is also more slippery than Deer Avenue. Ebony crows *caw-caw* as they limp along the street. This is a treacherous spot, so be careful, everybody, and walk only where you're supposed to. Keep your bodies straight and plant your feet firmly. Don't let your eyes wander, like some farmboy on his first trip to the city. If you do, you'll likely fall and make a spectacle of yourself. There's nothing worse than falling. Getting your clothes dirty will be the least of your worries if you wind up breaking a hip. Like I said, there's nothing worse than falling. Why don't we give our readers a break by resting before we walk any farther?

Here in Liquorland we have exceptional individuals who can drink without getting drunk, we have drunkards who steal their wives' savings to buy their next drink, and we have no-account hooligans who resort to thievery, mugging, and every imaginable form of trickery to the same end. I am reminded of the legendary Green Grass Snake Li Four, who was beaten to a pulp by the licentious monk, and Freaky Villain Niu Two, who was stabbed by the Black-Faced Monster. People like that are always hanging around Donkey Avenue – you can't miss them. See that fellow leaning against the doorway, a cigarette dangling from his mouth, and that one over there, liquor bottle in one hand as he gnaws on a donkey dick, called 'money meat' because it looks like old-fashioned coins, or that fellow with the birdcage, the one who's whistling? They're the ones I'm talking about. I tell you, friends, take care not to provoke them. Decent folk ignore bums on the street, just as new shoes avoid stepping on dogshit. Donkey Avenue is Liquorland's great shame as well as its great glory. You might as well not come to Liquorland if you never stroll down Donkey Avenue. This street boasts the shops of twenty-four donkey butchers. Ever since the Ming dynasty, owners of these shops have butchered their way through the entirety of the Manchu dynasty, plus all the years of the Chinese Republic. When the

Communists came to power, donkeys were labeled a means of production, and slaughtering them became a crime. Donkey Avenue fell on hard times. But in recent years, the policy of 'rejuvenate internally, open to the outside' has sparked a rise in the people's standard of living and an increase in meat consumption to improve the quality of the race. Donkey Avenue has sprung back to life. 'What dragon meat is to heaven, donkey meat is to the human world.' Donkey meat is aromatic; donkey meat is delicious; donkey meat is a true delicacy. Dear readers, honored guests, friends, ladies, and gentlemen, 'Sank you belly much,' 'Mistuh and Miss,' the saying 'Cantonese cuisine is tops' is nothing but a rumor someone down there cooked up to mislead the masses. Listen to what I have to say. Say about what? About dishes for which Liquorland is justifiably famous. When listing one item, ten thousand could be omitted, so please be forgiving. When you stand on Donkey Avenue, you see delicacies that cover Liquorland like clouds, more than the eyes can take in: Donkeys are slaughtered on Donkey Avenue, deer are butchered on Deer Avenue, oxen are dispatched on Oxen Street, sheep are killed on Sheep Alley, hogs meet their end in pig abattoirs, horses are felled in Horse Lane, dogs and cats are put to the knife in dog and cat markets . . . in mind-boggling numbers, so many the heart is disturbed, the mind thrown into turmoil, the lips chapped, the tongue parched. In a word, anything that can be eaten in this world of ours – mountain delicacies and dainties from the sea, birds and beasts and fish and insects – you'll find right here in Liquorland. Things available elsewhere are available here; things unavailable elsewhere are also available here. And not only available, but what is central, what is most significant, what is truly magnificent is that all these things are special, stylistic, historical, traditional, ideological, cultural, and moral. While that may sound boastful, in fact, it's anything but. In the nationwide craze over getting rich, our Liquorland leaders had a unique vision, a pioneering inspiration, a singular plan to put us on the road to wealth. My friends, ladies and gentlemen, nothing in this world, I think you'll agree, matches food and drink in importance. Why else would man have a mouth, if not to eat and drink? So people who come to Liquorland will eat and drink well. Let them eat for variety, eat for pleasure, eat for addiction. Let them drink for variety, drink for pleasure, drink for addiction. Let them realize that there's more to food and drink than the mere sustaining of life, that through food and drink they can learn the true meaning of life, can gain awareness of the philosophy of human existence. Let them understand that food and drink play an important role not only in the physiological process, but in the processes of spiritual molding and aesthetic appreciation.

Walk slowly, enjoy the sights. Donkey Avenue is a mile long, with butcher shops on both sides. There are ninety restaurants and inns, and all of them use the carcasses of donkeys in their fare. The menus are always changing, as new dishes vie for attention. The epitome of donkey gourmandism is reached in this place. Anyone who has sampled the fare of all ninety establishments need never again eat donkey. And only those people who have eaten their way up one side of the street and down the other can thump their chests proudly and announce: I have eaten donkey!

Donkey Avenue is like a big dictionary, filled with so much that even if my mouth were hard enough to drive nails through metal, I could never exhaust, finish, reach the end of the subject. If I don't tell my story well, it is because I babble nonsense or garbage. Please forgive and bear with me, please allow me to down a glass of Red-Maned Stallion to pull myself together. For hundreds of years, countless numbers of donkeys have been slaughtered here on Donkey Avenue. You can just about say that swarms of donkey ghosts roam Donkey Avenue day and night, or that every stone on Donkey Avenue is soaked in the blood of donkeys, or that every plant on Donkey Avenue is watered with donkey spirits, or that donkey souls flourish in every toilet on Donkey Avenue, or that anyone who has been to Donkey Avenue is more or less endowed with donkey qualities. My friends, donkey affairs are like smoke that shrouds the sky of Donkey Avenue and weakens the radiance of the sun. If we close our eyes we see hordes of donkeys of all shapes and shades running around and braying to the heavens.

According to local legend, late at night, when it is really quiet, when all is still, an extremely nimble, extremely handsome little black donkey (sex unknown) races from one end of the flagstoned avenue to the other, from east to west, then from west to east. Its handsome, delicate hooves, shaped like wine glasses carved out of black agate, pound the smooth flagstones, filling the air with a crisp, clear tattoo. This late-night sound is like music from Heaven, terrifying, mysterious, and tender all at the same time. Anyone hearing it is moved to tears, entranced, intoxicated, given to long, emotional sighs. And if there is a full moon . . .

That night, Yu Yichi, proprietor and manager of Yichi Tavern, his drumlike belly warmed by a few extra glasses of strong liquor, carried a bamboo chair outside to cool off under an old pomegranate tree. Waves of moonlight turned the flagstones into shiny mirrors. A chill breeze on that mid-autumn night sent the other people back into their houses, and if not for the effects of the alcohol, Yu Yichi would not have come outside either. Streets on which people had swarmed like ants were now transformed into scenes of tranquillity, invaded only by insect chirps, like razor-sharp darts that could pierce brass walls and iron barriers. The cool breeze blew across Yu's protruding belly, bringing him a sense of bliss. Gazing up at sweet pomegranates, big and small, and shaped like flower petals, he was about to fall asleep when suddenly he felt his scalp tighten and goose bumps erupt all over his body. His sleepiness disappeared in a flash and his body froze in paralysis – as if a kung-fu master had punched him in the solar plexus; of course, his mind remained clear and his eyes took in everything. A black donkey appeared on the street as if it had fallen from Heaven. It was a pudgy little animal whose body emitted light, as if it were made of wax. It rolled around on the street a time or two, then stood up and shook its body, as if trying to rid itself of non-existent dust. Then it jumped into the air, its tail raised, and started to run. It galloped from the eastern end of the street to the western end, and back, three round trips in all, so fast it was like a puff of black smoke. The crisp sound of its hooves drowned out the chirping of autumn insects. When it stopped and stood still in the middle of the street, the chirping recommenced. That is when Yu Yichi heard the barking of dogs in the dog market, the lowing of calves on Oxen Street, the bleating of lambs in Sheep Alley, the whinnying of ponies in Horse Lane, and the screeches of chickens from far and near: *gaawk – gaawk*

– *gaawk*. The donkey stood waiting in the middle of the street, its black eyes glowing like lanterns. Yu Yichi had heard stories about this little black donkey, but seeing it now with his own eyes shocked him nearly out of his skin, as he realized that legends are not simply made up out of thin air. Holding his breath and making himself as small as possible, he looked like a dead log, except for his staring eyes, as he waited to see how the story of this little black donkey would unfold.

Hours passed, until Yu Yichi's eyes were sore and weary, but the little donkey stood stock-still in the middle of the street, like a statue. Then, without warning, all the dogs in Liquorland erupted in a frenzy of barking – off in the distance, of course – snapping Yu Yichi out of his trancelike state, just in time for him to hear approaching footsteps on roof tiles and to see, almost immediately after that, a dark figure floating down over the street from a nearby rooftop; it settled onto the waiting back of the black donkey, which sprang to life and galloped off like the wind. Now, as a dwarf, Yu Yichi had not been given a chance to attend school, but as someone born into an educated family – his father had been a professor, his grandfather an imperial licentiate, and in generations past there were scholars who had passed the imperial examinations and were members of the Hanlin Academy – he had committed thousands of Chinese characters to memory and had read widely and eclectically. The scene he had just witnessed reminded him of a Tang dynasty tale about a shadowy knight-errant; from there his thoughts turned more philosophical: Even with the rapid developments in science, there exist countless phenomena that defy explanation. He tested his body: In spite of lingering stiffness here and there, he could still move. He felt his belly – it was wet, the effects of a cold sweat. Back when the dark figure was floating earthward, aided by the light of the moon, Yu Yichi had perceived that it was a young man, quite small in stature, his body covered in scaly skin that glinted in the moonlight. He held a willow-leaf dagger in his teeth, and had a bundle strapped to his back . . .

Dear readers, I can almost hear you grumbling: Why don't you stop running off at the mouth and take us to a tavern somewhere instead of having us circle Donkey Avenue over and over! Your grumblings are excellent, right on target, hit the nail right on the head. So let's pick up the pace, step lively; forgive me if I don't point out all the shops here on Donkey Avenue, even though there's a story behind them all, and even though each one of them has its unique calling. I'll shut up, no matter how much it pains me to do so. And so, let us ignore all those donkeys staring at us from both sides of the street and set our sights on our objectives. There are two types of objectives: major and minor. Our major objective is to march toward communism, where the ruling ideology is 'from each according to his abilities, to each according to his needs.' But if we march toward the end of Donkey Avenue, to an old pomegranate tree, we will reach our minor objective: the Yichi Tavern. Why, you ask, is it called Yichi Tavern? Listen up, and I'll tell you.

The tavern's proprietor, Yu Yichi (Twelve-inch Yu), is actually seventeen inches tall; like all dwarfs, he has never revealed his age to anyone, and trying to guess it would be folly. Within the memory of Donkey Avenue, this agreeable, amiable little dwarf has not changed his appearance or attitude in decades. He always returns looks of shock and amazement with sweet smiles. They are such charming, disarming smiles they tug at your heart and spawn feelings of sympathy you never knew you had. Yu Yichi makes a good living almost exclusively on the charm of these smiles. Coming from an intellectual family, he is very learned, with an array of knowledge on which he draws to entertain people on Donkey Avenue with his witty remarks. How unthinkably lonely and boring Donkey Avenue would be without Yu Yichi, who could actually lead a life of leisure with his natural talent alone. But being ambitious, he refused to settle for handouts, and took advantage of the winds of reform and liberalization to apply for a business license. He then produced a wad of money he'd been saving since who knew when and hired someone to remodel his old house for Yichi Tavern, which has become famous all over Liquorland. Yu Yichi's many ingenious ideas may well have been inspired by the classical novel *Flowers in the Mirror*, or could have originated in a book called *Overseas Wonders*. After the tavern opened, he placed a want ad in the *Liquorland Daily News*, looking for attendants who were under three feet tall. The ad, a highly publicized event at the time, initiated heated debates. Some people believed that a dwarf running a tavern was an insult to the socialist system and a smear on the bright five-star red flag. Following the increase of tourists in Liquorland, Yichi Tavern could easily become our city's greatest shame, one that would bring humiliation to the great Chinese nation. Others argued that the existence of a dwarf was a universal, objective phenomenon. But dwarfs in other countries relied on panhandling to survive, while ours supported themselves through their own labor, which is not a shame but a sign of glory. Yichi Tavern could help make our international friends understand the unsurpassable superiority of our socialist system. While the two sides were engaged in heated, unending debates, Yu Yichi tunneled his way into the City Hall compound through its sewers (the guards were too intimidating for him to enter through the main gate). Then he sneaked into City Hall, and into the office of the Mayor, with whom he had a long conversation, the contents of which must remain unknown to us. The Mayor sent him back to Donkey Avenue in her own luxurious Crown limo, after which the debates in the newspaper died down. My friends, ladies and gentlemen, we have reached Yichi Tavern, our objective. The drinks are on me today. Old Mr Yu is a friend of mine; we often get together to drink and to recite poetry. We have composed strange yet beautiful music for this colorful, dazzling world we live in. As a true brother who values friendship more than money, he will give us a twenty percent discount.

My honored friends, we are now standing outside Yichi Tavern. Please glance up at the gilded characters on the black signboard, each bursting with energy, like spirited dragons and lively tigers. This is the work of Liu Banping – Half-Bottle Liu – a famous calligrapher whose name tells of a true master who can't write without drinking half a bottle of good, strong liquor. Two pocket-sized waitresses, less than two feet tall, stand beside the door, one on each side, embroidered sashes across their chests and smiles on their faces. They are twins, who, after reading Yu Yichi's ad in the *Liquorland Daily News*, flew here from Shanghai on a Trident jet. They were born into a high-ranking cadre family, with a father so famous you'd be dazzled if I told you. So I won't. They could have counted on their father's power and position to live a life of leisure, wearing fancy clothes and eating delicacies. But they refused to do so, choosing instead to join the hustle and bustle here in Liquorland. The arrival of this pair of fairies came as such a surprise that the city's ranking Party members made a special trip in the pouring rain to greet them at Peach Spring Airport, some forty-five miles out of town. Accompanying the two fairies on their trip was their mother, that is, the wife of their heroic sire, plus a retinue of secretaries. It took the airport guest house two frantic weeks to prepare for the reception. But, my friends, please don't think that Liquorland did not get its money's worth, for that would be the near-sighted view, a mouse's vision of the world. Even though Liquorland went to considerable expense to welcome the fairies and their mother, our city has now established connections with the high-ranking official, who, merely by picking up his pen and drawing a few check marks, can bring us plenty of business and plenty of income. Do you know what we received when he casually wielded his pen on a visit last year? A low-interest loan of a hundred million, during a period of financial storms and tight credit. Imagine that, my friends, a hundred million, which we put to use promoting our Ape Liquor, building a magnificent China Brewery Museum, and organizing a celebration for the First International Ape Liquor Festival in October. If not for these two fairies, do you think he'd have stayed in Liquorland three whole days? So, my friends, it's no exaggeration to credit Mr Yu Yichi as a hero of Liquorland. I hear that the Municipal Party Committee is gathering material for permission to honor him as a model worker with a Labor Day decoration.

The two fairies of noble blood bow to us and smile radiantly. They have lovely faces and well-proportioned figures; except for being small, they are virtually flawless. We return their smiles out of respect for their noble birth. Welcome, welcome. Thank you, thank you.

Yichi Tavern, also known as Dwarf Tavern, is luxuriously appointed. When you step on the five-inch-thick wool carpet, your feet sink softly up to the ankles. Scrolls by famous painters and calligraphers hang on walls covered with birch panels from the Changbai mountains. Palm-sized goldfish swim lazily in an enormous aquarium. Pots of rare flowers bloom like a raging fire. In the middle of the room stands a lifelike little black donkey, which, upon closer observation, turns out to be a sculpture. Naturally it was only after the arrival of the two fairies that Yichi Tavern reached this level of popularity and prosperity. The leaders of Liquorland are not fools, and would never allow the darling daughters of a high-ranking dignitary to work in a shabby tavern run by some private entrepreneur. You know how things are these days, so I needn't waste time recounting the dramatic changes in Yichi Tavern over the past year. But you'll forgive me if I backtrack for a moment. Liquorland authorities built a small villa near Water Park in the downtown area for the two fairies before their mother returned to Shanghai. Each was also provided with a tiny Fiat. Did you happen to notice the Fiats parked beneath the old pomegranate tree as we came through the gate?

The maître d'hôtel, in red uniform and cap, comes up to greet us. He has the body of a two-year-old child, with facial features to match. He sways a bit when he walks on the thick carpet, his hips gliding from side to side, like a duckling wading through mud. He leads us along like a furry little puppy guiding the blind.

Climbing a staircase of red-lacquered pine, we reach the top landing, where the little red boy pushes open a door and steps aside, like one of the police uncles who direct traffic, his left arm held across his chest, his right arm hanging at his side. Both hands are stiff and straight, the left palm facing inward, the right palm outward, and both point in the same direction: the Grape Room.

Please come in, dear friends, don't be shy. We are honored guests for whom the elegant Grape Room is the salon of choice. While you are staring at clusters of grapes hanging from the ceiling, I happen to glance over at the little fellow who showed us in. His smiling, clouded eyes send poisonous rays our way. Like arrowheads soaked in poison, they will rot anything they touch. I feel a sharp pain in my eyes and suddenly seem to have gone blind.

During that brief moment of darkness, I cannot help but feel my heart palpitating. The little demon wrapped in a red flag that I created in my stories 'Meat Boy' and 'Child Prodigy' has suddenly appeared in front of me and is watching me with sinister eyes. That's him, that's him all right. Slender eyes, big, thick ears, kinky hair, and a two-foot body. In 'Child Prodigy' I described in detail the riot he instigated in the Special Purchasing Section of the Culinary Academy. In that story, I portrayed him as a little conspirator, a genius of strategy. I stopped after finishing the part about him and the children hiding in different parts of the campus after beating the guard – the 'featherless hawk' – to death. Originally, I planned for all the children to be caught and sent to my mother-in-law's Culinary Research Center, where they were to be boiled, steamed, or braised. Only the little demon escaped, by way of the sewer, but he fell into the hands of beggars scrounging scraps from the sewer, after which he began his legendary life anew. But instead of following my dictates, he rebelled and escaped from my story to join Yu Yichi's team of dwarfs. Wearing a scarlet wool uniform with a spotless white bow tie, a scarlet fore-and-aft cap, and black patent-leather shoes, he has materialized in front of me.

I mustn't neglect my guests, regardless of any unforeseen events that may occur, so I suppress the waves of turmoil raging in the depths of my heart and force a smile on my face as I sit down with you. The plush chair cushions, the snowy white tablecloth, the dazzling flowers, and the soft music take possession of our senses. Here I must insert a comment: The tables and chairs in Dwarf Tavern are very low, to ensure maximum comfort. An attendant hardly bigger than a bird walks up with a platter of disinfected hand towels. She is so fragile, so tiny that just carrying the platter takes all her strength; she elicits feelings of tender sympathy. By this time the little demon is nowhere to be seen, for, once he has carried out his duty, he must go back to greet the next batch of diners. Common sense, perhaps, but I can't help sensing some sinister, diabolical purpose to his disappearance.

My friends, in order to cash in on our 'twenty percent' discount, sit here for a moment while I go look up my old friend, Yu Yichi. Feel free to smoke or drink tea or listen to the music or gaze out the spotless windows at the landscaped back yard.

Gentle readers, at first I was going to join you in this sumptuous banquet, but the tavern is too small for this many people, and there are already nine of you here in the Grape Room. I'm deeply sorry. But openness in everything is absolutely essential to avoid the perception that I have ulterior motives. I know this tavern like a light carriage on a familiar road, and finding Yu Yichi is easy. But when I open the door to his office, I know I've come at the wrong time – my old friend Yu Yichi is standing atop his desk kissing a full-figured, buxom young woman. 'Oops, excuse me,' I blurt out, 'I forgot my manners, should have knocked.'

Yu Yichi jumps down off his desk, quick and nimble as a wildcat. When he sees my look of embarrassment, his comical little face creases into a smile. 'Doctor of Liquor Studies,' he says in a high-pitched voice, 'I should have known it was you. How's your research on Ape Liquor coming along? You don't want to miss the Ape Liquor Festival, do you? And your father-in-law is a fool to go up on White Ape Mountain and live with the apes.'

On and on he talks, until I'm sick of listening to him. But since I'm there to ask a favor, I must be patient and hear him out, forcing myself to appear captivated by what he is saying.

When he finally runs out of things to say, I volunteer, 'I brought some friends for a meal of donkey.'

Yu Yichi gets up and walks over to the woman. His head barely reaches her knees. She's a real beauty, and not, it seems, an innocent young maiden. She has the airs of a married woman. Her full lips are lightly coated with a sticky substance, as if she had just dined on escargots. He reaches up and pats her ample hindquarters. 'You go ahead, my dear,' he says, 'and tell Old Shen not to worry. Yu Yichi is a man of his word. If he says he'll do something, rest assured he'll do it.'

Not one to shy away from situations like this, the woman bends low, letting her pendulous breasts, which are about to burst out of her dress, drop so heavily on Yu Yichi's face that he winces as she gently picks him up. Judging only by size and weight, it looks like a mother cradling her son; but, of course, their relationship is much more complicated than that. Almost savagely, she plants a big kiss on his lips, then flings him down basketball-like onto a sofa against the wall. She raises her hand and says seductively, 'See you later, old-timer.' Yu Yichi's body is still bouncing on the springy sofa as the woman, wriggling her bright red backside, disappears around the corner. He shouts at her lovely back, 'Get lost, you vile fox spirit!'

Yu Yichi and I are now alone in the room. He jumps off the

sofa and goes to a large wall mirror to comb his hair and rearrange his tie. He even rubs his cheeks with his little claws, then spins around to face me, looking very dapper, like a man of great importance. If not for what had happened a moment earlier, I'd be too intimidated to joke with him. But: 'Hey, old pal, you do OK with the women. A case of the weasel screwing the camel, always going for the big ones,' I say, grinning cheekily.

He laughs a sinister laugh, his face swelling up in greens and purples, his eyes emitting a green light, his arms spread like the wings of an aging falcon ready to fly off. He looks absolutely terrifying. In all the time I've know him, I've never seen him like this. Maybe I hurt his feelings with my bantering a moment ago, and suddenly I feel remorseful.

'You little jerk.' He presses forward, grinding his teeth. 'How dare you mock me!'

I back away, fixing my gaze on his sharp claws, which tremble slightly from his towering rage, sensing that my throat is in peril. Yes, he could leap onto my neck at any moment, like a thunderbolt, and tear open my throat. 'I'm sorry, old man, really sorry.' My back presses up against the fabric-covered wall, and still I try to back up. Then I have a brainstorm. I reach up and give my own face a dozen savage slaps – *pa pa pa* – the sound hanging in the air; my cheeks burn, my ears ring, and I see stars. 'I'm sorry, old man. I don't deserve to live. I'm a lowly animal, I'm an asshole, I'm a black donkey prick.'

After my ugly performance, his face turns from greenish purple to pale yellow; his raised arms slowly fall to his sides; and I collapse in a heap.

He retreats to his black leather swivel throne, but instead of sitting, he squats on it. Removing an expensive cigarette from its case, he lights it with a lighter that spews a bright hissing flame, takes a long drag, and slowly blows out the smoke. He stares at the patterns on the wall, lost in thought, a deep, mysterious look in eyes that look like black-water pools. I huddle beside the door, terrified by my thoughts: How did this buffoon, a dwarf who had been the butt of everyone's joke, turn into the swaggering tyrant facing me now? And why am I, a dignified doctoral candidate, cringing before a hideous creature a foot and a half tall and

149

weighing no more than fifteen kilograms? The answer emerges like a shot out of the barrel of a gun, and there's no need to go into it.

'I'm going to fuck every pretty girl in Liquorland!' He rises out of his squatting position and stands on the swivel chair, raising his fist to proclaim solemnly, 'I'm going to fuck every pretty girl in Liquorland!'

Bursting with excitement, and grinning from ear to ear, he keeps his arm in the air for a long, long time. I can tell that the oars in his head are churning the waters of his mind, and that the ship of consciousness is being tossed about on the white-capped waves of his spirit. I hold my breath, for fear that I might shatter his reveries.

Finally he relaxes, tosses me a cigarette and asks genially, 'Know her?'

'Who?' I reply.

'The woman who just left.'

'No . . . although there was something familiar about her . . .'

'The TV hostess.'

'Oh, her.' I smack myself on the forehead, now that it's come to me. She stands there, microphone in hand, a sweet smile on her face, talking to us but saying little.

'This is the third!' he spits out savagely. 'The third . . .' Suddenly his voice turns husky and the light goes out of his eyes. In an instant, wrinkles cover a face that, up till then, had been babied until it was soft and lustrous as precious jade, and a body that was tiny to begin with shrinks even smaller. He sags into his throne-like chair.

In agony, I smoke my cigarette and watch this odd friend of mine, momentarily stumped for anything to say.

'I want to show all you . . .' His murmurs break the oppressive silence. He raises his head. 'Did you want to see me about something?' he asks.

'I brought some friends along, in the Grape Room . . .' I'm somewhat flustered. 'A bunch of poor scholars . . .'

He picks up the telephone and jabbers something. After hanging up, he turns back and says, 'Since we're old friends, I've arranged for an all-donkey banquet.'

Friends, talk about gourmet luck! An all-donkey banquet! Moved to the depths of my soul, I bow deeply. Perking up a bit, he goes from sitting to squatting, and the light comes back into his eyes. 'So you're a writer now, is that right?' he asks.

'Just some dog-fart essays,' I say, gripped by terror. 'Not worth mentioning. A little extra income for the family.'

'My dear Doctor,' he says, 'let's you and me do a little business.'

'What kind of business?' I ask.

'You ghost-write my autobiography,' he says, 'and I'll give you twenty-thousand cash.'

I am so excited my heart thumps wildly, but all I say is, 'I'm afraid my meager talents are inadequate for such an important task.'

Waving off my disclaimer, he says, 'Don't give me any of that false modesty. It's settled. You'll come here every Tuesday night and I'll relate my experiences to you.'

'Revered elder brother, money or not, as your inferior, it would be an honor to memorialize the life of such an extraordinary man. Money or not . . .'

'Can the hypocrisy, jerk,' he sneers. 'Money makes the devil turn the millstone. There may be people in this world who don't love money, but I've never met any. Which is why I can announce that I'm going to fuck every pretty girl in Liquorland!'

'Elder brother's charm has a lot to do with it.'

'Pah!' he blurts out. 'Up your old lady's you-know-what! Chairman Mao said, "It's critical to recognize one's own limitations." I've had enough of your bullshit, so get out of my sight.'

He takes a carton of Marlboros out of his desk drawer and tosses it to me. Holding the cigarettes in my hand, I thank him profusely, then get my ass back to the Grape Room, where I join you, friends, ladies and gentlemen, at the table.

Several dwarfs come up to pour tea and alcoholic beverages and to set the table with plates and chopsticks. They whirl around the table as if they were on wheels. The tea is Oolong, the liquor Maotai; no local flavor, but easily state-banquet quality. First to be served are twelve cold delicacies arranged in the shape of a lotus flower: donkey stomach, donkey liver, donkey heart, donkey intestines, donkey lungs, donkey tongue, and donkey lips . . . all donkey stuff. Friends, sample these delicacies sparingly and leave room for what follows, for experience tells me that the best is yet to come. Take note, friends, here come the hot dishes. You, the lady over there, be careful, don't burn yourself! A dwarf all in red – painted red lips and rouged cheeks, red shoes and a red cap, red from head to toe, like a red candle – rolls up to the table carrying a steaming platter of food. She opens her mouth, and out spills a flurry of words, falling like pearls: 'Braised donkey ear. Enjoy!'

'Steamed donkey brains, for your dining pleasure!'

'Pearled donkey eyes, for your dining pleasure!'

The donkey eyes, in beautifully contrasting black and white, lay pooled on a large platter. Go ahead, friends, dig in. Don't be afraid. They might appear to be alive, but they are, after all, just food. But, hold on, there are only two eyes but ten of us. How do we divide them up fairly. Will you help us out here, miss? The red candle girl smiles and picks up a steel fork. Two gentle pokes, and the black pearls pop, filling the platter with a gelatinous liquid. Use your spoons, comrades, scoop it up, one spoonful at a time. It may not be a pretty dish, but it tastes wonderful. I know there's another dish for which Yichi Tavern is famous. It's called Black Dragon Sporting with Pearls. The main ingredients are a donkey dick and a pair of donkey eyes. Today, however, the chef has used the eyes to make Pearled Donkey Eyes, so it looks like there'll be no *sporting* by the donkey dick this time. Who knows, maybe we're eating a female donkey.

Don't be shy, brothers and sisters. Loosen your belts, let your bellies hang out, eat till you burst. There'll be no toasting, since we're all family. Just drink to your hearts' content. And don't worry about the bill. Today you can bleed me.

'Donkey ribs in wine, for your dining pleasure.'

'Donkey tongue in brine, for your dining pleasure.'

'Braised donkey tendons, for your dining pleasure.'

'Pear and lotus root donkey throat, for your dining pleasure.'

'Golden whip donkey tail, for your dining pleasure.'

'Steamed and fried donkey intestines, for your dining pleasure.'

'Stewed donkey hooves with sea cucumbers, for your dining pleasure.'

'Five-spice donkey liver, for your dining pleasure.'

. . . and so on . . .

A medley of donkey dishes flows onto our table, filling stomachs that are now stretched taut as drums, and drawing rumbling belches out of the diners. Our faces are covered with a film of donkey grease, through which weariness shows, like donkeys worn out from turning a millstone. Comrades, you must be exhausted by now. I stop an attendant and ask, 'How many more dishes are there?'

'Twenty or so, I guess,' she replies. 'I'm not exactly sure. I just bring out what they give me.'

I point to the friends around the table. 'They're nearly full. Can't we skip some of the dishes?'

With a show of reluctance, she says, 'You ordered a whole donkey, and you've barely made a dent in it.'

'But we're stuffed,' I plead. 'Dear young lady, won't you please ask the kitchen to just bring out the best and forget the rest.'

The lady says, 'You disappoint me, but, OK, I'll talk to them.'

She is successful. Out comes the final dish.

'Dragon and Phoenix Lucky Together, for your dining pleasure. Enjoy!'

She wants us to enjoy the sight of the dish before beginning our dining pleasure.

One of our group, a sourpuss of a woman – and not very smart, either – asks the attendant, 'Which part of the donkey is this made of?'

Without hesitation, she answers, 'It's the donkey's sex organ.'

The woman blushes, but, unable to control her curiosity, asks, 'We only ordered one donkey, so how could there be . . .' She puckers up her lips to point at the 'dragon' and 'phoenix' on the plate.

'The chef felt terrible that you missed over a dozen dishes,' the waitress replies, 'so he added a set of female donkey's genitalia to create this dish.'

Please dig in, ladies and gentlemen, dear friends, don't be shy. These are the donkeys' jewels, as delicious as they are ugly. If you don't eat, it's your loss. If you do, it's still your loss, sooner or later, if you know what I mean. Come on, dig in, give it a try, eat eat eat Dragon and Phoenix Lucky Together.

As everyone wavers, their chopsticks raised, my old friend Yu

Yichi saunters into the dining room. I jump to my feet to introduce him to you:

'This is the famous Mr Yu Yichi, manager of Yichi Tavern, standing member of the Chinese People's Political Consultative Conference, standing member of the Board of Governors of the Metropolitan Entrepreneurs Association, provincial model worker, and candidate for national model worker. He is hosting today's banquet.'

All smiles, he walks around the table shaking hands and passing out perfumed business cards cramped with printing in Chinese and some foreign language. I can see that everyone warms to him at once.

He glances at the Dragon and Phoenix Lucky Together and says, 'So, you've even been given this dish. Now you can truly say you've eaten donkey.'

Expressions of gratitude emerge from around the table, my brothers and sisters, and every one of you has a smarmy grin on your face.

'Don't thank me, thank him,' he points to me, 'Dragon and Phoenix Lucky Together is not an easy dish to prepare. It's considered immoral. Last year, several renowned people made it known they wanted to try it, but were unsuccessful because they weren't up to par. So I can say, you have true gourmet luck.'

He downs three glasses of Black Pearl (a famous Liquorland drink that relieves indigestion) with each of us. A strong liquor, Black Pearl is sort of like a meat grinder, which produces rumbling noises in our stomachs.

'Don't worry about the rumblings down there. Doctor of Liquor Studies is here.' Yu Yichi points to me. 'Go on, have some, try it. Dragon and Phoenix Lucky Together loses its flavor when it's cold.' He picks up the dragon head with his chopsticks and places it in front of the lady who has expressed such an interest in donkey sex organs. Showing no modesty, she gobbles up the head in big mouthfuls, while everyone else attacks the dish with their chopsticks, finishing it off in no time, like a strong wind sweeping clouds from the sky.

He says, with a sinister smile, 'You won't be able to sleep tonight.'

Do you all understand what he meant by that?

My friends, ladies and gentlemen, this story has more or less reached its end, but you're such good friends that I want to chew the fat with you a bit longer.

That night, when the donkey banquet was finally over, we stumbled out of Yichi Tavern and into the late night air. Stars filled the sky and night dew covered the ground; a bluish, moist light was reflected off Donkey Avenue. Some drunken cats were fighting on people's roofs, causing the tiles to sing out. The cold dew was like a frost, sending leaves floating to the ground from trees on both sides of the street. Some of my friends, who were half drunk, started to sing revolutionary songs. Broken phrases like donkey lips and horses' mouths, southern tunes and northern melodies, not much gentler on the ears than the cats' screeches from the rooftops. I won't even dignify the rest of their ugly behavior with a comment. While all this was going on, we heard crisp hoofbeats at the eastern end of the street. Suddenly, a little black donkey with wine-glass-shaped hooves and lamplike eyes shot down the street and appeared in front us, like a black arrow. I was stunned, and so, apparently, were the others, since the singers closed their mouths, and so did those who were about to puke. Everyone's drunken eyes stared at the little black donkey, watching it gallop from the eastern end of the street to the western end, and then from the western end to the eastern end. After three complete trips, it stood quietly in the middle of Donkey Avenue, its body like shimmering ebony, but no sound escaped, as if it were a statue. Our bodies stiffened, we stood frozen to the spot, waiting to see if reality could verify legend. And sure enough, following some loud tile clattering, a black shadow flew down and landed on the back of the donkey. It was indeed a youngster whose bare skin shimmered like scales; he was carrying a bundle on his back and was biting down on a willow-leaf dagger that emitted a cold light.

V

Dear Mo Yan

Greetings!
I don't know how to express what I feel at this moment.
My dear, most respected mentor, your letter was like a
bottle of vintage liquor, like a thunderclap in spring, like a
shot of morphine, like a gigantic opium bubble, like a
pretty young thing . . . that brought spring to my life and
cheered me body and soul. I am not a hypocritically
modest gentleman; I know and dare to announce publicly
that I am bursting with talent that has been hidden away
like the Imperial Concubine of the Tang, like a steed that
has been forced to pull carts in a village. Now, at last, Li
Shimin, the Tang Emperor, and Bo-le, the true horse
breeder, have shown up hand in hand! My talent has been
recognized by you and Mr Zhou Bao, one of China's nine
renowned editors. I feel the frenzied joy of the poet Du Fu
when he packed his books to return to his war-torn home.
How to celebrate? Nothing except liquor would do, so I
took out a bottle of genuine Du Kang from the liquor
cabinet, uncorked it with my teeth, held the opening with
my lips while tipping my head back, and finished the
bottle without coming up for air. Happily, drunkenly, as if
floating on air, I picked up the pen to write my dear
mentor, in pursuit of a grand calligraphic style, inspiration
rushing like the tides, fanning out like a peacock's tail, like
a hundred flowers blooming.
    Sir, you took time out of your busy schedule to give my
humble work 'Donkey Avenue' a serious reading, for
which I am moved to tears of gratitude, until my face is
wet with tears and snivel. Now, please allow me to respond
to each of the issues you raised in your letter.
1. The little red demon who raised hell in the country of
meat children in my story is a real person in Liquorland.
Some of the rotten officials here are so utterly corrupt that

156

they violate the world's ultimate taboo by eating baby boys. This story was revealed to me by my mother-in-law, former associate professor at the Culinary Academy, and Director of the Culinary Research Center. She said there's a village in the Liquorland suburbs that specializes in producing meaty little boys, a place where the villagers don't give a second thought to the whole business. They sell their meaty little boys as if they were disposing of fattened little pigs, never troubled by gut-wrenching pain. I don't think my mother-in-law would lie about something like that. Since she'd gain neither fame nor profit by lying to me, why lie? No, she absolutely would never lie about it. I know this has severe consequences, and I could get into trouble if I were to write about it. But you have taught me that a writer should always bravely face life, risking death and mutilation in order to dethrone an emperor. So I went ahead with no concern for my own safety. Of course, I also know that literary works 'should originate from life yet rise above it,' and should create 'typical characters in typical circumstances,' so I made the image of the little red demon more colorful by adding some oil here, a little vinegar there, and a bit of gourmet powder here and there. The scaly boy was a little hero who, moving through Liquorland like a shadow, performed many good deeds, eliminating evil and eradicating the bad, stealing from the rich to give to the poor. He has come to the aid of all the rascals on Donkey Avenue, who treat him like a god. I haven't yet had a chance to behold his majestic countenance, but that doesn't prove he doesn't exist. Many people on Donkey Avenue have seen him, and everyone in Liquorland knows about him. Anything he does at night and where he did it is known all over town the next day. Whenever his name is mentioned, cadres grind their teeth, common citizens are beside themselves with joy, and the head of Public Security's legs cramp up. Sir, the existence of this young hero is a natural consequence of social development; his gallant behavior has actually achieved the goal of calming the people and venting their anger, which has led to an increase in social stability and solidarity. His existence helps redress imperfect laws that cater to those in power. Why do you think the people haven't risen up against Liquorland's corrupt cadres? The scaly boy, that's why. Everyone has been waiting to see him punish those corrupt officials. Being punished by him means being punished by justice, which means being punished by the people. The scaly boy has become the embodiment of justice, the enforcer of the people's will, the pressure valve of law and order. If not for him, Liquorland would be mired in chaos. He may not be able to stop the officials' corrupt behavior, but he can reduce the people's anger. In point of fact, he has been an invaluable aid to Liquorland's municipal government, but, ironically, some muddle-headed officials have called for his arrest.

Are the scaly boy and the little red demon the same person? Please forgive my presumptuousness, but I think your question is terribly naive. What does it matter if they're the same person or not? If they are, so what? And if they aren't, so what? The fundamental principle of literature is to create something out of nothing and to make up stories. My creation has not been altogether fashioned out of nothing, and is not entirely made up. To be honest, the scaly boy and the little red demon are identical and disparate at the same time. Sometimes one divides into two and sometimes two combine into one. Long separation ends in unification, long unification leads to separation. Heaven operates this way, so why not humans?

In your letter, you also claimed that the scaly boy's skills were portrayed with such grand exaggeration that they lost their veracity, a criticism I find hard to accept. In this day and age, when scientific breakthroughs occur daily, and humans can plant beans on the moon, what's the big deal about flying on eaves and walking on walls? Twenty years ago, our village showed a movie called *The White-Haired Girl Ballet*, in which the heroine walked on the tips of her

158

toes. We took that as a challenge: If you can walk on your toes, why can't we? Practice! If we can't master the skill in one day, we'll take two; if two days won't do, then three; if three days still aren't enough, then how about four days or five? Why can't we learn it in six days or seven? Eight days later, except for the really dumb Dog Two Li, a whole bunch of us kids had learned to walk on our toes. From then on, our mothers were forced to add thicker padding to the tips of our shoes. Now, if a group of no-talents kids like us could accomplish that, how about a genius like the scaly boy, who, additionally, bore a deep-seated hatred toward these people. He practiced his skills for vengeance; half the effort produced double the results.

You prattled on and on about kung-fu novels, but I haven't read a single one, and have no idea who Jin Yong or Gu Long are. I work only on serious literature in the style of Gorki and Lu Xun; strictly following the one and only true method of 'combining revolutionary realism with revolutionary romanticism,' I have not taken a single wayward step, not once. I would never do anything that required me to sacrifice principle in order to please a few readers. On the other hand, since even a serious novelist like yourself has fallen under the spell of kung-fu novels, your disciple – that's me – will definitely read a few; maybe I'll benefit from them. As for Ms Ladybug, I think I came across her name in a public toilet somewhere. Apparently, she likes to write scenes with a 'bloody flesh pillar growing out of the ground,' with strong sexual overtones. I haven't read anything by her. When I find time, I'll get one or two of her stories for bathroom reading. Ivan Michurin ran a brothel in God's botanical garden. Would Big Sister Hua, who wears the writer's laurel on her head, dare to open a brothel in the fiction garden of socialism?

2. You're concerned that my famous Donkey Avenue dish Dragon and Phoenix Lucky Together would attract flies. Please forgive my arrogance, but I think Mo Yan doth protest too much. What's filthy about a dish that even

famed critics and renowned musicians from Beijing shovel down their throats as fast as they can? What we are pursuing is beauty, nothing but beauty. It's not true beauty if we didn't create it. Creating beauty with beauty is not true beauty either; real beauty is achieved by transforming the ugly into the beautiful. This has two levels of significance. Let me explain. First, there's no beauty in sticking a donkey dick inside a donkey pussy and putting them on a plate, because they are dark as pitch, incredibly filthy, and they stink like hell. No one would eat them, that's for sure. But the head chef in Yichi Tavern soaks them in fresh water three times, bathes them in bloody water three times, and boils them three times in soda water. Then he strips the penis of its sinewy parts and plucks the pubic hair before frying them both in oil, simmering them in an earthen pot, and steaming them in a pressure cooker, after which he carves different patterns with his refined skills, adds rare seasoning, decorates the dish with bright-colored cabbage hearts, and, *voilà*, the male donkey organ is transformed into a black dragon and the female organ into a black phoenix. A dragon and a phoenix kissing and copulating, coiling around an array of reds and purples, filling the air with fragrance and looking so alive, a treat for the mind and the eye. Isn't that transforming the ugly into the beautiful? Second, donkey dick and donkey pussy are vulgar terms that assail one's sense of propriety and cause the imagination of the weak-willed to run wild. Now we change the former's name into dragon and the latter into phoenix, for the dragon and the phoenix are solemn totems of the Chinese race, lofty, sacred, and beautiful symbols that signify meanings too numerous to mention. Can't you see that this too is transforming the ugly into the beautiful?

Sir, suddenly I sense how similar the process of producing Donkey Avenue's most famous culinary dish is to the creative process in literature and the arts. Both originate from life yet transcend life. Both transform nature to benefit the human world. Both elevate the vulgar to the level of nobility, convert sensual desire into art, convert grain into alcohol, and turn grief into power.

Sir, I will never replace this dish, regardless of the scare tactics you choose to persuade me.

I believe that 'Ecstasy' and 'Red Locusts' are two of your best works. Those people who criticize you do so because they have eaten so many placentas and so many babies that the inner heat has risen and fried their brains. Why worry about what they say? The head of Liquorland's Writers Association is one of those who can't go without his placenta for even a day. He drinks a soupy mix of placenta and duck eggs, a whole bowlful, which is why his essays are heavy with 'human taste.'

3. Sir, Yu Yichi is so mysterious, I'm afraid of him. He wants me to write his biography and promises me a big payday, so I'm conflicted. But since you encouraged me to write, I'll embolden myself by gulping down the soup of courage. But now I want even more for the two of us to collaborate. You're famous enough that if you helped on the writing, Yu Yichi would be so overjoyed his ass would swing like a pendulum. You don't know how adorable he is when his ass swings, but just imagine a little Peke frolicking in the snow. He has deep pockets and is never stingy with his money, so you'll be amply rewarded for your troubles. Besides, you must come visit our Liquorland, take a tour to broaden your views. I think that would benefit your writing, just as a baby banquet is beneficial to one's health. No matter how you look at it, it's your loss if you don't visit Liquorland, if for no other reason than you won't otherwise get to sample Dragon and Phoenix Lucky Together.

4. As for the beginning section of 'Donkey Avenue,' since you praised its grandiloquence, what's wrong with a little 'nonsense'? There are so many publications full of tongue-twisting rubbish these days, why should I 'delete altogether' my 'grandiloquent nonsense'? I'm unwilling and unable to accept your recommendation.

5. The father of the twin dwarf sisters is indeed a leader in

the Central Government, so why ask me to downgrade him? Besides, even if I wanted to demote him to the head of a remote mountain village, would he do it? He'd likely fight me to the death over it. On the other hand, since literature and art are, after all, fabrications, if people want to identify the characters with real-life people, let them. That's not my problem. And if I have to pay with my life if his heart explodes from anger? Well, a life for a life, so be it. 'A true soldier fears not death, so do not attempt to frighten him with it.' 'Decapitation feels like the wind blowing off a hat.' 'Twenty years from now I'll be a hero again.'

Sir, please send my regards to Zhou Bao and Li Xiaobao, and ask the two gentlemen if they need any good liquor. Also, in October, Liquorland will host its first Ape Liquor Festival, a rare occasion not only in Liquorland but throughout Greater China. Vintage liquors from all over the world will be available to valiant individuals from all corners to drink to their hearts' content. All the delicacies in this world will await you – Mo Yan, my mentor – and you can wolf them all down. Your family is also invited. My father-in-law, Yuan Shuangyu, is the Vice-Director of the Technical Advisory Committee for this first annual Ape Liquor Festival, so you will want for nothing.

Wishing you good health, I am
Your disciple

Li Yidou
written in drunkenness

Chapter Five

I

Ding Gou'er wrapped his long arms tightly around the lady trucker's waist and crushed his lips skillfully against hers. She wrenched her head this way and that to break off the kiss, but he matched her, wrench for wrench, neutralizing her movements. And in the midst of those struggles he sucked both her fleshy lips into his mouth. She blubbered a series of curses: Goddamn it! Goddamn you! These goddamn its and goddamn yous were spit right into Ding Gou'er's mouth, where they were soaked up by his tongue, his gums, and his throat. Experience told him that the struggle probably wouldn't last long, that pretty soon her face would turn red and moist, she'd start breathing hard, her belly would heat up, and she'd melt in his arms like a tame little kitten. That's how women are. But what actually happened quickly proved he had blurred the distinction between the general and the specific. The woman was not incapacitated by the anesthesia in his mouth, and her struggle to resist did not abate just because he had her in a lip-lock; in fact, it increased and grew more frenzied. She clawed at his back, she kicked him in the legs, she kneed him in the groin. Her belly was hot as live cinders, her breath intoxicating as strong liquor. Incredibly aroused, Ding Gou'er was willing to subject his body to as much abuse as necessary before breaking off the kiss. He even tried to force his tongue between her clenched teeth. That was his downfall.

He never imagined that when she unclenched her teeth, it was just a ploy to allow his tongue to slip into her mouth. Then, with a sudden reclamping of her teeth, she drew a screech from the investigator, as a stabbing pain quickly spread from his tongue to every inch of his body. Ding Gou'er's arms flew off the lady trucker's waist, and he leaped away, a foul yet sweet taste emanating from a hot sticky liquid filling his mouth. He knew, as he clapped his hand over his mouth, that this spelled trouble. All of a sudden, no tongue. Bad news! In the investigator's long history of romantic conquests, this was his first tragic failure. You fucking daughter of a whore! he cursed inwardly, as he bent over to spit out a mouthful of blood. Stars lit up the sky, but the ground was hazy; he knew he'd spit out blood, even though he couldn't see the color of the stuff. What worried him most, of course, was the tongue itself, so he gently tried touching his teeth and lips; happily, it was still attached, but he detected a small gap on the tip. That's where the blood was coming from.

Ding Gou'er was enormously relieved that his tongue hadn't been bitten off. But he'd paid an annoyingly steep price for that kiss. He had to teach her a lesson, but how?

She was standing only a few feet away, looking straight at him, so close he could hear her labored breathing. He felt her body warmth through his thin shirt. She was staring at him, head held high, and now she was brandishing a monkey wrench. In the brightening starlight he took note of the angry expression on her animated face. Sort of like a naughty little girl. With a wry laugh, he grumbled:

'You've got sharp teeth.'

She was breathing heavily. 'I held back,' she said. 'I can bite through ten-gauge wire.'

This brief bit of dialogue brightened the special investigator's mood. The pain in his tongue turned to a dull ache. He reached out to pat her on the shoulder, but she jumped back in self-defense, raised the wrench over her head, and shouted. 'How dare you! Touch me and I'll split your skull open!'

'I'm not going to hit you, my pet,' he said, quickly drawing his hand back. 'I wouldn't dare. Let's talk this out peaceably, what do you say?'

'Pour the water into the radiator!' she commanded breathlessly.

As the night air grew heavy, Ding Gou'er felt a chill. Picking up his bucket and filling the radiator, as he was told, he was suddenly enveloped in a cloud of steam from the engine. That warmed him up. Water gurgling as it entered the radiator reminded him of a thirsty ox lapping up much-needed water. A shooting star tore through the Milky Way, insects were chirping all around, and the sound of waves beating against a distant shore came on the wind.

After they were back in the cab, he looked out at the bright lights of Liquorland, and was struck by feelings of loneliness, like a lamb that's strayed from the flock.

As he rested on the padded cushions of the lady trucker's sofa, Ding Gou'er was thoroughly intoxicated, he was enchanted. His sweat-soaked, alcohol-drenched clothing had been tossed out onto the balcony to continue sending their odors into the vast expanse of sky. His body was encased in a loose-fitting, downy-soft, warm and toasty bathrobe. That fine little pistol of his, along with several dozen bullets neatly stacked in their clips, rested on a tea table, the muzzle glinting a soft blue, the cartridges sparkling like gold. He was reclining on the sofa, his eyes narrowed to mere slits as he listened to the sounds of splashing coming from the bathroom and tried to picture hot shower water slipping down the lady trucker's shoulders and breasts. Everything that had occurred after his tongue was bitten was like a dream. He hadn't said another word after climbing into the truck, nor had she; instead he'd conscientiously and rather mechanically focused his attention on the roar of the engine and the sound of the tires on the road. The truck flew down the highway, Liquorland approaching very fast. Red lights, green lights, left turns, right turns. They entered the Brewer's College through a side gate and pulled into the parking lot. She got out of the cab; he followed her. When she walked, so did he; when she stopped, he did too. Although everything had a bizarre quality, somehow it seemed completely natural. He might as well have been her husband or her boyfriend, the way they sauntered into her apartment. Now, as he contentedly digested the wonderful meal she had prepared, he lay back on the sofa and sipped a glass of wine, enjoying the sights of her well-furnished living room and waiting expectantly for her to emerge from her shower.

From time to time a sharp pain in his tongue rekindled his vigilance. Maybe she was setting an even more insidious trap, maybe some ferocious man would suddenly appear, since this room had obviously been home to a male occupant. So what! I'm not leaving, even if two ferocious men appeared! He finished the glass of sweet wine and let himself sink into sweet reveries.

She emerged from the bathroom in a cream-colored bathrobe and bright red shower slippers. This was a woman who knew how to walk, the seductive sway of an exotic dancer. The wooden floor creaked beneath her feet. She was bathed in golden lamplight. Wet hair clung to her scalp, which was nice and round, like a perfectly shaped gourd that shone as it floated above her bathrobe in the halo of light. 'Grab prosperity with one hand, sweep away indecency with the other.' Curiously, this popular slogan popped into his head. She stood in front of him with crossed feet, her bathrobe loosely tied. A birthmark on her snowy white thigh looked like a watchful eye. The two mounds of flesh swelling up from her chest were also white. Ding Gou'er lay there, his eyelids drooping, enjoying the scenery and not moving a muscle. All he had to do was reach out and tug the belt around her waist for the lady trucker to be fully revealed to him. She was acting more like a lady of noble birth than a lady trucker. Having examined the house and its furnishings, the investigator was pretty sure that her husband was no lightweight. He lit another cigarette, a sly fox studying the bait in a trap.

'All looks and no action,' the lady trucker commented with annoyance. 'What kind of Communist Party member are you?'

'This is how undercover communists deal with female agents.'

'Really?'

'In the movies.'

'Are you an actor?'

'Studying to be one.'

Slowly she untied the belt of her robe, which fell around her feet when she shrugged her shoulders. Slim and graceful was the phrase that came to his mind.

Cupping her breasts with her hands, she asked, 'What do you think?'

The investigator replied, 'Not bad.'

'What now?'

'Continue to observe.'

She picked up his pistol, loaded it with a practiced hand, then stepped back to put some distance between them. The lamplight softened, encasing her body in gold. Not the whole body, of course; the rings around her nipples were dark red, her nipples like two bright red dates. Slowly she raised the gun, until it was aimed at the investigator's head.

He shuddered a bit, his eyes fixed on the blue steel of the muzzle and the black hole at the end. He was used to pointing guns at *other* people's heads, always the cat watching the mouse squirm under its sharp claws. Most of those mice, facing death, trembled with fear and peed their pants. Only a few could feign calmness, though a shaking fingertip or a twitch at the corner of the mouth usually exposed their fear. Now the cat had become the mouse; the judge had become the judged. He studied his own pistol as if it were the first time he'd seen it. The luster, like blue glazed tile, was as enchanting as the bouquet of vintage liquor, its smooth outlines displayed a kind of evil beauty. At this moment, it was God it was fate it was the Grim Reaper. Her large pale hand squeezed the carved handle, her long, slender index finger rested against the trigger, just a twitch away from driving the firing pin into the cartridge. Experience told him that a pistol in this state is no longer a piece of cold iron, but a living object with thoughts feelings culture morality. There is an enriched soul within – it is the soul of the gun holder. Without realizing it, this reverie relaxed him, until he was no longer focused on the muzzle, from which the bullet would emerge. It was just part of the gun. He took a leisurely drag on his cigarette.

An autumn wind blew in from the yard, gently billowing the silk drapes. Drops of cold condensation on the steamy bathroom ceiling fell noisily into the tub. He watched the lady trucker like a man appreciating a museum painting. To his surprise he discovered that a naked young woman holding a gun she was prepared to use could be incredibly sexy. At that moment, the pistol was no longer a simple handgun, but an organ of sexual conquest, a throbbing weapon. Ding Gou'er had never been one of those communists who can close their eyes in the presence of a woman. As we have already seen, he had a sex-crazed mistress. Now, to add some detail to the picture, he'd also had his share of one-night stands. In days past, he'd have easily held this little lamb in his grasp, like a ferocious tiger that had come charging down off the mountain. What gave him pause this time was: First, ever since arriving in Liquorland, he'd felt trapped in a labyrinth, confused and paranoid. Second, the tip of his tongue still ached. Facing this demonic butterfly, with her twisted personality, he dared not make a careless move, particularly since his head was in the sights of the business end of a pistol. Was there any guarantee this demon wouldn't pull the trigger? It's so much easier than biting someone – besides, it's civilized, modern, and filled with romance. The contrast between the roomy, well-appointed quarters the woman lived in and the grinding job she performed perplexed him. I nearly lost my tongue over a little kiss. What if I . . . who could guarantee the safety of the family jewels? Suppressing his 'bourgeois promiscuous inclinations' and rekindling his 'awesome proletarian righteousness,' he sat there, solid as Mount Tai, facing a bare-assed woman and the black muzzle of a pistol, so decorous and composed, a look of utter serenity on his face, that he could surely lay claim to the mantle of tragic hero the likes of which the world has seldom seen. Calmly he watched the scene change.

The lady trucker's face reddened, her excited nipples quivered, like the voracious mouths of tiny animals. The investigator could hardly keep from throwing himself on her and biting them. The sharp pain in his tongue kept him in his seat.

She sighed softly. 'I surrender,' she said.

She tossed the pistol down onto the table and raised her hands ostentatiously. 'I surrender,' she said again, 'you win . . .' With her arms in the air and her legs spread wide, all the points of entry were wide open.

'How can you be so blasé?' she asked the investigator in exasperation. 'Am I too ugly for you?'

'No, you're quite good looking,' he replied languidly.

'Then why?' She turned mocking. 'Not castrated, are you?'

'I'm afraid you'll bite it off.'

'Male praying mantises die when they mount the females, but that doesn't keep them from climbing on.'

'Don't give me that. I'm no praying mantis.'

'You goddamned coward!' the lady trucker cursed and turned her back on him. 'Get the hell out of here. I'm going to masturbate!'

The investigator flew off the sofa and grabbed her from behind, taking one of her breasts in his hand. She lay back in his arms, cocked her head, and grinned up at him. In spite of himself, he put his mouth next to hers, but his lips no sooner brushed up against her burning lips than stabbing pains re-attacked his tongue. 'Ouch!' he shouted, jerking his mouth out of harm's way.

'I won't bite you . . .' She turned and began to undress him.

Piece by piece, the investigator's clothes were peeled away. He pitched in to help, like a lone traveler confronted by a highwayman. First she removed his bathrobe and flicked it into the corner, then she relieved him of his shorts and undershirt, tossing them over an arm of the chandelier. He gazed up at them, suddenly wishing he could have them back. The desire to retrieve them was very strong. Wanting to 'pick the onions without delay,' he jumped a good thirty centimeters off the floor. He touched them with the tip of one finger of his right hand, but his feet were quickly back on the carpet. The next jump was forestalled by a leg sweep from the lady trucker, which put him flat on his back.

Before the investigator could come to his senses, the lady trucker had straddled him. Grabbing hold of his ears, she began bouncing up and down, raising a tattoo of sonorous slaps on Ding Gou'er's belly. His insides felt as if they were being crushed, and he shouted bloody murder. So the lady trucker reached out, picked up a smelly sock, and crammed it into his mouth. Her actions were violent and savage, not gentle or feminine. A foul, disgusting taste filled Ding Gou'er's mouth; he wanted to cry out. Is this supposed to be making love? It's more like hog-butchering. Just as his consciousness sent a command to his hands to shove this lady butcher off, she pinned his wrists to the floor, as if guessing what he had in mind. Ding Gou'er's emotions were a welter of confusion. He wanted to struggle, and he didn't want to. We've already seen why he wanted to struggle. And to find out why he didn't want to, we need look no further than down between his legs, where he was undergoing a test of blood and fire. So he closed his eyes and put his fate in God's hands.

And here is what happened: While the lady trucker, all hot and sweaty, was squirming and bouncing around on his belly, like a lovesick loach, snide laughter erupted high above him. Ding Gou'er opened his eyes, and was nearly blinded by a flurry of flash-bulb explosions, followed immediately by a series of shutter snaps, and finally the whirr of film rewinding inside an automatic camera. He sprang into a sitting position and swung at the passion-filled face of the lady trucker. His aim was perfect; with a loud crack and a frenzy of flash-bulb explosions, she fell over backwards, her shoulders settling slowly onto his upturned feet, her naked belly revealing many delicious secrets. More flash-bulb explosions, as the historical posture assumed by him and the lady trucker was photographed from every angle by her co-conspirator.

'All right, Comrade Ding Gou'er, special investigator, it's now time to have a little tête-à-tête,' Diamond Jin said tauntingly as he stuffed the roll of film into his pocket, crossed his legs, and settled comfortably into the sofa. He made the muscle on his right cheek twitch as he spoke, which Ding Gou'er found quite disgusting.

Pushing the dazed lady trucker off his body, Ding Gou'er tried to stand up, but his legs were so wobbly he moved like a paralytic.

'This is great!' Diamond Jin said, moving his cheek muscle. 'An investigator with awesome responsibilities paralyzed from the waist down from sexual overindulgence.'

Staring at the handsome, well-cared-for face, Ding Gou'er felt the fires of anger rage in his breast and spread throughout his body; his ice-cold legs felt as if thousands of tiny insects had suddenly come to life just under the skin. By propping himself on his arms, he somehow managed to stand, however wobbly. His plugged arteries snapped open, and as he began to move, he narrated his own actions: 'The investigator stands up and flexes his arms and legs. He picks up a hand towel and wipes down his sweaty body, including his belly, stained by love juices from the wife or the lover of Diamond Jin, Liquorland's Deputy Head of Propaganda. As he wipes down his naked body, he regrets his fears of a moment ago. I've committed no crime, except for falling into a trap laid by criminals.'

He tossed the hand towel into the air and watched it float to the floor in front of Diamond Jin, whose cheek muscle was, by now, twitching frantically, and whose face had turned the color of cold steel. 'That's quite a woman you've got there,' Ding Gou'er said. 'Too bad she threw in her lot with scum like you.'

He stood there waiting for Diamond Jin to explode in anger. But the man merely burst out laughing, guffaws of towering strangeness, which threw Ding Gou'er into a panic.

'What are you laughing at?' he demanded. 'Do you honestly think you can mask your guilt feelings with laughter?'

Diamond Jin stopped laughing abruptly, took a handkerchief out of his pocket to dry his eyes, and said, 'I ask you, Comrade Ding Gou'er, just who is troubled by guilt feelings? You wormed your way into my home and raped my wife, for which I have solid evidence.' He patted the pocket holding the film. 'An officer of the law,' he went on, 'who breaks the very laws he's sworn to uphold is guilty of a serious offense.' He sucked air in through the corner of his mouth. 'Now who has guilt feelings?' he said derisively.

Ding Gou'er ground his teeth. 'Your wife raped *me!*'

'That's the oddest thing I've ever heard!' Diamond Jin said, his cheek still twitching. 'A burly kung-fu master with a handgun raped by a defenseless female.'

The investigator turned to look at the woman, who was kneeling on the hardwood floor, her gaze clouded as if she were in a trance, fresh blood trickling from her nostrils. Shivers ran through Ding Gou'er's heart, as irresistible good feelings for the lady trucker's scorching belly returned in a rush, until his eyes stung and tears began to form. He knelt down to pick up the discarded bathrobe, then used it to wipe the blood from the woman's nose and mouth. If only he hadn't hit her so hard. He noticed two drops of water on the back of his hand. Great big opaque tears leaped noisily – *pi-pa pa-pa* – from her eyes.

Ding Gou'er lifted the lady trucker up in his arms, laid her on the bed, and covered her with a blanket. Then he jumped up, fetched his shorts from the chandelier, and put them on. After that, he opened the door to the balcony, retrieved the rest of his clothes, and got dressed. Diamond Jin's cheek twitched as he watched Ding pick his pistol up from the table, uncock the hammer, and stick it into his belt before sitting down. 'Let's lay our cards on the table,' Ding said.

'What cards are those?' Diamond Jin replied.

'Don't play dumb with me,' Ding Gou'er said.

'Not dumb, pained,' Jin said.

'Pained over what?' Ding asked.

'Pained over the realization that the ranks of cadres in our party have produced a degenerate like you!'

Ding: 'I'm a degenerate because I seduced your wife. That's degeneracy. But there are people who cook and eat little boys. And you can't be degenerate if you aren't even human! That's bestiality!'

'Ha ha ha . . .' Diamond Jin clapped his hands and laughed gleefully. 'This is just like *The Arabian Nights*,' he said when he finally stopped laughing. 'Here in Liquorland, we have a famous culinary dish of extraordinary imagination and creativity. Members of the Central Government have tried it, so have you. Therefore, if we're cannibalistic beasts, then you are too.'

With a sneer, Ding Gou'er said, 'If you have a clear conscience, why find it necessary to lure me into a sex-trap?'

'Only Higher-Procuratorate scum like you have the perverse imagination to come up with a thought like that!' Diamond Jin replied angrily. 'Now I'd like to report to your honor on behalf of our city's Party Committee and municipal government: We welcome Investigator Ding Gou'er of the Higher Procuratorate to our city. We are prepared to offer every assistance.'

'You could easily block my investigation, you know,' Ding Gou'er said.

Diamond Jin patted his pocket. 'What we have here, to be precise, is two willing fornicators. But even though your behavior has been despicable, you have broken no laws. And even though I have the power to send you crawling back to where you came from, like a lowly dog, individual interests must be subordinated to public interests, so I will not stop you from carrying out your mission.'

Diamond Jin opened his liquor cabinet, took out a bottle of Maotai, unscrewed the cap, and poured two tall glasses, emptying the bottle. He offered one to Ding Gou'er and raised the other in a toast: 'Here's to a successful investigation!' he said, clinking glasses with Ding Gou'er. He tossed his head back, and drank the liquor in one gulp. Holding up the now empty glass, he stared at Ding Gou'er, cheek twitching, eyes shining.

The sight of that twitching cheek muscle enraged Ding Gou'er, who held out his glass and, come hell or high water, drank every last drop.

'Good for you!' Diamond Jin shouted approvingly. 'Now you're acting like a real man!' Returning to the liquor cabinet, he removed an armful of liquor bottles, all name brands. 'Now let's see who's the *better* man,' he said, pointing to the bottles, which he deftly opened and began pouring from. Splashes of liquor turned the air aromatic. 'Anyone who doesn't drink is the son of a whore!' With his cheek twitching uncontrollably by now, Diamond Jin abandoned his sophisticated veneer in favor of a hardened, alcoholic look. 'Are you up to it?' he challenged, throwing his head back and emptying his glass. On and on the cheek twitched. 'Some people would rather be known as the son of a whore than drink a little liquor!'

'Who said I won't drink?' Ding Gou'er picked up his glass. *Glug-glug* – he drained it. A skylight opened up in his scalp and his consciousness was transformed into a demonic butterfly the size of a moon-shaped fan; it began to dance in the lamplight. 'Drink . . . fuck your mothers, all of them, drink every drop of Liquorland's . . .' He saw his hand grow to the size of a prayer mat and sprout a mass of fingers that reached out to the liquor bottles, which shrank to the size of carpentry nails, embroidery needles, then suddenly swelled to the size of large goblets, metal buckets, mallets. The lamplight changed, the butterfly tumbled in the air. Only the twitching cheek muscle stayed true to form. Drink! Liquor lubricates like honey. His tongue and gullet felt unimaginably good, better than words can describe. Drink! He sucked it up as fast as he could, then watched the clear liquid slip soothingly down his brown, twisting gullet. His feelings soared, following the contours of the wall.

Diamond Jin moved slowly in the lamplight, then took off abruptly, a virtual comet. The expression on his face cut a swath through the golden aura of the room like a razor-sharp saber, opening up a patchwork of seams in which he moved freely, slipping and sliding, until, just as abruptly, he vanished.

The multi-hued butterfly looked worn out, its wings getting heavier and heavier, as if weighted down by morning dew. Finally it settled on one of the chandelier arms, its antennae trembling tragically as it watched its skeleton crash heavily to the floor.

II

Dear Mo Yan, Sir

I'm concerned that I haven't heard from you for a long time. Is it because I went overboard regarding my achievements in my last letter, and all that wild talk upset you? If so, then your disciple is caught up in fear and trepidation, shivering in his boots, afraid even to sweat, guilty of crimes deserving a thousand deaths. 'A true gentleman forgives the trifles of a petty man, and the broad mind of an able minister can accommodate a ferry boat.' Please don't find fault with a child like me. I don't want to lose your affection under any circumstance. From now on I'll heed your every word, and will never again argue with you.

If you really believe that the dish Dragon and Phoenix Lucky Together has bourgeois liberalization tendencies, I'll delete it from my story 'Donkey Avenue,' and that's that. I can also look up Proprietor Yu of Yichi Tavern and ask him to remove the dish from his menu. A few days ago, when I mentioned you to him, his eyes lit up. He asked me, 'Is he the one who wrote *Red Sorghum*?' I said, 'Yes, that's him, my mentor.' He said, 'That mentor of yours is a true scoundrel who's always as good as his word, and I think highly of him.' I said, 'Who do you think you are, calling my mentor a scoundrel?' But he said, 'From me that's a compliment. At a time when sanctimonious hypocrites are everywhere, a "true scoundrel who's as good as his word" is rare as gold.' Sir, we cannot use ordinary logic on extraordinary people. This Mr Yichi is a true eccentric, a real mystery. Please don't take offense just because he talks like a guttersnipe.

I told him I'd asked you to help me with his biography, and he was delighted. He said that only Mo Yan is qualified to write his life story. When I asked him why, he said, 'Because Mo Yan and I are jackals from the same lair.' To which I argued, 'Mo Yan is one of the great young writers of his age. How can a dwarf like you be mentioned in the same breath?' With a sneer, he said, 'Calling him a jackal from the same lair is high praise from me. Do you know how many people would love to be considered a jackal from the same lair as me, but aren't?'

Sir, I hope you won't sink to his level. In these times, when everything's all topsy-turvy, even the city's 'number one Liquorland beauty,' the hostess of our local TV show, went to bed with him. That, as you can see, takes real skill. He has money, but lacks fame; you have fame, but no money. A perfect match. Sir, you don't have to pretend to be above worldly matters, just do a little business with him. He said that if you're willing to write his life story, he'll make it worth your while. I urge you to accept the assignment, both to earn a pile of People's Currency and to change your image of poverty and backwardness. Besides, Yu Yichi is a truly uncommon individual, and that has to pique your interest. Here's an ugly freak not much more than a foot tall who has vowed to f— every beauty in Liquorland, and has damned near f—ed them all. Now that's a mystery that has to get you thinking. With your literary genius and powerful writing style, *The Life of Yu Yichi* is bound to be a classic. He said that if you're willing to come to Liquorland to write his life story, he'll supply you with everything you need: You'll stay in Liquorland's finest hotel, drink Liquorland's finest liquor, dine on our finest cuisine, smoke name-brand cigarettes, sip famous tea. He even said – on the QT, understand – that if there are other pleasures you seek, he'll do whatever is necessary to make you happy. Sir, if you're concerned that the interviews will be too taxing, I'll be happy to do them for you. You won't find a better offer than this if you walk around with a lantern. So please don't hesitate another minute.

Sir, in order to further stir up your enthusiasm and convince you that Yu Yichi is your typical, lovable hooligan, I've written a story in the form of a chronicle, called 'Yichi the Hero.' I'd like your opinion of it. If you decide to come to Liquorland to write the biography, there's no need to give the story to anyone else. You'll be doing me a great favor, and I have nothing with which to repay your kindness. So we'll just count this story as a modest token of my esteem for you.

Wishing you
Good writing,
Your disciple

Li Yidou

III

Dear Elder Brother Yidou

Your letter and the 'chronicle-story' 'Yichi the Hero' arrived safely.

Your last letter was uncompromisingly candid. I admire that, so you have nothing to fear. I couldn't reply right away because I was out of town. Still no news regarding your stories, and I can only counsel patience.

Dragon and Phoenix Lucky Together is only a culinary dish. As such it has no class attributes, and thus cannot possibly be attacked for having bourgeois liberalization tendencies. There's no need to delete it from 'Donkey Avenue,' and certainly you needn't remove it from the Yichi Tavern menu. If I visit Liquorland someday, I want

176

to try this world-class gourmet treat, and how will I do that if it's not on the menu? Besides, these objects have such high culinary value that it would be a shame not to eat them, and stupid to boot. And since they must be eaten, there's probably no more civilized way to prepare them than as Dragon and Phoenix Lucky Together. Finally, even if you tried to take it off the menu, Proprietor Yu wouldn't permit it.

I'm getting more and more interested in this Yu Yichi character, and am willing in principle to work with him on his life story. He can set the fee. If he wants to give a lot, I'll take it; if he wants to give a little, I'll take that too; and if he doesn't want to give anything, that's OK with me. It's not money that attracts me to the project, but his celebrated experiences. I have the vague impression that Yu Yichi is the very soul of Liquorland, that he embodies the spirit of his age – half angel, half devil. Revealing the spiritual world of this individual could very well constitute my greatest contribution to literature. You may forward my initial response to Mr Yu.

I'm not going to flatter you on 'Yichi the Hero.' You call it a short story, but to me it's a hodgepodge, in every respect a mirror image of the scattered donkey parts in Yichi Tavern. In it you include a letter to me, excerpts from *Strange Events in Liquorland*, and the incoherent ramblings of Yu Yichi himself. It's as unconstrained as a heavenly steed soaring through the skies, completely out of control. In years past I've been criticized as being out of control, but compared to you, I'm the embodiment of moderation. We live in an age of strict adherence to law and order, and that includes the writing of fiction. For that reason, I do not intend to send your manuscript to *Citizens' Literature* – I'd be wasting my time. I'll hold on to it for the time being and return it when I visit Liquorland. I will, as you suggested, refer to the material in the story. Thanks for the generous offer.

One more thing: Do you have a copy of *Strange Events in Liquorland*? If so, please send it to me as soon as possible. You can make a photocopy if you're afraid it might get lost somewhere along the way. I'll reimburse you for the copying costs.

Wishing you
Peace,

Mo Yan

IV

Yichi the Hero, by Li Yidou

Please have a seat, Doctor of Liquor Studies, so we can have a heart-to-heart talk, he said with slippery intimacy as he sat on his haunches on his leather-covered swivel chair. The look on his face and the tone of his voice were like clouds at sunset, dazzlingly bright and in constant flux. He looked like a fearful demon, one of those patently evil, heretical knights-errant in kung-fu novels; my nerves were frayed as I sat on the sofa opposite him. You little rascal, he mocked, just when did you and that stinking rascal Mo Yan team up together? Cackling like a mother hen feeding her chicks (although I was trying to explain myself, not actually cackling), I said, He is my mentor, ours is a literary relationship. To this day I haven't met him face-to-face, one of the great regrets of my life. With a sinister heh heh heh, he said, Mo is not the real family name of that rascal Mo Yan, you know. His real family name is Guan, which makes him the seventy-eighth descendant of Guan Zhong, Prime Minister of the state of Qi during the Warring States period, or so he claims. In fact, that's pure bullshit. A writer, you say? To listen to him, you'd think he was some sort of literary genius. Well, I know everything there is to know about him. Astonished, I blurted out, How could *you* know everything there is to know about my mentor? To which he replied, Do nothing if you want nothing to be known. That rascal's been no good since he was a kid. At the age of six he burned down a production team's storage shed, at nine he fell under the spell of a teacher named Meng, following her around everywhere she went, to her great annoyance. At eleven he stole and ate some tomatoes, and got a beating when he was caught. At thirteen, for stealing some turnips, he was forced to kneel at Chairman Mao's statue and beg forgiveness in front of more than two hundred workers on a public project. The little rascal is good at memorizing things, and had a good time entertaining people with his wit, for which his father gave him such a whipping, his ass swelled up something awful. Don't you dare sully the name of my revered master! I protested loudly. Sully his name? Everything I've told you I got from his own writing! he said with a snide laugh. And a rotten scoundrel is just the person to write my life story. It takes an evil genius like him to understand an evil hero like me. Write to him and have him come to Liquorland as soon as possible. He'll get no shabby treatment from me, he said as he thumped his chest. Energized by the boastful pronouncement and loud thumping, he turned his expensive leather chair into a carousel. One minute I was looking into his face, the next at the back of his head. Face, back of the head, face, back of the head, a crafty, animated face and a nicely rounded gourd in the back, one crammed full of knowledge. As he whirled faster and faster, he began to levitate.

Mr Yichi, I said, I've already written to him, but I haven't received an answer. I'm worried he might not be willing to work on your life story.

With a sneer, he said, Don't you worry about that, he'll do it. There are four things you need to know about the little rascal: first, he likes women; second, he smokes and drinks; third, he's always strapped for money; and fourth, he's a collector of tales of the supernatural and unexplained mysteries that he can incorporate into his own fiction. He'll come, all right. I doubt there's another person on this earth who knows him as well as I.

As he twirled back down to the seat he said caustically, Doctor of Liquor Studies, just what sort of 'doctor' are you? Do you have any idea what liquor is? A type of liquid? Bullshit! The blood of Christ? Bullshit! Something that boosts your spirits? Bullshit! Liquor is the mother of dreams, dreams are the daughters of liquor. And there's something else I find relevant, he said as he ground his teeth and glared at me. Liquor is the lubricant of the state machinery; without it, the machinery cannot run smoothly! Do you understand what I'm saying? One look into that pitted face of yours tells me you don't. Are you going to collaborate with that little bastard Mo Yan in writing my biography? All right, then, I'll help you, I'll coordinate your activities. If you must know, no biographer worth his salt would waste time interviewing individuals, since ninety percent of what's gleaned through interviews is lies and fabrications. What you need to do is separate the real from the false, arrive at the truth by seeing what lies behind all those lies and fabrications.

I want you to know something, you rascal – and you can pass this on to that other rascal, Mo Yan – that Yu Yichi is eighty-five years old this year. A respectable age, wouldn't you say? I wonder where you two little bastards were way back when I was roaming the countryside, living off my wits. Maybe you were somewhere in the ears of corn, or the leaves of cabbage, or in salted turnips, or in pumpkin seeds, places like that. Is that little rascal Mo Yan writing his *The Republic of Wine*? It's nothing but the ravings of a fool, someone who has no concept of his own limitations. How much liquor did he consume before he felt qualified to write *The Republic of Wine*? I've put away more alcohol than he has water! Do you two know the identity of that scaly boy who rides a galloping steed up and down Donkey Avenue on moonlit nights? It's me, that's who, me. Don't ask where I come from. My hometown is a place lit up by dazzling sunlight. What, you don't see the resemblance? You don't believe I'm capable of flying on eaves and walking on walls? Permit me to give a demonstration, to open your eyes, as it were.

My dear Mo Yan, what happened next is the sort of thing that turns a person bug-eyed and tongue-tied. Rays of light shot out of that terrifying little dwarf's eyes, like glowing daggers, and with my own eyes I watched him shrink into himself right there on the seat of his leather-covered swivel chair, transforming himself into a shadowy figure that flew into the air, light as a feather. The chair kept spinning, until – *thunk* – it reached the end of the swivel rod. Our friend, the hero of this narrative, was by then stuck to the ceiling. All four limbs, his whole body, in fact, seemed equipped with suction pads. He looked like an enormous, disgusting lizard crawling across the ceiling, carefree and relaxed as can be. His muffled voice descended from the heights: Did you see that, little rascal? Well, that was nothing. My master could hang from the ceiling all day and all night without twitching. With that he floated down from the ceiling like a dark falling leaf.

Back in his chair again, he asked smugly, What do you say to that? Now do you believe in my skills?

His astonishing, frightful lizard trick had me in a cold sweat; it was as if I'd been given a glimpse of a dream world. It never occurred to me that the heroic young man on the magnificent steed was none other than this dwarf. My mind was thrown into confusion. An idol had been smashed, and my belly swelled with the expanding airs of disappointment. Sir, if you recall the description of the scaly youngster in my story 'Donkey Avenue' – the bright moonlight, the magical little black donkey, the clattering of roof tiles, and the willow-leaf dagger clasped majestically between the youngster's teeth – you'd be disappointed, too.

You don't believe me, he said, and you can't stand the idea of me and that scaly youngster being one and the same – I see it in your eyes – but that's how it is. You probably want to ask where I learned these remarkable skills, but I can't tell you. To be honest, if you're willing to treat your own life more lightly than a goose feather, there's nothing you can't learn.

He lit a cigarette, but rather than puff on it, he blew a series of smoke rings, then strung them together with a single jet of smoke. The smoke rings held their shape as they hung in the air. His hands and feet never stopped moving. He was like one of those little apes that make their home on White Ape Mountain. Rascal, he said as he swiveled in his chair, let me tell you and Mo Yan a story about alcohol. I didn't make it up – making up stories is your business.

He said:

Once upon a time the proprietor of a tavern here on Donkey Avenue hired a skinny twelve-year-old as an apprentice. An oversized head topped the boy's long, skinny neck; he had big black eyes as deep as bottomless pits. He was a hard worker – fetching water, sweeping the floors, cleaning the tables, whatever he was asked to do – and extremely capable, to the immense satisfaction of the proprietor. But there's another side to the story, a strange side: From the first day the little apprentice entered the tavern, there was a notable discrepancy between the consumption of liquor from the vats and the money that wound up in the till, which greatly puzzled the proprietor and his employees. One night, after the vats had been filled to the brim with fresh liquor from several lined baskets, the proprietor hid near by to see if he could solve the puzzle. Nothing happened during the first half of the night, and the proprietor was about to fall asleep when he heard the tiniest of noises, like the muffled footsteps of a cat. Pricking up his ears and growing alert, he waited to see what would happen. A shadowy figure glided up. After waiting for such a long time, the proprietor's eyes had gotten used to the dark, so he easily identified the dark figure as that of his apprentice. The youngster's eyes were an emerald green, like those of a cat. He was panting excitedly as he removed the lid from one of the vats, buried his mouth in the alcohol, and began sucking it up. As the astonished proprietor watched the level go down and down, he held his breath so as not to give himself away. After helping himself to a goodly amount of alcohol in several of the vats, the apprentice tiptoed away. Having solved the riddle, the proprietor got up silently and went to bed. The next morning, when he checked his stock, he saw that twelve inches of alcohol was missing from each of the vats. He had witnessed a capacity for alcohol that defied explanation. As an educated man, he knew that the belly of the apprentice was blessed with a treasure known as a liquor moth, and that if he could get his hands on one and introduce it into his liquor vat, not only would it eternally replenish itself, but the quality of his liquor would increase many times over. So he had the apprentice bound up next to the vats. Giving him nothing to eat or drink, he ordered his employees to stir the liquor in the vat, over and over, filling the air with its aroma and the pitiful shouts of the apprentice, who twisted and turned in agony. That went on for seven days, after which the proprietor released the apprentice, who immediately pounced onto one of the vats, stuck his head into the liquid and drank thirstily. All of a sudden, there was a loud splash, as a red-backed, yellow-bellied toadlike creature fell into the vat.

Know who that young apprentice was? Yu Yichi asked gloomily. Seeing the look of agony on his face, I asked tentatively, Was it you?

Who the fuck do you think it was? Of course it was me! If that proprietor hadn't stolen the treasure in my belly, I might very well have turned into a god of wine.

You're not doing so bad as it is, I consoled him. You have wealth and power; you eat and drink whatever you like, and you take your enjoyment where you please. I don't think even a god of wine has it that good.

Bullshit! After he stole my treasure, my capacity for drink was history. Which is the only reason I succumbed to the tyranny of that rascal Diamond Jin.

Deputy Head Jin must have one of those liquor moths in his belly, I said, since he can walk away sober after a thousand cups of the strong stuff.

Bullshit! Him, a liquor moth? All he's got is a mass of liquor tapeworms. With a liquor moth you become a god of wine; with liquor tapeworms, the best you can hope for is a wine demon.

Why didn't you just swallow the liquor moth back and be done with it?

That shows what you know. Ai! That liquor moth was so thirsty it was barely in the vat before it choked to death. Sorrowful memories were turning his eyes red.

Elder brother Yichi, tell me the name of that proprietor, and I'll trash his tavern.

Yu Yichi burst out laughing, and when he had finished, he said, You poor muddled little rascal, did you really believe all that? I made it up, every word of it. How could there be anything like a liquor moth? That was just a story I heard my tavern proprietor tell. All tavern owners dream of owning a vat that never goes dry. But it's pure fantasy. I worked in that tavern for years, but I was too little for any heavy work, and the proprietor was always grumbling over how much I ate and how dark my eyes were. He finally sent me on my way. After that I just knocked around, sometimes begging food, and sometimes selling my labor for something to eat.

You've tasted the bitter life, but now you're a man among men.

Bullshit bullshit bullshit . . . after a string of 'bullshit's, he spat out spitefully, Can the clichés! That might work with most people, but not with me. Millions of people all around the world have suffered and been mistreated, but those who become men among men are as rare as phoenix feathers and unicorn horns. It's all a matter of fate, it's in your bones. If you're born with the bones of a beggar, that's what you'll spend your life as. Damn it, I don't want to talk to you about these things anymore, it's like playing the lute for an ox. You're not smart enough to understand any of it. The only thing you know is how to turn grain into liquor, and just barely, at that. Like Mo Yan, who knows only how to write fiction, and just barely, at that. The two of you – mentor and disciple – are a couple of stuffed-up assholes, two turtle-spawn bastards. By asking you to write my biography I'm honoring your ragtag wicked thoughts. Clean out your ears and pay attention, you rascal, while your revered ancestor tells you another story.

He said:

Once upon a time, an educated little boy was watching a performance by two acrobats, one of them a beautiful maiden of twenty or so. The other was an elderly deaf-mute, by all appearances the girl's father. She was the only performer; the elderly deaf-mute just rested on his haunches off to the side to keep watch over her props and costumes, for which there was no obvious need – the old fellow was clearly superfluous. And yet, without him, the troupe was somehow incomplete, so he was anything but expendable. He served as a contrast to the beautiful young maiden.

Her opening routine included producing an egg out of thin air, then a pigeon, then making things appear and disappear – some big, some small – things like that. Energized by the swelling crowd, which formed a dense wall around her, she announced, Ladies and gentlemen, devoted supporters, your servant will now perform a peach-planting. But before I begin, let's open with a quotation from Chairman Mao: Our literature and art serves the workers, peasants, and soldiers. She picked a peach pit up from the ground, planted it in a patch of rich soil, and spit a mouthful of water over it. Grow! she commanded. Lo and behold, a bright red peach bud rose from the ground, higher and higher, until it became a full-fledged tree. Then the crowd watched as flowers blossomed

184

on the branches and peaches began to grow. In no time they were ripe, an off-white color with tiny red mouths around the stems. The girl picked several of the peaches and handed them to onlookers, none of whom dared try one. Except for the little boy, who took one from her and gobbled it down. When asked how it tasted, he replied it was delicious. The girl invited the onlookers to taste the peaches a second time, but once again they just stood there, eyes popping, not daring to try one. With a sigh and a wave of her hand, she made the tree and the peaches disappear, leaving behind a vacant patch of soil.

The performance over, the girl and the old man gathered up their things to leave, while the boy watched on longingly. She acknowledged his attention with a smile, showing off her red lips and white teeth, just like a peach, so enchanting him she nearly snatched the soul right out of his body. Little brother, she said, you were the only one who ate one of my peaches, which shows that our fates are linked somehow. How's this? I'll leave you an address, and anytime you find yourself thinking about me, that's where you can find me.

The girl took out a ball-point pen, found a slip of paper, and scratched out an address, which she handed to the boy. He put it in a safe place, treating it as a cherished treasure. But when the girl and the old man walked off, he followed them, as if in a trance. Several li later, the girl stopped and said, Go home, little brother. We'll meet again. Tears slipped from his eyes and down his cheeks. With a red satin handkerchief, she dried his tears, then blurted out abruptly, Little brother, your parents are coming for you!

Quickly turning to look, he saw his mother and father hobbling along after him, waving their arms and moving their lips, as if shouting, though he didn't hear a sound. And when he turned back, the girl and the old man had vanished without a trace. He turned back again, and his parents had also vanished without a trace. Throwing himself to the ground, he cried like a baby. After a long while, exhausted from so much crying, he sat up and stared off blankly. Then, once he'd had enough of that, he lay back down and looked up into a sky as blue as any ocean, where puffy white clouds floated lazily by.

After returning home, the boy was in the grip of lovesickness:

he wouldn't eat and wouldn't talk, drinking only a single glass of water daily and getting thinner and thinner, until he was skin and bones. Sightless when his eyes were open, when he closed them, he saw the lovely maiden standing beside him, the smell of musk on her breath, passion filling her eyes. Dear elder sister, he would shout, I miss you more than I can bear! Turning to put his arms around her, he'd open his eyes, and there'd be nothing there. Since it was clear to the boy's anxious parents that he was wasting away, they sent for his uncle, a learned man with keen eyes, shrewd of mind, far-sighted, judicious, and resolute. One look at the boy was all he needed to know the source of his illness. Elder sister, brother-in-law, he sighed, my nephew's illness cannot be cured by medical potions, and if he keeps deteriorating at this rate, nothing can save him. That's why I think it's best to 'treat the dying horse as if it were alive and well.' Give him his freedom. If he finds the girl, maybe they'll be joined together. If he doesn't, he might give up the quest. The boy's tearful parents, knowing they had no choice, accepted the uncle's recommendation.

The three grownups went to the boy's bedside, where the uncle said, Nephew, I've convinced your parents to let you go in search of the girl.

Leaping out of bed, the boy prostrated himself at his uncle's feet and kowtowed over and over. A pink color quickly returned to his cheeks, probably from excitement.

Son, the boy's parents said, your ambitions are too great for someone so small. We underestimated you, and have decided to take your uncle's suggestion to let you go search out that alluring genie. Our elderly servant, Wang Bao, will accompany you. We hope you find her, but if you don't, come home and put an end to our worries. We will find a lovely girl from a good family for you. Finding a two-legged toad is impossible, but the world is filled with two-legged girls, so don't think there's only one tree to hang from.

The boy, objecting to his parents' suggestion, told them that the conjuring girl was the only one for him, that not even fairies from the Nine Heavens could take her place.

But his father, a man of considerable experience himself, advised the boy: My son, you're under the spell of that demon-girl. You cannot tell what's inside a stuffed dumpling by looking at its folds, and a girl's qualities are not revealed in her face. Beauty and ugliness vanish as soon as you close your eyes.

Naturally, the boy refused to come to his senses, for he was in the grip of passion, and nothing his parents said had any effect on him. Finding themselves powerless, they fed their little donkey, prepared enough provisions for half a month, and gave Wang Bao, the elderly servant, detailed instructions. Their preparations complete, amid a flood of tears, a host of anxieties, and seemingly endless dawdling, they saw the boy out of the village and onto the road.

Sitting astride his donkey and wobbling from side to side as if mounting the clouds and riding the mist, the boy thought only of the prospects of seeing the girl before long. Elated by this thought, he grew so animated on the donkey that people who saw him said he'd taken leave of his senses.

Many days passed, and the provisions he'd brought were exhausted, as was the money he'd been given. No one along the way could direct him to Apricot Blossom Cave on Westwind Mountain. The old servant urged him to turn around and head home, but to no avail. He kept heading west, his determination never flagging. So Wang Bao sneaked off, begging for food on the way back home. Then the donkey died. But the boy kept going, alone and on foot, as the days waned and his road neared its end. Finally, he sat down on a roadside boulder and wept, though his thoughts of the girl remained as strong as ever. He was startled out of his weeping by a loud noise, just before the earth opened up and the boulder plunged downward, carrying him with it. He opened his eyes to find himself in the welcoming arms of the girl he was looking for. Overwhelmed by rapture, he passed out . . .

That boy was me! Yu Yichi announced with a sly grin. I spent many days with a performing troupe, where I learned sword-swallowing, tightrope walking, fire-spitting, and more. Traveling performers live wonderful lives, mysterious and romantic. Whoever writes my life story should narrate this period with all the flair and color he can manage.

Mo Yan, sir, this Yu Yichi is a master of imagination, rich in creative powers. I had the feeling I'd run across the story he just told me somewhere or other, maybe during my reading of *Tales from the Scholar's Studio* or *Tales of the Supernatural*. Then, not long ago, I was browsing through *Strange Events in Liquorland* and ran across the following passage, which I have copied out for you:

In the early years of the Republic, a performer came to Wine Fragrance village, a woman whose beauty matched that of the Moon Goddess. Among the villagers crowding around to watch her was a young man surnamed Yu, whose given name was Yichi and whose nickname was Lapdog. Born to well-to-do parents in their forties, for whom he was a pearl in the palm, he was thirteen at the time, a gifted, intelligent boy, and lovely as fine jade. When the girl bestowed a smile on him, his heart took flight. Then the girl began her performance by summoning the wind and the rain, spitting out clouds and mist, to the raucous delight of her audience. She produced a tiny bottle, the thickness of a single finger, and held it up for all to see, saying: This is the cave-home of genies. Who among you will accompany me on a trip inside? The people gaped at one another, exchanging bewildered glances, wondering how two fully grown humans could possibly enter a bottle no thicker than a human finger. It must be hocus-pocus to trick the audience. But Yichi, captivated by the girl's beauty, leaped out of the crowd. I'll enter the bottle with you, he said. The crowd laughed at his foolishness. Young man, the girl said, you have a pure and wonderful disposition, and a strange fragrance emanates from your body. Clearly, you are no ordinary mortal, and entering the bottle with you is proof that our fates have been linked over three lifetimes. With that she raised her hand, forming her fingers into an orchid, from which puffs of smoke emerged. Ripples swept through the onlookers, like moon shadows, splintering and flickering without coming together. Yichi felt his wrist grasped by the girl, whose fingers were like threads, whose skin was satiny, soft and yielding. She whispered into his ear, Follow me, a sound like the gentle chirping of a swallow, her breath heavy with the smell of musk. She tossed the bottle into the sky, streaked with colorful rays of sunset and a host of auspicious auras. The mouth of the twirling bottle began to expand, the bottle grew and grew until it was at least ten feet long and shaped like a moon gate. Yichi drifted slowly inside with the girl. A flower-bedecked path, shaded by green pines, exquisite birds and marvelous animals frolicking all around. Yu was swept into an intoxicated stupor, lust burned in his heart. He grabbed the girl's hand and pulled her to him, wanting to perform the dance of love. With a giggle, she said, Aren't you afraid the village elders will laugh at you? She raised her hand and pointed outside the bottle, where he saw the onlookers craning their necks to observe what was going on inside. Momentarily startled, Yu felt his passion flag. But it quickly returned, and while his passions raged, he was too choked up to speak. The girl said, The depth of your emotions moves me. If my lowly origins do not disturb you, or my repulsive appearance, then I ask you to return to Apricot Blossom Cave on Westwind Mountain one year from today, when I will prepare my bed to receive you. Yu's emotions surged wildly and he was rendered speechless. With another wave of the girl's hand, he found himself once again under a bright sky, the tiny bottle lying in the palm of her hand. He detected a peculiar floral redolence on his clothing.

Back when the girl had first grasped Yu's wrist, the onlookers watched as his body shrank, then the girl's, until they were a pair of mosquitoes flitting into the bottle, which then floated upwards and began to circle in the air, like magic. They were stunned by what they saw.

The girl planted a gourd seed in the rich soil, spit a mouthful of fragrant saliva on the spot, and commanded, Grow! A bud appeared, turned into a tendril, and sprouted leaves as it stretched dozens of feet into the sky. It grew where it willed itself to grow, twisting and coiling like a column of smoke. With a sack over her shoulder, the girl began to climb the stalk, from one leaf to the next, until she had gone ten feet or more. She stopped, looked down, smiled, and said to Yu, Don't forget to keep your promise. Then she flew upwards, causing the leaves to quiver as she passed, and was soon out of sight. The stalk that had grown out of the gourd seed turned to dust that fluttered to the ground. The crowd stood there speechless before finally leaving the scene.

Yu returned home, but could not get the girl's beauty out of his mind. Neither eating nor drinking, he lay stiffly in bed day and night, shouting over and over in his delirium, as if in the presence of ghosts and demons. His frightened parents sought help from a parade of doctors, all of whom were mystified by a tenacious illness that defied medical treatment. Yu continued to deteriorate, body and soul, until he arrived at the brink of death. His parents, reduced to tears, were at their wits' end, when suddenly they heard the tinkle of a horse-bell at the door, followed by a shout,

It's I, the boy's uncle! The words still hung in the air when a strapping young man burst through the door. After completing his bows, he said, Brother-in-law, elder sister, have you been well since last we met? Looking into his face, with its high nose, wide mouth, yellow hair, and blue eyes, unlike other Chinese, the mother was too startled to speak. The man strode over to the boy's bed and announced, My nephew is seriously afflicted with lovesickness. Can potions or medical treatment cure him of that? You doddering oldsters will surely send my nephew to his death! Ill for many days, Yu lay with his eyes closed, barely breathing, as if he were already slipping into death, cut off from the outside world. The visitor bent down to check his condition. He announced with a sigh, Such pallor on a face so young and tender shows that my nephew is sick at heart. Producing three red pellets, he placed them in Yu's mouth, which immediately brought color to his cheeks and restored his heavy breathing. Then, clapping his hands thrice, the visitor announced, Foolish youngster, the anniversary of your promise, which you have anxiously awaited for so long, has nearly arrived. Do you not want to be there at the appointed hour? Yu's eyes popped open, bright and radiant, and he leaped out of bed. Thumping himself on the forehead, he exclaimed, If not for your help, uncle, I would have missed my rendezvous with the girl. You must leave, the visitor said, you must leave at once. He turned and strode out the door. Without stopping to change his clothes, comb his hair, or put on his shoes, Yu ran after his uncle. His parents called out tearfully, but he paid them no heed.

The visitor sat on his horse beside the road, waiting for Yu. Reaching down with his long arms, he lifted Yu up onto his mount, as if he were a newborn chick. Then he struck the horse with his riding crop; the animal whinnied once and was off like the wind. Yu sat astride the horse, holding on tightly to its mane, the wind whistling past his ears. Open your eyes, nephew, he suddenly heard his uncle say. When he did, he saw that he was in the Gobi Desert, surrounded by dry, withered grass on the rocky terrain, with nary a soul in sight. Without a word, his uncle smacked his horse and galloped off like a puff of smoke, leaving not a trace.

Yu sat on the rocky ground, alone and in tears. Suddenly he felt the rocks give way and heard a series of thunderous claps. Golden beams of light filled his eyes, so startling him that he swooned dead away. When he next awoke, he felt dainty fingers on his face, spreading their redolence in the air around him. He opened his eyes, and there before him was the girl. Tears of joy fell from his eyes. I have waited for you for such a long time, the girl said.

(Here five hundred words have been excised.)

Strolling hand in hand, they saw a garden with a profusion of unusual trees and rare flowers. One particular tree, large with palm-sized leaves, was covered with fruit shaped exactly like baby boys. At the mid-day meal, a golden-hued baby boy sat in the center of a platter, so perfectly lifelike that Yu dared not touch it with his chopsticks. How can a young man, over five feet tall, be such a coward? the girl said as she picked up her chopsticks and stuck them into the baby's penis, which, along with the rest of the body, crumbled under the assault. She picked up a piece of arm and ate it, chewing and grinding like a tiger or a wolf. Yu was more frightened than ever. With a sneer, the girl said, This boy is not a boy at all, but a boy-shaped fruit, and I am not pleased by your posturing. Wanting to please her, Yu forced himself to pick up an ear and put it into his mouth, where it melted and flooded his taste buds with indescribably delicious flavors. Emboldened by this discovery, he attacked the food like a hungry wolf or a starving tiger. The girl covered her mouth as she giggled. She said, Before you knew the flavor you were frightened as a lamb, but now you are ravenous as a wolf! Yu was too busy eating to reply; with grease and oil smeared across his face, he was a sight to behold. The girl brought out a flagon of liquor, saturating the air like perfume. She said, This is brewed from fruit gathered by apes and monkeys in the mountains. It is among the most sought-after anywhere . . .

Mo Yan, sir, you've probably read enough for one sitting, and I've certainly copied all I can for the moment. But I should remind you that eating infant boys and drinking Ape Liquor, both of which are mentioned in this nonsensical article, constitute two significant current events in Liquorland; you could even say they are the two keys to the mystery of Liquorland. The author of *Strange Events in Liquorland* is unknown, and I have only recently learned of its existence. For a few years now, it has circulated among the public in a hand-copied version, and I hear that the Propaganda Department of the Municipal Party Committee has ordered it confiscated. So I speculate that the author must be a contemporary, someone who is very much alive, right here in Liquorland. The protagonist of the piece is also called Yu Yichi! So I suspect that he is the author.

Mr Yu, you are confusing me something awful. First you work in a tavern, then you're a scaly young warrior who comes and goes like a shadow, and then you're a clown in a performing troupe. Now you're the prestigious owner of a tavern – your life is a mixture of truth and untruth, filled with countless transformations. How is anyone to write your life story?

He laughed uproariously. Who'd have guessed that such loud, crisp laughter could emerge from the chicken-breast chest of such a tiny dwarf. He tapped on the telephone buttons, making the little computer inside whirl dizzily. Then he tossed a teacup made of fine china from the town of Jingde toward the ceiling, sending it and the tea inside, aided by the pull of gravity, crashing and splashing onto the gorgeous, and expensive, wool carpet. Reaching into a drawer, he withdrew a stack of color photographs and flapped them in the air, making them flutter like a swarm of gaudy butterflies. Do you know these women, he asked smugly. I picked up the photos and studied them greedily, a hypocritical look of shyness on my face. Every one of the women was a beauty, totally naked, and they all looked familiar. He said their names were on the back. There I found the women's work units, their ages, their names, and the dates they had sex with him. They were all from Liquorland. He was very close to realizing his glorious aspiration.

So, Doctor of Liquor Studies, this crowning success by an ugly little dwarf ought to earn him the right to have his biography written, don't you think? Have that rascal Mo Yan get his ass over here as soon as possible. Wait too long and I might kill myself.

I, Yu Yichi, age unclear, stand seventy-five centimeters tall. Born into poverty, I wandered from place to place. I hit my stride in my middle years, serving as Chairman of the Metropolitan Entrepreneurs Association, earning distinction as provincial model worker, assuming proprietorship of Yichi Tavern, anointed as a candidate for Party membership, and having sex with twenty-nine of Liquorland's most beautiful women. I have a mental state beyond the imagination of mortal men, and abilities that surpass the best of them. I also have a rich supply of the sort of experiences that are the stuff of legend. My biography will rank as the world's most phenomenal book. Tell that rascal Mo Yan to make up his mind at once. Will he write it or won't he? Shit or get off the pot.

Chapter Six

Ding Gou'er sensed the gold-trimmed Gate of Hell open with a loud rumble. To his astonishment he discovered that Hell wasn't the dark, shadowy place mythology had made it out to be. No, it was dazzling, drenched simultaneously in rays from the red sun and the blue moon. Schools of beautifully striped, armored sea creatures, with soft, lithe limbs circled his body as it floated aimlessly. He sensed that a pointy-mouthed, multi-hued fish was nibbling at his anus, gently removing his hemorrhoids with the surgical skill of a trained proctologist. The butterfly of his con-sciousness returned to the body from which it had separated itself for so long, bringing a coolness to his brain. The special investigator, intoxicated for so long, opened his eyes: Sitting beside him was the lady trucker, naked as the day she was born, rubbing down her body with a sour-smelling liquid on a sponge she used to wash her truck. He, too, was stark naked, as he quickly discovered, lying on a sparkling teakwood floor. Images of the recent past seeped into his mind. He tried to get up, but couldn't. The lady trucker was carefully rubbing down her breasts, absorbed in her task, as if alone, like a mother about to suckle a baby. As if in slow motion, glistening tears welled up in her eyes, formed two threads, slithered down her cheeks, and fell directly onto her purplish nipples. A divine emotion rose in the investigator's heart. He was about to say something, when the lady trucker threw herself on him and sealed his lips with hers. Then, for the second time, he sensed that fish were schooling in the air around him – he could smell them. He sensed the essence of alcohol that had flourished in his body saturate hers. He awoke. With an eerie scream, she collapsed in a heap on the floor.

The investigator stood up on rubbery legs; still light-headed, he supported himself with his hand on the wall to keep from falling down again. Never had he been so drained of energy – feeling a void inside, he had become skin and no bones. Opaque steam rose from the lady trucker's body, like a freshly steamed fish. The steam vanished and was replaced by chilled sweat that oozed from her pores and puddled on the hardwood floor. What a pitiful sight she was as she lay there in a swoon; pity grows in the heart like poisonous weeds. Still, the investigator wasn't about to forget the woman's sinister and vicious side. Ding Gou'er felt like emptying his bladder all over her, like an animal in the wild, but he quickly drove that perverse thought out of his mind. Reminded of Diamond Jin and of his own sacred mission, he clenched his teeth with steely determination. Get out of here! My taking your wife to bed was a moral lapse, but cooking and eating children is a truly heinous crime. Gazing back at the lady trucker, he saw her as a target of flesh belonging to Diamond Jin. I hit the bull's-eye of that target, and the bullet of righteousness still flies through the air. He opened the dresser, selected an olive green wool suit, and put it on. It fit perfectly, as if it had been custom-made for him. I've slept with your woman, he was thinking, now I'm wearing your clothes, and when it's all over, I'll have your life. He retrieved his pistol from his own dirty clothes and pocketed it. Then he ate a raw cucumber straight from the refrigerator and took a big swig from a bottle of Zhangyu wine. It was soft and silky as a lovely woman's skin. As he turned to leave, the lady trucker rolled over and balanced herself on all fours, like a frog or a crawling infant. The look of wretched helplessness in her eyes reminded him of his own son, which filled his heart with paternal love. He walked over to pat her on the head.

'You poor thing,' he said, 'you poor little darling.'

She wrapped her arms around his legs and gazed up at him tenderly.

'I'm leaving,' he said. 'I'll not allow your husband to get away with his crimes.'

'Take me with you,' she said. 'I hate him. I'll help you. They eat infants.'

She stood up, dressed quickly, and took a bottle from the cabinet. In it was some ocher-colored powder.

'Know what this is?' she asked.

The investigator shook his head.

'It's infant powder,' she said. 'They use it as a tonic.'

'How's it made?' the investigator asked.

'It's produced by the hospital's Special Nutrition Unit,' she replied.

'From live babies?'

'Yes, live ones. You can hear them crying.'

'Come on, we're off to the hospital.'

She took a cleaver out of the cabinet and handed it to him.

With a laugh, he tossed it onto the table.

That drew a crisp cackle out of the lady trucker, sort of like a laying hen, or a wooden wheel rolling over cobblestones. Then with a smile like that of a bat, she threw herself at him again, wrapped her arms tenderly around his neck, and, with the same tenderness, wrapped her legs around his knees. With a struggle, he managed to pry her off, but she was right back at him, like a bad dream that won't go away. The investigator hopped all over the place, monkey-style, trying to keep away from her.

'Jump on me one more time,' he panted, 'and I'll put a bullet in you!'

Stunned for a moment, she cried out hysterically, 'Go ahead, put a bullet in me! Do it, you ingrate, put a bullet in me!'

She ripped open her blouse, sending a purple Plexiglass button to the floor, where it hit with a crisp *ping* and began rolling around like a tiny animal, first one way, then the other. Whatever force moved it seemed undeterred by the pull of gravity or the friction of the hardwood floor. Stomping on it angrily, the investigator felt it slip around under his foot, tickling him through his sock and thick-soled shoe.

'What kind of person are you? Did Diamond Jin instruct you to do this?' The sentimental attachment the investigator felt for the woman after sex was already dissipating; as his heart began to harden, it turned the color of cold steel. 'If so, then you're a co-conspirator,' he said with a sneer, 'and have eaten infants along with them. Diamond Jin must have ordered you to block my investigation.'

'What an ill-fated woman I am . . .' She began to sob, then cried openly, her face awash with tears, her shoulders heaving. 'Five times I've been pregnant, and each time he's sent me to the hospital in my fifth month for an abortion . . . he ate every one of the aborted fetuses . . .'

Overcome by the grief of despair, she wobbled and was about to topple, when the investigator reached out to steady her; she reacted by falling into his arms and nibbling at his neck. Then she bit him – hard. With a screech of pain, the investigator drove his fist into her belly. She croaked like a frog and crashed to the floor, face up. Her teeth were sharp, as Ding Gou'er knew from experience. He touched his wounded neck and drew back two bloody fingers, while she lay on the floor, eyes open. But as the investigator turned to leave, she rolled over to block his way. 'Dear elder brother!' she wailed. 'Don't leave me, let me kiss you . . .' That gave him an idea: fetching a length of nylon rope from the balcony, he bound her to the chair. Struggling mightily to get free, she screamed:

'Goddamned gigolo, I'll bite the life out of you, you goddamned gigolo!'

The investigator took out a handkerchief, gagged her with it, then ran out as if his life depended on it, slamming the door behind him. Dimly he could hear the chair legs banging against the hardwood floor, and was afraid that the tenacious lady bandit might come after him, chair and all. His flying feet slapped against the concrete stairs, raising a deafening noise. In spite of the fact that the lady trucker lived in a low building, the staircase kept winding and winding, as if leading him down to the depths of Hell. As he was negotiating a bend in the stairs, he ran headlong into an elderly woman coming up the stairs. Her protruding belly felt like a leather sack filled with some sort of liquor; instead of yielding to the pressure, the liquid merely shifted. He then watched as she fell backwards on the steps, frantically waving her stubby arms. Her face was very large and very pale, like a head of cabbage tucked away for the winter. Inwardly cursing his bad luck, the investigator felt a clump of toadstools suddenly sprout in his brain. Hopping down onto the landing, he reached out to help the woman to her feet. She was moaning, her eyes closed, the sound mild yet bleak. Feeling guilty, the investigator bent down and put his arms around her waist to help her up. Not only was she heavy, she wouldn't stop rolling around, and the effort to lift her up swelled the blood vessels in the investigator's head to bursting point. A stabbing pain shot through the spot on his neck where the lady trucker had bitten him. Finally, the old woman cooperated by wrapping her arms around his neck, and together they managed to get her to her feet. But her greasy fingers on his wounded neck caused such excruciating pain that he broke out in a cold sweat. Her breath smelled like rotten fruit, so unbearably foul that he loosened his grip, sending her sprawling back onto the stairs, where she jiggled like a burlap sack filled with mung-bean noodles; she was holding on to his trousers for dear life. Noticing that the backs of her hands glistened with fish scales, suddenly he watched as two fish – one a carp, the other an eel – wriggled out of a plastic bag she'd been carrying. The carp flopped crazily on the stairs, while the eel – yellow face, green eyes, two erect, wiry whiskers – wriggled along stealthily, sluggishly. The water in the sack spilled slowly onto the stairs, soaking one step, then the next. He heard himself ask dryly:

'Are you OK, old lady?'

'I broke my hip,' she replied, 'and tore up my intestines.'

Hearing her describe her injuries in such detail, the investigator knew that a whole lot of trouble was about to come crashing down on his unlucky head once again. He was in a bigger pickle than even that hapless carp; naturally, the carefree eel was infinitely better off than he. His first thought was to get away from this old woman, but instead he bent over and said:

'I'll carry you to the hospital, old auntie.'

The old woman replied:

'My leg's broken, and my kidneys have been damaged.'

He sensed an air of poison swelling in his gut. The carp flopped up onto his shoe. His foot flew, and so did the fish, right into the metal banister.

'You owe me a fish!'

He stomped on the eel as it slithered by.

'I'll carry you to the hospital!' he repeated.

The old woman hung on to his legs for dear life.

'Don't even think about it!'

'Old auntie,' he said, 'your hip's broken, your leg's broken, your intestines are all torn up, and your kidneys have been damaged. If you don't go to the hospital, you'll die right here. Is that what you want?'

'If I do, I'll take you along with me,' the old woman said resolutely. He felt her grip grow more powerful.

The investigator sighed forlornly. Looking down at the stairs and at the two dying fish, then out at the gloomy gray sky beyond the broken window, he didn't know what to do. Just then the strong smell of alcohol drifted in through the window, along with the *clang-clang* of sheet metal being struck. Suddenly chilled to the bone, he longed for a drink.

Grim laughter burst over him and the old woman, then footsteps. The lady trucker was coming downstairs, one baby step at a time, standing up straight and carrying the chair behind her.

He greeted her with an embarrassed laugh. Instead of being alarmed, he was actually happy to see her. Better to be burdened by a young woman than an old one, he was thinking. He smiled. And that smile calmed his mind, as if the sun of hope had just broken through the haze of despair. He noted that she'd already bitten through the handkerchief he'd tied around her mouth, increasing his admiration for the sharpness of her teeth. The chair tied to her body slowed her progress, its rear legs bumping against the stairs with each descending step. He nodded to her, she nodded back. Coming to a stop alongside the old woman, she swung her body like a tiger whipping its tail around, slamming the chair into the woman. He heard her demand ferociously:

'Let him go!'

The old woman looked up and mumbled what sounded like a curse before letting her arms drop. Freed at last, the investigator stepped back to put some distance between him and the old woman.

She said to the old woman:

'Do you know who he is?'

The old woman shook her head.

'He's the Mayor.'

Clambering to her feet, the old woman grabbed the banister and shuddered.

Moved by her plight, the investigator hurried to say:

'I'll take you to the hospital for a checkup, old auntie.'

The lady trucker said:

'Untie me.'

He did, and the chair fell to the floor. As the lady trucker was flexing her arms, the investigator turned and ran. He heard her footsteps behind him.

As he ran out the front door, he caught his sleeve on a waiting bicycle. *Craaash!* The bicycle hit the ground. *Riiiip.* There went his coat. The mishap slowed him down just enough for the lady trucker to lasso him around the neck with her rope. She drew the noose tight and choked the breath right out of him.

She dragged him outside as if he were a dog or some other dumb animal. A steady drizzle falling into his eyes clouded his vision as he reached up to loosen the rope's choke-hold. Something round flew past, scaring the hell out of him. Then he saw a shaven-headed little boy run past, soaked to the skin and covered with mud, as he chased down his football. He cocked his head and pleaded:

'Dear little woman, let me go. I'd hate for anybody to see me like this.'

With a flick of the wrist, she drew the noose even tighter.

'Aren't you good at running?' she said.

'I won't run, I won't, not if my life depended on it.'

'Promise you won't abandon me, that you'll take me with you?'

'I promise, I give you my word.'

She loosened the rope to let the investigator slip his head out of the noose. He was about to give her hell when dulcet sounds emerged from her tender lips:

'You, you're like a little boy. Without me to look after you, you're at the mercy of everyone out there.'

Touched by her words, which sent warm currents swirling through his belly, the investigator welcomed the shower of happiness that settled over him like a spring rain, wetting not only his eyelids, but his eyes as well.

The fine drizzle wove a soft, dense net around the buildings, the trees, everything. He felt her reach out and take hold of his arm, heard a crisp click, and watched a pink umbrella snap open in her other hand and rise above them, covering their heads. As if it were the most natural thing in the world, he put his arm around her waist and took the umbrella from her, like any considerate husband. He wondered where the umbrella had come from, but his suspicions were quickly driven away by happiness.

The sky was so dark and misty, he couldn't tell if it was morning or afternoon. A watch would have helped, but his had been stolen by the little demon. The fine rain beat a light tattoo on the umbrella. It was a sweet but melancholy sound, like a fine French wine – sad, sentimental, anxious, worried. He wrapped his arm more tightly around her, until he could feel her cold, clammy skin under her satin pajamas; there was a gentle squirming in her stomach. Huddled closely together, they walked down the Brewer's College asphalt path between rows of Chinese ilex trees, with their glistening leaves, like the orange nails of pretty girls. Milky white steam carrying the fragrance of burned coal rose from the towering mounds of coal outside the mine. The heavy air pushed back the hideous black smoke trying to force its way out of smokestacks, turning it into black dragons that coiled and writhed in the lowering sky.

They walked together out of the Brewer's College compound and strolled arm-in-arm in the shade of the willow trees on the bank of a little river from which opaque steam and the fragrance of alcohol rose. From time to time, drooping willow branches scraped the nylon shell of the umbrella, sending large drops of rain skittering down across the ribs. The narrow path was covered by drenched golden-yellow leaves. Abruptly the interrogator lowered the umbrella and stared at the green willow branches.

'How long have I been in Liquorland?' he asked.

The lady trucker replied:

'You're asking me? Who do you expect me to ask?'

The investigator said:

'This is no good. I must get to work.'

The corner of her mouth twitched. In a mocking tone, she said:

'Without me, you'll never get to the bottom of anything.'

'What's your name?'

'What is it with you?' she said. 'You've slept with me, and you don't even know my name?'

'Sorry,' he said. 'I asked, but you wouldn't tell me.'

'You never asked me.'

'I sure did.'

'No you didn't.' She kicked him. 'You never asked.'

'OK, OK, I never asked. So I'm asking now.'

'Forget it,' she said. 'You're Hunter and I'm Mickey. We're partners. How's that?'

'Good old partner,' he said, patting her on the waist, 'where do we go now?'

'What do you want to investigate first?'

'A gang of rotten criminals, headed by your very own husband, who kill and eat infants.'

'I'll take you to see someone who knows everything there is to know here in Liquorland.'

'Who?'

'I won't tell you unless you kiss me.'

He gave her a peck on the cheek.

'I'll take you to see the proprietor of Yichi Tavern, Yu Yichi.'

Arm-in-arm they strolled out onto Donkey Avenue under a dark sky; the investigator's gut feeling told him that the sun had already settled behind the mountains – no, it was just then sinking behind them. Drawing upon his imagination, he pictured the fabulous scene: the sun, an enormous red wheel, forced earthward, radiates thousands of brilliant spokes to dress the rooftops, the trees, the faces of pedestrians, and the cobblestones of Donkey Avenue in the tragically valiant colors of a fallen hero. The despot of the Kingdom of Chu, Xiang Yu, stands on the bank of the Wu River, holds his spear in one hand and the reins of his mighty steed in the other as he gazes blankly at the angry waters rushing by. But at this moment there was no sun above Donkey Avenue. Immersed in the enveloping mist, the investigator was mentally engulfed by melancholy and sentimentalism. Suddenly he was struck by the absurdity of his trip to Liquorland – absolutely ridiculous, a ludicrous farce. Floating in the filthy water of a ditch running alongside Donkey Avenue were a rotten head of cabbage, half a clove of garlic, and a hairless donkey tail, silently clumped together and giving off muted rays of green, brown, and blue-gray under the dim streetlights. The investigator mused agonizingly that these three lifeless objects should be taken together as symbols for the flag of a kingdom in decay; even better, they could be carved on his own tombstone. As the sky pressed down, he saw the drizzling rain in the artificial yellow light, like floating threads of silk. The pink umbrella looked like a colorful toadstool. He felt hungry and cold, sensations that erupted into his consciousness after he'd seen the clump of garbage in the roadside ditch. At the same time, he was aware that the seat and cuffs of his trousers were soaked through, his shoes were caked with mud and filling up with water, producing a squishing noise as he walked, like a loach slurping through mud in a riverbed. On the heels of these strange sensations, his arm was frozen numb by the icy coldness of her body, except for his hand, with which he attempted to touch her belly, the source of the sorry rumblings. She was wearing only pink pajamas and a pair of fuzzy bedroom slippers. As she shuffled along, the appearance was not so much of walking as of being carried along by a pair of mangy cats. The long history of men and women, he thought to himself, was actually very much like the history of class struggle: sometimes the men are victorious, sometimes the women, but in the end the victor is also the vanquished. His relationship with this lady trucker, his thoughts continued, was sometimes a game of cat and mouse, while at other times it was a case of two wolves, one with short forelegs, the other with short hind legs, working together. They made love, but they also fought like mortal enemies, the weights of tenderness and ferocity striking a perfect balance. His little thing must be frozen solid, he thought; he also imagined that she was frozen solid. Reaching up to touch one of her breasts, he discovered that something that had once been nice and springy had turned into something as cold and hard as the metal weight on a hand scale, like an unripe banana or an apple stored in an icebox.

'Cold?' His question was patent nonsense, but he forged ahead: 'Why not go to your place. I can carry out my investigation after the weather warms up.'

Her teeth were chattering, but she said stiffly:

'No!'

'I'm concerned that the cold might be too much for you.'

'I said no!'

Holding the hand of his close comrade in arms, Mickey, the crack detective Hunter walked silently down Donkey Avenue on a cold, drizzly autumn night . . . These were the thoughts running through the head of the investigator, like lyrics flashing across the screen in a karaoke bar. He was mighty, Herculean; she was stubborn and intractable, but could be affectionate and passionate when she wanted to be. Donkey Avenue was virtually deserted. Potholes filled with water like frosted glass gave off a dull glimmer. Just how long he'd been in Liquorland he couldn't say, but he'd spent all that time on the periphery of the city; the city itself was a mystery, one that finally beckoned to him on this late night. For the investigator, Donkey Avenue, with its long history, brought to mind the sacred conduit between the legs of the lady trucker. He quickly criticized himself for this objectionable association. He was like a pale adolescent suffering from compulsive behavior, incapable of restraining the shocking metaphor spinning in his head. Wonderful memories fluttered toward him. He was vaguely conscious of the likelihood that the lady trucker was destined to be his true lover, and that his body and hers were already linked by a heavy metal chain. He sensed that he had already foolishly developed feelings for her, which ran the gamut from hate to pity and to fear; this was love.

There were few lights on the street, now that most of the shops were closed. But there were plenty of lights in the compounds behind the shops. Loud, dull noises emerged from one compound after another, and the investigator wondered what the people were doing there. The lady trucker supplied the answer:

'They butcher the donkeys at night.'

In what seemed like a split second, the roadway turned treacherous; the lady trucker slipped and fell hard on her backside. He fell alongside her when he tried to help her up. Together they broke the umbrella, snapped the ribs; she flung it into the ditch, as the drizzle turned into a hailstorm, the air around them suddenly cold and clammy. Chilled air bored through the spaces between his teeth. He pressed her to move on. Donkey Avenue, narrow and gloomy, had become a place of horror, a lair of criminal activity. Hand in hand with his lover, the investigator entered the tiger's lair. He saw the words with extraordinary clarity. A herd of glossy donkeys came down the street toward them, blocking their way at the very moment they spied the large signboard – Yichi Tavern – beneath a red light.

The donkeys were huddled closely together. A rough count revealed twenty-four or twenty-five of the animals, every one of them glossy black, down to the last hair. Drenched by the rain, their bodies glistened. Well fed, with handsome faces, they looked to be quite young. Either to combat the cold or because they detected something frightful in the air of Donkey Avenue, they huddled as closely together as possible. When those in the rear pushed their way deeper into the herd, they invariably forced out some of those in the middle. The sound of their donkey hides scraping together was like prickles jabbing the investigator's skin. The heads of some of the donkeys, he saw, were low; others held their heads high. But every one of them was twitching its floppy ears. They pressed forward, squeezing in and being squeezed out, their hoofs clip-clopping and sliding on the cobblestone road, raising a sound of applause. The herd was like a mountain in motion as it passed in front of them, followed, he saw, by a black youngster hopping along behind them. He noted a distinct resemblance between the black youngster and the scaly youngster who had stolen his things. But as he opened his mouth to shout, the youngster let loose with a piercing whistle so sharp it sliced through the heavy curtain of night and initiated an eruption of braying in the donkey herd. Experience told the investigator that when donkeys brayed they planted their feet and raised their head to focus their energy into the sound. These donkeys, to his surprise, ran as they brayed. A strange, heart-gripping phenomenon. Letting go of the lady trucker's hand, he burst forward, unafraid, determined to get his hands on this donkey-herding youngster; but all he managed to do was crash heavily to the ground, cracking the back of his head on the cobblestones. His ears swelled with a strange buzzing as two huge yellow orbs danced before his eyes.

By the time the investigator regained consciousness, the herd of donkeys and the youngster driving them along were nowhere to be seen. All that remained was the lonely, dreary strip of Donkey Avenue stretching ahead of him. The lady trucker gripped his hand tightly.

'Did you hurt yourself?' she asked, obviously concerned.

'I'm all right.'

'I don't think so. You took quite a fall,' she sobbed. 'You must have a concussion or something.'

Her words brought the realization of a splitting headache. Everything looked like a photographic negative. The lady trucker's hair, her eyes, and her mouth were pale as quicksilver.

'I'm afraid you're going to die . . .'

'I'm not going to die,' he said. 'Why are you trying to jinx me by talking about dying when my investigation is just getting started?'

'Jinx you?' she fired back angrily. 'I said I was afraid you'd die.'

His pounding headache drained any interest he had in keeping up the conversation, and he reached out to touch her face in a conciliatory gesture. Then he rested his arm on her shoulder; like a battlefield nurse, she helped him cross Donkey Avenue. Suddenly, the eyes of a sleek sedan snapped on; stealthily, the car pulled away from the curb, freezing the two of them in its headlights. There was murder in the air – he felt it. He pushed the lady trucker away, but she sprang back and wrapped her arms around him. But there would be no murder, not tonight, because as soon as the sedan moved out into the middle of the street, it sped past, its white exhaust beautiful to behold in the glare of red tail-lights.

They were right in front of the Yichi Tavern, which was brightly lit, as if there were a celebration going on inside.

Standing beside the flower-bedecked front door were two serving girls less than three feet tall. They wore identical red uniforms, sported the same beehive hair style, had nearly identical faces, and wore the same smile. To the investigator, there was something artificial about the twin girls; they looked like mannequins made of plastic or plaster. The flowers between them were so lovely they, too, seemed artificial, their perfection lifeless.

They said:

'Welcome to our establishment.'

The tea-colored glass door flew open, and there in the center of the room, on a column inlaid with squares of glass, he saw an ugly old man being propped up by a grimy woman. When he realized that it was a reflection of him and the lady trucker, he gave up all hope. He was about to turn and leave when a little boy in red hobbled up with amazing speed and said in a tinny voice:

'Sir, Madam, are you here for dinner or just some tea? Dancing or karaoke?'

The little fellow's head barely reached the investigator's knee, so in order to converse, one had to throw his head back, while the other was forced to bend down low. Two heads – one large, the other small – were face to face, with the investigator occupying the commanding position, which helped to lighten his mood. He was struck by the spine-chilling look of evil in the boy's face, despite the benign smile that all tavern service people are trained to effect. Evil of that magnitude is not easy to mask. Like ink seeping through cheap toilet paper.

The lady trucker answered:

'We want to drink, and we want dinner. I'm a friend of your manager, Mr Yu Yichi.'

The little fellow bowed deeply:

'I recognize you, Madam,' he said. 'We have a private room upstairs.'

As the little fellow led the way, the investigator was taken by how much the little creep resembled one of the demons in the classic novel *Monkey*. He even fantasized that the tail of a fox or a wolf was hidden in the crotch of his baggy pants. The polished marble floor made their muddy shoes look especially grimy, rein-stilling feelings of inferiority in the investigator. Out on the dance floor, beautifully decked-out women were dancing cheek-to-cheek with men whose faces glowed with health and happiness. A dwarf in a tuxedo and white bow tie, perched atop a high stool, was playing the piano.

They followed the little fellow up the winding staircase and into a private room, where two tiny serving girls ran up with menus. The lady trucker said:

'Please ask Manager Yu to come up. Tell him Number Nine is here.'

While they waited for Yu Yichi, the lady trucker demonstrated a lack of decorum by taking off her slippers and wiping her mud-caked feet on the spongy carpet. Then she sneezed, loudly, from the effects of the stuffy air. When one of her sneezes wouldn't come, she looked up at the light, squinted, and screwed up her mouth to help it along. The look disgusted the investigator, who was reminded of a donkey in heat when it sniffs the odor of a female donkey's urine.

In one of the between-sneeze lulls, he asked:

'Are you a basketball player?'

'Ah-choo – what?'

'Why Number Nine?'

'I was his ninth mistress, ah-choo –'

II

Dear Mo Yan, Sir

Greetings!

I have passed your message to Mr Yu Yichi, who gleefully replied, 'Now what do you say? I told you he'd write my biography, and that's what he's going to do.' He also said that Yichi Tavern's doors are always open to you. Not long ago, the municipal government earmarked a large sum of money for repairs to Yichi Tavern. It's open twenty-four hours a day, and is richly appointed, lavish and sumptuous. With a modicum of modesty, you might say it's three-and-a-half star quality. Recently they entertained some Japanese, and the little runts went home happy as clams. Their group leader even wrote a piece for The Traveler magazine, in which Yichi Tavern scored very high. So when you come to Liquorland, you can stay at Yichi

Tavern and enjoy untold pleasures without spending a cent.

I had a lot of fun with my chronicle-story 'Yichi the Hero.' In my last letter I said it was my gift to you, to which you can refer when you write his biography. Still, I'm keeping an open mind about what you said. My failing is that I have too rich an imagination, and sometimes I lose control and digress so much I lose sight of the principles of writing fiction. From now on, I'll take your critique to heart, and work like the devil to write fiction worthy of the name.

Sir, I hope with all my heart that you will pack your things soon and come to Liquorland. Anyone who passes up the opportunity to visit Liquorland has wasted his time on this earth. In October we'll hold the first-ever Ape Liquor Festival. It will be a lavish, unprecedented spectacle, with something exciting planned every day for a month. It's not something you'll want to miss. Of course, the second annual festival will be held next year, but it won't be nearly as stirring as the first, or as epochal. My father-in-law has been up in White Ape Mountain, south of the city, living with the apes for three years just so he can learn the secrets of Ape Liquor, and has nearly gone native up there. But that's the only way he'll ever find out how to prepare the stuff, just as there's only one way to write a good novel.

Some years back I came across a copy of that book you want, *Strange Events in Liquorland*, at my father-in-law's place, but I haven't seen it since. I phoned a friend at the Municipal Party Committee's Propaganda Department, and asked him to find a copy for you, no matter what it takes. The little booklet is filled with vicious innuendo, which is all the proof I need that it was written by a modern contemporary. Whether that person is Yu Yichi is open to question. As you said, Yu is half genius, half demon. Here in Liquorland he is both vilified and praised, but because he's a dwarf, few people are willing to engage him in a real 'knives and spears' struggle. That's why nothing seems to bother him, and why he can get away with murder. He's probably taken good and evil about as far as either of them will go. Now, I'm a man of meager talents and limited knowledge, not nearly up to grasping this individual's inner world. There's gold here, just waiting for you to come claim it.

It's been a long time since those stories of mine were submitted to *Citizens' Literature*, and I'd be grateful if you'd give the editors another nudge. At the same time, you're free to invite them to our first annual Ape Liquor Festival. I'll do my best to arrange for their room and board. I'm confident that the generous citizens of Liquorland will make them feel right at home.

Last, but not least, I'm sending you my latest story, 'Cooking Lesson.' Before writing it, Sir, I read virtually everything written by the popular 'neo-realist' novelists, absorbing the essence of their work and adapting it to my own style. I hope you'll send this story to the editors of *Citizens' Literature*, since I firmly believe that by continuing to submit my work to them, sooner or later I'll touch the hearts of this pantheon of gods who spend their days in jade palaces gazing up at the sky to watch the Moon Goddess brush her hair.

Wishing you continued success with your writing, I am

Your disciple

Li Yidou

III

Cooking Lesson, by Li Yidou

Before she went crazy, my mother-in-law was a graceful beauty – even though she was in her middle years. There was a time when I felt she was younger, prettier, and sexier than her daughter, who was my wife. At the time, my wife worked on the special column desk of the *Liquorland Daily News*, where she published some exclusive interviews that drew strong reactions. She was dark and skinny, her hair was yellow and brittle, her face was a rusty brown, and her mouth reeked like stinking fish. By contrast, my mother-in-law was plump, her skin was white and soft, her hair was so black it seemed to ooze oil, and her mouth emitted the fragrance of barbecue the day long. The striking difference between my wife and my mother-in-law, when put side by side, naturally reminded one of the struggle between classes. My mother-in-law was like the well-kept concubine of a big landowner, whereas my wife was like the eldest daughter of an old, dirt-poor peasant. No wonder the hatred between them was so deep seated they didn't speak to each other for three years. My wife would rather sleep out in the newspaper yard than go home. Every time I went to see my mother-in-law, my wife would become hysterical, cursing me with languge unfit to print, as if I were visiting a prostitute, not her own mother.

To tell the truth, in those days, I did indeed harbor vague fantasies over my mother-in-law's beauty, but these evil thoughts, bound up by a thousand steel chains, had absolutely no chance to develop and grow. But then my wife's curses were like a raging fire burning through those chains. So I confronted her:

'If one day I sleep with your mother, you will bear full responsibility.'

'What?' she asked, enraged.

'If you hadn't called my attention to it, I'd have never considered the possibility of someone making love with his own mother-in-law,' I said venomously. 'The only real difference between your mother and me is our ages. We're not related by blood. Besides, recently your own newspaper ran an interesting story about a young man in New York named Jack who divorced his wife and married his mother-in-law.'

My wife let out a scream, her eyes rolled back, and she fainted dead away. I hurriedly splashed a bucket of cool water over her and pricked the area between her nose and upper lip and the spot between her thumb and index finger with a rusty nail. Finally, after half an hour, she came to sluggishly. With staring eyes, she lay in the mud like a stiff, dry log. The shattered lights of despair in her eyes sent chills down my spine. Tears welled up in her eyes and flowed toward her ears. At this moment, I thought, the only thing to do was apologize with all my heart.

Calling her name affectionately, while holding back my disgust, I kissed her nauseatingly stinky mouth, at the same time conjuring up thoughts of her mother's mouth, which always smelled like barbecue. No taste-treat could compare with taking a sip of brandy and kissing her mother's mouth; it would be like washing down fine barbecue with good brandy. Strangely enough, age had not eroded the attraction of youth in that mouth, which was moist and red even without lipstick, and was filled with sweet mountain grape juice. Her daughter's lips, on the other hand, weren't even on a par with the skins of those grapes. In a drawn-out, thin voice, she said:

'You can't fool me. I know you love my mother, not me. You married me only because you fell in love with her. I'm just a stand-in. When you kiss me, you're thinking about my mother's lips. When you're making love with me, you're thinking about my mother's body.'

Her sharp words were like a paring knife that was flaying my skin. In anger I said – I patted her face softly, pulled a long face – and said:

'I'll slap you if you keep spouting that nonsense. You're letting your imagination run wild, you're hallucinating. People would laugh if they saw you. And your mother would explode with anger if she knew what you were saying. I am a Doctor of Liquor Studies; a dignified, imposing man among men. No matter how shameless I might be, I'd never dream of doing something even an animal wouldn't stoop to do.'

She said:

'Yes, you've never done it, but you want to. Maybe you'll never do it as long as you live, but you'll be thinking about it the whole time. If you don't want to do it during the day, you'll want to do it at night. If you don't want to do it when you're awake, you'll want to do it in your dreams. You won't want to do it while you're alive, but you'll want to do it after you're dead.'

I stood up and said:

'That's an insult to me, to your mother, even to yourself.'

212

She said:

'Don't you dare get angry. Even if you had a hundred mouths, and even if those hundred mouths all spat out sweet words at the same time, you'd never succeed in deceiving me. Ai, What's the point in going on? Just to be an obstacle, to be despised by others, to suffer? Why not just die? That would solve everything . . .

'When I die you two can do whatever you want.' With her stumpy little fists, which looked like donkey hooves, she pounded her own breasts. Yes, when she was lying on her back, all that showed on her concave chest were two nipples in the shape of black dates. On the other hand, my mother-in-law's breasts were as full as those of a young woman, showing no signs of withering or sagging. Even when she wore a thick, double-knit sweater, they arched like doughty mountains. The reversal of figure between a mother-in-law and a wife had pushed the son-in-law to the edge of the abyss of evil. How could they blame me? Losing control of myself, I started to scream. I don't blame you, I blame myself. She uncurled her fists and tore at her clothes with a pair of talons; the buttons popped off, exposing her bra. My god! Like a footless person wearing shoes, she was actually wearing a bra! The sight of her scrawny chest forced me to turn away. I said:

'That's enough! Stop this madness. Even if you were to die, there's still your father to worry about.'

She pushed herself up into a sitting position, as terrifying lights shot from her eyes.

'My father is only a front for people like you,' she said. 'He cares about nothing but liquor, liquor liquor liquor! Liquor is his woman. If my father were normal, why would I need to worry so much?'

'I've never seen a daughter like you,' I said, feeling powerless.

'That's why I'm begging you to kill me.' Kneeling on all fours, she banged her bone-hard head on the cement floor and said, 'I'm on my knees begging you, I'm banging my head to implore you. Please kill me, Doctor of Liquor Studies. There's a brand-new stainless-steel knife in the kitchen. It's sharp as the wind. Bring it over and kill me. Please, I beg you, kill me.'

She raised her head and arched her neck, which was long and thin, like that of a plucked chicken; greenish purple, the rough skin was marked by three black moles, and the swollen veins throbbed. Her eyes were rolled halfway up, her lips hung slack, her forehead was covered with dirt through which small drops of blood seeped, and her hair was as matted as a magpie's nest. How could this thing be called a woman? But she was my wife, and to tell the truth, her behavior horrified me. After horror came disgust. Comrades, what could I do? She sneered, her mouth like a tire tread, and I was afraid she was losing her mind. 'My dear wife,' I said, 'the saying goes: "Once a couple, the feelings between two people are deeper than the ocean." We've been husband and wife for many years, so how could I have the heart to kill you? I'd be better off killing a chicken, since then, at least, we could make a pot of soup. But if I killed you, I'd have to eat a bullet. I'm not that stupid.'

With a hand on her own neck, she said softly:

'Are you really not going to kill me?'

'No, I'm not.'

'I think you ought to,' she said, drawing her finger across her throat, as if she were holding the knife that was sharp as the wind. 'Ssst – one light touch, the veins of my neck would open up, and bright, fresh blood would spurt like a fountain. After half an hour, I'd be nothing but a transparent layer of skin. And then,' she continued, a sinister smile on her face, 'you could sleep with that old demon who eats infants.'

'Bull – fucking – shit!' I cursed savagely. Comrades, it wasn't easy for an elegant, refined scholar like me to utter such filth. She drove me to it. I was so ashamed. 'Shit on your mother!' I cursed. 'Why should I kill you? Why would *I* kill *you*? You never let me in on anything good, and now you come to me with something like this. Anyone can kill you, I don't care, as long as it's not me.'

Angrily, I stepped aside. I may not be able to deal with you, I was thinking, but at least I can get away. I picked up a bottle of Red-Maned Stallion and – *glug glug* – poured it down my throat. But I didn't forget to watch her movements out of the corner of my eye. I saw her get up lazily, a smile on her face, and walk toward the kitchen. My heart skipped a beat. Hearing the water running noisily from the tap, I tiptoed over and saw her holding her head under the gushing water. She was gripping the edges of the greasy sink, her body bent at a ninety-degree angle, her upturned backside skinny and lifeless. My wife's backside looks like two slices of dried meat that have been curing for thirty years. I'd never compare those two slices of dried meat with the two orbs of my mother-in-law's derriere. But with those orbs jiggling in my mind, I finally realized that my wife's jealousy was not completely groundless. Snowy white, and obviously cold, the water poured down the back of her head, then crashed loudly like foamy waves. Her hair was transformed into shreds of palm bark coated with opaque bubbles. She was sobbing under the water, sounding like an old hen choking on its food. I was worried she might catch cold. For a brief moment, my heart was filled with sympathy for her. I felt I'd committed a grave crime by tormenting a weak, scrawny woman like that. I went up and touched her back; it was very cold. 'That's enough,' I said. 'Don't torture yourself like this. It doesn't make sense to do things that anger our friends and please our enemies.' She straightened up in a hurry and glared at me with fire in her eyes. She didn't say a word for a good three seconds, frightening me so much I backed off. I saw her snatch the gleaming knife, just bought at a hardware store, from the rack, make a half circle across her chest, aim the point at her neck, and push down.

Without a thought for myself, I rushed up, grabbed her wrist, and wrested the knife out of her hand. I was disgusted by her behavior. 'Damn you, you're ruining my life.' I flung the knife heavily onto the cutting board, burying it at least two fingers deep into the wood; pulling it out would have taken tremendous strength. Then I smashed my fist into the wall, which shook from the force. A neighbor yelled, 'What's going on in there?' I was as enraged as a golden-striped leopard prowling its cage. 'I can't take it any more,' I said. 'I can't fucking go on living like this.' I paced the floor, dozens of times, and concluded that I had no choice but to stay with her. Getting a divorce would be like checking myself in at the crematorium.

'Let's clear things up right now,' I said. 'We'll have your father and mother settle this once and for all. While we're at it, you can ask your mother if anything ever happened between her and me.'

She wiped her face with a towel and said:

'Let's go, then. If you people who have committed incest aren't afraid, I certainly have nothing to fear.'

'Anyone who refuses to go is a goddamned turtle spawn,' I said. She said:

'Right. Anyone who refuses to go is a goddamned turtle spawn.'

Dragging and tugging at each other, we walked toward the Brewer's College. On the way, we ran into a government motorcade welcoming foreign guests. On motorcycles leading the way sat two policemen in brand new uniforms, shiny black sunglasses, and snowy white gloves. We stopped quarreling for a minute and stood like a couple of trees alongside a locust beside the road. The powerful, reeking stench of rotting animals drifted over from the ditch. Her clammy hand was gripping my arm tightly, timidly. I sneered at the foreign guest's motorcade while feeling disgust over her clammy claw. I could see her incredibly long thumb, with green dirt packed under the hard nail. But I didn't have the heart to shrug off her hand, for it was seeking protection, like a drowning person clutching at a straw. Son of a bitch! I cursed. A bald old woman in the crowd moving out of the way of the motorcade turned to look at me. She was wearing a baggy sweater with a row of large white plastic buttons down the front. I experienced gut-wrenching disgust over those large white plastic buttons, feelings that went back to my childhood, when I had a case of the mumps. A smelly nosed doctor whose chest was embellished with large white plastic buttons had touched my cheeks with slimy fingers like octopus tentacles, making me throw up. The woman's big fat head rested heavily on her shoulders, her face was all puffy, her teeth yellow as brass. When she cocked her head to look at me, I shuddered. I was turning to leave when she rushed up to us in short, mincing steps. It turned out she was a friend of my wife. She grabbed my wife's hands affectionately and shook them hard, pressing her heavy torso upward until the two of them seemed about to start hugging and kissing. She was like my wife's mother. So, naturally, I thought about my mother-in-law and about the terrible joke of her having given birth to such a daughter. I walked alone toward Liquorland's Brewer's College; I wanted to ask my mother-in-law if her daughter was an abandoned child she had gotten from an orphanage or if she was switched at birth by nurses at the maternity hospital. And what would I do if that really were the case?

My wife caught up with me. She was giggling as if she'd completely forgotten that she'd tried to cut her own throat only moments before. She said:

'Hey, Doctor, do you know who that old woman was?'

I said I didn't.

'She's the mother-in-law of Section Chief Hu of the Municipal Party Organization Department.'

I snorted.

'What are you snorting about?' she said. 'Stop looking down on people, and considering yourself to be the smartest person in the world. I want you to know that I'm going to be the head of the newspaper's Culture and Life section.'

'Congratulations,' I said, 'new Chief of the Culture and Life section. I hope you'll write an article describing your personal experience in throwing a tantrum.'

She stopped, shocked by my comment. '*I* threw a tantrum? I'm as good as any woman who ever lived. If anyone else knew her husband was playing hanky-panky with her own mother, she'd have already poked a hole in the sky!'

I said, 'Let's hurry up and go ask your father and mother to settle this.'

'I'm such a fool,' she said, standing there as if she'd just awakened from a dream. 'Why should I go with you? Why should I go to see you and that old flirt make eyes at each other? The two of you may be shameless, but not me. There are as many men in this world as there are hairs on a cow's hide, so why should I give a damn about you? You can sleep with whomever you want. I don't care any more.'

She turned and walked away nonchalantly. An autumn wind shook the treetops, sending golden leaves floating silently to the ground. My wife was walking among the poetry of autumn, her dark back making an uncanny connection with the notion of delicacy. Surprisingly, her nonchalance provoked a slight sense of loss in me. My wife's name was Beauty Yuan. Beauty Yuan and the falling leaves of autumn formed a melancholic lyrical poem, producing a bouquet like the General Lei liquor from Yantai's

Zhangyu Distillery. I stared at her, but she didn't turn around, a case of 'pursuing justice without looking back.' In truth, I may have been hoping she would look back, but the chief-to-be of the Culture and Life section of the *Liquorland Daily News* never did. She was going off to her new position. Chief Beauty Yuan. Chief Yuan. Chief.

The chief's back disappeared among the red-walled, white-tiled buildings of Seafood Alley, from which a cluster of spotted doves fluttered into the blue sky, where three large yellow balloons floated, dragging bright red ribbons embroidered with big white letters. A man stood there in a daze. It was me, Doctor of Liquor Studies, Li Yidou. Li Yidou, you're not going to jump into the roiling, liquor-laced Liquan River, are you? No, why should I? My nerves were as tough as a cowhide that's been tanned with caustic soda and Glauber's salt, neither to be worn down nor torn to shreds. Li Yidou, Li Yidou, striding forward with his head held high, his chest thrown out, in an instant he had walked into the Brewer's College and was standing in front of his mother-in-law's door.

I really needed to get to the bottom of things. Maybe I'd have a fling with my mother-in-law – which, in fact, she might not be. It would be an ocean-draining upheaval in my personal life, no doubt about that. A note was posted on the door:

'This morning's cooking lesson will be held in the lab at the Gourmet Section.'

I had long heard that my mother-in-law, with her superior cooking skills, was the shining star of the Culinary Academy, but I'd never seen her in class. Li Yidou decided to attend his mother-in-law's class, to witness his mother-in-law's awe-inspiring stature.

I walked through the small rear gate of the Brewer's College and entered the campus of the Culinary Academy. The fragrance of liquor still lingered, the aroma of meat now permeated the air. In the courtyard, many strange and exotic flowers and trees, with their eyelike leaves, squinted at me, Doctor of Liquor Studies, an ignoramus where plants are concerned. A dozen or so campus cops in blue uniforms moved about lazily in the yard, but when they saw me, their spirits were invigorated, like hounds spotting their quarry. Their ears, like thin pancakes, stood straight up, heavy snorts escaped from their nostrils. But I wasn't afraid of them, for I knew they'd return to their lazy former selves as soon as I spoke my mother-in-law's name. The structure of the campus was very intricate, similar to Suzhou's Rustic Statesman Garden. A gigantic rock the color of pig's liver stood in the middle of the path for no obvious reason, with an inscription in yellow that read, 'Graceful Rock Points to the Sky.' After receiving permission from the campus cops, I strolled around until I found the Gourmet Section, then walked past row after row of iron railings, passing the exquisite building for raising meat boys, passing artificial hills and a fountain, passing the training room for exotic birds and strange animals, and finally entering a dark cave that led to a luminous spot. It was a restricted area. A young lady handed me some work clothes. She said, 'Your people are videotaping the associate professor,' mistaking me for a reporter from the local TV station. As I was putting on the cone-shaped hat, I detected the fresh smell of soap. Just then, the woman recognized me. 'Your wife, Beauty Yuan, and I were high-school classmates. Back then my grades were much better than hers, but now she's a famous reporter, while I'm a lowly doorkeeper,' she said, dejectedly, looking at me with resentment in her eyes, as if I were the one who had cut short her promising future. I nodded apologetically, but her sad face immediately turned proud. 'I have two sons,' she boasted, 'both smart as whips.' I replied viciously, 'Don't you plan to send them to the Gourmet Section?' Her face turned purple, and since the last thing I wanted was to look at another purple-faced woman, I headed over toward the lab. I could hear her grind her teeth as she cursed, 'One of these days, someone will give you cannibalistic beasts exactly what you deserve.'

The doorkeeper's comment sent shock waves through my heart. Who were those cannibalistic beasts? Was I one of them? I thought back to what the Liquorland dignitaries had said when the famous dish was being served: What we're eating is not human, but a gourmet dish prepared with special techniques. The creator of this gourmet dish was my beautiful mother-in-law, who was now lecturing to her students in a spacious, well-lit lecture hall. She was standing at the podium, framed by bright lamplight. I could see her large, round, moonlike face, which was as smooth and brilliant as a china vase.

Reporters were indeed videotaping her lecture. One of them, surnamed Qian, a fellow with a pointy mouth and monkey cheeks, was director of the special newspaper column. I'd drunk at the same table as him once. With a video camera on his shoulder, he was sauntering back and forth in the lecture hall. His assistant, a short, pale, fat fellow carrying lights and dragging black cords, followed Qian's orders to aim the white-hot lights, sometimes on my mother-in-law's face, sometimes on the chopping board in front of her, and sometimes on the students who were concentrating on her lecture. I found a vacant seat and sat down, feeling the tender, loving rays from her big grayish-brown eyes stop on my face for a couple of seconds. Slightly embarrassed, I lowered my head.

Five words carved deeply into the desk leaped into my eyes, 'I WANT TO FUCK YOU.' Like five rocks dropped into my mind, they created surging waves. I felt my body go numb; like a frog given electric shocks, my limbs trembled, whereas a certain spot in the center began to stir ... My mother-in-law's well-paced, pleasant talk, like tidal waves, rushed up closer and closer, wrapping my body in a giant warm current and sending spasms of excitation surging up and down my spine, faster and faster ...

... Dear students, has it ever occurred to you that, owing to the rapid development following the four modernizations and the constant upping of people's living standards, eating is no longer simply something to fill one's stomach, but an esthetic appreciation? Hence, cooking is not simply a skill, but is also a profound art. A master chef these days needs hands more dextrous than a surgeon, a sense of color keener than a painter, a nose sharper than a police dog, and a tongue more sensitive than a snake. A chef embodies a blending of all the arts. Concomitant with this, the standards of gourmet diners are rising. Diners have expensive tastes, they like new things and despise old stuff, wanting one thing in the morning and changing their minds in the evening. It is extremely hard to please their taste buds. But we must study hard to produce new dishes that satisfy their needs. This is closely tied to the prosperity of Liquorland and, of course, to the bright future of every one of you here. Before we begin today's lecture, I want to recommend a special, rare dish to you –

Picking up an electronic pen, she wrote two words on the magnetic board with a flourish: STEAMED PLATYPUS. She turned sideways to face the students as she wrote, polite and charming. Then she threw down the pen and pushed a button under the podium, causing a cloth screen to pull back slowly, the way a general pushes a button to reveal a battle map. Behind the screen was a large water tank in which several small platypuses with glossy fur and webbed feet swam nervously. She said, Now I'm going to give you the ingredients and the actual cooking procedures, so please take notes. This ugly little animal embarrassed the learned and erudite Engels, our great proletarian leader, for it was an aberrant phenomenon in evolution, the only known mammal that lays eggs. The platypus is the one truly exotic animal. So we must take exceptional care during cooking, in order not to waste such a rare animal with a procedural mistake. Therefore, I suggest that, before we make platypus, we should practice on turtles. Now, let me give you the actual cooking method:

Take a platypus, kill it and hang it upside down for about an hour to drain the blood. Please note that you should use a silver knife and cut from under its mouth to make sure the point of entry is as small as possible. After draining the blood, put the platypus in water heated to 75 degrees Celsius to strip the hide. Then carefully remove the innards, the liver, the heart, and the eggs (if there are any). Use special care when removing the liver, making sure you don't puncture the gallbladder. Otherwise the platypus will become inedible and useless. Take out the intestines and turn them inside out to clean thoroughly with salt water. Then wash the mouth and feet with boiling water, rub off the rough shell over the beak and the rough skin between the toes. Make sure to keep the webbing between toes intact. After cleaning, lightly cook the innards in hot oil and stuff them inside the platypus. For sauce, add salt, garlic, shredded ginger, chili pepper, sesame oil – remember not to use any MSG – and slowly cook over a low fire until it turns dark red and gives off a peculiar odor. If the situation permits, sauté the eggs and innards together, then stuff them back inside the platypus. If there are larger, better-formed eggs, you can make them into a separate gourmet dish by following the recipe for braised turtle eggs.

After introducing the recipe for platypus, she brushed back her hair, like one of the nation's top leaders preparing to make an important announcement, and stared at the students, who, in turn, felt her warm gaze touch their faces. I sensed that my mother-in-law had touched my soul. With great seriousness, she said, Now we move on to the cooking methods for braised baby. I felt as if a rusted awl had been driven through my heart, and currents of cold liquid poured into my chest, where they congealed and pressed against my organs, putting me on tenterhooks, while sticky, cold sweat seeped into the palms of my hands. Every one of her students' faces turned red, excitement accelerating the beating of their hearts. Like a group of medical-school students performing their first dissection of human genitalia, they feigned nonchalance, but their efforts were wasted – excitement was revealed by twitching muscles on their cheeks and nervous coughs. My mother-in-law said, This is the Culinary Academy's pride and joy. We cannot give everyone an opportunity for hands-on practice, because the ingredient is so difficult to come by and so incredibly expensive. I'll show you the procedure in detail, and you must watch attentively. At home you can use a monkey or piglet as a substitute.

She first stressed that a chef's heart is made of steel and that a chef should never waste emotions. Rather than being human, the babies we are about to slaughter and cook are small animals in human form that are, based upon strict, mutual agreement, produced to meet the special needs of Liquorland's developing economy and prosperity. In essence, they are no different than the platypuses swimming in the tank waiting to be slaughtered. Please put your minds at ease, and do not let your imagination run wild. You must recite to yourselves a thousand times, ten thousand times: They are not human. They are little animals in human form. Gracefully she picked up a switch and banged it several times against the tank: In essence they are no different than platypuses.

She picked up the phone on the wall and barked a command into the receiver. Then she put down the phone and said to the students: This, of course, is a famous dish that one day will shock the world, so we cannot tolerate the slightest carelessness in the creative process. Generally speaking, the emotional pressure an animal experiences before being slaughtered affects the amount of glycogen in the meat, which in turn decreases the quality of the finished product. Therefore, an experienced butcher always prefers ending the animal's life with lightning speed, in order to improve the quality of the meat. In comparison with average domesticated animals, meat boys are more intelligent, so we must try everything possible to maintain their happy spirit, thus preserving the quality of the main ingredient of this famous dish. The traditional method of slaughtering was to brain them with a club, but this method bruises the soft tissues and can even smash the skull, thereby affecting the appearance of the finished product. It has gradually been replaced by anesthetization with ethanol. The Brewer's College has just distilled a new liquor that is sweet and not too strong, but has an unusually high alcoholic content, which is perfect for our purposes. Experience has shown that anesthetizing the meat boys with alcohol before slaughtering reduces the milk odor that used to be the most troublesome aspect of the cooking process, and lab tests have shown that the nutritional value of anesthetized meat boys increases dramatically. Once again she reached for the receiver on the wall, and said:

Send it in.

That's all my mother-in-law said, and without fanfare; five minutes later, two young women in snowy white hospital gowns and square caps carried a naked meat boy into the lecture hall in a specially designed gurney. The women would have been considered good looking, but their pale faces made me squirm. They set the gurney on the chopping block, then stepped aside, their arms hanging down stiffly. My mother-in-law bent over to inspect the pink meat boy, poked him in the chest with a soft, dainty index finger, and nodded with satisfaction. Then she stood up to remind the students one more time, with great solemnity: You must never ever forget that this is just a little animal in human form. She'd barely gotten the words out when the little animal in human form on the gurney rolled over. The students let out a suppressed gasp. Everyone, myself included, thought the little guy was about to sit up; fortunately he didn't. He simply rolled over and spread his sweet, even snores all over the lecture hall. His round, chubby, bright pink face was turned toward the students, and, naturally, me. What we saw was a beautiful, healthy little boy with black hair, long eyelashes, a tiny nose like a clove of garlic, and a little pink mouth. His pink lips were smacking slightly, as if he were sucking on candy in his dream. My wife and I had been married for three years, but we had no children. I adored them, and had the urge to run up to the chopping block at the front of the lecture hall and scoop up this little guy, then kiss his face and his belly button, touch his little pecker, and bite his cute little feet. They were pudgy feet, with meaty folds where they joined his legs. From the looks on the students' faces, particularly the dazed, mesmerized females, I could tell that they were experiencing the tender warmth of love for the little guy. For that reason, my mother-in-law's voice, which had turned cold, reverberated in the lecture hall again, overwhelming the little guy's even snores. Let me make it clear to you. You must eradicate all the unhealthy emotions in your hearts. Otherwise, we cannot continue with this lecture. Grasping his arm, she turned him 180 degrees, until he was facing the platypuses in the glass tank and showing us his little butt. My mother-in-law poked him and said, He's not human, not human at all.

As if to protest her comment, the little guy released a mighty fart that was totally inconsistent with the size of his body. The students, slightly fazed, gaped at each other for about fifteen seconds, before laughter erupted in the hall. My mother-in-law tried to keep her face taut, but couldn't do it. Finally, she too was laughing along with the students.

She banged the table, trying to still the laughter. She said, These little things have all kind of tricks. The students were about to laugh again, but she stopped them. No more laughter. This is the most important lesson in your four years of college. As long as you can command the skill of cooking meat boys, you'll never have to worry about a thing, no matter where you go. Don't you all want to go abroad? So long as you can handle this superior dish, it's as good as holding a permanent visa in the palm of your hand. You can conquer the foreigners, be they Yanks, Krauts, or whatever.

Her words apparently hit home, for they renewed their concentration, every one of them holding a pen in one hand and pressing down a notebook with the other, eyes fixed on my mother-in-law. The meat boy is sleeping so soundly, she said, he'll be blissfully unaware of anything we do. Not a hint of protest. With a wave of her hand, she summoned the two women in white, who had been standing in the corner awaiting her command. They came over to help lift up the meat boy and place him in a specially designed rack shaped like a birdcage, on top of which was a hook connected to a suspended ring. With the help of the two women in white, the cage-like rack was hoisted into the air. The meat boy lay in his caged prison, one white, pudgy little foot sticking out from under the rack; it was a lovely sight. My mother-in-law explained, The first step is to drain the blood. But I must tell you that, for a while, some comrades believed that keeping the blood made the meat boy taste better and raised his nutritional value. Their theory was based upon the Korean practice of never making a cut to drain the blood when they cook dog meat. But after repeated tests and comparisons, we have concluded that a meat boy tastes much better and is tenderer when his blood is drained. It is a simple procedure: the more blood you drain from a meat boy, the better his color will be. When a meat boy's blood is not completely drained, the finished product will have a dark color and a pungent odor. Therefore, you must not treat this phase lightly. My mother-in-law reached out and grabbed the foot hanging down from the rack with her left hand; the little boy babbled something or other. The students' ears all pricked up as they tried to figure out what he wanted to say. My mother-in-law said, We must choose the right place to cut to ensure the completeness of the meat boy. Generally we cut the bottom of a foot to expose an artery, which we then sever to induce the flow of blood. As she was talking, a glistening knife shaped like a willow leaf materialized in her right hand and was aimed at the meat boy's little foot . . . Nervously closing my eyes, I thought I heard the little guy cry out loud on the rack as desks and chairs in the hall began to bang against each other. With a mighty howl, the students stormed out of the hall. But when I opened my eyes, I realized it was all in my head. The meat boy didn't cry, didn't scream, and there was already an opening on his foot. In a strangely beautiful manner, a string of bright red drops of blood like gemstones hung down to merge with a glass jar under his foot. The lecture hall was unusually quiet. All the students – male and female – their eyes bulging, were staring at the meat boy's foot and the string of blood that hung from it. The camera from the local TV station was also trained on the foot and the blood beneath it, which sparkled in the bright lights. Gradually I heard the students' heavy breathing, deep like the swelling tide, and the clear, crisp, ear-pleasing sounds of blood dripping into the jar, like a creek flowing through deep ravines. My mother-in-law said, The meat boy's blood will be completely drained in about an hour and a half. The second step is to remove the innards while keeping them intact. The third step is to loosen the hair with water heated to 70 degrees . . . I really don't feel like describing my mother-in-law's actual cooking lesson, which was boring and nauseating at the same time. Since night was falling, Doctor of Liquor Studies' brain, which was full of wonderful ideas, and stimulated by alcohol, had to concentrate on creating a story entitled 'Swallows' Nests' instead of wasting his talent on a banquet for cannibals.

Chapter Seven

I

The lady trucker's comment knifed into the investigator's heart. He pressed his hand against his breast like a love-struck teenager and bent over in agony. He saw her pink feet, which were livelier than her hands, rubbing back and forth across the carpet. His heart was inundated with a wicked passion. Clenching his teeth, he cursed – 'Slut!' – before turning and striding toward the door. He heard a shout thud into his back: 'Where do you think you're going, you whoremonger? Who the hell do you think you are, bullying a woman that way?' He kept walking. A sparkling drinking glass whizzed past his ear, bounced off the door, and landed on the carpet. Turning to look back, he saw her standing there, thrusting her chest out and breathing heavily, moisture glistening in her eyes. Beset by mixed emotions, he struggled to keep his voice under control: 'How could you be so shameless as to sleep with a dwarf? Was it for money?' She burst into tears, sobbing and sobbing, until suddenly she raised her voice, hoarse yet shrill, setting the metal decorations of the frosted-glass hanging lamps tinkling loudly. She tore open her blouse, began pounding her breasts, scratching her face with her fingernails, tearing her hair, and smashing her head against the cream-colored wall. In the midst of her frenzied self-abuse, she shrieked hysterically, nearly bursting the investigator's eardrums:

'Get out – get out – get the hell out –'

The investigator was scared witless. Nothing like this had ever happened to him before. He felt as if the Angel of Death were rubbing his nose with its cold hand and red-painted nails. Spurts of urine ran down his leg. He knew how inelegant, not to mention uncomfortable, it was to be pissing his pants, yet he couldn't help himself. It was all that kept him from falling apart. But even as he was pissing his pants, he experienced the joy of shedding an enormous emotional burden. Voice cracking with emotion, he said:

'Don't do that . . . please, I beg you . . .'

Unmoved by his plea or by his loss of bladder control, the lady trucker forged ahead with her self-abuse and loud wails. As she banged her head with increased vigor, the wall protested loudly, until it seemed inevitable that it would soon be splattered with her brains. The investigator ran over and threw his arms around her waist, only to have her straighten up and break his grip. Now she changed tactics: instead of banging her head against the wall, she began tearing at the back of her hands with her teeth, as if gnawing on a pig's foot. She was really digging in, not play-acting, for soon her hands were a bloody mess. The investigator, in an act of desperate futility, fell weakly to his knees and began knocking his head on the floor in supplicating kowtows.

'Dear woman,' he said. 'Does that help, calling you dear woman? My dearest woman, don't be offended by someone as worthless as I. Be forgiving, like a wise and tolerant prime minister. Pretend that what you heard was a fart, a loud, stinky fart.'

Surprisingly, that did the trick. She stopped chewing the backs of her hands, closed her eyes, opened wide her mouth, and bawled like a baby. The investigator straightened up. Then, like something right out of the movies, he started slapping his own face – hard – first one cheek, then the other, berating himself as he did:

'I'm not human, I'm a bastard, a bandit, a hooligan, a dog, a wriggly maggot in a vat of shit. Smack, I'll smack you to death, you lousy son of a bitch . . .'

The first few slaps stung, but by the fourth or fifth one, it was about the same as hitting a piece of cowhide – no pain, no sting, just numbness. Several slaps more, and even that disappeared, leaving only the horrible, loud smack, as if he were slapping the carcass of a debristled hog or the ass of a dead woman. And he kept it up, one vicious slap after another, gradually feeling an odd sense of pleasure from this act of self-vengeance. At some point, he stopped berating himself, and the energy conserved by not speaking was transferred to his hand, increasing the force of each slap and turning up the volume of the resounding smacks. He watched as her mouth closed and the wails died out; she watched his performance as if in a trance. The investigator was pleased with himself. So after a few more vicious slaps, he dropped his hands. He heard a commotion on the other side of the door. Very tentatively, he asked:

'You're not mad at me any more, are you, young lady?'

She didn't move. With staring eyes, a gaping mouth, and an expression that sent shivers through the investigator, she simply stood there like a malevolent statue. Slowly he got to his feet and began to sweet-talk the woman, masking the anger in his heart, as he edged toward the door. 'Don't be mad at me anymore, please don't be mad. I've always had a filthy mouth, as filthy as any asshole. My mouth has always gotten me into trouble, and nothing I do seems to help.' His backside brushed against the door. 'You didn't deserve that, and I apologize with all my heart.' He applied pressure on the door with his backside. It creaked loudly. 'I'm the lowest of the low, a disgusting creature, I mean it,' he mumbled as a cool breeze brushed against his back. Giving her one last look, he slipped through the narrow opening and let the door close behind him. With her now on the other side, he ran toward the far end of the corridor without a second thought; but halfway there he was met by a neatly dressed little man rushing along behind a tiny serving girl. With a long stride he virtually leaped over both short people's heads, ignoring the girl's frightened shriek. Finally reaching the end of the corridor, he turned the corner and pushed open a greasy door, where he was greeted by a potpourri of smells – sweet, sour, bitter, spicy – and a cloud of hot steam that swallowed him up. A bunch of little men were rushing around in the steamy room, coming in and out of view as they bustled about like a covey of little sprites. Some, he saw, were carving, others were plucking hairs and feathers, yet others were washing dishes, and others still were mixing ingredients. Chaotic at first appearance, there was a distinct sense of order there. He tripped over something, and discovered it was a string of frozen donkey vaginas. He immediately thought of Dragon and Phoenix Lucky Together and the all-donkey banquet. Several of the little kitchen helpers stopped what they were doing to size him up with curious looks. Backing quickly out of the room, he turned and ran until he spotted a staircase, which he descended, guiding himself along by holding on to the banister. When he heard a woman's heart-stopping scream, what was left in his bladder ran down his leg. Deathly silence followed that single scream, and an unhappy thought flashed through his mind. 'To hell with her!' Without a thought for the gaily dressed boys and girls dancing nimbly across a dance floor laid with Laiyang Red marble, and unavoidably shattering the beautiful rhythms of the dance music, like a whipped, mangy dog smelling of rancid piss, he crashed through the main hall of Yichi Tavern, a place noted for scenes of debauchery.

Only after hotfooting it into a darkened little lane did it dawn on him that the twin dwarfs in the doorway were so surprised and frightened by his passage that they screeched bloody murder. Leaning against the wall to catch his breath, he looked back at the bright lights of Yichi Tavern. A neon sign over the door kept changing color, turning the slanting raindrops red, then green, then yellow; meanwhile, he was aware that he was standing in the cold rain of an autumn night, leaning up against a frigid stone wall. Only the walls of a cemetery could be that cold, he was thinking. After all the misfortunes that had tied him inextricably to Liquorland, if tonight could not count as an escape from the jaws of death, at the very least he'd made it out of the tiger's lair. Strains of lovely music from Yichi Tavern drifted over on the wind and faded out in the night air. As he strained to listen to the music, pangs of sorrow touched his heart and chilled tears of self-pity spilled from his eyes. For a brief moment he fancied himself to be a little prince in distress; but there was no princess to rescue him. The air was cold and damp; his aching hands and feet told him that the thermometer had dropped below zero. Liquorland's weather had abruptly turned cruel and unfeeling; the raindrops froze on their way down, splintering when they hit the ground, then skittering around to form slicks all over the street. A solitary automobile slid and skidded its way along a distant roadway illuminated by streetlights. The memory of a herd of black donkeys running up Donkey Avenue returned like an ancient dream. Had it really happened? Does such a bizarre lady trucker truly exist?

Has an investigator by the name of Ding Gou'er really been sent to Liquorland to investigate a case of child-eating? Is there even such a person as Ding Gou'er? If so, is that really me? He rubbed the wall with his hand; it was icy cold. He stomped the ground with his foot; it was hard as a rock. He coughed; pains shot through his chest. The sound of his cough carried far into the distance before being swallowed up by the darkness. This proved that it was all real, and the oppressive feelings lingered on.

The icy raindrops falling on his cheek were refreshing, like an itch being scratched by a kitten's claws. He sensed that his face must be burning up, which reminded him of his shameless face-slapping exhibition. Feelings of numbness returned, then a stinging sensation. The numbness and the stinging sensation were followed by thoughts of the lady trucker's hideous face, which swayed back and forth in front of his eyes and wouldn't go away. Her hideous face was replaced by a lovely one, which also swayed back and forth in front of his eyes and wouldn't go away. Then came the image of the lady trucker and Yu Yichi, side by side, and after that feelings of anger and jealousy, side by side, merging like a strange, inferior liquor that began to poison his soul. As his mind cleared, he realized that the unthinkable had occurred: He'd fallen in love with the woman, and now their lives were bound together like a pair of locusts on a string.

The investigator pounded the stone wall of the cemetery or the martyrs' shrine, or whatever it was, with his fist. 'Slut!' he cursed. 'Slut! Rotten slut! A rotten slut who'll drop her pants for a dollar!' The searing pain in his knuckles lessened the ache in his heart, so he doubled up his other fist and drove it into the stone wall. Then it was his head's turn.

A powerful beam of light trapped him. A pair of patrolmen asked sternly:

'What do you think you're doing?'

He turned around slowly and shielded his eyes with his hand. Suddenly his tongue froze and he lost the power to speak.

'Search him.'

'What for? He's nuts.'

'Knock that off, you hear me?'

'Go on home. Any more of that and we'll take you in.'

The patrolmen walked off, leaving the investigator surrounded by inky blackness. He was cold and hungry. He had a splitting headache. The darkness brought him back to his senses, the patrolmen's brief interrogation reminded him of his glorious past. Who am I? I'm Ding Gou'er, a famous investigator of the provincial Higher Procuratorate. Ding Gou'er is a middle-aged man who has rocked and rolled in brothels, so he has no business going ga-ga over a woman who's slept with a dwarf. That's absurd! he grumbled as he took out his handkerchief to stop the flow of blood from his forehead and spat out several mouthfuls of bloody saliva. If news of my ridiculous behavior made it back to the Procuratorate, my brothers there would die laughing. He reached down to see if that critical piece of metal was still there; it was, and he felt much better. Time to go find some lodging for some food and a good night's sleep, then back to work tomorrow. I won't rest till I have this gang by the tails. Forcing himself to walk straight ahead, without turning back for a last look, he left the Yichi Tavern and its demonic activities behind him.

The investigator had barely started walking down the dark lane when his feet flew out from under him and he fell backward, banging his head loudly on the cold, slippery ground. Climbing slowly to his feet, he set out again, staggering and reeling with each step he took on the rugged, icy terrain; it was the most treacherous footing he'd experienced. When he turned to glance behind him, the bright lights of Yichi Tavern filled his eyes and stabbed at his heart. Like a wild animal brought down by a hunter's rifle, he fell to the ground with a moan; blue flames burned inside his brain, hot blood rushed to his head and swelled his skull until it seemed about to pop, like an over-inflated balloon. The forces of agony pried open his mouth; he felt like howling, but as soon as the first howl broke from his throat, it rolled and rumbled atop the stones in the roadway like a wooden-wheeled water-wagon. Prompted by the rumbling sound, his body began to roll around on the ground uncontrollably, first chasing the wooden wheels, then rolling out of the way so they wouldn't crush him, then being transformed into a wooden wheel and fastening itself to other wooden wheels; as he rumbled along with those other wooden wheels, he could see the street, the wall, trees, people, buildings

. . . all turning round and round, over and over, in an endless revolution, from 0° to 360°. During his tumbling performance, a sharp object jabbed him painfully in the waist. The pistol. Taking it out of his waistband, he wrapped his hand around the familiar handle, and his heart began beating wildly, as past glories flooded into his mind. Ding Gou'er, how could you have fallen so low? Rolling around in the dirt like a common drunk. You've turned into a pile of urban garbage, and all for the sake of a woman who's slept with a dwarf. Is it worth it? No, it isn't! Get up, stand on your own two feet, show a little dignity! His head spun as he propped himself up with his hands. The bright lights of Yichi Tavern were very seductive. One glimpse of those bright lights ignited green flames in his brain, snuffing out the light of rationality. He turned away from those evil lights, which illuminated drug use and carnal indulgence, and shone down on monstrous crimes, as powerfully seductive as a whirlpool, while he was but a single blade of grass on the edge of that whirlpool. He gouged the tender flesh of his thigh with the muzzle of his pistol, hoping to drive away the fanciful thoughts with sharp pain. On his feet again, he walked slowly into the darkness, groaning with each step.

The narrow lane seemed to go on forever. There were no lights to show the way, but dim starlight at least lent form to the walls alongside him. Snow and rain fell more heavily in the dark night, accompanied by a soft, heart-warming rustle that hinted at pine and cypress beyond the walls, and symbolized the ghosts of individuals sacrificed over the years in this place. If tens of thousands could be martyred for the good of the people, is there any form of suffering the living cannot cast aside? By paraphrasing this famous line by Mao, the pain in his heart abated a bit. The lights of Yichi Tavern had been swallowed up behind several layers of buildings, the lane sandwiched between two stone walls had been swallowed up by his tangled thoughts; time passed inexorably, the dark night pressed onward through the icy rain and the rustlings; the barely discernible barking of a dog somewhere added to the sense of mystery in this town in the darkness of night. Without being aware of it, he emerged from the small cobblestone lane, and was greeted by the hiss of a gas lamp up ahead. He headed straight for it, like a moth drawn to the light.

A portable stand selling wonton was framed in the halo of lamplight; flashes of gold leaped from an oven where kindling crackled and popped, and sent burning cinders into the air; he detected the odor of charred beans and heard the gurgling of wonton boiling in a pot. Its fragrance tugged at his soul. He couldn't begin to calculate how long it had been since he'd last eaten, but his coiling intestines complained loudly, and his legs were too rubbery to support him any longer. He shuddered, cold sweat dotted his forehead, and he collapsed face-down in front of the wonton stand.

As the old wonton peddler was picking him up by the arms, he said:

'Gramps, I need some wonton.'

The old fellow sat him down on a campstool and handed him a bowl of wonton. Grabbing the bowl and the spoon, and not caring whether it was hot or cold, he wolfed it down. But with one bowlful nestling in his stomach, his sense of hunger was stronger than ever. Even four bowlfuls failed to satisfy his hunger, but when he looked down, some of the wonton cut loose from his stomach and made the return trip.

'More?' the old fellow asked.

'No more. What do I owe you?'

'No need to ask,' the old fellow answered with a sympathetic look in his eyes. 'If it's convenient, you can give me four cents. If not, just count it as my treat.'

Stung by the patronizing reply, the investigator fantasized that he had a crisp new hundred-dollar bill in his pocket, its edges sharp as a razor, which he would flick with his finger to make it snap, then fling it at the old man, before flashing him a superior look, turning on his heels, and walking off whistling, the sound slicing through the vast night like a dagger, teaching the old man a lesson he'd never forget. Unhappily, the investigator was broke. When he wolfed down the wonton, he simultaneously wolfed down his embarrassment and awkwardness. One piece after another, the wonton rose from the investigator's stomach, only to be chewed up and sent back down. Now, finally, he could taste them. With a sense of deep sadness, he thought, I've turned into an animal that chews its cud. Anger welled up as he recalled the scaly little demon who had stolen his wallet, wristwatch, cigarette lighter, papers, and electric shaver; recalled the oily Diamond Jin; recalled the bizarre lady trucker; recalled the celebrated Yu Yichi. And as he recalled Yu Yichi, he envisioned the lady trucker's firm, voluptuous body, and the green flames of jealousy burned anew. Hurriedly he extracted himself from these dangerous recollections and returned to the awkward scenario of having eaten a vendor's wonton without being able to pay for it. For a measly four cents, I've descended to the level of a beggar. A hero brought low by a few coins. He turned his pockets inside-out – no money, not a cent. His shorts and T-shirt were both hanging from the chandelier in the lady trucker's place, which he'd fled like a rat running from danger. The cold night air chilled him to the bone. With nowhere to turn, he took out his pistol and laid it gently in a white ceramic bowl with blue flowers. Light glinted off the blue steel barrel. He said:

'Gramps, I'm an investigator sent down by the province. I ran into some bad people who stole everything I had, all except for this pistol. This ought to prove I'm not someone who goes around eating food without paying for it.'

The old fellow, slightly flustered, picked up the bowl with both hands.

'A man of action,' he said eagerly, 'a real man of action. It's my good fortune that you've chosen *my* wonton. Now please take this thing back, it scares me.'

After retrieving his pistol, Ding Gou'er said:

'Old fellow, since you only wanted four cents, you must have known I was penniless. Supplying me with all the wonton I could eat, even though you knew I was penniless, can only mean that you took me for a bad person who could put you out of business if he felt like it. You didn't serve me that wonton because you wanted to, and I can't let this misunderstanding go unchecked. Here's what we'll do. I'll leave my name and address, and if you ever find yourself in a pickle, look me up. Do you have a pen?'

'I'm an illiterate old wonton peddler. Why would I have a pen?' the fellow said. 'Besides, Boss, I know you're an important person, here on an undercover assignment. You don't need to leave your name and address. All I ask is that you spare my life.'

'Undercover assignment? Bullshit! I'm the unluckiest man alive. And I'm going to find a way to pay for that wonton, come hell or high water. Tell you what . . .'

Pushing a release button on his pistol, he removed the ammunition clip, took out a single bullet, and handed it to the old fellow.

'You can keep this as a souvenir,' he said.

Frantically waving off the gesture, the old fellow said:

'No, I really can't. A few bowls of inedible wonton, Boss, what can it be worth? Just the opportunity to meet a good and decent man like you is my great fortune, enough to last me three lifetimes, no, I really can't . . .'

Unwilling to let the old fellow prattle on and on, the investigator grabbed his hand and forced him to take the bullet. The old man's hand was hotter than blazes.

Just then he heard a snicker behind him, like the sound of an owl on a tombstone, which scared him into hunching his head down into his shoulders. Another spurt of urine ran down his leg.

'Some investigator!' It was an old man's voice. 'I see an escaped convict!'

Trembling with fear, he turned to see who it was. There beside the trunk of a French kolanut tree stood a skinny old man in a tattered army uniform, pointing a double-barreled shotgun at him; a long-haired tiger-striped dog sat motionless and menacingly on its haunches beside him, eyes like laser beams. The dog frightened the investigator more than the man did.

'Gramps Qiu, I've disturbed you again,' the peddler said softly to the old man.

'Liu Four, how many times have I told you not to set up shop here? And still you refuse to listen to me!'

'Gramps Qiu, I didn't mean to anger you, but what can a poor man do? I have to come up with my daughter's tuition. I'll do anything for my kids, but I don't dare go into the city, because they'll fine me if they catch me, and there goes half a month's income.'

Gramps Qiu waved his shotgun in the air. 'You there,' he said sternly, 'toss that pistol over here!'

Like an obedient child, Ding Gou'er tossed the pistol over to to where Gramps Qiu was standing.

'Put your hands up!' Gramps Qiu demanded.

Slowly Ding Gou'er raised his hands, then watched as the skinny old man whom the aging wonton peddler had called Gramps Qiu held his shotgun in one hand to free up the other. Then, bending his legs while keeping his upper body straight – so he could shoot if necessary – he picked up the six-nine service pistol. Gramps Qiu studied the gun from every angle, before announcing disdainfully, 'A beat-up Luger!' Ding Gou'er, seeing his opportunity, said, 'I can tell you're a weapons expert.' The old man's face lit up. In a high and scratchy yet infectiously powerful voice, he said, 'You're right there. I've handled at least thirty, maybe even fifty different weapons in my time, from the Czech rifle to the Hanyang, the Russian submachine gun, the tommy gun, the nine-shot repeater . . . and that's only the rifles. As for handguns, I've used the German Mauser, the Spanish Waist-Drum repeater, the Japanese Tortoise Shell Mauser, the Chinese Drumstick revolver, and three kinds of Saturday-night specials, not counting this one here.' He tossed Ding Gou'er's pistol into the air and caught it on its way down, in a nimble practiced fashion that belied his years. He had an elongated head, narrow eyes, a hooked nose, no eyebrows and no sideburns; his deeply wrinkled face was dark as a tree trunk that's been charred in a kiln. 'This pistol,' he said scornfully, 'is better suited for women than for men.' The investigator replied evenly, 'It's very accurate.' The old man examined it again, then said authoritatively, 'It's fine within ten meters. More than that, it isn't worth shit.' To which Ding Gou'er replied, 'You know your business, Gramps.' The old man stuck Ding Gou'er's pistol into his waistband and snorted contemptuously.

The wonton peddler said, 'Gramps Qiu is a veteran revolutionary. He's in charge of Liquorland's Martyrs' Cemetery.'

'No wonder,' Ding Gou'er said.

'What about you?' the old revolutionary asked.

'I'm an investigator for the provincial Higher Procuratorate.'

'Let's see your papers.'

'They were stolen.'

'You look like a fugitive to me.'

'I know I look like one, but I'm not.'

'Can you prove it?'

'Call your Municipal Party Secretary, or your Mayor, or your Police Chief, or your Chief Prosecutor, and ask if they know a special investigator by the name of Ding Gou'er.'

'Special investigator?' The old revolutionary couldn't suppress a giggle. 'Where'd they find a dogshit special investigator like you?'

'I was brought down by a woman,' Ding Gou'er said. Intending to laugh at himself, he was surprised by the heart stabs this simple admission produced. Falling to his knees in front of the wonton stand, he began pummeling his already bloody head with his already bloody fists and screeching, 'I was brought down by a woman, by a woman who slept with a dwarf . . .'

The old revolutionary walked up, poked Ding Gou'er in the back with his shotgun, and demanded:

'Get your ass up!'

Ding Gou'er looked up through his tears at the dark, elongated head of the old revolutionary, as if seeing a friend from home or like an underling looking at his superior or, most fitting of all, like a son laying eyes on his father for the first time in years. In the grip of strong emotions, he wrapped his arms around the old revolutionary's legs and said tearfully, 'Gramps, I'm a useless sack of shit to have been brought down by a woman . . .'

The old revolutionary jerked Ding Gou'er to his feet by his collar. His shiny, tiny eyes bored mercilessly into the wretched man for about half as long as it takes to smoke a pipeful, before he spat on the ground, drew the pistol from his waistband, and threw it down at his feet. Then he turned and swaggered off without so much as a grunt. The big yellow dog followed on his heels, also without a grunt, its damp fur glistening like a coat of tiny pearls.

The wonton peddler laid the shiny bullet down next to the pistol, picked up his stand, turned down the gas lantern, hoisted the whole rig onto his shoulder, and walked off without a sound.

Standing petrified in the dark, Ding Gou'er watched the man's retreating back until all he could see was pale yellow lamplight, flickering like a will-o'-the-wisp; the canopy of the French kolanut overhead kept the raindrops off him and made a rustling sound that seemed louder now that the other people had left, taking the lamplight with them. In a state of utter stupefaction, he managed to stay upright; he had the presence of mind to pick up his pistol and the bullet. The night air was cold and damp, he ached all over, and he was a stranger in a strange land; he felt as if his day of reckoning had arrived.

The menacing look in the old revolutionary's eyes had implied that Ding Gou'er was not up to snuff, and felt a need to pour out his heart to the man. What power could, in such a short time, transform a man so tough he could eat nails and shit springs into a mangy cur who had lost his soul? And was it possible that an ordinary-looking woman could possess that power? The answer was no, so putting all the blame on her was unfair. Something mysterious was going on here, and the old man who patrolled the night with his dog was at the heart of that mystery. Sensing that great wisdom was contained in that elongated head, Ding Gou'er made up his mind to go looking for him.

He set out on legs that had turned stiff, heading in the direction the old man and his dog had taken. From off in the distance came the sound of night trucks driving across a steel bridge, a steady *clang-clang* that deepened the night and its mystery. The road rose and fell beneath his feet, and at the top of one particularly steep hill, he sat on the ground and slid down. When he looked up, he saw a pile of broken bricks in the halo of a streetlight. A layer of white, like frost, blanketed the pile. A few steps more, and he was standing beside an ancient gateway. A light burning in the window of the battlement above illuminated a wrought-iron gate and a white placard on which red letters proclaimed:

LIQUORLAND MARTYRS' CEMETERY

He rushed up to the gate and grabbed hold of the steel rods rising above the gate, like a man in jail; they were sticky enough to peel the skin right off his hands. The big yellow dog ran up to the gate, barking frantically, but he held his ground. Then the loud, scratchy voice of the old revolutionary emerged from the other side of the battlement; the dog stopped barking and hopping around, then hung its head and wagged its tail. The old revolutionary appeared before Ding Gou'er, shotgun slung over his shoulder, the brass buttons on his overcoat emblematic of his commanding authority.

'What the hell are you up to?' he demanded sternly.

With a loud sniffle, Ding Gou'er replied tearfully, 'Gramps, I really am a special investigator for the provincial Higher Procuratorate.'

'What are you here for?'

'To investigate a very serious matter.'

'What serious matter might that be?'

'A gang of cannibalistic dignitaries are cooking and eating infants.'

'I'll kill every last one of them!'

'Don't go off half-cocked, Gramps. Let me in and I'll tell you the whole story.'

The old revolutionary swung open a small side gate. 'Squeeze in through there,' he said.

Ding Gou'er hesitated, because he'd spotted some fine yellow hairs stuck in the corner.

'Are you coming in or not?'

Ding Gou'er bent down and slipped through the gate.

'Stuffed bellies like you can't hold a candle to my dog.'

As Ding Gou'er followed the old revolutionary into a gate house, he was reminded of the gate house at the Mount Luo mine and the gateman with the wild mop of bristly hair.

The gate house was ablaze with light, the walls a snowy white. A fire-heated brick bed occupied half the room's space; a wall as wide as the bed separated it from a stove on which a wok rested. Pine kindling kept the fire roaring and filled the air with its fragrance.

The old revolutionary unstrapped his shotgun and hung it on the wall, removed his overcoat and tossed it onto the bed, then rubbed his hands and said:

'Burning firewood and sleeping on a heated bed is my one special privilege.' He looked at Ding Gou'er and asked, 'After decades of making revolution, which left me with seven or eight scars the size of ricebowls, don't you think I deserve it?'

So mellowed by the pervading warmth that he was about to doze off, Ding Gou'er replied, 'Yes, of course you do.'

'But that rotten son of a bitch Section Chief Yu wants to have me start burning acacia instead of pine. I've made revolution all my adult life, even had the head of my prick shot off by the Jap devils – I'll never have sons or grandsons to carry on my line – so what's the big deal in burning a little pine in my old age? I'm already eighty, how many pine trees can I use up in the years left to me, hm? I tell you, if the King of Heaven came to earth, he couldn't stop me from burning pine!' Waving his arms and slobbering, the old fellow was getting increasingly agitated. 'What was it you said just now? Something about people eating infants? Cannibals? They're worse than animals! Who are they? Tomorrow I'll go kill every last one of them! I'll shoot 'em first and make my report later. At worst I'll get a demerit or two. I've killed hundreds of people in my lifetime, all of them bad – traitors, counter-revolutionaries, invaders – and now that I'm old, it's time to kill a few cannibalistic animals!'

Ding Gou'er itched all over; his clothes reeked of moist, steamy ashes. 'That's what I'm here to investigate,' he said.

'Investigate, my ass!' the old revolutionary cackled. 'Take 'em out and shoot 'em, I say! Investigate, my ass!'

'Gramps, we're living under a system of laws these days. You can't just go around shooting people without hard evidence.'

'Then get on with your investigation. What the hell are you hanging around here for? What happened to your class consciousness? What happened to your work ethic? The enemy's out there eating infants, and you're in here getting toasty warm! I'll bet you're a Trotskyite! A member of the bourgeoisie! A running dog of imperialism!'

This flood of invective from the old revolutionary snapped Ding Gou'er out of his dreamy stupor, as if his head had been splattered with dog's blood, his chest filled with roiling waves of heat. He tore off his clothes, until he was standing there naked, except for his scuffed shoes. Squatting down in front of the stove, he stirred the fire inside and added some oily pine kindling, sending white smoke reeking of pine up his nostrils; he sneezed, and it felt good. Draping his clothing over pieces of kindling, he held it up to the fire to dry; it sizzled like a reeking donkey hide. The fire also heated his bare skin, making it sting and itch. The more he scratched and rubbed himself, the better he felt.

'Have you got fucking scabies?' the old revolutionary asked. 'I got scabies once from sleeping in a haystack. The whole platoon got them. Itch? We scratched and rubbed until we bled. It didn't help. Even our damned insides itched, and we weren't a fighting unit anymore. We lost men without a fight. The assistant squad leader of Squad 8, Ma Shan, had a brainstorm. He bought a bunch of green onions and garlic, smashed them to a pulp, then added some salt and vinegar, and rubbed it all over our bodies. It stung like hell, it numbed the skin, it felt like a dog scratching its balls. I've never felt anything so good! All those fucking mites, gone just like that with a home remedy. You get sick, the government takes care of you. That's how it's done. I hung my head on my belt and fought for the revolution, so by rights they should take care of me . . .'

The investigator detected a note of bitterness, a grumbling tone in the old revolutionary's words, a history of revolutionary hardship and suffering. What was supposed to have been a chance to pour out his heart had elicited a litany of grievances from the old-timer. Sadly disappointed, he was beginning to realize that no one can really rescue anyone else, that everyone has his own problems, and talking about them doesn't help – the hungry man's belly is just as empty, the thirsty man's mouth stays just as dry. He shook out his clothes, knocked off some of the dried mud, and got dressed. The hot fabric burned his skin, transporting him to Seventh Heaven. But now that he was swathed in comfort, his spiritual suffering swelled, as a picture of the naked lady trucker and the pigeon-breasted, bow-legged humpback together in bed flashed into his head, clear as day and lifelike as a movie, the sort of thing he'd seen once through a keyhole. The longer he let the picture roll, the livelier it got, and the richer. The lady trucker was the golden color of a plump female loach, covered with oily, slippery mucus that gave off a subtle and not very pleasant odor. Yu Yichi, that warty little toad, was pawing her with his webbed feet, frothy bubbles popping in the corners of his mouth as he croaked and croaked . . . Ding's heart was like a leaf shuddering in the wind; how he wished he could rip open his chest, gouge out that heart, and fling it in her face. Slut slut filthy slut! He could, it seemed, see, and see conclusively: Investigator Ding

Gou'er, majestic as a statue hewed from pure marble, kicks in the cream-colored door with the tip of his leather shoe. There in front of him a bed, a solitary bed, on which the stupefied lady trucker and Yu Yichi sit – he rolls off the bed like a toad, his belly covered with hideous red spots – he stands cowering at the base of the wall – pigeon breast, humped back, bowed legs (or knock-kneed), an oversized head, white eyes, a crooked nose, no lips, yellow teeth with wide gaps, a mouth like a black hole that gives off a festering stench, big, dry, almost transparently thin and slightly yellow, twitching ears, black apelike arms that nearly scrape the ground, bushy hair all over his body, mutant-looking feet with more than the usual supply of toes, not to mention his black-as-ink donkey dick – How could you possibly sleep with a hideous creature like that?

The investigator, unable to restrain himself, howled loud and long. What did you say? What the hell did you say? the old revolutionary, Gramps Qiu, asked. The big yellow dog started to bark.

Then she shrieks in alarm and jerks the blanket up over her naked body – like you see in the movies all the time – under the blanket her body quakes – at that moment he lays eyes on the flesh he knows so well . . . voluptuous . . . firm . . . sweet smelling . . . as if ten thousand arrows have pierced his heart, a sorrow he's never known before – a blue light flashes before his eyes, his face the color of cold steel with rigid lines, a sneer, skin like ice – he raises his pistol, slips his finger into the trigger guard, waves the pistol slightly, turning it handsomely, takes careful aim, and – *pow!* – a loud explosion, and the mirror behind Yu Yichi's head disintegrates, sending glittering, splintering shards of glass raining to the floor – Yu Yichi lies petrified on the floor – then the investigator holsters his weapon, turns without a word – do *not* look back – and strides out of Yichi Tavern – Forgive me forgive me she wails as she kneels on the floor, wrapped in the bedsheet – do *not* look back – and he walks down the sun-drenched Liquorland street, between crowds of people staring at him with a mixture of reverence and fear – men and women, young and old, one of the old women looking exactly like his mother, with tears in her eyes, her haggard lips quivering. Child, she says, my child – a girl in a virginal white dress, long golden tresses flowing over her shoulders, pushes her way through the crowd, eyes beneath thick, curly lashes glistening with tears, her arching breasts heaving, gasping for breath as she elbows her way through the tightly packed crowd, shouting in a tearful yet still sweet voice, Ding Gou'er – Ding Gou'er – but Ding Gou'er does not turn to look, he keeps his eyes straight ahead, striding forward with resounding, determined steps, heading into the sunlight, into the bright-colored sunset, onward and onward, until he becomes one with the red wheel of the sun . . .

The old revolutionary laid his hard hand on Ding Gou'er's shoulder. The investigator, having become one with the sun, shivered as he struggled to regain consciousness. His heart was pounding; the tears of a tragic hero welled in his eyes.

'What goddamned demon possessed you?' the old revolutionary asked scornfully.

Quickly wiping his eyes with his sleeve, the embarrassed investigator laughed drily.

In the wake of his turbulent fantasy, he felt as if cracks had suddenly appeared in his chest amid the melancholy that lay there, while his exhausted brain felt weighted down, and there was a dull ringing in his ears.

'It looks like you've got a fucking cold,' the old revolutionary said. 'Your face is as red as a monkey's ass!'

The old revolutionary reached into the fire hole beneath his bed and took out a white bottle of liquor with the brand stamped in red. He waved it in front his guest's eyes. 'This'll do it. The alcohol will kill the virus and get rid of the poison in your body. Alcohol is good medicine, it'll cure what ails you. Back when I crossed the Red River four times with Mao Zedong, we passed through Maotai township twice. I had to drop out because of a case of malaria, so I hid in a distillery. When the Kuomintang "white bandits" opened fire outside, I was quaking. Drink up, it'll chase away the fear! So, *glug glug*, I downed three bowlfuls, one right after the other. Well, it not only calmed me down, but it gave me courage and stopped the shakes. I picked up a board, ran out of the distillery, and clubbed two of the white bandits to death. Then I took one of their rifles, ran off, and caught up with Mao's troops. Back then, Mao Zedong, Zhu De, Zhou Enlai, and Wang Jiaxiang all drank Maotai. When Mao drank it, his mind was sharp as a tack and full of strategies. If not for that, his small band of soldiers would have been wiped out easily. So Maotai liquor played a key role in the Chinese revolution. You probably think it was chosen as our national liquor by a fluke, right? Hell no, it was to commemorate it! And after a lifetime of making revolution, I ought to be able to drink a little Maotai. That son of a bitch Section Chief Yu wants to cut off my supply and replace it with – what's it called? – Red-Maned Stallion. Well, he can stick it up his grannie's you know what!'

The old revolutionary poured some liquor into a chipped ceramic mug, tipped back his head, and drank it down. 'Now it's your turn,' he said. 'Genuine Maotai, down to the last drop.' Seeing tears in Ding Gou'er's eyes, he said scornfully, 'Scared? Only turncoats and traitors are scared to drink, afraid they'll get drunk and tell the truth or divulge some secrets. Are you a turncoat? A traitor? No? Then how come you're scared to drink?' He downed another mugful, the liquor gurgling as it cascaded down his throat. 'Don't worry, I'm not going to force you! I suppose you think I came about this little bit of Maotai easily! Well, that Trotskyite Section Chief Yu watches me like a hawk. On the ground a phoenix is worse off than a chicken, and a tiger on the open plain is at the mercy of dogs!'

Ding Gou'er found the bouquet of the liquor irresistible; emotional moments are made for drinking good liquor. He snatched the mug out of the old revolutionary's hand, put it up to his lips, took a deep breath, and sent a flood of liquor straight down to his stomach. A spray of pink lotuses blossomed in front of his eyes, spreading their thought-provoking light in the surrounding haze. It was the light of Maotai, the essence of Maotai. In that split second, he watched the world turn incredibly beautiful, including Heaven and earth and trees and the virgin snow on the Himalayan peaks. With a satisfied laugh, the old revolutionary took back his mug and refilled it; the liquor gurgled as it spilled across the mouth of the bottle, setting his ears ringing and making his mouth water. The old revolutionary's face was suffused with indescribable benevolence. As Ding reached out, he heard himself say, 'Give it to me, I want more.' The old revolutionary was jumping around in front of him, nimble as a young man. 'I'm not giving you any more, it's too hard to get.' 'I want some,' he bellowed, 'I want it. You're the one who woke the serpent of gluttony in me, so why you won't you give me any more?' The old revolutionary slugged down another mugful. Fuming, Ding grabbed the mug, with the man's finger still firmly in the handle. He heard the sound of teeth against ceramic and felt a wetness on his skin as the cold liquor spilled over his hand. As his anger rose in the struggle over the mug, his knee recalled a trick his buddies had taught it: with the calf bent backwards, you propel yourself into your enemy's groin. When he heard the old revolutionary cry out, the mug passed into his hand. Impatiently he poured the mugful of liquor down his throat. Wanting still more, he looked around for the bottle, which lay on its side on the floor like a handsome young battle casualty. He was suddenly wracked by inconsolable grief, as if he had somehow killed the young man. Wanting to bend down to pick up the white-skinned bottle with its red sash – to help the handsome young man to his feet – inexplicably, he fell to his knees. And the handsome young man rolled over to a corner of the wall, where he righted himself and began to grow, taller and taller until he stood over three feet tall and stopped growing. He knew that was the liquor's soul – Maotai liquor's soul – standing in the corner, smiling at the investigator. Jumping to his feet to grab it, he managed only to bang his head against the wall.

As he was luxuriating in the sensation of the room spinning around him, he sensed a cold hand grab him by the hair. He guessed whose hand it was. He followed the pain in his scalp upward, his body acting like a pile of pig's guts, slipping and sliding on the floor – cold and slippery and coiled and nauseatingly foul – now being uncoiled and straightened, though he knew that the minute the old revolutionary let go, the mass of pig's guts would slump back to the floor, dripping wet. The big hand turned, bringing him face to long swarthy face with the old revolutionary, and he saw that the benevolent smile had been replaced by a fossilized scowl. The cold-blooded nature of class contradictions and class struggle was driven home. You counter-revolutionary son of a bitch, I give you liquor, and you pay me back by kneeing me in the balls! You're worse than a dog. If a dog drinks my liquor, it wags its tail to show its gratitude. The old revolutionary sprayed him with saliva, stinging his eyes so badly he cried out in pain; two great paws landed on his shoulders. The dog had his neck in its mouth, its bristly fur was jabbing into his skin; involuntarily he tucked his neck into his shoulders, like a tortoise sensing danger. He felt the heat of the dog's breath and smelled its sour stink. The feeling that he was a mass of coiled pig's guts returned abruptly, and a white-hot terror rose in his heart. Dogs gobble up pig's guts like a child slurps up rice noodles. Terror-stricken, he cried out, just before blackness closed in around him.

How much later he didn't know, the investigator, believing himself blinded by the dog, opened his eyes to light once again. It spread like the sun breaking through the clouds, and then – *bang* – all the sights of the Martyrs' Cemetery gate house pounded into his eyes at once. He saw the old revolutionary sitting under a lamp polishing his double-barreled shotgun, absorbed in his task, working earnestly and meticulously, like a father bathing his one and only daughter. The striped hunting dog was sprawled lazily in front of the stove, its long snout resting on a pile of pine kindling, as it stared at the sweet-smelling golden flames, looking pensive, sort of like a philosophy professor. What was it thinking? The investigator was mesmerized by the dog, which was immersed in deep thought. The dog watched the flames as if in a trance, he watched the dog as if in a trance, as gradually the brilliant tableau inside the dog's head – one he'd never seen before – began to take shape in his own head, accompanied by peculiar and amazingly moving music – like drifting clouds. He was stirred to the depths of his soul, his nose throbbed as if it had met a fist and come out second best. Two trickles of tears materialized on his cheeks.

'Not much hope for you, I see,' the old revolutionary said, looking him over. 'We take the seed from tigers and wolves, and all we get are some snotty worms.'

Once again he dried his eyes with his sleeves and pleaded his case: 'Gramps, I was brought down by a woman . . .'

With a look of disappointment, the old revolutionary put on

his heavy overcoat, strapped his shotgun over his shoulder, and summoned his trusty companion: 'Dog, let's go make our rounds and leave this worthless wretch to his tears.'

The dog got lazily to its feet, cast a sympathetic glance at the investigator, and followed the old revolutionary out of the gate house. The door's hinge snapped it closed with a bang, but not before a damp, very cold night wind slipped in to make him shiver. Loneliness and fear. 'Wait for me,' he shouted, as he pulled the door open and chased after them.

The electric light over the doorway transformed them into shadowy figures. A cold rain fell, the sound crisper and denser than ever, probably because the night had deepened. Instead of walking out through the main gate, the old revolutionary headed toward the heart of the cemetery, directly into gloomy darkness. The dog was on his heels, he was right behind the dog. For a while, the electric light made it possible to discern the shapes of cypresses trimmed to look like pagodas bracketing the narrow cobblestone path; but before long, they too were swallowed up by the converging darkness. Now he knew what it felt like not to be able to see his fingers in front of his face. And the darker it became, the louder the sound of raindrops on the trees; the chaotic, intense tattoo first threw his mind into turmoil, then emptied it. Only from the sounds and smells up ahead did he gain an awareness of the old revolutionary and his yellow dog's existence. Darkness is so heavily oppressive, it can crush a man flat. Securely in the grip of fear, the investigator could detect the smell of martyrs' graves hidden amid the green pines and emerald cypresses. To his mind, the trees were sentries standing there holding their shoulders and harboring ill will toward him, with sneers on their faces and evil in their hearts; downy spirits of the brave departed sat on the weedy graves at their feet. Sobered up by raw terror, he reached for his pistol, his hand coated with cold sweat. A weird screech tore through the darkness, followed by flapping sounds moving past him. A bird, he assumed, but what kind of bird? An owl, maybe? The old revolutionary coughed; the dog barked. The two sounds, securely anchored in the mortal world, brought the investigator a measure of comfort; he coughed, loudly, and even he discerned the blustery tone. Up ahead in the darkness, the old revolutionary's laughing at me, he assumed. And so is that philosophical running dog of his. He saw two green lights in the darkness ahead, and if he hadn't known it was a dog, he'd have sworn the eyes belonged to a wolf. He began to cough, uncontrollably, when a flash of light blinded him. Covering his eyes with his hand, he opened his mouth to protest, just as the light moved off in another direction and lit upon a carved white tombstone. The words looked to have been freshly painted in shocking red, but the redness so clouded his vision, he couldn't read them. The light went out as abruptly as it had come on; he still saw spots in front of his eyes, and his brain was awash in red, like the blazing pinewood fire in the stove back at the gate house. He heard the old revolutionary's heavy breathing up front, as the noisy, chilling rainshower died out suddenly, and an earth-shattering clap near by nearly frightened him out of his wits. He wondered what could have caused the explosion, but only for a moment. All that mattered was, from the instant the light shone on the martyr's tombstone, an enormous wave of courage surged into his body and drove out the jealousy of sickness wine, the evil weakness of widow wine, and the restlessness and anxiety of love wine, turning them all into a sour stench, into reeking urine. Then vodka, spirited as a proud stallion galloping across a Cossack plain, became him; and cognac, rough and unconstrained, yet with a fine edge to its roughness, rich in the spirt of adventure, rich in audacity, like a Spaniard addicted to the danger of bullfighting, became him. As if, after eating a mouthful of red chilis, sinking his teeth into a bunch of green onions, gnawing on a stalk of purple-skinned garlic, chewing up a hunk of aged, dried ginger, or swallowing a whole jar of black pepper, he would feel like an oil-fed fire, like flowers on a piece of brocade; his spirits would soar like the tail feathers of a rooster – a true cocktail – as he picked up his six-nine service pistol, which had been created with the same loving care as the finest Great Yeast liquor, and charged ahead, his strides as menacing as cheap grappa, as if, in the blink of an eye, he could be back at Yichi Tavern, where he would kick in the jade-white door, raise his pistol, aim it at the lady trucker, who was sitting in the lap of the dwarf Yichi, and – *pow pow* – two heads would shatter. The sequence of events unfolded like the world-famous

Knife Liquor: full-bodied and strong, with a sweet, tart flavor, it zips down the gullet like a razor-sharp knife slicing through tangled rope.

II

Dear Elder Brother Yidou

I received your latest letter and the story 'Cooking Lesson.'

As for visiting Liquorland, I've already broached the subject with my superior. He's not particularly keen on letting me go, since I'm in the military. Besides, I've just been promoted from captain to major (I lose two stars and gain a bar, and since I think three stars and a single bar would look much better, I'm not as pleased as I might be), and I should go down to company headquarters to eat and live and drill with the troops, so I can write stories or 'reportage' that reflect the lives of our soldiers in this new age. Going into the provinces to find material puts me under the jurisdiction of local administrators, which complicates matters, even for Liquorland, which has attracted so much attention in recent years because of everything that's been going on there. I'm not ready to give up yet, and will keep trying. There are plenty of fine-sounding excuses I could come up with.

Liquorland's first annual Ape Liquor Festival should be an interesting, successful event. While everybody's drinking and having a good time, saturating the air with the bouquet of good liquor, I hope this pudgy body of mine can make an appearance among the tipsy, drink-besotted alcoholic troops.

I've reached an impasse in my novel. That slippery investigator from the Higher Procuratorate is fighting me every step of the way. I don't know whether to kill him off or have him go mad. And if I choose to finish him off, I can't decide whether he should shoot himself or die in a drunken stupor. I got him good and drunk in the previous chapter. And because I'm having trouble reconciling all these tormenting problems, I went ahead and got good and drunk myself. But instead of enjoying a good buzz, all I got was a vision of Hell. It's a lousy place, I tell you.

I spent a whole night reading 'Cooking Lesson' (I read it several times). I'm finding it harder and harder to comment upon your stories. But if forced to say something, I guess I'd more or less repeat what I've said before: that it lacks a consistency of style, that it's too capricious, that the characters aren't well developed, and that sort of thing. I think that instead of bringing up the same old thing again and again, I'm better off keeping my mouth shut. Nonetheless, I did as you asked and made a special trip to *Citizens' Literature*. Zhou Bao and his co-editor were away from the office, so I left the story on their desk with a note. You'll have to trust to luck on this one, but my gut tells me it'll be hard to publish. You and I have never met, but since we're like old friends by now, I'm giving it to you straight.

I'm convinced you can write a first-rate story that will be just right for *Citizens' Literature*. It's just a matter of time. It'll happen sooner or later, so don't be disappointed or downcast.

By my calculations, you've sent me a total of six stories to be forwarded for consideration; that includes 'Yichi the Hero,' which I have here. If I come to Liquorland, I probably should retrieve the manuscripts from *Citizens' Literature*, so I can return them to you in person. Sending them by mail is risky and bothersome. Every time I go to the post office, I'm a bundle of nerves for days after confronting the stony faces of the ladies or gentlemen at the windows. It's as if they're waiting to unmask a spy or nab a bomber, or something. They make you feel as if the package you want to mail is filled with counter-revolutionary tracts.

Don't worry if you can't find a copy of *Strange Events in Liquorland*. Plenty of oddball books like that have

251

appeared in recent years, most simply thrown together to make money. They're pretty much worthless.

Wishing you
Good writing!

Mo Yan

III

Dear Mo Yan, Sir

Greetings!
Just knowing there's a chance you'll visit Liquorland has me jumping for joy. I look forward to your visit with the anticipation of 'Waiting for the stars, waiting for the moon, I long to see the sun rise over the mountain.' Some classmates of mine work for the Municipal Party Committee and for the government (not menial jobs, either, but official posts, some more important than others), so if you need a formal invitation from either organization, or something along that line, I can ask them to help out. Chinese in leadership positions are impressed by official seals, and I'll bet it's no different in the army.

   As for the stories, I must admit I'm disappointed *and* downcast. No, it's more than that – I've got a bone to pick with Zhou Bao and Li Xiaobao. They've sat on those manuscripts, without even a letter of acknowledgment, which doesn't say much about their attitude toward people. I know they're busy, and that if they answered every letter from an amateur writer, they wouldn't have time for anything else. I understand that perfectly well, but I'm angry just the same. If they won't do it for the sake of the monk, then do it for the sake of the Buddha. After all, I've got you to recommend me. Sure, I know it's not healthy, that low morale is harmful to the creative process, and I'm working hard to keep my morale problem in check. Being one of those who will 'Never give up till he sees the Yellow River,' and 'Never calls himself a man till he reaches the Yangtze,' I'm determined to keep writing, undaunted by setbacks.

Everyone at the college is up to his ears in preparations for the Ape Liquor Festival. The department has given me the job of using the sickness wine in our storeroom to make an alcohol base and distill a special liquor for sale during the Ape Liquor Festival. If I'm successful, I can expect substantial monetary rewards. That's very important to me. Of course I won't abandon my stories for the sake of monetary rewards. No, I'll keep writing, devoting ten percent of my energy to working on the sickness wine, and the other ninety percent to my fiction.

I'm sending you my latest, a story called 'Swallows' Nests.' Your criticisms are welcome. I've summed up my feelings toward my earlier work: I believe that the reason my stories haven't been published has to do with intervening in society. So I've corrected that failing in 'Swallows' Nests.' It's a story far removed from politics and from the capital. If this one doesn't get published, then I've been 'abandoned even by Heaven'!

Peace, as always,
Li Yidou

IV

Swallows' Nests, by Li Yidou

Why does my mother-in-law never age or lose her beauty, and why does she still have arching breasts and a curvaceous derriere even though she's over sixty? Why is her belly as flat as fine steel plate, without an ounce of fat? Why is her face as smooth as the mid-autumn moon, not a wrinkle anywhere, and why are her teeth so white and clean, neither broken nor loose? Why is her skin as smooth and silky as priceless jade? Why are her lips bright red, why does her kissable mouth always smell like barbecue? And why is she never sick, unvisited even by the symptoms of menopause?

As a son-in-law, maybe I'm out of line, but as a dyed-in-the-wool materialist, I say what needs to be said. And what needs to be said here is, although my mother-in-law is in her sixties, she could produce a dozen little brothers-in-law and sisters-in-law for me if the law permitted and she was willing. Why does she seldom fart, and on those rare occasions when she does, why, instead of smelling bad, do her farts actually smell like sugar-fried chestnuts? Generally speaking, a beautiful woman's belly is filled with bad odors; in other words, beauty is only skin deep. How, then, can my mother-in-law be not only pretty on the outside, but fragrant and appetizing inside as well? All these question marks have snared me like fish hooks, turning me into a balloon fish that has blundered into choice fishing waters. They torment me as much as they probably bore you, dear readers. You're probably saying, Can you believe the way this Li Yidou guy is auctioning off his own mother-in-law? My dear friends, I am not 'auctioning off' my mother-in-law, I am studying my mother-in-law. My research will greatly benefit the human race, and I shall not falter, even if it angers my mother-in-law.

At first I assumed it was primarily because she was born into a family of swallows'-nests gatherers that I inherited a mother-in-law like Oloroso sherry – a beautiful, uniform color, a rich, invigorating bouquet, full-bodied yet mellow, a sweet, silky flavor, a wine well suited for cellaring, and one that improves with age – rather than one like some rustic wine made of sweet-potatoes, with a murky color, a pungent, disagreeable aroma, flat and characterless, and a flavor not much different from insecticide.

In line with a current trendy narrative strategy, I may now say that our story is about to begin. But before entering the story proper, which belongs both to me and to you, please allow me three minutes to impart some specialized know-how you will need in order to avoid obstacles as you move along. I had planned to write just enough for you to read for a minute and a half, and leave the rest of the time for you to think. So let's cut the crap about stuff like 'As soon as the fox starts thinking, the tiger laughs,' or 'You can't stop the sky from hailing or your mother from marrying,' which, as everyone knows, was a comment by Mao when Lin Biao was trying to get away. Let them laugh. If a few hundred million of them laughed themselves to death, there'd be no need for birth control and my mother-in-law could use her still healthy organs to present me with some little brothers-in-law or sisters-in-law. Please, no more BS. OK, no more BS. I hear your angry shouts, and take note of your impatience, like the prairie liquor produced in Inner Mongolia. You're still a lot like a bottle of that roiling 120-proof Harbin liquor made from sorghum chaff, the one that packs such a wallop.

Collocalia restita, Aves class, the rain-swallow family, is about 18cm long, has black or brown feathers with a blue sheen, and a gray-white belly. Its wings are long and pointed, its legs short and pink, with four front-facing talons. Gregarious, insectivorous, they build their nests in caves. The male secretes saliva from glands in the throat; once it has solidified, it is called 'swallow's nest.'

Collocalia restita are found in Thailand, the Philippines, Indonesia, Malaysia, and deserted islands off the coastal provinces of Guangdong and Fujian in southeast China. Early June is when they build nests to raise their young. But before that, the male and female mate following an animated courtship, after which the male perches on the cave's stone wall, flicking its head back and forth as it secretes the saliva, like spring silkworms spinning silk. Threads of transparent, sticky saliva stick to the stone wall and solidify to form swallow's nest. According to reports from observers, the male bird neither sleeps nor eats during this nest-building process, which demands of the bird that it flick its head tens of thousands of times. It is an arduous process, more difficult than shedding one's heart's blood. The first nest, formed completely with bird saliva, contains virtually no impurities, so its color is pure white and crystal clear and its quality so fine that it is commonly referred to as 'white nest' or 'official nest.' When this nest is removed, the bird will make a second one, but an insufficient amount of saliva forces it to mix in its own feathers. And, since the bird has to exert itself to produce more saliva, it is often streaked with blood. The end result, which is of lower quality, is called 'feathered nest' or 'bloody nest.' If the second nest is also removed, the bird will make yet a third one, but it has no culinary value, since it is mainly made of algae, with little saliva.

The first time I saw my mother-in-law, she was using a silver needle to remove impurities from a nest soaked in soda water: blood, feathers, and seaweed. Now we know that was a 'bloody nest.' Pouting like an angry platypus, my mother-in-law grumbled, Would you look at this, how can this be called a swallow's nest? It's nothing but a jumbled feather nest, a magpie's nest, or a crow's nest. Calm down, said my teacher, Yuan Shuangyu, as he took a sip of the blended liquor he himself had made – it had the elegant, noble bouquet of orchids. In this day and age, everything's adulterated. Even the swallow has learned the trick. In my view, ten thousand years down the road, if humans are still around, swallows will be using dog shit to build their nests. The fermenting bird's nest jiggled in her hands. She was looking at her husband, my future father-in-law, dumbstruck. I can't imagine how something as repulsive as a dog's brain could be more valuable than gold. Is it really as wondrous as you folks claim? He sized up the thing in her hand with a cold look. She said, You don't know anything about anything, except liquor. Her face reddened slightly as she threw down the bird's nest and took off to who-knows-where like a little whirlwind. It was my first visit to my wife's house. She said her mother wanted to show off her culinary skills, and I was surprised and perplexed to see her fling the bird's nest away like that and just walk off. But the old man said, Never mind, she'll be back. She knows swallow's nests as well as I know liquor. We're both top in our fields.

As my father-in-law predicted, my mother-in-law returned before long. Having removed all the impurities from the nest, she made some bird's nest soup for us. My father-in-law and my wife refused to drink any; he said it smelled like chicken shit, she said that, given the smell of blood, it was a bowl of heartless soup replete with extreme cruelty, emblematic of the fact that human beings are the source of all evil. My wife, who has a heart filled with abundant love, was applying for membership in the Worldwide Animal Protective League in Bonn. At the time my mother-in-law said, Little Li, don't pay any attention to these fools. Their so-called love of humanity is a sham. Confucius said that a gentleman should stay away from the kitchen, but he never had a meal without meat sauce. One must be meticulous about fine food and choice meats. When he accepted students, he demanded ten packets of dried meat in lieu of tuition. If they don't want any, that's fine, let's drink ours. My mother-in-law said, We Chinese have been eating swallows' nests for a thousand years. It's the most valuable tonic in the world. Don't underestimate its nutritional value just because it's ugly, for it can aid a child's growth and development, maintain a woman's youthful appearance, and prolong an old man's life. Not long ago, a Professor Ho of Hong Kong's Chinese University discovered an ingredient in swallows' nests that prevents and cures AIDS. If she ate swallow's nest, my mother-in-law said, pointing to my wife, she wouldn't look like she does. To which my wife replied angrily, I'd rather look like this than eat *that* stuff. Turning to stare at me, she said, Tell me, is it good? Not wanting to offend my wife *or* my mother-in-law, I muttered, What can I say? How should I put it? Ha ha ha ha ha. My wife said, Aren't you the slick one! My mother-in-law put some more into my bowl and looked at her daughter provocatively. My wife said, You'll both have nightmares. Like what? my mother-in-law asked. My wife said, Flocks of swallows pecking at your brains. My mother-in-law said, Little Li, just drink your soup, and ignore this daffy girl. She ate a crab yesterday, so why isn't she afraid that crabs will attack her nose with their pincers? She went on, When I was a little girl, I hated people who gathered swallows' nests. But after moving to the city, I realized that my hatred was groundless. More and more people are eating them these days, because there are so many more rich people. But money is no guarantee that you can get your hands on top-quality 'official nests.' The best nests, the Siamese Tributes from Thailand, never get past Beijing. These blood nests are the best that people in small cities like Liquorland can hope for. And they sell for eight thousand a kilogram in People's Currency, well out of reach for the average person. All this she said with appropriate gravity and at least a hint of braggadocio. Swallows' nests may be wonderful, and all that, but, honestly, it doesn't taste very good, and I'd much prefer something as satisfying as braised pork.

Unstintingly, my mother-in-law continued my education on swallows' nests. After dealing with their nutritional value, she moved on to preparation, which didn't interest me much. What did interest me was the story she told of gathering swallows' nests, the story of her family, her story.

My mother-in-law was born into a family with a long history of gathering swallows' nests. When she was still in her mother's womb, she heard the painful chirpings of the swallows and absorbed the nutrients of their nests. Her mother was a gluttonous woman whose appetite grew even more rapacious when she was pregnant. She often ate swallows' nests behind her husband's back and was never discovered, because she was so skilled at stealing food. My mother-in-law said her mother was born with a set of teeth that were harder than steel, teeth that could chew through tough dry swallows' nests. She never stole a whole nest – her husband always kept count – but would skillfully gnaw off an inch or so from the bottom of each nest where it had been scarred by knives during removal, leaving undetectable marks. My mother-in-law said her mother ate nothing but the best 'official nests,' for those that hadn't gone through the refinement process were the most nutritious. My mother-in-law said that all prized food items lose a significant amount of their nutritional content in the cooking process. Progress, she said, always comes at a cost. Humans invented cooking to please their taste buds, and sacrificed their fierce, brave nature. The reason Eskimos who live near the North Pole have such strong bodies and the ability to endure extreme cold is unquestionably tied to the fact that they eat raw seal meat. If one day they master the complicated and delicate culinary techniques of the Chinese, they will no longer be able to live there. My mother-in-law's mother ate a great amount of raw swallows' nests, so my mother-in-law was a healthy newborn with dark black hair and pink skin, a voice far louder than any baby boy, and four teeth in her mouth. Her father, being a superstitious man who believed that a newborn baby with teeth will bring bad luck to the family, dumped my mother-in-law outside in the weeds. It was the middle of winter. Although it's never terribly cold in Guangdong, the December nights can still be bone chilling. My mother-in-law slept through the night there in the weedy cold, and survived, which changed her father's mind; he carried her back into the house.

According to my mother-in-law, her mother was very pretty; according to my mother-in-law, her father was born with bushy downward-slanting eyebrows, deep-set eyes, a flat nose, thin lips, and a goatee on his pointy chin. My mother-in-law's father was older than his years and skin and bones due to long hours of climbing steep hills and squeezing between cliffs, while her mother sneaked nutritious swallows' nests daily, which gave her a rosy complexion and fair skin from which water could be squeezed, like lilies in June. When my mother-in-law was a year old, her mother ran off to Hong Kong with a swallows'-nests merchant, so my mother-in-law was raised by her father. She said that after her mother ran off, her father cooked a swallow's nest for her every day; it's safe to say that she grew up on swallows' nests. My mother-in-law said she didn't have a single bite of swallow's nest when she was pregnant with my wife, because that was in the early sixties, when life was so difficult. Which is why my wife looks like a black monkey. My wife would improve if she ate swallows' nests, but she refuses. Still I knew it would have been difficult even if she'd wanted some, because my mother-in-law had only been director of the Gourmet Section of the Culinary Academy for a short while, and it would have been virtually impossible to acquire any swallow's nest prior to assuming the directorship. The inferior swallow's nest she made for me had not come through normal channels, which showed that she was quite fond of me, fonder than my wife was. I married my wife in part because her father was a teacher who had been good to me, and one of the major factors keeping me from divorcing my wife has been my affection for my mother-in-law.

By drinking swallow's nest soup and eating baby swallows, my mother-in-law grew into a strong, healthy child. At the age of four, her height and intelligence reached the level of a normal ten-year-old, and she was convinced that her swallows diet was the reason. My mother-in-law said that, in some respects, she was nurtured and raised by male swallows and their precious saliva, since her own mother was afraid to breast-feed her, given the presence of the four teeth with which she was born. 'What kind of mammal would do that?' she said grudgingly. She contended that humans were the cruelest, most ruthless mammals of all, for only a human would refuse to breast-feed her own baby.

My mother-in-law's family lived in a remote corner of the southeastern coast. On clear days, she sat on the beach, within sight of the shadowy, steel-green islands whose giant, rocky caves were home to the swallows. Most of the villagers were fishermen; only my mother-in-law's father and six uncles gathered swallows' nests for a living, as had their ancestors. It was a dangerous, profitable occupation. Most families couldn't have managed it even if they'd wanted to. That is why I stated earlier that my mother-in-law grew up in a swallows'-nests gathering family.

My mother-in-law said her father and uncles were all strong, exceptionally fit men without an ounce of fat, nothing but lean, protein-rich, ruddy-colored muscles that looked as if they were twisted hemp. Anyone with muscles like that must be more than an ape. Her father actually kept two apes, which he called their teachers. During the off seasons, her father and uncles lived on the income from nests collected the previous year, while making preparations for the next round of nest-gathering. Nearly every day, they took the apes up the mountain and had them scale cliffs and climb trees while they themselves imitated the actions. My mother-in-law said that some nest-gatherers on the Malay Peninsula had tried to train apes to gather nests, but weren't very successful. The apes' unreliability affected production. She said that even in his sixties, her father was agile as a swallow and could climb slippery bamboo stalks like a monkey. In any case, due to their genes and to their training, everyone in my mother-in-law's family was adept at scaling cliffs and climbing trees. My mother-in-law said that the most outstanding climber was her youngest uncle, who, with skills like a gecko, could climb a cliff several meters high, bare-handed, without the help of any equipment, in pursuit of swallows' nests. She said she'd nearly forgotten what the other uncles looked like, but clearly remembered this uncle. His body was covered with aging skin like fish scales; he had a lean, dry face, in which two deep-set blue eyes reflected sparkles of melancholy.

My mother-in-law said she was seven years old the first summer she accompanied her father and uncles to the islands to gather swallows' nests. They owned a double-masted boat made of pine and covered with thick layers of paulownia varnish that gave off the fragrance of a forest. A southeastern wind blew that day, sending long, billowing waves chasing after each other. The white sand on the beaches shone bright in the sunlight. My mother-in-law said she was often startled awake by a blinding white light in her dreams. In her bed in Liquorland she could hear the waves from the south sea and smell the seawater. Her father, smoking a pipe, was directing his brothers to load supplies, fresh water, and green bamboo poles on board the boat. Finally, one of her uncles brought over a burly male water buffalo with a strip of red satin tied to its horns. The animal's eyes were bloodshot, white froth gathered at its mouth, as if wild with anger. The kids from the fishing village came out to see the nest-gathering boat set sail. Among them were some of my mother-in-law's playmates, Sea Swallow, Tide Birth, Seal . . . An old woman stood on a rock at the entrance of the village shouting, Seal, Little Seal, come home. Reluctantly, the little boy left, but before he walked off, he said to my mother-in-law, Yanni, can you catch a swallow for me? If you get a live swallow, I'll trade you one of my marbles. He showed her the marble clasped in his palm. I was surprised to learn that my mother-in-law had such a wonderful pet name, Yanni – Swallow Girl. Good heavens! It was the same name as Mrs Karl Marx. Mother-in-law said sadly, That boy, Little Seal, is now a military commander. Obviously, she was airing her dissatisfaction with my father-in-law. What's so great about a military commander? my wife said. My father's a college professor and a distilling specialist, every bit as impressive as some little military commander! My mother-in-law glanced over at me. She always sides with her father, she complained. It's the Electra complex, I said. My wife stared daggers at me. My mother-in-law said, On the day the boat set sail, the most exciting event was getting the buffalo on board.

Buffaloes are very intelligent, she said. Particularly when they're not neutered. Knowing what was in store for it, the animal's eyes turned red as soon as it neared the pier. Panting heavily, it tugged mightily on the harness, nearly jerking my uncle off his feet. My mother-in-law said, A narrow gangplank connected the boat at a slant to the stone steps of the pier. Beneath it only muddy seawater.

The buffalo's front hooves stopped at the edge of the gangplank and it refused to move another inch. My uncle tugged with all his might, like a baby at the nipple, until the steel nose ring stretched the buffalo's nose to bursting point; the pain must have been unbearable. But the buffalo held its ground and refused to go on board. In a life-and-death struggle, what does it matter to lose a nose? My mother-in-law said that her other uncles rushed up to help get the buffalo aboard, but no matter how hard they pushed they couldn't budge it. Not only that, the buffalo kicked out angrily and crippled the leg of one of her uncles.

My mother-in-law said her youngest uncle was not only stronger than his brothers, but more intelligent as well. He took the rope from his brother and walked the buffalo along the beach while talking to the animal, leaving a trail of their footprints in the sand. Finally, he removed his shirt, covered the buffalo's head, and led it back to the gangplank all by himself. The wooden plank sagged heavily from the weight of the animal, turning it into a bow. The animal knew it was walking a dangerous path, for it placed its hooves as carefully as a circus goat on a tightwire. Once the buffalo was aboard, the people boarded, and the gangplank was cast off. With a *whoosh*, the sails were set. Her youngest uncle removed his shirt from the buffalo's head. The animal was quaking, its hooves skittering on the deck. It let out a mournful cry. Gradually, the land disappeared, and the island loomed larger and larger, shrouded in mist and fog, a fairy mountain, a mythical palace.

My mother-in-law said that after her father and uncles anchored their boat in a cove, her youngest uncle took the buffalo ashore. The expression on everyone's face was grave, almost religious. As soon as they set foot on the desolate, thorn-covered ground, the irritable buffalo turned as docile as a lamb. The blood-red color vanished from its eyes, replaced by a deep ocean blue, the same color as her youngest uncle's eyes.

My mother-in-law said it was dusk when they landed on the deserted island. Red lights flickered on the sea, flocks of circling birds filled the air with deafening shrieks. The party of gatherers slept under the night sky, hardly speaking to one another. Early the next morning, after breakfast, her father said, Let's do it. The mysterious, risky job of gathering swallows' nests had begun.

A great many dark caves dotted the island. My mother-in-law said that her father set up an altar outside a large cave, burned a bundle of spirit money, kowtowed several times, then commanded, Kill the sacrificial animal! His six brothers rushed up and shoved the buffalo onto its side. Strangely enough, the powerful buffalo put up no resistance; rather than being pushed off its feet by the six men, it was as if it lay down on its own. Its legs simply crumpled, as if made of dough, and it fell to the ground, where it lay quietly, its powerful neck resting on the rocky surface, connected awkwardly to its gigantic head with its steel-green horns, as if they were welded together. The way it lay there showed that it was willing to accept its fate of serving as a sacrifice to the god of the cave. My mother-in-law said she vaguely sensed that the swallows' nests were the private property of the god of the cave, and that her father and uncles were offering this powerful buffalo as trade with the god, which must have been a ferocious monster, if it could eat a whole buffalo. My mother-in-law said that just thinking about it terrified her. After pushing the buffalo to the ground, her uncles stood aside, and she saw her father remove a glistening ax from his waistband. Holding it in both hands, he walked up to the animal. Her heart, seemingly in the grip of a massive hand, was barely able to start again after each beat. Her father mumbled something, a look of fear danced in his black eyes. Suddenly she felt immensely sorry for her father and for the buffalo. She sensed that this man, who was as skinny as a monkey, was as pitiable as the buffalo that lay stiffly on the rocky ground: this was not something that either the butcher or the butchered wanted, but both were driven by an overpowering force to do what must be done. When my mother-in-law saw the immense, oddly shaped opening of the cave, heard the strange noises coming from inside, and felt the ominous air spewing from the mouth, she was inspired by the thought that what scared the daylights out of both her father and the buffalo was the god inside. She saw the buffalo's tightly closed eyes, the long lashes squeezed by the eyelids into a thin line. An emerald-green fly was picking at something in the corner of its moist eye. My mother-in-law was so troubled by the disgusting fly that the corners of her eyes began to itch, but

263

the buffalo didn't so much as twitch. My mother-in-law's father walked up alongside the buffalo, looking around as if in a trance. What was he thinking? My mother-in-law said that, as a matter of fact, he saw nothing, that looking around was a sign that his mind was empty. Holding the ax in his left hand, he spat into his right palm, then switched the ax to his right hand and spat into his left palm. Finally, he held the ax in both hands and shifted his legs slightly, as if trying to stand more firmly. He took a deep breath and held it; as his face darkened and his eyes bulged, he raised the ax high over his head and brought it down hard. My mother-in-law heard a thump as the ax split the buffalo's head. Her father exhaled and stood there weakly, as if his body were falling apart. A long time passed before he bent down to pry the ax from the buffalo's head. The animal let out a dull cry; it made several attempts to stand up, but failed. It was unable to raise its head, for the ligaments in its neck were severed. Then different parts of its body began to twitch, one after another, seemingly beyond the control of its brain. My mother-in-law's father raised his ax again and chopped down savagely, enlarging the wound above the buffalo's neck. He made a 'hey-hey' sound as he hacked away, each chop right on target, making the wound deeper and deeper, until black blood spewed from the buffalo's neck. The smell of hot, raw blood streaked into my mother-in-law's nostrils. Her father's hands were covered in blood; she could feel the slipperiness of the ax in the way her father repeatedly dried his hands with grass. Following the further enlargement of the wound, fresh blood splashed over her father's face. Bubbles gurgled out of the buffalo's severed windpipe. With her hands around her own neck, my mother-in-law turned away; when she turned back, her father had already chopped off the head. He threw down the ax, picked up the head by its steely horns with his bloody hands, and carried it over to the altar outside the cave. What puzzled my mother-in-law was the buffalo's eyes, which had been tightly closed before it died, but were now wide open. Still as blue as the ocean, they reflected the people around them. My mother-in-law said her father stepped back after arranging the buffalo's head on the altar. Mumbling something unintelligible, he knelt on the ground and kowtowed by the cave opening. Her uncles also knelt down on the rocky ground and kowtowed to the cave opening.

After the sacrifice was completed, her father and uncles went into the cave with their tools, leaving her outside to guard the boat and equipment. My mother-in-law said that silence followed their entry into the cave, like a stone sinking to the bottom of the sea. Terrified of facing the buffalo's head with its staring eyes and the body from which blood continued to flow, she gazed out to where the sea and the sky merged. The mainland had disappeared behind the sea. Flying over the island were many giant birds whose names she didn't know. Some fat, chattering rats crawled out from cracks between rocks and swarmed over the buffalo's corpse. My mother-in-law tried to drive them away, but they jumped half a meter high, and turned their attack to my mother-in-law, who was just a little girl at the time. As the rats began clawing at her chest, she ran screaming into the cave.

Crying out for her father and uncles, she threaded her way through the darkness. Suddenly the cave lit up in front of her and seven blazing torches appeared above her head. My mother-in-law said that her father fashioned torches out of treetops soaked in resin during the off season. The torches were about a meter long, with a thin handle that could be held in the mouth. My mother-in-law said she stopped crying as soon as she saw the light from the torches, for a sacred and grave force clutched her throat. Compared to the work her father and uncles were engaged in, her petty fears weren't worth mentioning.

It was a gigantic cave, about sixty meters high and eighty meters wide, but these estimates of size came from my mother-in-law's adult assessment of a childhood memory. Exactly how long the cave was, she couldn't say. There were sounds of water flowing in the cave and dripping from the ceiling; a cool breeze blew. She looked up at the torches burning above her; the flames were reflected on her father's and uncles' faces, particularly her handsome, youngest uncle, whose skin had turned amber. His face even had the texture of amber; it was a moving, unforgettable sight, like the champagne called Italian Widow Wine, which is refreshing and rich, with a wonderful aftertaste that surpasses all others. Holding a crackling torch in his mouth and pressing his body against an indentation in the rocky cliff, he stretched his knife toward a sparkling, creamy-white object – a swallow's nest.

My mother-in-law said that what first caught her attention when she entered the cave wasn't the resin torches above her head, or her young uncle's handsome face lit up in the flame, but the flocks of swallows flying all over the cave. Startled by the fires, they came flying out of their nests, but were unwilling to stray too far from them. The flapping wings in the cave were like brilliant flowers on mountain slopes, like swarms of circling butterflies. Their chirping sounds filled the cave, as if they were weeping blood and crying blood. My mother-in-law said she could hear the bitterness and anger in their voices. Her father, perched atop tall green bamboo stalks high above her head, reached the other side of the cave, where over a dozen nests had crystallized. With a strip of white cloth wrapped around his head, her father lifted up his face, his dark black nostrils flaring, looking like a roasted piglet. He reached out with a white-handled knife and, with a single stroke, cut down a nest, which he caught in the air and placed into the sack with a forked opening that hung at his waist. Several little black things fell off and landed at my mother-in-law's feet with a light pop. Bending down and feeling around with her hand, she picked up pieces of broken eggshell with yolk and egg white clinging to them. My mother-in-law said she was deeply saddened. She also felt terrible watching her father risk his life to gather swallows' nests dozens of meters above the ground, supported by only a few rickety stalks of green bamboo. Swarms of swallows rushed toward the torch in her father's mouth, as if trying to put out the fire to protect their nests and their offspring; but they were always forced back at the last minute by the heat. Their wings quickly veered off just as they were about to be singed by the flames; blue feathers flickered in the light of the fire. My mother-in-law said her father paid no attention to the harassing swallows. Even when their wings slapped against his head, his eyes were still trained on the nests stuck to the cliff; one by one he scraped them off with steady, accurate, determined skill.

My mother-in-law said her father and uncles slid down from the bamboo stalks leaning against the cliff when their torches were about to burn out. They gathered together and lit up another batch of torches, while they emptied the nests in their bags and stacked them on a sheet of white cloth. She said that the usual arrangement was that her father only gathered nests for the duration of a single torch. His younger brothers continued working for the duration of three more torches, while he stayed down to guard the nests from the rats. In the meantime, he rested his already weakened body. They were surprised and pleased when my mother-in-law appeared. In a scolding voice, her father asked why she'd entered the cave on her own. She said she was afraid to be alone outside the cave. My mother-in-law said that as soon as she uttered the word 'afraid,' her father's expression changed abruptly. He slapped her and said, Shut up. She said she learned later that no one was allowed to use words like 'falling,' 'slipping,' 'death,' or 'afraid.' Otherwise, they would meet with a great calamity. She started to cry from being slapped. Her youngest uncle said, Don't cry, Yanni. I'll catch a swallow for you later.

The men smoked a pipeful, wiped their sweaty bodies with the bags at their waists, then stuck the torches between their teeth and went back into the depths of the cave. Her father said, Now that you're here, guard the nests while I go up to work through another torch.

My mother-in-law said her father went off with a torch held between his teeth. She saw running water on the cave floor, and snakes swimming in the water; the floor was littered with rotten bamboo stalks and vines. Layers of swallows' droppings covered the rocks on the cave floor. Her eyes followed her youngest uncle, since he had promised to catch a live swallow for her. She saw him climb up several green bamboo stalks and, as if on flying feet, quickly reach a height of a dozen or more meters. He found a foothold on a crack in the cliff, then bent down, lifted up the bamboo stalk under his feet and stuck it into the crack; then he lifted up another one, which he laid sideways, and another to prop up the others. Now three bamboo stalks formed a profoundly scary scaffold. Stepping on this tottering overpass, her youngest uncle approached the arched firmament, where a dozen extra large, white swallows' nests hung from a mushroom-shaped stalactite. When the other swallows were fleeing their nests, these swallows, seemingly undisturbed, stayed where they were. Maybe they knew their nests were built in an absolutely safe spot. The heads of two sprightly swallows stuck out from one of the nests. Several more of the birds were hanging upside down from the stalactite, their heads moving rapidly as they pulled the snowy white, crystal-clear threads to weave their delicate, elegant nests. They probably didn't know that her youngest uncle's hands and feet were negotiating the cold, slippery cliff like a large, scary lizard, inching closer and closer to them. My mother-in-law said the swallows used their forward-facing talons to grip the rocks, toiling and suffering the hardships of building a nest. Their short beaks were like a nimble weaver's shuttle, moving swiftly back and forth on the arched surface. After pulling the shiny threads for a while, they would tense their bodies, flap their wings, jerk their tail feathers, and cough up more of the precious saliva from their throats, which they held in their beaks to pull into shiny threads again. In an instant, the threads crystallized to form transparent, white jade. My mother-in-law said that the process was a rare sight in nature, but those dignitaries and eminent personages could never understand the nests' true value, unaware of the hardships the birds endured; nor did they know the difficulty undertaken by the nests' gatherers.

My mother-in-law's youngest uncle was hanging nearly upside down on an outcropping of the mushroom-like stalactite. It was incomprehensible that, using only his feet, he could hold on to a grooved surface that was so slippery. The torch hung sideways, its flame burning bright above his head. The bag around his waist also hung upside down, like two torn flags drooping shyly in the rain. Obviously, he couldn't open his mouth to speak, but his situation also made it impossible for him to put the nests into his bag. My mother-in-law said that her father, who had already slid down from the cliff, was now holding the torch and looking up at his youngest brother, whose very life was suspended upside down from the ceiling, ready to pick up the nests as soon as they hit the ground.

My mother-in-law said she's never seen nests that big since, not once. They were ancient nests. She said that all swallows instinctively build their nests on top of previous ones. As long as the nests aren't damaged, the birds can build a new one the size of a conical hat. And, of course, the undamaged nests are made of pure saliva, with no impurities – top-quality nests.

He stretched out his hand, which held a sharp, triple-edged razor. His body was stretched to a frightening length, like a snake. My mother-in-law said she saw shiny beads of sweat dripping down from the ends of his hair. His razor was nearly touching the edge of the giant nest; it did, it touched it! His body stretched even longer, his razor jabbed at the base of the nest, his hand sawing the razor back and forth, while sweat poured from his head. The swallows flew out of the nest; displaying unusual courage, they crashed into his face again and again, showing no fear for their own lives. My mother-in-law said that the nest was firmly anchored to the rock surface, particularly since it was an ancient nest, and actually seemed to be growing out of the rock itself. That made her youngest uncle's task particularly difficult; ignoring the frenzied swallows that were smacking against his face, he kept a cool head and a firm hand, gritting his teeth and closing his eyes to persevere. He bit his lip and tasted his own blood.

My mother-in-law said, My God, it was like a hundred years had passed. The colossal nest finally started to tip over and hung by a thread; one more cut, and it would fall off, like an enormous piece of white gold.

Little uncle, try a little harder! my mother-in-law cried out despite herself. Following her cry, his body thrashed forward and the white nest fell from the rock. Drifting and whirling in the air, after the longest time, it landed at her and her father's feet. Tumbling down with the fallen nest was her little uncle, the one with unsurpassable skills. Normally he could glide down from a height of several feet without hurting himself; but this time he was too high and his body was twisted the wrong way. His brains splashed all over the swallow's nest; the torch was still burning when it fell to the ground, sputtering out only after it hit the shallow water on the cave floor.

My mother-in-law said that her father also fell to his death in a cave five years after her youngest uncle. But the job of gathering swallows' nests didn't stop just because someone died. She could not continue her father's line of work, but didn't want to depend on her uncles either. So, on one hot summer day, carrying the colossal nest stained with her uncle's blood, she set off on a long journey of her own. She was fourteen years old.

My mother-in-law said that, under normal circumstances, she could never have become a famous chef of swallows' nests, for those heart-breaking, soul-stirring scenes flew past her eyes every time she plucked impurities from a nest with a needle. She was able to cook every nest with extreme respect and care only because she knew the bitter hardships – those of the swallows and those of the nest-gatherers – behind each one. She had gained invaluable experience in regard to swallows' nests. But deep down she was uneasy. The connection between the nests and human brains made her uncomfortable, feelings that disappeared only after Liquorland accomplished the glorious coup of cooking and eating meat boys.

Clearly worried, my mother-in-law said, The demand for swallows' nests in mainland China rose sharply in the 1990s, while the occupation of gathering the nests in southern China all but disappeared. Now the gatherers take modern equipment like hydraulic lifts into the caves, which not only destroy the nests but kill the swallows in the process. There are, in fact, no more nests to be harvested in China. Under these circumstances, China must import huge quantities of nests from Southeast Asia to supply the demands of the Chinese people, and that has caused the price of swallow's nest to skyrocket. In Hong Kong, each kilogram costs twenty-five hundred US dollars and the price keeps going up. That, in turn, has driven the gatherers in other countries into a gathering frenzy. In the old days, my father and his brothers only harvested nests once a year, but now gatherers in Thailand harvest them four times annually. Twenty years from now, children will no longer know what a swallow's nest looks like, my mother-in-law said as she finished the soup in her bowl.

I said, As a matter of fact, even today, there are no more than a thousand Chinese children who have tasted swallow's nest. The availability of the stuff doesn't matter to the average person, or to the masses. So why worry about it?

Chapter Eight

I

Dear Elder Brother Yidou

I received and have read your story and your letter.

After reading 'Swallows' Nests,' a parade of thoughts thronged my mind. When I was a child, my granddad told me that when rich people sit down to eat, their tables are filled with things like camel's hooves, bear's paw, monkey brains, swallow's nest, and things like that. I've seen a camel, and I have no reason to doubt that their big, meaty hooves make for good eating, though I've never had the good fortune of tasting one. Once, as a child, I ate a horse's hoof my second brother secretly cut off of a dead horse and brought home from his production brigade. Of course, we didn't have a famous chef to prepare it, so my mother just boiled it in water with some salt. There wasn't much meat on it, so I filled up on the broth. Still, it left a lasting impression, one I invariably bring up with my brother when we're together at New Year's, as if the delightful flavor still lay on my tongue. That was in 1960, at the beginning of the famine, which is probably why the memory has stayed with me so long. As for bear's paw, a couple of years ago an industrialist invited me to dinner at his home, and when the last dish was carried in, a plate of black lumpy things, he announced with great solemnity, This is bear's paw, brought specially all the way from Heilongjiang. Excitedly, I picked up a piece with my chopsticks, put it in my mouth, and savored it slowly. It was sticky and mushy, neither particularly fragrant nor particularly foul-tasting, sort of like a pig's leg tendons. But I raved about it to my host anyway. He picked up a piece, tasted it, and announced, It didn't swell the way it should. He criticized the chef for not being up to par. I was too embarrassed to ask him what he meant by 'swell.' Some time later, I asked a friend who worked in a Beijing restaurant what it meant to 'swell' something. He told me I'd eaten dried bear's paw, which had to swell first. Fresh bear's paw, on the other hand, doesn't require it, but it's still hard to prepare. If you obtain some fresh bear's paw, he said, you have to dig a hole in the ground, line it with pieces of limestone, then put the bear's paw inside and cover it with more limestone, which you douse with warm water until it's hot enough to crack; that's the only way to loosen the bristly hairs enough to pluck them out. He said that eating bear's paw requires patience, since the softer it is, the better it tastes. If it's planned for dinner, you need to begin stewing it at dawn. That's too much trouble, if you ask me. I recall that my granddad also said that, since bears stop eating in the winter, they lick their paws to quell any hunger pangs, which is why they're so treasured. But I have my doubts about that. As for monkey brains, I used to think they were just that, the brains of a monkey. But then someone said it was a sort of tree fungus. That's something I've never eaten, although I have taken monkey brain fungus tablets for my stomach problem. Not long ago, I met someone from a pharmaceutical company on the train, and he said there was no way they could gather enough monkey brain fungus to meet the demand, so they simply lace it with wood-ear fungus or dried mushrooms. That surprised me, since I never dreamed that even medicine was adulterated. If they'll adulterate medicines, what can we expect to be unadulterated? The last thing I want to talk about are those frightful swallows' nests. I've never seen one and never eaten one. In the novel *Dream of the Red Chamber*, every time Lin Daiyu's consumption acts up, she drinks swallow's-nest soup, which means it's good stuff, and far too expensive for most people. But I never thought it was *that* expensive. Most of us could work half a lifetime and still not earn enough to buy a couple of catties of swallow's nest. And after reading your story, it's something I never want to try, partly because of the expense, but also because it involves such cruelty. I'm not one of those hypocritical 'swallow-ists,' but it pains me to think of one of those golden swallows making a nest out of its own saliva. My level is about on a par with 'my wife' in your story. I doubt that swallow's nest is as mystical as 'my mother-in-law' says. Swallow's nest is popular in Hong Kong, but if you look at the people walking the streets of Hong Kong, you'll see that most of them are short and scrawny. In Shandong, where we eat sweet-potato cakes and thick green onions, you'll have no trouble finding tall people, and even though not every one of our women is a raving beauty, you won't have any problem finding one. It should be obvious that the nutritional value of those things can't come close to baked sweet potatoes. Spending that kind of money to eat something that dirty sounds pretty stupid to me. The cruelty of destroying a swallow's home to get one of the nests moves it beyond stupidity. In recent years, and especially since I've been reading your stories, I've discovered that the Chinese have indeed racked their brains in the pursuit of new and exotic foods. Needless to say, most of those who have the wherewithal to pamper their palates don't need to spend their own money to do so, while most people just stuff their bellies with whatever they have at hand. We live in an age of mountains of victuals and oceans of potables, and the petty bureaucrats in your stories are more overweening than Liu Wencai, who dined exclusively on webbed ducks' feet. This has become commonplace lately. Not many years ago, people still wrote breezy columns or drew political cartoons satirizing this trend, but you don't even see them anymore.

But back to the issue at hand. In my view, 'Swallows' Nests' is still too political, and if I were you, I'd empty my belly of every vestige of passion and rewrite it. Gathering swallows' nests, an ancient and endangered profession replete with mystery and legend, could make a wonderful story. For emphasis, focus on the mystery and the legends.

My superior has more or less agreed to let me visit Liquorland. But I can't leave until I've finished the draft of my novel. I've committed the date of your first Ape Liquor Festival to memory, and will be finished in time to attend.

I'm returning your manuscript by express special delivery. Please let me know when it arrives.

Wishing you success with your writing,

Mo Yan

II

Dear Mo Yan

Your letter and the express special delivery package with my manuscript arrived. You really didn't have to spend all that money – first-class registered mail would have been fine. A few extra days wouldn't have made any difference to me, since I am now writing a story I call 'Liquor Fairy,' and any changes to 'Swallows' Nests' will have to wait.

You got so emotional over my 'Swallows' Nests,' even returning to your childhood, when you ate a boiled horse's hoof, that even if it never finds its way into print, it has already justified its existence – without it, would you ever have written me such a long letter?

As you wrote in your letter, the nutritional value of swallows' nests has been greatly exaggerated, and I think the best you can say about it is it's a bird secretion high in protein. It has no magical properties, for if it did, the few people who eat the things, as many as four or five a day, would surely have found the secret of immortality by now. I've eaten it once, just the way I wrote in my story. When you come to Liquorland, I'll arrange for you to sample some. The actual eating isn't as important as the experience, of course.

I'll try to control my passion better. Given the current state of affairs, no one can stem the raging tide, and when you think about what society has come to, everyone shares the blame. My job has made it easy for me to sample the finest wines and liquors in the world, most of which are nearly as expensive as swallow's nest. Common folk have probably never seen, let alone tasted, wines like Gevrey-Chambertin and de la Romanée-Conti from France, or Lay and Doktor from Germany, or the Italian Barbaresco or Lacryma Christi. They're true treasures, every one of them, unquestioned wines of the gods, pure ambrosia. Please come, and make it soon. I may not be able to boast of much, but it won't be difficult to see that you drink only the best while you're here. Better that you and I drink the stuff than those corrupt, greedy officials.

There's so much I want to tell you, but since you'll be in Liquorland soon, I'll save it till we can talk face to face. After we toast each other, we can talk to our hearts' content.

I'm enclosing my latest story, 'Ape Liquor,' and await your criticisms. I was going to make it longer, but I've been so tired the past few days, I decided to wrap it up where it was. You don't need to mail it back after you've read it. Just bring it along when you come to Liquorland. I'm going to take a day off, then start another story. After that I'll make changes to 'Swallows' Nests.'

Wishing you the best,
Your disciple

Li Yidou

III

Ape Liquor, by Li Yidou

Ape Liquor is Yuan's Liquor. Who was its distiller? My father-in-law, Yuan Shuangyu, a professor at the Brewer's College in Liquorland. If Liquorland is a glossy pearl in the heart of our glorious motherland, then the Brewer's College is the pearl of Liquorland, and my father-in-law the pearl of the Brewer's College – the most lustrous, the most brilliant. It has been the grand opportunity of a lifetime to become the elderly gentleman's student and then his son-in-law. So many people envy and covet my good fortune. When I was giving this story a title, I pondered for the longest time, unable to decide whether I should call it 'Ape Liquor' or 'Yuan's Liquor.' I finally decided to call it 'Ape Liquor,' for the time being, even though it might smack somewhat of Fauvism. My father-in-law is an erudite man who possesses an upright character. In his search for Ape Liquor, he was willing to live among the apes on White Ape Mountain, eating the wind and sleeping in the dew, combed by breezes and bathed by the rain, until success was his at last.

In order for my teetotaling readers to gain an understanding of my father-in-law's erudition, I shall have to copy out a large portion of the handouts he gave us for a class he taught on The Origins of Liquor.

At the time I was a young, know-nothing student; entering the sacred temple of liquor from a poor peasant family, I knew next to nothing about alcoholic spirits. When my father-in-law walked grandly up to the podium, carrying a cane and dressed in a white suit, I was of the opinion that liquor was just spiced-up water. What could this old fellow say about it that was worthwhile? Standing at the podium, he began to laugh before saying a word. Amid his laughter, he took a small flask out of his pocket, removed the stopper, and took a drink from it. Then he smacked his lips and asked, Students, what am I drinking? Someone said, Tap water, someone else said, Boiled water, another said, Clear liquid, and yet another said, Liquor. I knew it was liquor – I could smell it – but I muttered, Urine. Good! My father-in-law said, slapping the podium with his hand. Whoever said liquor, please stand up. A girl with braided hair rose from her seat. Blushing bright red, she took a look at my father-in-law, then lowered her head and played with the tips of her braids – a common habit among girls with braids, something they learned from the movies. My father-in-law asked, How did you know it was liquor? In an almost imperceptible voice, she said, I could smell it . . . Why is your sense of smell so keen? my father-in-law asked. The girl's blush deepened, her face seemed to be burning up. Well? Why? my father-in-law asked. In an even lower voice, she said, I . . . I've had a keen sense of smell these past few days . . . My father-in-law slapped his forehead, as if suddenly enlightened, and said, OK, I get it. You can sit down. What did he 'get'? Do you know? I didn't, not until much later, when he told me that girls have a particularly keen sense of smell during their periods, and also a more active imagination. That's why so many important discoveries in human history have been so closely linked with the female menstrual cycle. Now, the student who said urine, please stand up, my father-in-law said gravely. I felt a sudden buzzing in my ears, and saw stars flying in front of my eyes, as if I'd been clubbed. I hadn't realized an old fart like that could have such good hearing. Stand up. Don't be shy! he said. My embarrassment attracted the attention of the entire class, including the girl with braids, who was having her period – her name was Jin Manli, a typical name for a female secret agent. I'll discuss what happened between the two of us in another story. Later on she became one of my father-in-law's graduate students – Damn, this mouth of mine, which is fouler smelling than dogshit, has got me into trouble again. Li Yidou, Li Yidou, what did your parents say before you left home? Didn't they tell you to speak less and listen more? You and that mouth of yours, even a medicinal plaster couldn't keep it shut. Like a gorged woodpecker that dies stuck in a tree, its beak is its undoing – I stood up in total embarrassment, not daring to raise my head. What's your name? Li Yidou. No wonder you have such a vivid imagination; you're the Liquor God Reincarnate. The class broke up laughing. He stilled the laughter with his hands, took a drink of the liquor, smacked his lips, and said, Sit down, Li Yidou.

Frankly speaking, I like you very much. You're different from the others.

I sat down in total confusion, while watching my father-in-law recap his flask, shake it vigorously, and hold it up to the light to enjoy the sight of the bubbles inside. He said in a lilting voice, Dear students, this is a sacred solution, an indispensable liquid in human life. At present, in a time of reforms and liberalization, its functions increase daily. It is no exaggeration to say that without liquor the revitalization of Liquorland would just be empty talk. Liquor is sunshine, it is air, it is blood. Liquor is music, painting, ballet, poetry. A distiller of liquor is a master of many skills. I hope that a master distiller will emerge from among you to gain glory for our country with a gold medal from the World's Fair in Barcelona. A while ago I heard someone scorn our profession by saying that it had no future. Students, I can tell you that one day, even if the earth is destroyed, the molecular essence of liquor will still be flying around the universe.

Amid rousing applause, my father-in-law raised his flask high, with a solemn, even divine expression on his face, like that look on a hero's face we so often see in the movies. I was ashamed over having blasphemed such a significant liquid by calling it urine, even though it all becomes urine sooner or later.

The origin of this celestial liquid is still a riddle today, my father-in-law said. Several thousand years of liquor have converged to form the Yellow River and the Yangtze River, but we cannot locate its source. We can only speculate. In their spectrum analysis of the universe, Chinese astronomers have discovered vast quantities of alcohol molecules in outer space. Recently an American astronaut detected the strong aroma of alcohol inside her spacecraft, which brought waves of euphoric sensation, as if she were slightly drunk. I ask you, where did these alcohol molecules come from? Where did the scent detected by the astronaut come from? Another planet? Or might it have been dissipated remnants from right here in Liquorland? Students, spread the wings of your imagination!

My father-in-law continued, Our ancestors attributed the invention of liquor to deities and made up beautiful and moving stories about it. Please look at your handouts.

The ancient Egyptians believed that liquor was discovered by Osiris, guardian of the dead. Liquor was offered as sacrifice to the ancestors, to raise their souls from suffering and give them wings on which to fly away to Paradise. Even those of us who are still alive feel a sensation of flying when we're drunk. Therefore, the essence of liquor is the spirit of flying. The ancient Mesopotamians made Noah the brewer's laureate. They said he not only created the human race anew but also gave humans the wonderful gift of liquor in order to avoid disasters. The Mesopotamians even identified the place where Noah made his liquor – Erivan.

The ancient Greeks had their own god of liquor; his name was Dionysus, the specialist in liquor among the Olympian gods and goddesses. He represented wild ecstasy, the unfettering of all shackles, the releasing of a soaring free spirit.

Religions that place great stock in spirituality have different explanations for the origin of liquor. Buddhism and Islam are replete with antipathy toward liquor, declaring it to be the source of all evil. On the other hand, Christianity considers liquor to be Jehovah's blood, the material embodiment of His dedication to the salvation of the world. Christians believe that drinking wine will help them connect with God, correspond with God. It is profound that the Christian doctrine treats wine as a kind of spirit, even though we all know that liquor is a substance. But let me remind you all that anyone who treats liquor only as a material object will never become a true artist. Liquor is spiritual, a belief whose traces still remain in many languages. For instance, in the English language hard liquor is called 'spirits,' while the French language labels liquor with a high alcoholic content 'spiritueux.' These terms share a linguistic root with 'spiritual.'

But we are materialists, after all. We emphasize the fact that liquor is spiritual simply because we want to let our minds spread their wings and fly high. When they are tired from flying, when they settle back to earth, they must still seek the origins of liquor among a pile of ancient written records. This is enormously satisfying work. An alcoholic beverage called 'Soma' and another called 'Baoma', both used in sacrificial rites, are mentioned in India's oldest religious text and literary collection, the *Veda*. The Hebrew Old Testament often mentions 'sour wine' and 'sweet wine'. Our ancient oracle bones record, 'This liquor □ to Dajia □ □ to Ding,' meaning an offering of liquor to the dead, Dajia and Ding. There is another word on an oracle bone, *chang*, which Ban Gu of the Han Dynasty, in his 'Interpretation of the White Tiger,' interpreted this way: *Chang* is a brew made of the fragrance of all plants. *Chang*, meaning fine liquor, is synonymous with unrestrained, satisfying, enjoyable, unstoppable, unhindered: as in unrestrained access, unrestrained good cheer, unrestrained talking, unrestrained passage, unrestrained imagination, unrestrained drinking . . . Liquor is the embodiment of this free realm. So far, the earliest known record of liquor found in other parts of the world is a cork excavated from a prehistoric tomb in Egypt. On it we find the seal of Ramses the Third's brewery (1198–1166 BC).

Let me give you more examples of early written records on liquor. For instance, 'li' in Chinese means a kind of sweet liquor; 'bojah' in ancient Hindu is a liquor made of grain extracts; in an Ethiopian tribal language, liquor made from barley is called 'bosa'. 'Cer visia' in old Gallic, 'Pior' in old German, 'eolo' in old Scandinavian, and 'bere' in old Anglo-Saxon are all terms for beer in various ancient people's languages. Fermented mare's milk was called 'koumiss' by ancient nomads on the Mongolian steppe, and 'masoun' by the Mesopotamians. Mead was called 'melikaton' by the ancient Greeks, 'aqua musla' by the ancient Romans and 'chouchen' by the Celts. The ancient Scandinavians often gave mead as a wedding gift, which is the origin of 'honeymoon,' a term still in use all around the world. Written records such as these can be found everywhere in ancient civilizations, and it is impossible to list them all.

Quoting a big chunk of my father-in-law's handout has probably annoyed the hell out of you. Sorry. I'm bored out of my skull too, but I have no choice. Please bear with me a little longer, it'll be over soon, just another minute. Regrettably, we can only go back to circa the tenth century BC to ascertain the origins of liquor through written records. It is perfectly legitimate to speculate that the origins of liquor predate recorded history, since many archeological finds provide sufficient evidence. The history of liquor exceeds ten thousand years, excavated evidence for which includes a clay liquor tripod from Longshan, China, beautifully crafted 'zun' and 'jia' wine vessels from Da Wen Kou, and the liquor rites on a fresco found in Spain's Altamira caves.

Students, my father-in-law said, liquor is an organic compound, naturally produced as one of Nature's ingenious creations. It is made of sugar transformed by enzymes into alcohol, plus some other ingredients. There are so many plants with sugar content that they will never be exhausted. Fruits with high sugar content, like grapes, are easily broken down by enzymes. If a pile of grapes is brought to a low, moist place by the wind, water, birds or animals, the proper amount of water and the right temperature can activate the enzymes on the skins to turn grape juice into sweet, delicious liquor. In China, an old saying goes, 'Apes make liquor.' The ancient text 'Evening Talks in Penglong' records the following: 'There are many apes in Mount Huang. In the spring and summer, they pick flowers and fruits, and place them in a low place among rocks, where the mixture ferments into liquor with an aroma that can be detected for several hundred paces.' An 'Occasional Note from Western Guang' in *Miscellaneous Jottings* records: 'Apes abound in the mountains of such Western Guang prefectures as Pingle. They are skilled in plucking flowers to make liquor. When woodcutters enter the mountains, those who find their nests can retrieve several pints of liquor. It is fragrant and delicious, and has been named Ape Liquor.' Now if apes knew how to pick a variety of fruits and put them in a shallow place to brew liquor, how much more likely is it for our human ancestors? Other countries have stories similar to that of apes making liquor. For instance, French brewers generally believe that birds collect fruit in their nests, but unforeseen incidents prevent them from swallowing the fruit. As time passes, birds' nests become containers for making liquor. Humans must have been inspired by birds and beasts in their pursuit of the secrets of making liquor. The natural appearance of liquor and the emergence of plants with sugar content probably occurred at about the same time. So it is safe to say that, before there were humans, the earth was already permeated with the aroma of liquor.

So when did humans actually start distilling liquor? The answer to this question lies in the discovery by humans of the existence of liquor in Nature. Some of the boldest ones, or those who were dying of thirst, drank the liquor in shallows among the rocks or from the birds' nests. After tasting this marvelous elixir and experiencing great pleasure, they flocked off to look for more shallows among the rocks and for more birds' nests. The motivation to make their own liquor naturally occurred after they had drunk all the liquor they could find. Imitation followed motivation; they copied monkeys by throwing fruit into shallows and into birds' nests. But they didn't always succeed; sometimes the fruit dried up and sometimes it simply rotted away. Many times humans abandoned their quest to learn from the apes, but the overpowering seductiveness of the elixir enticed them into summoning their courage and starting over again with their experiments. Eventually, their experiments succeeded, and a fruity liquor was created with Nature's help. Ecstatic, they danced naked in their fire-lit caves. This process of learning how to make liquor occurred simultaneously with a mastery of planting crops and domesticating animals. When grains replaced meat and fish as the people's main staple, they began experimenting with the fermentation of grains. The motivation for these experiments might have been accidental, or might have come as a revelation from God. But when the first drop of liquor formed from steam accumulating in an earthenware still, human history turned a new, magnificent page. It was the start of the glorious age of civilization.

That ends my lecture, my father-in-law announced.

Now that class was over, my father-in-law gulped down the remaining liquor in his flask and smacked his lips repeatedly. Then he put it in his pocket, stuffed his briefcase under his arm, and, after casting me a mean yet meaningful glance, walked out of the classroom, head held high, chest thrust out.

Four years later, I graduated from college and took an exam to become my father-in-law's graduate student. The title of my thesis was 'Latin American "Magic Realist" Novels and the Distilling of Liquor.' It won high praise from my father-in-law, and I passed the oral defense with ease. It was even sent to the *Journal of Brewer's College*, where it was published as the leading essay. My father-in-law accepted me as his Ph.D. student and happily approved my area of research: How are a distiller's emotions manifested in the physics and chemistry of the distilling process, and how do they affect the overall taste of a liquor? My father-in-law believed that my topic, with its fresh angle, was both highly significant and highly interesting. He suggested that I spend a year in the library, reading all the relevant books and collecting sufficient materials, before sitting down to write.

Following my father-in-law's instructions, I threw myself, body and soul, into my studies at the Liquorland Municipal Library. One day I found a rare book called *Strange Events in Liquorland*, which included an article that particularly interested me. I recommended it to my father-in-law. How could I have known that it would affect him so profoundly that he would go off to White Ape Mountain to live with the apes? I'll quote the entire story here for you; read it if you want to, skip it if you don't.

In Liquorland there lived an old man surnamed Sun, who had a fondness for drink. Blessed with a great capacity for liquor, he consumed several pints at each sitting. He had once owned ten acres of fertile land and tiled houses with dozens of rooms, but they all went to pay his drinking expenses. His wife, surnamed Liu, took the children and remarried. The old man wandered the streets, with matted hair, a dirty face, and tattered clothes, a common beggar. When he saw someone buying liquor, he begged some by kneeling in front of the person and kowtowing until his forehead bled. It was a pitiful sight. Suddenly one day, a white-haired old man with a young face materialized in front of him and said, 'A hundred li southeast of here is a tree-lined mountain called White Ape Mountain, where apes have created ponds overflowing with wine. Why not take yourself there to drink? Is it not better than begging here?' Hearing those words, Sun kowtowed without a word of thanks and left like a whirlwind. Three days later, he reached the foothills of the mountain, and when he looked up, he saw a dense growth of trees but no path. So he climbed by holding on to vines and roots. Gradually he entered thickets where ancient trees reached the sky and blocked out the sun, the forest floor a mass of entangled vines and roots, where birds' cries came in waves. A giant animal appeared before him. It was the size of an ox, with electrifying eyes and thunderous roars that shook the plants and trees. Terrified, Sun tried to run away, and in his haste, fell into a deep ravine. Hanging upside down from a tree, he thought he would surely die. Then the aroma of wine entered his nostrils, quickly revitalizing him. He climbed down the tree and, following the aroma, came to a place overgrown with shrubs, where strange flowers and rare fruit hung from the treetops. A little white ape was picking a cluster of amber-like purple fruit. When it bounded away, the old man followed it to an open space. He saw a giant rock several feet wide, with a hollow in the middle, at least a yard deep. The little ape threw the fruit into the hollow area with a crackling sound like broken tiles. The smell of wine billowed upward. Moving closer to take a look, he saw that the hollow was filled with vintage wine. A group of apes came up carrying large leaves like rounded fans, folded into the shape of plates, which they used to scoop up the wine. Before long, they were all engaged in laughable behaviors: stumbling around, baring their teeth, and casting flirtatious looks. When the old man approached them, the apes retreated several feet, shouting angrily. But he paid no heed. He rushed up, thrust his neck into the hollow, and began sucking up wine like a whale. He did not rise for a long time, and when he did, his insides had been cleansed, his mouth was filled with a wonderful taste, and he felt like a weightless immortal. He then imitated the apes' drunken behavior: jumping up and down, shouting and yelling. The apes quickly followed his example, and they all got along very well. From then on, he remained in the area near the rock, sleeping when he was tired and drinking as soon as he woke up, sometimes playing games with the apes. He enjoyed himself so much that he did not want to go back down the mountain. People in his village all thought he was dead, telling tales about him that were known even to children. Decades later, a woodcutter entered the mountains and met up with Sun, whom he mistook for a mountain deity, because Sun had white hair with a young complexion, a healthy body, and high spirits. The woodcutter knelt to kowtow to Sun, who looked him over and asked, 'Is your name Sanxian?' The woodcutter replied, 'Yes.' Sun said, 'I am your father.' As a child, the woodcutter had heard that his father was a drunk who was tricked into going up the mountain, where he died. He was surprised and bewildered to encounter his father on this day. The old man related his adventures and recalled incidents of days past among the family. Finally believing the story, the woodcutter asked the old man to return to the village so he could take care of him. But the old man laughed and said, 'Is there a wine pond in your house from which I can drink at will?' He told his son to wait while he went off through the treetops, swinging on vines like a nimble ape. After a short while, he returned with a section of bamboo, the ends of which were stuffed with purple flowers. He handed it to his son, saying, 'There is ape wine inside the bamboo. It can improve your health and help you maintain a youthful appearance.' His son took the bamboo home, where he removed the seal and poured the contents into a basin. It was deep blue, like indigo, with a strong, rich bouquet unmatched in the human world. Being very filial, the woodcutter filled a bottle with the liquid and gave it to his father-in-law, who in turn gave the wine to his master, a gentryman named Liu. Mr Liu saw the wine and was greatly surprised. He asked about its origin. The servant told Mr Liu what his son-in-law had told him. Mr Liu reported to the provincial governor, who sent dozens of people to comb the mountain. After several months, they found only overgrown trees and thickets of thorny plants, and returned with nothing to report.

When I finished reading the story, I felt I had stumbled upon a rare treasure, so I quickly made a copy at the service desk, which I took to my father-in-law's place to present it to him. It was an evening three years ago. When I arrived, my father-in-law and my mother-in-law were having a quarrel over dinner. A storm raged outside, with thunder and lightning. Blue bolts of lightning, like long, crackling whips, beat on the windows and rattled the glass. I shook the water out of my hair. My nose stung from being pelted by hailstones mixed with rain, and tears welled up in my eyes. My mother-in-law took one look at me and said angrily:

'A married daughter is like spilled water. You solve your own problems. This isn't civil court.'

I knew she'd gotten the wrong idea, but before I could explain, I was interrupted by a powerful sneeze. In the midst of my nasal spasm, I heard my mother-in-law grumble:

'Are you one of those men who treat liquor as their wives? Are you . . .'

I didn't understand what she meant at the time, but, of course, I do now. Back then I just saw a grumbling woman whose face was turning reddish purple, her heart apparently filled with loathing. She seemed to be talking to me, but her eyes – stiff, focused, frozen, and cold as snake eyes – were fixed on my father-in-law. I'd never seen a look like that before, and even now, when I recall it, a chill skips across my heart.

My father-in-law was sitting properly at the dinner table, maintaining the airs of a college professor. Under the warm lamplight, his gray hair looked like the fine threads of a silkworm, but with each bolt of blue lightning outside the window, it was transformed into strands of cold, green soybean noodles. He ignored my mother-in-law and kept drinking alone. It was a bottle of Italian Widow Champagne, a golden liquid like the smooth, warm bosom of a western girl, strings of tiny bubbles sizzling like the sound of her whispers. The fruity bouquet of the wine was elegant, pleasant, and refreshing; the more you smelled it, the longer the aroma stayed with you. It was magnificent beyond imagining. Gazing at this kind of wine was better than staring at the naked body of a western girl; smelling this kind of wine was better than kissing a western girl; drinking this kind of wine . . .

He lovingly caressed the smooth, green, jadelike bottle with one hand and fondled a tall-stemmed glass with the other. His long, slender fingers toyed with the glass and the bottle with erotic tenderness. He raised the glass to eye level to let the bright lamplight shine on the softly tinted liquid, and as he admired it, a hint of impatience showed in his eyes. Holding the glass under his nose to sniff it, he held his breath and opened his mouth joyously. Then he took a tiny, an absolutely tiny, sip, barely moistening the tip of his tongue and his lips, as rays of excitement shot from his eyes. Pouring the glassful into his mouth and holding his breath, he kept the liquid in his mouth without swallowing for a moment. Puffed-out cheeks made his face rounder than usual, his chin pointier. I was surprised to note that he had no beard, not a single whisker. Those weren't the lips and chin of a man. He swished the liquid around in his mouth, which must have brought him great joy. Red spots appeared on his face, like unevenly applied rouge. The way he held the liquor in his mouth so long affected me physically – I heard the sound of rushing water. A bolt of lightning turned the room green. Amid that green spasm, he swallowed the wine, and I watched it travel down his throat. Then he licked his lips, and his eyes moistened, as if he were crying. I'd seen him drink in class before, and there was never anything unusual about it. But at home, he turned sentimental, and that was quite unusual. Watching my father-in-law caress his glass and admire the liquid in it somehow spawned images of a gay man; although I'd never actually seen a gay man, I believed that what gay men did when they were alone must be similar to how my father-in-law treated his bottle, his glass, and his wine.

'Disgusting!' My mother-in-law threw down her chopsticks and cursed aimlessly, then stood up, went to her room, and locked the door behind her. I was embarrassed. At the time I had no idea what had disgusted her, but now I know.

His enjoyment ruined, my father-in-law stood up by holding the edge of the table. Staring at the green bedroom door, lost in thought, he didn't move for the longest time. But the expression on his face kept changing, from disappointment to agony and finally to anger. The look of disappointment was accompanied by a long sigh; he recapped the bottle and sat down on a sofa by the wall, looking like the shell of a man. Suddenly feeling pity for the old man, I wanted to console him, but didn't know what to say. Then I thought about the strange story tucked in my briefcase, which reminded me of the purpose of my visit. I took the story out and handed it to him. I'd never gotten into the habit of calling him 'Papa,' always addressing him as 'Teacher.' While this bothered my wife, fortunately he didn't mind. He said it was easier and more natural for me to call him 'Teacher,' and that it was hypocritical, even sort of creepy, for a son-in-law to call his father-in-law 'Papa.' I poured him a cup of tea, but the water was lukewarm, and the leaves floated on the surface. I knew that tea didn't interest him much, so it didn't really matter whether the water was hot or not. He pressed down on the cover with his palm as a way of thanking me, then asked in a half-hearted manner:

'Did you have another fight? Well, go on, just keep fighting!'

From that brief comment, I could sense his feelings of helplessness regarding the married lives of two generations of the family. A halo of sadness shrouded the small living room. Handing him the copy of the story, I said:

'Teacher, I found this in the library today. It's very interesting. Please take a look.'

I could tell he was uninterested in the article and in this son-in-law who stood there in his living room. He probably wanted me to leave, so he could be free to collapse on the sofa and lose himself in the aromatic aftertaste of the Italian Widow Champagne. It was only out of courtesy that he didn't drive me away, and also out of courtesy that he reached out a languid hand, like a sexually overindulgent man, and took the paper from me.

'Teacher,' I said encouragingly, 'it's an article about apes making alcoholic beverages. And not just any apes, but the ones on White Ape Mountain near Liquorland.'

Reluctantly, he raised the paper and lazily skimmed it, his eyes like old cicadas squirming on a willow branch. Had he stayed that way, I'd have been sorely disappointed, knowing that I didn't understand him at all. But I *did* understand him, and I knew the article would pique his interest and lift his spirits. I wanted to make him happy, not to benefit myself, but because I felt that deep inside the old man's mind hid an innocent little animal, which was neither a dog nor a cat, one with smooth, shiny fur, a short snout, big ears, a bright red nose, and squat legs. This little animal held my attention, as if it were my own twin brother. Of course, these feelings were absurd, groundless, and incomprehensible. As I figured, his eyes lit up, his languid body stirred, and excitement showed through his reddening ears and trembling fingers. I thought I saw that little animal leap out of his body, jumping and gliding in the air three feet above his head, along tracks like strings of silk. I was truly happy, I was truly delighted, I was truly ecstatic, I was truly elated.

He took another quick look at the sheets of paper, then closed his eyes, his fingers unconsciously tapping the paper in a series of tiny clicks. He opened his eyes and said:

'I'm going to do it!'

'Do what?'

'After all the years you've been with me, you have to ask?'

'Your student lacks talent and knowledge, and cannot fathom the profundity of your words.'

'Clichés, all clichés!' he said unhappily. 'I'm going up to White Ape Mountain to search for Ape Liquor.'

As excited and uneasy emotions raged through my subconscious, I sensed that a long-anticipated event was about to occur. Tidal waves were about to engulf life as calm as stagnant water. A fascinating story just made for drinking parties would soon spread throughout Liquorland, and would immerse the city, the Brewer's College, and me in an atmosphere of romance formed by the integration of elite and popular literatures. And all this would come about as a result of my accidental discovery in the Municipal Library. My father-in-law would soon depart for White Ape Mountain in search of Ape Liquor, followed by throngs of the curious. But all I said was:

'Teacher, you know that stories like this are usually fabrications by idle literati. We should treat them as fantasies, and not take them too seriously.'

He had already risen from the sofa and was pulling himself together, like a soldier setting off for the battlefield. He said:

'My mind's made up, so say no more.'

'Teacher, it's such a momentous decision, shouldn't you at least discuss it with my mother-in-law?'

He cast me a cold glance and said,

'She has nothing to do with me anymore.'

He removed his watch and eyeglasses, walked to the front door as if heading off to bed, opened it with determination, and slammed it shut behind him. The thin layer of wood sent the two of us into two separate worlds. The sounds of wind and rain and thunder and the cold, damp air of a rainy night that entered the house when he opened the door suddenly stopped with the sound of the door slamming shut. Dumbfounded, I stood there listening to the disappearing sounds of his slippered feet scraping against the sand and scraps of paper on the cement stairs. The sound grew weaker and weaker, then died out completely. His departure left a gaping hole in the living room. I was still standing there, big and tall, but felt somehow that I had stopped being human and was less significant than a cement pillar. It had all happened so fast it felt like an illusion; but this was no illusion, for his watch and his eyeglasses, still warm, lay on the tea table, the two sheets of paper I'd handed him were still lying on the sofa where he'd thrown them, and the bottle and the glass he'd been caressing still stood forlornly on the dining table. The filament in the fluorescent lamp was hissing; the old-fashioned clock hanging on the wall continued to mark time – *tick-tock tick-tock*. Even though there was a door between us, I could hear my mother-in-law breathing, as, I assumed, she lay in bed, her head cradled in her arm, like a peasant woman slurping hot porridge.

After considerable thought, I decided to tell her everything. I tested the door first, then knocked loudly. In between the raps, I heard rustling noises that quickly turned into a loud sobbing intermingled with the snorts of nose-blowing. Where, I wondered, did she deposit the stuff from her nose? This highly insignificant thought bounced stubbornly in my head, like a pesky fly that wouldn't be shooed away. It occurred to me that she must already know what had happened out here, but still I said uneasily:

'. . . he's gone . . . said he was going to White Ape Mountain for Ape Liquor . . .'

She blew her nose again; where *did* she wipe the snot? The sobbing was replaced by rustling sounds. I had a picture of her getting out of bed and staring at the door or at the wall, where their engagement picture, which I had so admired, hung. Framed in ornate black wood, it looked like a portrait of an ancestor that is passed down from generation to generation. At the moment frozen in the frame, my father-in-law was still a handsome man whose lips curled up at the corners to reveal a humorous, engaging personality. His hair was parted down the middle, a white line like a scar left by a sharp knife that divided his head in two. His neck invaded the space above my mother-in-law's head, his pointy chin no more than three centimeters from her sleek, neatly combed hair, thus symbolizing both the authority and love of a husband. Under the oppression of the indispensable authority and love of her husband, her face was round, with bushy eyebrows, a silly little nose, and a firm, exuberant mouth. At the time, my mother-in-law looked a bit like a handsome young man dressed in women's clothes. Her face still showed some of the rash qualities of her nest-gatherer lineage – undeterred by hardships, undaunted by any cliff – contrasting sharply with her present lazy, sensuous, pampered self, akin to the Imperial Consort Yang Guifei. Why had she turned out like this? And how had the two of them produced such an ugly daughter, one who could shame the whole Chinese nation? The mother was carved out of ivory, the daughter molded from mud. I believed that sooner or later I'd find the answer to this question. It had been so long since the glass in the frame had been cleaned that a succession of stealthy spiders had weaved their delicate webs over it. Fine dust was caught in the lattice-work. What was my mother-in-law thinking as she stared at this relic? Was she recalling bygone happy days? But I didn't know if they'd ever had happy days. It's my theory that any couple that has stayed married for decades must be calm people who are in complete control of their emotions. At best, the happiness experienced by this type of couple is dusk-like: slow, ambiguous, acrid, and sticky, a bland, murky happiness like sediment at the bottom of a liquor vat. Those who get divorced three days after their wedding are more akin to red-maned stallions; their emotions burn like a prairie fire, enough to light up the world around them and bake it until it oozes grease. The cruel sun at high noon, a tropical storm, a razor-sharp sword, strong liquor, a paint brush dipped in a full palette. These marriages are the spiritual wealth of the human race, while the former become gooey mud, numbing the human ability for enlightenment and slowing down the process of historical development. That is why I had second thoughts about what my mother-in-law was thinking; instead of recalling bygone happy days, it was far more likely that she was recalling my father-in-law's unsavory behavior, which had disgusted her over the decades. The facts would soon prove that my speculation was correct.

I knocked on the door one more time.

'What do you think we should do?' I asked. 'Bring him back or report to the school authorities?'

There was silence for a minute, absolute silence; even her breathing stopped, making me very uneasy. Suddenly she let out a loud, piercing cry, her voice like a sharpened bamboo stalk, totally incompatible with her age, her identity, and her usual dignity and elegance. The incompatibility created a powerful discrepancy, which terrified me. I was worried she might go so far as to hang her naked self from one of the nails in the room, like a cooked swan. Which nail would that be? The one from which the picture hung? Or the one holding the calendar? Or the one for hats? Two were too flimsy, the other both flimsy and short; since none could sustain my mother-in-law's budlike body, with its snowy white skin, my fears were superfluous. But her remarkable cry had sent a chill down my spine, and I thought that the only way to still her voice was to keep rapping on her door.

As I continued, I tried to explain things and comfort her. At the moment, she was like a ball of tangled camel hair, and it was essential to console her with patient, rhythmic knocks and smooth talk like Wujia herbal liquor, which has a soothing effect and aids the body's circulation. What exactly did I say? I guess it was something along the lines of: My father-in-law had embraced a lifelong desire to rush up to White Ape Mountain one night. He was willing to sacrifice his life for liquor. I told her that his departure had nothing to do with her. I said that he would very likely find his Ape Liquor, thereby making a great contribution to mankind, enriching an already splendid liquor culture, turning a new page in mankind's distilling history, bringing glory to our nation, making a name for the Chinese, and generating revenue for Liquorland. I also said, 'No one can catch a cub without entering the tiger's lair.' How could he obtain Ape Liquor if he didn't go up the mountain? Besides, I told her, I believed that my father-in-law would return one day, whether he found the ape liquor or not, to live out his years with her.

My mother-in-law screamed:

'Who cares if he comes back? I don't want him to come back! I'll be disgusted if he comes back! I hope he dies up on White Ape Mountain. I hope he turns into a hairy ape!'

Her words made my hair stand on end; cold sweat seeped from every pore of my body. Prior to this moment, I'd only vaguely sensed that they lived in disharmony, and that there were some minor frictions. I'd never dreamed that her hatred for her husband was deeper than that which a poor peasant feels for the landowner, deeper than a worker's enmity toward a capitalist. The creed that 'Class hatred is stronger than Mount Tai,' which had been pounded into me for decades, crumbled. If one person's hatred for another could reach such proportions, it was an unquestioned form of beauty, a magnificent contribution to humanity. How closely it resembled a purple, poisonous poppy blooming in the swamp of human emotions; as long as you don't touch or ingest it, it will exist as a form of beauty, possessing an attraction that no kindly, friendly flower could ever have.

Then she began recounting my father-in-law's misdeeds – every word, every sound, was filled with blood and tears. She said:

'How can he call himself human? How can he call himself a man? For decades, he has treated his liquor like a woman. It was he who started the evil practice of comparing a beautiful woman to vintage liquor. Drinking has taken the place of sexual intercourse. He has devoted all his sexual appetite to liquor, to his bottles, to his wine glasses . . .'

'Dr Li, I'm not really your mother-in-law. I never gave birth – how could I? Your wife was an abandoned infant I picked out of a trash can.'

The truth was out. I let out a deep breath, as if a big load had been lifted from my chest.

'You're an intelligent person, Doctor. Sand in the eyes doesn't throw you off the track. You must have sensed that she wasn't my biological daughter. That is why I think we can become close friends, and I can tell you everything. Doctor, I'm a woman, not a stone lion outside the Palace Museum, or a weather vane on a rooftop, and surely not a lowly, androgynous worm. I have a woman's desires, but I am denied any . . . Who can know the pain I feel?'

I said:

'Then why haven't you divorced him?'

'I'm weak, I'm afraid of people's scorn . . .'

I said:

'That's absurd.'

'Yes, it is. But the absurd days are over now. Doctor, I can tell you why I never divorced him. It was because he distilled a strong herbal liquor especially for me, which he called "Ximen Qing," after the licentious hero of classical novels. Drinking this liquor creates mind-blowing illusions, some even better than sex . . .'

I detected a sweet shyness in her voice.

'But when you showed up, the power of the liquor mysteriously disappeared.'

I didn't feel like rapping on the door anymore.

'There's this woman who, like a bear's claw drenched in spices, has been stewing over a low heat for decades. Now she has finally ripened. Her fragrance is overpowering. Don't tell me you can't smell it, my dear Doctor . . .'

The door opened wide. The aroma of braised bear's paw rolled out in waves. I held tightly to the door frame, like a drowning man with a death-grip on a ship's railing . . .

IV

After the swarthy dwarf was shot, his body flew upwards, as if he were about to fly away. But the hot lead had destroyed his central nervous system, and his limbs twitched spastically. The spasms made one thing abundantly clear: He could no longer call forth the mystical powers described in Doctor of Liquor Studies' story 'Yichi the Hero,' where he soared into the air and stuck to the ceiling like an oversized lizard. Quite the opposite: after jerking a few centimeters into the air, he slid off the lady trucker's lap and landed on the floor, where Ding Gou'er watched him struggle to straighten himself out, his thigh muscles stretched as taut as utility wires in a gale. Blood and brain matter oozing from the hole in his head fouled the polished floorboards. Then one of his legs began to jerk in and out like the neck of a rooster as the knife enters; his body, wracked by powerful spasms, spun around in smooth, easy circles. After about a dozen revolutions, his legs quit banging the floor, and what happened next was this: The spasmodic flailing stopped, but he began to quake. At first the trembling involved his whole body, creating a steady twang; but then it became localized, his muscle groups acting like sports fans performing the wave. Starting from the tip of his left foot, it moved up to his left calf then to his left thigh then to his left hip and then to his left shoulder, where it crossed over to his right shoulder and moved down to his right hip then to his right thigh then to his right calf then to the tip of his right foot, and from there changed direction and headed back to the starting point. This movement continued for a long while before the trembling stopped altogether. Ding Gou'er heard a loud release of air from the dwarf's body just before it went limp and lay spread out on the floor.

Dead as a doornail, he looked like a leathery alligator in a swamp. Not for a second while he was watching the death-throes of the dwarf did Ding lose sight of the lady trucker. At the instant when the dwarf slid to the floor from her glossy, bare knees, she fell over backwards onto the inner-sprung mattress, which was covered by a snow-white bedsheet and a jumble of odd-shaped pillows and cushions. The pillows were down-filled, Ding Gou'er noted as he watched delicate goose feathers ooze from the seam of a large pillow with pink floral borders and soar skyward when the pillow was crushed by her falling head. Her legs spread wide and hung limp over the side of the bed as she lay face-up, a posture that stirred the sediment in Ding Gou'er's mind. Reminded of the lady trucker's wild passion, he felt stabs of jealousy, and even as he bit down on his lower lip, wicked thoughts consumed him, sending pains like those of a mortally wounded hunter's prey tearing through his heart. Agonizing moans slipped through his clenched teeth. He gave the dwarf's lifeless body an angry kick, then threw himself onto the bed alongside the lady trucker, the smoking gun still in his hand. Her sprawled body reawakened love–hate feelings toward her; he hoped she was dead yet prayed that she had just fainted from fear. Lifting up her head, he saw a faint sparkle of light reflected off barely glimpsed shell-like teeth between soft yet brittle, slightly parted lips. Scenes from that late autumn morning at the Mount Luo Coal Mine flashed before the investigator's eyes; back then those lips crushing down on his mouth had felt cold, yielding, devoid of elasticity, and altogether weird, like clumps of used cotton wadding . . . there between her eyes he spotted a dark hole the size of a soy bean, around which tiny metallic filings were arrayed; he knew they had come from a bullet. His body rocked to one side, as once again he felt a sickeningly sweet liquid rise up into his throat. As he threw himself at her feet, a stream of fresh blood spewed from his mouth, painting her flat belly a bright red.

I've killed her! he thought, terror-stricken.

He reached out and felt the hole with his forefinger. It was hot to the touch, the splintery skin around it scraped his fingertip. It was a familiar feeling. By jogging his memory, he finally managed to recall the youthful sensation of feeling a new tooth with the tip of his tongue. Then he was reminded of the time he scolded his son for doing the same thing. The little boy, with his moon face and big, round eyes, looking slovenly no matter how new or clean his clothes might be, a book bag strapped to his back, a red bandanna tied haphazardly around his neck, a willow switch in one hand, walked up to him, moving a loose tooth around with his tongue. The investigator patted him on the head, for which he was rewarded by a crack across the leg from the willow switch. Stop that! the boy had demanded unhappily. Who said you could pat the top of my head? Don't you know that can make a person stupid? He cocked his head and squinted, a no-nonsense look. With a laugh, the investigator said, You stupid little boy, a pat on the head can't make you stupid! But playing with new teeth with your tongue will make them grow in crooked. . . powerful nostalgia sent his juices nearly to the boiling point, and as he jerked his hand back, tears spilled from his eyes. Softly intoning his son's name, he thumped his own forehead and cursed:

You son of a bitch! Ding Gou'er, you son of a bitch. How could you do something like this?

The little boy stared at him disgustedly, then turned and walked off, his chubby little legs pumping. He was quickly swallowed up in the cross-traffic.

Murder's a tough rap to beat, he thought to himself. But I want to see my son one last time before I die. Then his thoughts drifted to the provincial capital, which seemed at this moment to be on the other side of the world.

He picked up his pistol, which had only one bullet left, and ran out the gate of Yichi Tavern; the two dwarf gatewomen grabbed his clothes as he passed, but he shook them off and darted among the cars on the street, risking life and limb. He heard the jarring sound of screeching brakes to his left and right, and one car probably bumped his hip as he ran; but this only spurred him on, until he reached the safety of the pedestrian lane. He heard a chorus of noises from the Yichi Tavern gate; people were shouting. Following the leaf-strewn pedestrian lane, he ran for all he was worth, sensing vaguely that it was early morning, and that the rain-washed sky was filled with blood-streaked clouds. A cold rain that had fallen all night long made it slippery going; a coat of icy dewdrops beautified the low-hanging branches. In what seemed like no time, he found himself on the familiar cobblestone street. Opaque steam rose from the roadside ditch, on the surface of which floated delicacies like roasted pig's head, fried meatballs, turtle shell, braised shrimp, spicy pig's knuckles. Some old-timers in rags were fishing the delicacies out of the water with nets on long poles. Their lips were greasy, their faces flushed, bearing witness, he thought, to the nutritive value of the garbage they salvaged. Some passersby on bicycles reacted with disgust just before, with shrieks of alarm, they careened into the ditch. They and their bicycles shattered the calm surface and sent the heavy smell of distiller's grains and animal carcasses into the air, nearly making him gag. He hugged the wall as he ran, but lost his footing on the rocky road. Shouts and heavy footsteps behind him. Scrambling to his feet and turning to look, he saw a crowd jumping up and down, and shouting loudly, but not daring to chase after him. He continued on his way, more slowly now, his heart pounding so hard his chest ached. There on the other side of the stone wall was the familiar Martyrs' Cemetery, over which the white canopies of towering pagoda evergreens lent an aura of purity and sanctity.

Why am I running? he was thinking as he ran. Heaven casts its net wide. I can run but I can't hide. And still his legs kept churning. He spotted the giant ginkgo tree, and under it the old wonton seller, standing straight as the tree itself; puffs of steam rising from his wonton baskets blotted out his face, like the hideous countenance of the moon fronted by floating clouds. He vaguely recalled the old man standing there holding a copper bullet as payment for the wonton he had consumed. He ought to retrieve that bullet, he thought to himself as the taste of pork-and-scallion wonton rose from his stomach; early winter scallions are the best, and the costliest. Hand in hand, he and she are buying groceries in the provincial capital's open-air market, where vegetable peddlers from the outskirts hunker down behind their baskets and poles to chew on cold stuffed buns, which leave their teeth spotted with bits of scallion. The old man opened his hand to show off the beautiful bullet that lay in his palm, a supplicating look showing through the mist that was trying to obscure his face. As he strained to figure out what the old man wanted, a dog's barks shattered his concentration. The big striped canine appeared before him like an apparition, without warning, although its barks seemed to be coming from far, far away, rolling across the tips of grass in a distant meadow and losing most of their timbre by the time they got to this point. He watched as the dog's heavy head sagged in a strange nod; it opened its great mouth, but no sound emerged, producing a dreamlike, furtive effect. Under the bright red morning sun, faint shadows from the sparse leaves on the ginkgo tree cast a loose net over the dog's body. He could see that the look in the animal's eyes was non-threatening; its barks were a friendly hint or a sign for him to get moving again. He mumbled something to the old wonton peddler, but a gust of wind carried the sound off. So when the old-timer asked him what he said, he stammered:

I want to go find my son.

Nodding to the dog and giving it a wide berth, he walked to the back of the ginkgo tree, where he spotted the elderly caretaker of the Martyrs' Cemetery, leaning against the tree and cradling his shotgun, its muzzle pointing into the tree's canopy. The same look – a friendly hint or a sign to get moving again – showed in the old man's eyes. Deeply touched, he bowed respectfully to the old-timer before running over to a block of cold, uninviting, and apparently deserted buildings up ahead. A shot rang out behind him. He hit the ground instinctively, then rolled sideways to take cover behind the chilled leaves in a bed of roses. Then another shot. This time he looked back to see where it had come from, just in time to see the canopy of the ginkgo tree shudder and several yellow leaves flutter earthward in the reddish rays of sunlight. The old cemetery caretaker was still up against the tree, not moving a muscle. Blue smoke curled from both barrels of his shotgun. By then the big yellow dog had shambled over from the other side of the tree and was crouching beside the caretaker, its eyes reflecting the sun's rays like gold nuggets.

Before entering the block of buildings, he crossed a desolate sidewalk park where some old men were out airing birds in cages and some kids were jumping rope. Tucking his pistol into his waistband and acting as if he hadn't a care in the world, he sauntered past them and headed for the buildings. But the minute he reached his objective, he discovered he'd made a big mistake, for he'd walked into the middle of an early morning flea market. Crowds of peddlers were hunkering down beside their second-hand goods, which included used clocks and watches, Mao Zedong badges and plaster busts from the Cultural Revolution, and things like old wind-up gramophones. Plenty of sellers, but not a single buyer. The peddlers eyed each infrequent passerby greedily. It felt like a trap to him, a lure for the unwary, and that the peddlers were actually plainclothes cops. And the more closely Ding Gou'er observed them, the more a lifetime of experience told him that's exactly what they were. Alertly, he retreated to a spot behind a white poplar to observe the goings-on. He saw seven or eight youngsters, boys and girls, sneak out from behind one of the buildings, their expressions and demeanor telling Ding Gou'er that this was a group of kids involved in some unlawful activity. The girl in the center, wearing a knee-length gray coat, a red cap, and a necklace of Qing dynasty brass coins, was their leader. All of a sudden, he noticed the wrinkles in the girl's neck and detected the acrid smell of foreign tobacco on her breath, so close it was as if she were nearly on top of him. He focused his attention on her, watching the lady trucker's features slowly take form on the face of this unfamiliar girl, the way a cricket emerges from the thin casing of its cocoon. A trickle of rose-colored blood oozing from a bullet hole between her eyes ran down her nose and dripped from the tip to divide her mouth into two equal halves; from there it slid to her navel, down and down, neatly cleaving her body in two and forcing gurgles out of her internal organs. With a shout of alarm, the investigator turned and ran, but no matter how fast his legs churned, they could not take him out of the flea market. Finally, he hunkered down in front of a peddler selling used handguns and pretended to be a customer, as he examined the rusty old guns laid out in front of him. He sensed that the girl who had been cloven in half was standing behind him wrapping herself in green paper bindings. She worked very fast; at first she was wearing cream-colored rubber gloves as her hands flew through the air, but before long, they were yellow blurs that were quickly swallowed up in wet green paper the color and consistency of seaweed. The green was such a transcending green it exuded a powerful life force. And then the paper bindings began to move on their own, and in a matter of seconds had her wrapped in a tight cocoon. He felt a chill on his back, but tried to act nonchalant, picking up a beautifully crafted revolver and trying to spin its rusty cylinder. It wouldn't budge. He asked the peddler, Do you have any aged Shanxi vinegar? The peddler said he didn't. Disappointed, he heaved a sigh. The peddler said, You act like a pro, but you're actually a rank amateur. I don't have any aged Shanxi vinegar, but I do have some Korean white vinegar, which is a hundred times better at removing rust than the Shanxi stuff. He watched the peddler reach into his shirt with a pale, delicate hand and feel around as if looking for something. Ding Gou'er caught an occasional glimpse of two little glass bottles tucked into a lacy pink bra. They were green, but frosty, not see-through, the sort of bottle so many famous foreign liquors come in. The frosty green looked especially expensive; even though they were obviously made of glass, somehow they didn't look it, which was why they were so precious. Capitalizing on the structure and logic of this sentence, he came up with a parallel: Even though it was obviously a real boy on the platter, somehow it didn't look it, which was why it was so precious. Finally, the hand brought one of the bottles out of its hiding place in the bra. Some squiggly writing was stamped on the bottle. He couldn't read a word of it, but his vanity forced him to blurt out cockily: That's either 'hoo-wis-key' or 'ba-lan-dee', as if he'd never met a foreign language he couldn't handle. This is the Korean white vinegar you wanted, the peddler replied. Taking the bottle from him, Ding glanced up and saw an expression that was identical to that of his superior when he'd handed him the carton of China cigarettes. A closer look showed that the two men weren't all that similar, after all. The peddler smiled, flashing a pair of glittering canines that made him look infantile. He opened the bottle, releasing a frothy head. How come this vinegar looks like beer? he asked. Are you trying to say that beer is the only liquid in the world that froths? the peddler replied. Ding pondered that for a minute. Crabs aren't beer, but they froth at the mouth, he said, so you're right and I'm wrong. When he poured some of the frothy liquid over the revolver's cylinder, his nostrils were assailed by the strong smell of alcohol. Bathed in the frothy bubbles, the revolver made clicking sounds, like a big green crab; and when he reached out to touch it, something nipped his finger painfully, like a scorpion sting. Are you aware, he demanded in a loud voice, that dealing in firearms is against the law? With a sneer, the peddler said, Do you honestly think I'm a peddler? Thrusting his hand into his shirt, he pulled out the bra and shook it in the air; the outer layer fell away to reveal a pair of shiny, American-made, stainless steel spring handcuffs. With the investigator looking on, the peddler was transformed into a bushy-browed, big-eyed, hawk-nosed, brown-stubbled, garden-variety police captain, who grabbed Ding Gou'er's hand and – *click click* – snapped the cuffs on his and Ding's wrists. You and I are now joined at the wrist, neither of us can get away. Unless, that is, you've got the strength of nine oxen or a couple of tigers, and can carry me over your shoulder. Blessed with strength born of desperation, Ding Gou'er picked up the burly police captain and threw him over his shoulder, as if he were no heavier than a paper cut-out. By then, the froth had evaporated, revealing a silvery revolver, rust-free. With no strain he bent over and picked up the pistol, feeling its heft in his wrist and its warmth in his palm. What a handgun! he heard the police captain say with a sigh from where he lay, across Ding's back. With a mighty shrug of his shoulder, he flipped the man into the air and smack into an ivy-covered wall. The intertwining tendrils, some thick and some thin, created patterns on the wall; red leaves here and there lent it considerable beauty. He watched as the police captain bounced slowly off the wall and landed flat on his back right at his feet. The handcuffs, stretched like a rubber band, were still fastened to both men's wrists. These are American handcuffs, the police captain said. If you think you can break loose, forget it! As panic began to grip Ding Gou'er, he stuck the muzzle of the revolver up against the virtually transparent metal and pulled the trigger. The recoil jerked his arm upward, and the pistol nearly leaped out of his hand. He looked down. Not a scratch on the handcuffs. He tried again, with the same result. With his free hand, the police captain took a pack of cigarettes and a lighter out of his pocket. The cigarettes were American, the lighter Japanese, both top quality. You Liquorland folks have a pretty high standard of living, don't you? The police captain sneered. In times like this, he said, gluttony claims the bold and starvation takes the timid. With banknotes flying all over the place, it's just a matter of whether or not you've got the guts to reach out and grab them. If that's true, Ding Gou'er said, it must also be true that you Liquorland people really do cook and eat little boys. Cooking and eating little boys is no big deal! the police captain replied. Have you ever eaten one? Ding Gou'er asked him. Don't tell me *you* haven't, the police captain retorted. What I ate was a fake boy made from a variety of materials, Ding Gou'er replied. How do you know it wasn't real? the police captain asked. How could the Higher Procuratorate send such a numbskull to us? Good brother, Ding Gou'er said, I won't lie to you. I've fallen under the spell of a woman in recent days. I know, the police captain said. You killed her, that's a capital offense. I know, Ding Gou'er admitted, and now all I want is to return to the provincial capital to see my son once more before turning myself in. That's a worthwhile reason, the police captain said. Pity the poor parents. All right, I'll let you go. Bending down and opening his mouth, he bit through the handcuffs. Unfazed by Ding Gou'er's bullets, the hard metal parted like a soggy noodle in the man's mouth. Good brother, the police captain said, you're wanted in the city, to be captured alive. I'm taking a big chance by letting you go, but I have a son of my own, and I know what you're feeling, which is why I'm letting you go. Bending low in gratitude, Ding Gou'er said, Good brother, I'll never forget your kindness, not even if I wind up in the Nine Springs of Hell.

The investigator took off running, and as he passed by a large gateway, he spied a courtyard crowded with luxurious sedans, into which some men dressed to the nines were climbing. Sensing trouble, he turned down a narrow lane, where he came across a little girl who repaired shoes. She wore a blank expression, as if deep in thought. As he was standing there, a heavily made-up woman jumped out from under a colored plastic banner above a café door and blocked his way. Come inside for a bite to eat, sir, she said, and something to drink. Twenty percent off everything. She sidled up next to him, her face exuding passion the likes of which he seldom saw. I don't want anything to eat, Ding Gou'er said, and nothing to drink. But the woman grabbed his arm to drag him inside. You don't have to eat or drink anything, she said, just come in and take a load off your feet. With rising anger, he sent her sprawling in the dirt. Big Brother, she bawled, come out here, this hooligan hit me! With a fearful jump, Ding Gou'er tried to leap over the prostrate woman, but she wrapped her arms around his legs and wouldn't let go. He fell on top of her in a heap. Scrambling to his feet, he kicked her savagely. She grabbed her stomach and rolled on the ground in agony. As he looked up, a hulking man with a liquor bottle in his left hand and a meat cleaver in his right ran out of the café. This was big trouble, so he spun around and took off flying, at least that's how it felt to him, with the form and speed of a track star – no pounding heart, no gasping for breath. When he finally turned to look back, he saw that the man had given up the chase and was taking a piss alongside a concrete utility pole. Now exhaustion crept in; Ding Gou'er's heart was racing and he was covered by cold, sticky sweat. His legs were too rubbery to take another step.

The ill-fated investigator followed his nose to a three-wheeler, where its owner, a young man, was frying wheatcakes and an old woman, probably his mother, was standing alongside taking money from the customers. He was so hungry, he could feel his stomach reaching up to his throat for something to eat. But he was broke. A green military motorcycle roared up and screeched to a stop alongside the three-wheeler. Panic-stricken, the investigator was about to run for his life when he heard the sergeant in the sidecar say to the peddler: Hey, Boss, fry us up a couple of those wheatcakes. The investigator heaved a sigh of relief.

The investigator studied the two soldiers: the taller of the two had big eyes and bushy brows, the shorter one had more delicate features. They stood around the stall shooting the breeze with the young fellow frying wheatcakes, a comment here, a response there, a bunch of bullshit passing back and forth. The young fellow brushed some hot sauce on top of the steaming wheatcakes. His customers flipped the cakes from one hand to the other as they ate, noisily, tastily, arduously, and in no time, they had wolfed down three apiece. The short soldier reached into his overcoat and took out a bottle of liquor, which he handed to his comrade. Want a drink? he asked. With a giggle, his tall comrade said, Might as well. Ding watched as the soldier stuck the neck of the comely little bottle into his mouth and took a hearty drink. Then he noisily sucked in a mouthful of air and smacked his lips. Good stuff, he said, terrific stuff. His short comrade took the bottle, tipped his head back, and drank. His eyes nearly closed in rapture. A moment later, he said, Goddamned good stuff, this is more than just liquor! The tall soldier went over to the motorcycle and took two thick scallions out of the sidecar. After peeling off the roughage, he handed one to his short comrade. Try this, he said, genuine Shandong scallion. I've got some peppers, the short one said, pulling some bright red peppers out of his pocket. Genuine Hunan chilis, he said proudly. Want some? You're not a revolutionary if you don't eat chilis, and if you're not a revolutionary you must be a counter-revolutionary. True revolutionaries eat scallions, the tall one countered. Their hackles up, they advanced toward each other, one brandishing scallions in the air, the other waving a handful of chilis. The tall one poked his comrade in the head with his scallions, the short one crammed his chilis into his comrade's mouth. The wheatcake peddler rushed up to keep things from getting out of hand. No fighting, comades. You're both really revolutionary, as I see it. The soldiers backed off, huffing and puffing with anger, which had the wheatcake peddler in stitches. Ding Gou'er, appreciating the humor of it, started laughing too. The peddler's mother walked up to him. What are you laughing at? You look like a troublemaker to me. No I'm not, Ding Gou'er was quick to reply, I'm really not. Who but a troublemaker would laugh like that? Like what? Ding Gou'er asked. With a flick of the wrist, the old woman produced a tiny round mirror, as if snatching it out of thin air, and handed it to Ding Gou'er. See for yourself, she said. He was shocked by what he saw. There between his eyes was a bloody bullet hole and, as he could see, a shiny yellow bullet moving around in the convolutions of his brain. With a gasp of alarm, he dropped the mirror as if it were a piece of hot steel; it hit the ground and spun on its edge, projecting a shiny dot of light on the faded red surface of a distant wall. A close examination of the words on the wall showed that it was a ridiculous slogan: Eliminate The Evils Of Alcohol And Sex. Abruptly understanding the implications of the slogan, he walked up to the wall and

304

touched the painted words, which also burned his finger, like red-hot steel. When he turned back, the two soldiers were gone, so were the wheatcake peddler and his mother; the motorcycle stood there looking sad and lonely. He walked up and found a bottle of liquor in the sidecar. Picking it up and giving it a shake, he watched a multitude of bubbles, like little pearls, rise to the top. The liquid was green, as if made from mung beans. The bouquet of fine liquor seeped up through and around the cork, which he removed; a sense of comfort washed over him as he inserted the cool neck of the bottle into his overheated mouth. The green contents slid down his throat like a lubricant, drawing whoops of joy from his stomach and intestines, like a schoolchild holding a bouquet of flowers. His spirits revived, as would seedlings watered by cool rain after a long drought, and before he knew it, he had drunk every drop. Wishing there were more, he took one last rueful look at the bottle before tossing it away, mounting the motorcycle, and gripping the handlebars; he stomped down on the starter and felt the motorcycle come restlessly to life, like a proud steed – snorting loudly, pawing the ground, and flicking its tail, ready to run. The second he released the brake, the motorcycle bumped its way up onto the road, then, with a triumphant roar, took off like a shot. It felt as if the motor between his knees knew precisely what he wanted, there was no need for him to drive; all he had to do was sit tight and hold on to keep from being thrown. The roar of the engine turned into the whinnying of a horse; he felt the warmth of his steed's belly between his thighs and smelled the intoxicating odor of animal sweat. They left one gleaming vehicle after another in their wake, while those coming in their direction stared in wide-eyed terror before pulling over to the side of the road to get out of the way. An icebreaker cleaving its way through an arctic floe or a steamship knifing through the ocean. He was drunk from exhilaration. Several times he was sure they were going to crash, could, in fact, hear the other vehicles' screams of terror, but somehow disaster was always headed off in the nick of time; with a margin of error no greater than the thickness of a needle, at the last moment, these objects parted like jelly and moved out of the way of him and his mighty steed. A river appeared up ahead; there was no bridge, naturally. Water roared down the deep ravine, sending icy whitecaps into the air. He pulled back on the handlebars, and the motorcycle rose skyward; suddenly feeling as light as a sheet of paper, he was twisted and crumpled by strong gusts of wind, while enormous glittery stars above him seemed so close he could reach out and touch them. Am I on my way to Heaven? he wondered. If I am, does that mean I've become an immortal? He sensed that something he'd always thought would be incredibly difficult to achieve was suddenly and easily within his grasp. He watched as a spinning wheel fell away from the motorcycle. Then another, and another. He shrieked in terror, the sound bouncing off treetops like the passing wind. He hit the ground, the wheel-less motorcycle lodged itself inelegantly in the crotch of a tree, startling a bunch of squirrels that began gnawing at the machinery on which he had sat. Never imagining that squirrels' teeth were *that* sharp, so strong they could chew through metal as if it were little more than rotten tree bark, he shook his legs to get the kinks out, and was glad to see he'd come through the crash-landing unscathed. He got to his feet and took a dazed look around. Winding round the trunks of towering trees surrounding him were lush tendrils of climbing vines on which large flowers like purple paper cut-outs bloomed. The vines were home to clusters of grape-like fruit, both purple and green, all plump and juicy, and so perfectly shaped as to have been carved from fine jade. The semi-transparent skins could barely contain the juices inside; you couldn't ask for better wine grapes. Dimly he recalled that the lady trucker, or maybe some other nameless, pretty girl, had told him that a white-haired old professor was living up in the mountains, where he and the apes were brewing the finest liquor the world had ever seen. Its skin was smoother than that of a Hollywood starlet, its eyes more enchanting than those of an angel, its lips sexier than the painted lips of a ravishing queen. It was more than liquor, it was a creation of the gods, born of divine inspiration. His attention was caught by pillars of bright light amid the branches, where white mist curled, and apes leaped around: some bared their teeth and made hideous faces; others were grooming their companions, picking off lice and ticks. A big, husky male, whose bushy white eyebrows made him an elder, plucked a leaf from a branch, rolled it into a tube, put it up to his lips, and blew through it, producing a shrill whistle. All the apes quickly gathered round, forming three lines in comic imitation of humans, then stood more or less at attention, looking left and right to dress ranks. This is great, the investigator mused. Their military formation was a joke, what with their bowed legs, stooped posture, and heads that were thrust way out in front; but, after all, they were apes, and he couldn't be too picky. It takes humans at least six months of rigorous training to meet honor-guard standards, which includes tying their legs together, stuffing boards down their pants, and sleeping without a pillow at night. No, he thought, I can't be too picky. Their raised tails looked like clubs. Many of the fruit-laden branches were propped up with sticks to keep them from snapping off. The same held true for the apes. When people get old, they need canes. In Beijing there's a Front Cane Lane, which must mean there's also a Rear Cane Lane; now if lanes need canes, front and rear, what about apes? They have them in the rear only, and when they climb a tree, their bright red bottoms are out there for all to see. Following a pep talk by the old ape, they broke ranks and began climbing the vines, swinging back and forth as they picked the purple and green grapes, each as big as a ping-pong ball. As he licked his lips, bitter saliva gathered in his mouth. He reached out to pick some grapes, but they were just beyond his reach. Meanwhile, the apes, grapes piled on their heads, shinnied down the vines and noisily dumped the grapes into an open well. The bouquet of alcohol, lovely as a beautiful woman, rose from the well in what seemed to be clouds of sticky mist. Craning his neck to peer down into the well, he saw the golden orb of the moon reflected in what looked like a bronze mirror lining the bottom. The apes hung by their arms, a whole line of them, like you read about in stories. It was a beautiful sight, all those cute, cuddly apes, with their weird expressions. If only he had a camera, he was thinking, this picture would rock the world of photojournalism and earn him a big-time international award worth 100,000 US, which would convert into 600,000 of People's Currency, enough for him to eat and drink in style for the rest of his life and still have plenty left over for his son to go to college and get married. The boy's teeth had grown in already, two big incisors with a gap between them, which gave him the appearance of a dippy little girl. All of a sudden, the apes began dropping into the well, splintering the moon's watery reflection and sending splashes of gold flying, making rustling noises as they stuck to the sides of the well like dollops of syrup. Moss grew on the stone walls alongside a type of fungus known as supernatural grass, which is golden red. A red-crested heron swept down and carried off one of the supernatural grass stalks, then stuck out its legs, stretched its wings, and flew into the bright moon. No doubt taking it as a gift to Chang'e, the goddess of the moon, a celestial body covered by soft golden sand in which two tracks of human footprints, left there by American astronauts, will last for half a million years. Two astronauts, a pair of spectral wanderers. The sun's reflection on the moon is too bright for human eyes to endure. He stood beneath the moon, his hair transformed into golden threads, clean-shaven but dressed in rags, his face battered and bruised; he carried an oaken bucket in one hand and a wooden ladle in the other. Scooping liquor from the bucket, he poured it slowly onto the ground, where it formed semi-transparent honey-colored ribbons of liquid that quickly turned gummy, like newly made rubber. It looked so tasty he could hardly wait to sample it. Are you that professor from Liquorland's Brewer's College, the one who's supposed to be not quite right in the head? he wanted to ask. He said, I am China's King Lear, standing beneath the captivating moon. King Lear stood in a violent rainstorm cursing Heaven and earth, while I stand in the moonlight singing the praises of mankind. Ancient fairy tales sooner or later become reality, liquor is mankind's greatest discovery. Without it there would be no Bible, there would be no Egyptian pyramids, there would be no Great Wall of China, no music, no fortresses, no scaling ladders to storm others' fortresses, no nuclear fission, no salmon in the Wusuli River, and no fish or bird migrations. A fetus in its mother's womb can detect the smell of liquor; the scaly skin of an alligator makes first-rate liquor pouches. Martial-arts novels have advanced the brewer's art. What was the source of Qu Yuan's lament? There was no liquor for him to drink. Drug peddling and drug use are rampant in Yunnan. Why? Because the liquor there is inferior. Cao Cao forbade the production of liquor as a grain-conservation measure; a perfect example of a wise man doing something stupid. How can anyone prohibit liquor? Prohibiting the production and consumption of liquor is on a par with prohibiting sexual intercourse while urging an increase in population – it can't be done. Avoiding the stuff is harder than breaking free of the pull of gravity; the day an apple falls up is the day liquor can be prohibited. The lunar craters look just like liquor cups of unsurpassed excellence, the Roman Coliseum could be converted into a giant fermentation cellar. Sour-Plum Wine, Bamboo-Leaf Green, Imperial-Scholar Red, Out-of-Bottle Redolence, Sunny Spring, Intoxicated Emperor, Almond Village, Lotus-Blossom White . . . these are all pretty good liquors. But compared to my Ape Liquor, it's night and day. Someone once said you can enhance liquor with human piss. That's an imaginative manifestation. In Japan, treating ailments with urine has gained considerable popularity; they say you can ward off a host of diseases by drinking a cup of your own urine every morning. The legendary physician Li Shizhen had a good point when he said that a child's urine can lower internal fires. True connoisseurs of liquor do not need to snack when they drink, so Diamond Jin and his ilk show what inferior drinkers they are by cooking infants to go with their liquor . . .

Chapter Nine

I

Dear Mo Yan, Sir

Greetings!

If I'm not mistaken, I've sent you eight of my stories, yet I haven't heard a word from the venerable editors of *Citizens' Literature*. In my view, giving an aspiring young writer the cold shoulder like that is highly inappropriate. Since they have opened shop, they have an obligation to treat anyone who submits a manuscript with dignity and respect. As the saying goes, 'Heaven turns and the earth spins; you go up, and I go down,' or 'For two mountains to meet is unlikely, but for two people it is a common occurrence.' Who knows, Zhou Bao and Li Xiaobao might find themselves in front of the business end of my rifle one day. From now on, Sir, I refuse to contribute to *Citizens' Literature*. We may be poor, but not in strength of character. It's a big world out there, and there's a forest of publications, so why hang myself on that particular tree? Don't you agree?

Preparations for our first annual Ape Liquor Festival are well underway. I also came up with a plan to revitalize reserve stocks of our sickness wine, which I took to the Municipal Alcoholic Beverage Quality Control Group, where several tasters sampled the stuff after cleansing their palates, and determined that it had a unique taste, comparable to a delicate, melancholic beauty. The Municipal Alcoholic Beverage Naming Association gave this liquor the name Sick Xi Shi, after the legendary beauty. I didn't think that was appropriate, since the word 'sick' is clearly inauspicious, and can only produce dark clouds in the hearts of consumers, which will in turn have an adverse effect on sales. I urged them to change Sick Xi Shi to Xi Shi's Frown or in Daiyu Buries Blossoms, since both of those include beautiful women, but sound warmer, more tender, and appeal to people's affectionate nature. But the folk at the Municipal Alcoholic Beverage Naming Association, who are jealous and conservative by nature, were unyielding about the name Sick Xi Shi. My patience exhausted, I went, liquor in hand, to see the Mayor's secretary, who was so deeply moved by my gift of fine liquor and my unflagging sense of honor that he took me to see the Mayor, who, after hearing my tale, pounded the table and jumped to her feet, wide-eyed and scowling. She pounded the table again before sitting down and picking up the telephone. She shouted into it for a moment or two, until the head of the Alcoholic Beverage Naming Association came on, and got a royal chewing out from a woman who speaks with the force of justice, bold and assured, unyielding even if Mount Tai were to crush down on her. I couldn't see the man on the other end of the line, but I could picture the scene: The head of the Alcoholic Beverage Naming Association seated on the floor with his legs folded, bean-sized drops of sweat dotting his forehead. The Mayor sang my praises, saying that my efforts on behalf of the first annual Ape Liquor Festival constituted great meritorious service to all of Liquorland. Then she asked, in a tender voice, about my family background, my work, my hobbies, and my relations with my teachers and my friends; I felt as if a spring had burst forth in my heart. I told her everything, holding back nothing. The Mayor was particularly concerned with your situation, Sir, and personally extended an invitation to attend our Ape Liquor Festival. When I brought up the matter of travel expenses, she gave a mildly contemptuous snort and said, The dregs from liquor bottles in Liquorland alone would be enough to take care of ten Mo Yans.

Sir, I've decided to hand the naming rights for this liquor to you. Xi Shi's Frown or in Daiyu Buries Blossoms, it's your choice. Unless, of course, you can come up with something even better. The Mayor has said she'll give you a thousand in gold for every word. Naturally, we'd like you to write some promotional copy for this liquor, so we can advertise it in prime time on CTV, whatever the cost. We want to introduce Xi Shi's Frown or in Daiyu Buries Blossoms to every individual in the nation, nay, to everyone in the world. You can see the importance of what you write; it must be light and humorous, yet filled with moving images, so that anyone watching TV will feel as if they were face to face with little sister Lin Daiyu or with big sister Xi Shi: Crinkled brow, hands held to her breast, a hoe over her shoulder, pursed cherry lips, she glides along like a willow frond swaying in a breeze. Who would have the heart not to buy it? Especially the lovesick, the lovelorn, and those excitable young men and women with a modicum of literary taste, who would pawn their own trousers to buy it and drink it and enjoy it and use it to cure their love maladies, or sugar-coat it to present to their lovers as a material blitzkrieg with psychological overtones or a psychological stimulus with material overtones in order to get what they want. With the guidance of your sentimental, bleeding-heart advertising copy, this sickness wine will be transformed into an abnormal taste of love capable of producing soul-stirring obsessions, and will anesthetize the feeble hearts of China's hordes of underdeveloped petit-bourgeois boys and girls who pattern themselves after the characters in the romantic novels of which they are so fond, giving them ideals, hope, and strength, and keep them from killing themselves over their emotions. This will become *the* liquor of love, which will stun the world; its flaws will be transformed into conspicuously unique qualities. Sir, it is a fact that many tastes are acquired, not innate; no one is willing to call bad something the rest of the world calls good; great authority is vested in the preference of the masses, like the power the Director of the Municipal Party Organization Department wields over a grass-roots Party cadre; if he says you're good, you're good whether you're good or bad; if he says you're bad, you're bad whether you're bad or good. Besides, drinking liquor, as with the consumption of all food and drink, is a habit that becomes a mania: always preferring something new over something old, always ready to take a risk, always seeking a more intense high. Much gourmandism results from anti-traditionalism and a disdain for the law. When one tires of eating fresh, white tofu, one turns to moldy, gummy, stinky tofu or pickled tofu; when one tires of eating fresh, tasty pork, one dines on rotten, maggot-ridden meat. Following that logic, when one tires of imbibing ambrosial spirits and jadelike brews, one seeks out strangely bitter or spicy or sour or dank flavors to excite the taste buds and the membranes of the mouth. So long as we lead the way, there isn't a liquor made we can't sell to the public. I hope that while you're writing your novel, you'll make time to write something along these lines. With the grandiose comments of our Mayor as security, your efforts will be well rewarded. You might even earn considerably more for this modest advertising copy than for six grueling months of writing fiction.

In recent days I've been busily involved in a magnificent idea revealed by the Mayor during our discussions: She would like me to head up a writing group charged with the creation of a set of 'liquor laws.' Naturally, these will constitute the basic laws concerning liquor in all conceivable aspects. I'm not exaggerating when I say that, if successful, this will usher in a new era where liquor is concerned, one that will light the way for thousands of years, producing a halo that will shine down on ten thousand generations. This will be a creation of historical proportions. I cordially invite you to join our liquor-law drafting group. Even if you are unable to participate in the actual writing, you can serve as chief adviser. Please do not deny me in this endeavor.

I hope you'll forgive me for writing such a disjointed, hopelessly muddled letter, for which liquor is to blame. I'm enclosing a story I wrote last night when I was in my cups. I invite your criticisms. It's up to you whether or not you submit it for publication. I wrote it in pursuit of the auspiciousness of a certain number. I have always revered the number nine, and this piece, entitled 'Liquorville,' is my ninth story; and, of course, the word liquor has the same sound as the number nine. I hope it is like a bright new star, lighting up my dark past and the rugged path that lies ahead of me.

I await your arrival. Our mountains await your arrival, as do our waters, our young men, and our young women. Those young women resemble flowers from whose mouths emerge a redolence of liquor that is like heavenly music . . .

With reverence, I wish you
Peace and happiness,
Your student

Li Yidou

II

Liquorville, by Li Yidou

Whether you travel by airplane, steamship, camel, or donkey, you can reach Liquorville from any spot on earth. There is no shortage of beautiful places in the world, but few of those places are more beautiful than Liquorville. Actually, the word 'few' is too vague – I prefer the word 'none.' The citizens of Liquorville are straightforward. Just like an explosive projectile, except that the casing of a projectile is filled with coiled wire, while the wires inside Liquorville residents run straight from their mouths down to their rectums, without a single twist or curve. That should tell what you need to know about the disposition of Liquorville residents. To state the issue even more clearly, Liquorville is the capital of Liquorland. I hope my explanation doesn't lead to any misunderstandings.

The fragrance of liquor emanating from Liquorland can be detected for a hundred li in any direction, and even people with a blunted sense of smell can detect it from fifty li. Don't accuse me of witchcraft if I reveal that, when Boeing jets fly over Liquorland, they perform loop-the-loops, in spry yet intoxicated innocence, never, however, jeopardizing their safety. Comrades, ladies, gentlemen, friends, you needn't be anxious, for while you sit in the safety of your airplanes, you are like spry yet intoxicated cute little puppies; the wonderful, exotic aroma is an open invitation to enjoy your experience of passing, of soaking up one of the world's most captivating smells as you pass over Liquorland.

The municipal government and Party headquarters are located smack in the center of Liquorville. A towering white liquor vat stands in the heart of the Party compound, while a towering black cask has been placed in the middle of the government compound. Please, folks, don't assume there's a note of sarcasm there, because there isn't. Since the era of reforms and liberalization was launched, Party committees and government offices everywhere, in order to speedily improve the people's lives, have racked their brains, devised proposals, and come up with plans to integrate the current local realities with Party spirit to create workable scenarios and schemes: Those in the mountains live off the mountains, those near water make their living from the water, those with fine scenery develop the tourist industry, those with tobacco land produce tobacco . . . after rolling like the wind and clouds for over a decade, this has produced Ghost City, Tobacco Capital, Fireworks Town . . . here in Liquorland the liquor is plentiful and of excellent quality, so the Municipal Party Committee and the government have established a Brewer's College, and are making plans for a distillery museum, expanding twenty distilleries, and building three gigantic distilleries that incorporate the finest of the world's distilling art. With liquor as the engine, we have spurred the development of special services for our male visitors, the restaurant business, the raising of exotic birds and animals . . . now the fragrance of liquor floats above every nook and cranny of Liquorland. There are thousands of inns and taverns in Liquorville, their bright lights shining day and night above the sound of glasses clinking noisily; Liquorland's fine liquors and superb victuals draw hordes of visitors, diners, and drunks, domestic and international, to take tours, to drink, and to eat fine food, although the most important visitors are liquor distributors who carry our fine liquor and sterling reputation to every corner of the earth. Our excellent liquor travels abroad, excellent greenbacks make the trip back. In recent years, Liquorland's annual tax bill has soared into the hundreds of millions, a huge contribution to the nation, while, at the same time, our citizens' standard of living has kept improving. Our people now live comfortably, are on their way to becoming well off, and dream of the day when they can call themselves rich. What, you ask, is meant by 'rich'? 'Communism,' that's what. Now that you've read to this point, dear readers, you understand why the Municipal Party Committee and government built their huge vat and cask.

Having dispensed with idle talk, dear readers, it's time for my story to get on track and for me to return to Liquorville. While you, ladies and gentlemen, take in the lovely sights of Liquorland and enjoy the fragrant smell of its liquor and sample its wonderful flavor, please listen to what I have to say and enjoy to your hearts' content drinking songs sung by our lovely maidens. No need to be polite. When good friends drink together, a thousand cups is too little; when the talk is not congenial, half a sentence is too much. The rack in front of you is filled with Liquorland's finest brews, the table behind it piled high with delectables. I invite you to eat and drink as much as you can, as much as you need. It's free, all of it. As executive director of the publicity preparatory committee, I had originally intended to collect fifty cents from each of you as a symbolic donation for today's meal, but the Mayor said that was the hypocritical equivalent of erecting a memorial archway to the chastity of a prostitute, that since fifty cents wouldn't be enough for half a donkey dick, why ask for anything? Besides, you are all honored guests who have traveled far to get here; by charging you for food, people everywhere would laugh until their teeth fell out, and dentists would be the only ones to benefit – which reminds me: Liquorville's Dental Academy task force has developed a tooth-filling material that never wears out, so if any of you need dental work, please take care of it while you're here, free of charge. This material is impervious to cold, heat, sour or sweet flavors; never again will any food stand up to your teeth when you chew, no matter how stubborn. But back to the subject at hand. People have been distilling liquor here in Liquorville for at least 3,000 years, as we learn from archaeological excavations. I call your attention to the video: Beneath this site, called Moonbeam Heap, lie the ruins of an ancient city, and from it over 3,000 relics have been recovered, half of them liquor vessels: this is a goblet, this one a jug, this is a liquor urn, this a drinking bowl, this a tumbler, and this one is a tripod liquor bowl . . . you name it, it's there. Experts have dated the site as being 3,500 years old, which puts it at the end of the Shang dynasty. Even back in those ancient times, this was a place where glasses clinked loudly and the aroma of fine liquor hung in the air. These days an odious trend has gripped the world of liquor: everyone seems to be trying to make a tiger's skin out of a personal banner. If the legendary Yu got drunk on your liquor, the great emperor Kangxi got drunk on mine; if the consort Yang Guifei was infatuated by your liquor, then the emperor Han Wudi stumbled around after drinking mine . . . and so on and so forth, creating an absurd tradition and bringing great harm to many. Here in Liquorville we seek truth from facts and always prove our case. Friends, take a look at this brick. It's not an ordinary brick. No, it's a portrait from the Eastern Han, dug up right here in Liquorville. The painting depicts the distilling of liquor, and from it we are happy to learn that, way back then, in Liquorland the production of alcoholic beverages already involved cooperative labor. A woman at the top of the painting is holding a large pot over a liquor vat in her left hand and stirring the cooling water with her right. A man to her right is heating the water in the vat. The man standing to the left of the liquor trough carefully watches the flow of liquor. At the bottom of the picture, a man with two buckets on a carrying pole is responsible for ensuring that there's enough water . . . this painting graphically shows how liquor was produced thousands of years ago, and corresponds perfectly to a description of the process in the chapter 'Sorghum Wine' in the novel *Red Sorghum* by my mentor, Mr Mo Yan. Now please look at the second brick, called

'The Wineshop.' Wine jugs line the street in front of the shop, the proprietor stands behind the counter, and two prospective customers in the upper left-hand corner are rushing joyfully toward the shop. Now the third brick, named 'The Banquet.' Seven people are seated around a table, three in the middle and two on either side, a proper banquet. Glasses and goblets are arrayed in front of dishes piled high with food. The diners are raising their glasses and urging one another to eat and drink, just the way we do now. Well, I've prattled on long enough. These three bricks constitute firm and powerful evidence that Liquorville is the fountainhead of liquor and the liquor culture of the Chinese race, thoroughly discrediting rumors about the history of alcoholic beverages – into the dustbin with Great Yu Bottle and Xiang Yu Wine Glass. Or, the consort Yang Guifei left Liquorland to get married, and Han Wudi is a son of Liquorland. All you boasters and liars, quickly pour your drinks into the river. The liquor of Liquorville is the liquor of history; the liquor of Liquorville is soaked in the classics of Han culture.

Comrades, the liars have overlooked the common knowledge that the distilled spirits in their bottles first appeared in the Han dynasty, and that only fermented spirits were available during the reign of the Great Yu. The Han dynasty brick paintings prove that a revolution in the production of alcohol was launched right here in Liquorland.

Friends, just as water flows day and night in Sweet Spring River, the fine liquor of Liquorville flowed uninterrupted for a long time, eventually entering an age of maturity. In the early years of the Qing dynasty, a distillery by the name of Great Blessings appeared, as did a liquor of unknown origins named Charming Gaits. From this emerged a distillery called Blessings and Charm, which produced Liquorville's finest brew: Great Clouds and Rain.

Legend has it that during the Shunzhi reign of the Qing lived a petty innkeeper by the name of Yuan Yi, whose honorific was Sanliu, or Three Six. He began by selling liquor, then went into the distilling business. Expert at assimilating the traditional technologies of Liquorville's distillers, he aspired to become famous in the distiller's art. Unhappily, he died before he could realize his ambitions. Not until his great-great grandson's generation would his cherished wish come true. During the Qianlong Emperor's reign in the Qing dynasty, Yuan's great-great grandson, whose name was Jiuwu, or Nine Five, called upon his ancestor's experience and his own rich understanding of the marketplace to set up shop on Daughter's Well Street by the Temple of the Immortal Matron out beyond Liquorville's East Gate.

Rumor had it that the eye of the sea existed beneath the Temple of the Immortal Matron, and that if it were ever disturbed, Liquorville would fall into the sea. In order to avert a watery disaster, the people pooled their money to erect a temple, then built a golden Matron and placed her atop the eye of the sea. Clouds of incense smoke filled the Temple of the Immortal Matron, especially on the eighth day of the fourth lunar month. On that day, a festive atmosphere accompanied the burning of incense. Young ladies from good families came out in droves, as did roughnecks who mingled with them to fondle their breasts and pinch their bottoms, eliciting shrieks of protest. Truly this was a treasured place to buy and sell liquor – the *feng shui* was just right. So Nine Five Yuan bought a piece of land near the Temple of the Immortal Matron and set up shop under the name Blessings and Charm. He also built a distillery beside Daughter's Well.

Daughter's Well was only one li distant from the Temple of the Immortal Matron. Its water came from Sweet Spring River; after passing through the natural filtration of sand and rocks, it bubbled up clear, sweet, and icy cold. It was considered Liquorville's finest well. Popular legend had it that a beautiful woman had drowned in the well, and that after her death she turned into a cloud that enveloped the well and would not disperse. But Yuan's great-great grandson had not forgotten that Daughter's Well had been the source of fine water for Charming Gaits of an earlier era; not only was he a master of the distiller's art, but, naturally, a man of superior historical vision as well. Drawing on the water from Daughter's Well for his new brew was significant for Blessings and Charm not only because 'water is the lifeblood of liquor,' but also because it had produced Charming Gaits, and, even more significantly, since 'the gods are the soul of liquor,' it contained the richness of historical culture.

Extraordinary ambition, extraordinary skills, and extraordinary well water led naturally to extraordinary beginnings. Great Clouds and Rain had no sooner come on the market than it was proclaimed a great success. Blessings and Charm was as busy as a marketplace, with workers and scholars and old hands and petty hooligans beating a path to the door. A poet by the name of Li Sandou – Three-Pint Li – wrote two poems in praise of the qualities of Great Clouds and Rain. Here they are:

Spring has long dwelt in the Temple of the Immortal Matron,
Fragrant well water is transformed into puffy clouds.
The face of a beautiful woman is a sight to behold,
But a great brew has a man in its thrall.

With water for clothing and a cloud as his face,
Liu Ling lies naked, drunk as a lord.
Having drunk clouds and rain, there's no need to dream,
For it's better than Song Yu's romance with a fairy.

Admittedly replete with roughneck airs, the poems succeed admirably in capturing the unique appeal of Great Clouds and Rain.

There in front of the Temple of the Immortal Matron, in Blessings and Charm, with a shop in front and a distillery in the rear, beverage and consumer found it easy to meet. Devout pilgrims could see the large gold placard with its black lettering long before they reached the Temple: elegant yet unconventional, the wildcap handiwork belonged to Hairy Turtle Jin, the nationally renowned calligrapher. The scrolls on either side of the door had been chosen by the eminent scholar, Miss Ma Kuni. They read:

Enter with knitted brows and divided feelings
Leave holding a loving heart in cupped hands

The shop was elegantly furnished, the embodiment of gentility. The central scroll, which hung from the main wall, was a colorful painting by one of Liquorland's foremost artists, Miss Li Mengniang. It depicted the consort Yang Guifei drunk and in a state of dishabille, her buxom body glistening, especially her nipples, which were as red as cherries. Coming to this place to drink brought pleasure both to the mind and to the eye.

The drinking utensils were unique among all the wineshops in Liquorville. Here the goblets were fashioned as shapely women's legs; they came in one-ounce, three-ounce, and eight-ounce sizes, to suit the customers' wishes. Holding one of those legs and sampling its liquid contents brought unique pleasures. Beautiful, splendid. Beauteous splendor beyond compare.

Quality liquor, elegant surroundings, and a fine reputation produced an unending supply of strange tales and amusing anecdotes.

Legend has it that on a cold winter night during the Guangxu Reign of the Qing dynasty, as swirling snowflakes covered the ground, the proprietor of Blessings and Charm was about to close up shop when, in the hazy darkness, a man with a lantern, wearing a thick coat of snow, entered the shop and said that his lady guest had asked for some Great Clouds and Rain; he had braved the snowstorm to come for some. As luck would have it, they had sold out that day, and the proprietor could only convey his abject apologies. But the customer refused to leave, so moving the proprietor that he sent his apprentice to the storeroom to fetch more. But when the storeroom door swung open, releasing the fragrance locked up inside, the customer was unable to resist its appeal and ran inside with his lantern. In his attempt to block the customer's way, the apprentice bumped the lantern, setting fire to its paper cover, which quickly spread to the storeroom itself, resulting in a disastrous conflagration. Flaming, flowing dragons of liquor, burning blue and bright, brought destruction not only to the storeroom and the shop, but to the Temple of the Immortal Matron across the way, reducing it to a pile of ashes. Keep in mind, dear readers, that it snowed heavily that night, turning the ground into rivers of splintered color. The surpassing beauty of blue tongues of fire snaking through the snowy landscape defies description. After the fire was out, its origin and progress took on the airs of mystery and wonder in the telling and retelling, so that when Blessings and Charm was rebuilt, its reputation and fiery demise brought in more business than ever. What had been a disastrous fire was transformed into a magnificent advertisement.

Great Clouds and Rain was not only mellow, sweet, clean, and delicious, it also had an incomparable redolence. One late spring day, one of the distillery workers accidentally dropped a lined basket of new liquor on the ground; as the contents flowed to the street, sending its redolence skyward, tears welled up in the eyes of strolling red-cheeked boys and girls, who began to wobble and weave. Just then, a passing flock of birds lost their bearings and fell out of the sky. Sinking fish and falling swallows [great feminine beauty], bewitching souls and spell-binding spirits. A thousand tender emotions. Ten thousand types of womanizing. As the poem goes:

> A cup of Great Clouds and Rain moistens the throat,
> Ten thousand scenes appear before your eyes.
> This liquor should exist only in heaven,
> How often can people taste such a glorious elixir?

Honored guests, friends, I've already laid out the attributes of our Great Clouds and Rain. I need only add the following: My father in law, Professor Yuan Shuangyu of the Liquorland Brewer's College, is the great-great-great-great-great grandson of Mr Nine Five Yuan, the creator of Great Clouds and Rain! As a professor at the Brewer's college, he has been generous in demonstrating the amazing skills handed down by his ancestors. Under his leadership, and with the concern and guidance of the Municipal Party Committee and government, we here in Liquorland have ridden the mighty steeds of reform and liberalization. In a mere ten years, building upon the foundation we inherited, we have created at least a dozen new liquors that compare favorably with Great Clouds and Rain, some actually surpassing it in quality. Such brands as Overlapping Green Ants or Red-Maned Stallion or Love at First Sight or Fire Clouds or Ximen Qing or Lin Daiyu Buries Blossoms . . . but even more inspiring is the fact that my father-in-law, Professor Yuan, went up to White Ape Mountain alone, his hair matted, his face dirty, an old man with a ruddy complexion, making friends with the apes and learning from beasts in the wild, absorbing the apes' wisdom, continuing his ancestor's tradition, and drawing lessons from outsiders' experience, making the past serve the present, foreign things serve China, and apes serve humans, until, at last, success was his and he could take his place as a world leader with his city-toppling ape wine.

Ape wine will be solemnly introduced at the first annual Ape Liquor Festival!

A thousand ounces of gold is easily obtained, a single drop of Ape Liquor cannot be begged!

Friends! Don't hesitate another second, come to Liquorland, and hurry!

Do not pass up this opportunity!

III

Dear Elder Brother Yidou

Your manuscript arrived safely.

As luck would have it, a publishing friend of mine dropped by, and I showed him 'Liquorville.' When he finished, he pounded the table and shouted, This has real potential. He said that if you can expand the story to seventy or eighty thousand words and add some graphics and photographs, you can publish it as a book. His house will assign it a number and assume editorial responsibility. All your city has to do is come up with a subvention and guarantee the purchase of ten thousand copies. He said that since you'll have to prepare promotional materials for attendees to the first annual Ape Liquor Festival, why not include copies of an illustrated book? It will provide everyone with an accessible, readable history of Liquorland that they can keep for a long time. I think it's a terrific idea. Talk it over with your mayor. You'll probably have to give the publisher about 50,000 yuan, a trifling amount for Liquorland, wouldn't you say? Please let me know as soon as possible, whatever you decide. That friend of mine was so interested in the concept that I gave him your address before he left. He may contact you directly.

As for naming your new brew and participating in the liquor-laws drafting group, since the potential benefits are apparent, I see no reason for false modesty. I accept your invitation. As soon as I put the finishing touches on my novel, I'll leave for Liquorland. We can work out the details of all these matters then.

Best wishes for success in your writing,

Mo Yan

IV

. . . wah wah wah! When Ding Gou'er's thoughts turned to Diamond Jin and all those baby boys who were eaten then excreted into toilets, feelings of personal responsibility and a sense of right and wrong, like the brilliant stars of the Big Dipper, lit up his consciousness, which had been flitting and fleeing in the darkness. At such times, he experienced sharp pains in the helixes of his ears and the tip of his nose, as if they had been pierced by poison darts. Instinctively he sat up – the sky spun, the earth tumbled, his head was as big as a willow basket – and forced his puffy eyelids open; four or five large gray shadows leaped away from his body and landed with dull, meaty thuds. At the same time he heard a high-pitched chirping. A strange bird? Some wild beast? The investigator imagined a grouse or a wild rabbit, even a flying dragon or a flying squirrel. A pair of flashing green eyes poked through the blurry background in front of him. He strained to roll his glassy, crusted eyes and moisten them with the secretions of his tear glands; the tears that glistened across his eyeballs carried the smell of cheap booze. After rubbing his eyes with the back of his hand, the scene grew clearer. The first thing he could make out was a clutch of seven or eight large gray house rats glaring angrily and disgustingly at him through pitch-black eyes. The investigator's stomach lurched at the sight of their pointy snouts, stiff whiskers, sagging bellies, and long, thin tails; his mouth opened, and out spewed a noxious stew of exotic foods, good liquor, and something very near to excrement. His throat felt as if it had been slit by a sharp knife, his nose ached, and his nostrils were stopped up by slimy objects that hadn't quite made it out. Then a shiny, black fowling piece hanging on the wall caught his eye, and it was just the right image to bring him out of his dark funk. His thoughts turned immediately to his panicky flight from danger so long ago, and to the spectral old man engaged in the illegal sale of wonton, and to the old revolutionary caretaker of the Martyrs' Cemetery, and to the dancing spirit of Maotai liquor, a red sash across its chest, and to the fiercely intimidating golden-coated dog . . . his mind was working full-speed, but his thoughts were a hopeless tangle, as if all the flowers were blooming at once. Like a dream, but not entirely; lifelike and fantastic at the same time. Thoughts of the voluptuous lady trucker thudded into the investigator's mind, just as a large rat jumped onto his shoulder and, with incredible agility, took a bite out of his neck, forcing him to wipe his mind clean of all those random thoughts and concentrate on the here and now. With a shake of his body, he sent the rat flying, as a shriek came of its own accord up out of his throat, but was driven back where it came from by the bizarre scene in front of him. His mouth fell slack, his eyes had a dazed look. There, on his back on the brick bed lay the old revolutionary, blanketed by a dozen or more large rats. His nose and ears had already been gnawed off by the hungry rats – maybe it wasn't really hunger that drove them on – and his lips had been chewed away, exposing his discolored gums. The mouth, which had once launched strings of witty remarks, was ugly beyond imagining, and the old man's skull, shorn of its extraneous protrusions, presented a hideous sight. The rats, meanwhile, were working themselves into a frenzy as they attacked the old revolutionary's hands. The white bones of hands that had once been so adept at wielding a rifle or a club looked like stripped willow branches, absent the skin that had once covered them. The investigator harbored good feelings toward the hardened old revolutionary, who had come to his aid when he needed it most. Rousing his weary body, he rushed up to drive away the rats, but was so startled to see their eyes change color as he bore down on them, from pitch black to a soft pink, then to a dark green, that he stopped in his tracks and backed off, all the way to the wall, where he watched as the rats bared their teeth, frothed at the mouth, and glared with rage, closing ranks to form an attack unit ready to charge. Feeling the fowling piece against his back, the investigator had a sudden inspiration. He spun around, grabbed the gun, took aim, and wrapped his finger around the trigger, standing at the ready, as if facing a menacing horde.

'Don't move!' the investigator shouted. 'One step closer and I'll blow you away!'

The rats exchanged glances and gestures, mocking the investigator, who all but exploded in anger:

'You fucking rats!' he swore. 'Now you'll find out who you're dealing with!'

The words were barely out of his mouth when an explosion tore through the room, like a thunderclap. A flash of fiery light sent clouds of gunsmoke rolling in the air. When the smoke cleared, the investigator was relieved to see that a single shot had decimated the rat ranks; those that survived the blast cursed their parents for not giving them four more legs, as they scurried across roofbeams, clung to cross beams, flew on eaves and walked on walls, until, in a matter of seconds, they were gone without a trace. The investigator was alarmed to note that, while the blast from his fowling piece had killed or scattered the rats, it had also blown holes in the old revolutionary's face, which now looked like a sieve. Hugging the shotgun to his chest, he fell back against the wall and slid to the floor on rubbery legs, his heart screaming out in agony. The old revolutionary obviously died under an assault by those rats, he reasoned, but who would believe him after seeing the man's face all pitted with buckshot? People would jump to the conclusion that he had died from a shotgun blast to the face, which had then been further disfigured by rats. Ding Gou'er Ding Gou'er, this time you could jump into the Yangtze and not come out clean. The Yangtze is muddier even than the Yellow River. 'When a sage appears, the Yellow River turns clean. Families everywhere gather to sail lanterns made of gourds and melons. What kind? White gourds, watermelons, and pumpkins. What kind of lanterns, what kind? Cucumber, squash, and brain gourd lanterns.' This childhood folk song crisply and mysteriously pounded the eardrums of the distraught special investigator, distant at first, then nearer and nearer, getting clearer and clearer, louder and louder, until it expanded into a full-blown chorus of brilliant juvenile voices, like floating clouds and flowing water. And there, standing in the conductor's spot in front of the boys' chorus, more than a hundred members strong, was the son from whom he had been parted for so long. The boy was wearing a snow-white shirt and sky-blue shorts, like a cottony cloud floating in the sky, or a single gull soaring through the sea-blue heavens. Two rivulets of murky fluid, like warm liquor, flowed from the investigator's eyes, soaking his cheeks and the corners of his mouth. He stood up and reached out to his son, but the blue and white little fellow drifted slowly away from him, the boy's image in his eyes replaced by the ghastly scene he and the rats had created, a false yet indescribable scene of murder that was destined to rock Liquorland.

Drawn by the enchanting expression on his son's face, the investigator walked to the gate of the Martyrs' Cemetery and saw the big dog with the tiger-like demeanor, which had once caused his hair to stand on end; it lay on its side under a dark green poplar tree, its legs thrust out stiffly, blood trickling from its mouth. Startled out of his wits, the investigator bent down and squeezed through the dog door. There wasn't another soul on the ancient, pitted asphalt road, in the center of which a solitary concrete utility pole cast a lengthy shadow down the road. Blood-red rays of the setting sun fell on the investigator's face as he stood up dejectedly. He stood there for a long while deep in thought, yet thinking about nothing tangible.

The rumble of a train passing through the center of Liquorland gave him an idea. Walking down the road, he dimly sensed that he was heading in the direction of the railway station. But a river turned golden by the sun's late-afternoon rays blocked his way. It was a gorgeous river scene, with colorful, creaky boats slipping across the surface into the sun. The men and women on one of the boats appeared to be lovers, since only lovers would have their arms around each other as they gazed straight ahead in silent infatuation. A burly woman in an old-style dress stood on the stern, straining and stretching as she worked the scull back and forth, shattering the golden glaze of the river and stirring up the stench of decaying bodies and the smell of heated distillery grains that permeated the water. In the eyes of the investigator, her labors seemed somehow artificial, as if she were acting on stage, not performing her task on a boat. Her boat glided past, followed by another, and another and another and another. All the passengers were love-struck young men and women, and all the women on the sterns performed their tasks with the same artificial air. The investigator felt sure that the passengers and the women sculling them along must have undergone some sort of rigorous training in a technical school. Unawares, he fell in behind the river-going contingent, following along on a road paved with octagonal cement blocks. On that late-autumn day, most of the leaves on the riverside willows had fallen to the ground; the few that clung to their branches seemed cut out of gold foil; beautiful and precious. As he followed the progress of the boats, Ding Gou'er felt more and more at peace, all mortal concerns disappearing from his consciousness. Some people walk toward the morning sun; he was walking toward the setting sun.

At a bend in the river a broader expanse of water appeared in front of him. Lamps were already showing in the windows of ancient buildings. One after another, the boats tied up at the shore. The love-struck young men and women went ashore and were quickly swallowed up by the city's bustling streets. The investigator had no sooner entered the city than he sensed that he was in an historical artifice. The pedestrians glided along like ghosts. Their aimless floating made him feel light as a feather; his feet didn't touch the ground, it seemed.

Eventually he followed people into a Temple of the Immortal Matron, where he saw a clutch of beautiful women on their knees kowtowing to the golden statue of a large-headed, fleshy-eared Matron. They were sitting on their heels. Infatuated, he admired their high-heeled shoes for the longest time, imagining the holes they poked in the ground. A little bald-pated monk hiding behind a column, slingshot in hand, was shooting the upraised hind-quarters of the women with muddy spit wads. He never missed, to which the yelps emerging from beneath the Matron's knee paid witness. And after each yelp, he clasped his hands, closed his eyes, and recited a Buddhist incantation. Wondering what the little monk was thinking, Ding Gou'er walked up and flicked the top of his head with his middle finger. That too produced a yelp – in a *girl's* voice. Suddenly he was surrounded by dozens of people, accusing him of hooliganism and of taking liberties with the little nun, just like Ah-Q, the hero of Lu Xun's story. A policeman grabbed him by the neck and dragged him out of the temple, where he gave him a shove and a kick in the rear. Ding Gou'er found himself on all fours on the steps of the temple, like a dog fighting over shit; his lip was split, his front tooth was loose, his mouth was filling up with brackish-tasting blood.

Afterwards, as he was crossing an arched bridge, he saw sparkles on the surface of the water; they came from flickering lanterns. Large boats were sailing past, songs were being played and sung aboard the boats, and the whole scene seemed like a night procession of genies and fairies.

After that he entered a tavern and spotted a dozen or more men in wide-brimmed hats sitting around a table feasting on liquor and fish. The fragrance of both assailed his nostrils and had him salivating in no time. Stopped from going up to beg something to eat and drink only by his sense of shame, his ravenous hunger soon got the upper hand; spotting an opening, he rushed the table like a hungry tiger pouncing on its prey. Then, grabbing a bottle of liquor in one hand and a whole fish in the other, he turned and ran out the door. A commotion erupted behind him.

A while later, he hid in the shade of a wall to drink his liquor and eat his fish. Little but bones remained of the fish, so that's what he chewed up and swallowed. He drank every last drop of liquor in the bottle.

Later still, he wandered the area, gazing at the reflections of stars in the river and at the big, red moon, which looked like a golden-fleeced baby boy leaping out of the water. Sounds of aquatic delights were louder than ever; when he looked to see where they were coming from, he spotted a hulking pleasure-boat sailing slowly toward him from upriver. Backlit by a profusion of cabin lights, young women in old-style clothing were singing and dancing on the deck, pounding drums and blowing panpipes. In the cabin, a dozen or so neatly dressed men and women were sitting at a

329

table playing finger-guessing games as they drank the fine liquor and feasted on the exotic foods arrayed in front of them. They were gobbling up the food – men and women alike. Different times, different styles. A woman with blood-red lips was gorging herself like an old sow, not coming up for air. Just watching her eat made Ding Gou'er dizzy. As the pleasure-boat neared, he could make out the passengers' features and smell their fetid breath. He saw familiar faces. There was Diamond Jin, the lady trucker, Yu Yichi, Section Chief Wang, Party Secretary Li . . . even someone who looked remarkably like Ding himself. All his good friends and kinfolk, his lovers and his enemies, appeared to be participants at this cannibalistic feast. Why a cannibalistic feast? Because the *pièce de résistance*, placed in the middle of a large gilded platter, all oily and redolent, was a plump little boy with a captivating smile.

'Come here, my dear Ding Gou'er, come over here . . .' He detected a mischievous yet undeniably fetching undertone to the lady trucker's voice as she called out tenderly, and he saw her wave enticingly with a lily-white hand. Behind her, the stalwart Diamond Jin was bending down whispering to the diminutive Yu Yichi, the condescending smile on his lips answered by Yu Yichi's knowing sneer.

'I protest –' Ding Gou'er screamed as, with a final burst of energy, he dashed toward the pleasure-boat. But before he got there, he stumbled into an open-air privy filled with a soupy, fermenting goop of food and drink regurgitated by Liquorland residents, plus the drink and food excreted from the other end, atop which floated such imaginably filthy refuse as bloated, used condoms. It was fertile ground for all sorts of disease-carrying bacteria and micro-organisms, a paradise for flies, Heaven on earth for maggots. Feeling that this was not the place where he should wind up, the investigator announced loudly, just before his mouth slid beneath the warm, vile porridge, 'I protest, I pro –' The pitiless muck sealed his mouth as the irresistible force of gravity drew him under. Within seconds, the sacred panoply of ideals, justice, respect, honor, and love accompanied a long-suffering special investigator to the very bottom of the privy . . .

Chapter Ten

I

Dear Elder Brother Yidou

I've asked someone to buy me a ticket on the September 27th train to Liquorland. According to the timetable, I arrive at 2:30 on the morning of the 29th. I know it's a terrible hour, but it's the only train I can take, and I'll just have to trouble you to meet me then.

I've read 'Ape Liquor,' and have many thoughts about it. We can talk when I get there.

Best wishes,

Mo Yan

I I

As he lay in the relative comfort of a hard-sleeper cot – relative to a hard-seater, that is – the puffy, balding, beady-eyed, twisted-mouthed, middle-aged writer Mo Yan wasn't sleepy at all. The overhead lights went out as the train carried him into the night, leaving only the dim yellow glare of the floor lights to see by. I know there are many similarities between me and this Mo Yan, but many contradictions as well. I'm a hermit crab, and Mo Yan is the shell I'm occupying. Mo Yan is the raingear that protects me from storms, a dog hide to ward off the chilled winds, a mask I wear to seduce girls from good families. There are times when I feel that this Mo Yan is a heavy burden, but I can't seem to cast it off, just as a hermit crab cannot rid itself of its shell. I can be free of it in the darkness, at least for a while. I see it softly filling up the narrow middle berth, its large head tossing and turning on the tiny pillow; long years as a writer have formed bone spurs on its vertebrae, turning the neck stiff and cold, sore and tingly, until just moving it is a real chore. This Mo Yan disgusts me, that's the truth. At this moment its brain is aswarm with bizarre events: apes distilling liquor and dragging down the moon; the investigator wrestling with a dwarf; golden-threaded swallows making nests from saliva; the dwarf dancing on the naked belly of a beautiful woman; a doctor of liquor studies fornicating with his own mother-in-law; a female reporter taking pictures of a braised infant; royalties; trips abroad; cursing people out ... What pleasure can he get from the jumble of thoughts filling his mind, I wonder?

'Liquorland, next stop, Liquorland,' a skinny little conductress announces as she sways down the corridor, slapping her ticket pouch as she passes. 'Next stop, Liquorland. Reclaim your tickets, please.'

Quickly Mo Yan and I merge into one. He sits up in his middle berth, which means that I sit up as well. My belly feels bloated, my neck stiff; I'm having trouble breathing and I have a terrible taste in my mouth. This Mo Yan is so filthy he's hard to swallow. I watch him take a metal tag out of a gray jacket he's worn for years and reclaim his ticket, then he jumps clumsily out of the middle berth and searches out his smelly shoes with smelly feet that resemble a pair of hermit crabs looking for new shells. He coughs twice, then wraps his filthy water mug in the filthy rag he uses to wash his face and feet, stuffs it into a gray travel bag and sits spellbound for a few minutes, staring at the hair of the pharmaceutical saleswoman sleeping noisily on the lower berth across from him. Finally he gets up and staggers in the direction of the door.

When I step down off the train, my attention is caught by the contrast of white raindrops dancing in the murky yellow lamplight. The station platform is deserted except for two shuffling men in blue overcoats. Conductors huddle silently in the car doors like chickens in a henhouse that have somehow made it through another long night. The train is still, seemingly abandoned. The roar of water from behind the train indicates that the tanks are being refilled. Up front, the headlight blazes. A uniformed man beside the train pounds the wheels with a mallet, like a woodpecker going through the motions. The cars, all soaking wet, are panting, and the tracks, reaching out to distant stations in the bright headlight, are also soaking wet; by all appearances, it has been raining for quite a while, though I wasn't aware of it on the train. Back when I was leaving Beijing my bus passed through Tiananmen Square, where bright sunlight brought the golden chrysanthemums and fiery red flowers to life. Sun Yat-sen, who stood in the square, and Mao Zedong, who hangs from the wall of the Forbidden City, were exchanging silent messages past the five-star flag hanging from a brand-new flagpole. I read in the paper that the pole is over forty meters high, and while it doesn't appear to be that high, it surely must be, since no one would dare cut corners in erecting this sacred column. I've cooled my heels in Beijing for nearly ten years, wrapped in the skin of the writer Mo Yan, so I have a good feel for the place. Geologically, it's in good shape, with no faults running beneath it. Now here I am, in Liquorland, and it's raining. When going from one place to another, you sure can't count on the weather. I never considered the possibility that the Liquorland train station would be so peaceful, so very peaceful, amid a gentle rainfall, the bright, warm and golden lamplight, shiny railroad tracks, chilled but refreshingly clean night air, and a darkened tunnel running beneath the tracks. The little train station has the feel of a detective novel, and I like it . . . When Ding Gou'er was walking down the passage beneath the tracks, the agreeable odor of the braised infant boy was still in his nostrils. Dark red, shiny grease ran down the face of the tiny, golden-bodied fellow, a smile of impenetrable mystery hanging in the corners of his mouth . . . I watch as the train roars to life and chugs out of the station. Not until the red caboose lantern disappears around the bend, not until the rumble comes from far into the dark night, like a disembodied illusion, do I pick up my bag and start walking on the bumpy floor of the underground tunnel, which is dimly lit by a few low-wattage bulbs. Since my bag has wheels, I set it down to drag behind me. But the noise from the wheels throws my heart and mind into an uproar, so I pick it up and carry it over my back.

My footsteps are greatly magnified in the tunnel, making me feel empty inside . . . Ding Gou'er's experiences in Liquorland had to have been closely linked to this underground tunnel. There ought to be a secret marketplace for buying and selling meat children here somewhere; there ought to be a bunch of drunks, hookers, beggars, and half-crazed dogs hanging around, for this is where he was given some important clues . . . Unique descriptions of scene play a significant role in the success of fiction, and any first-rate novelist knows enough to keep changing the scenes in which his characters carry out the action, since that not only conceals the novelist's shortcomings, but also heightens the reader's enthusiasm in the reading process. Caught up in his thoughts, Mo Yan turns a corner and spots an old man curled up in a corner, a tattered blanket wrapped around his shoulders. Alongside him lies a green liquor bottle. It comforts me to know that in Liquorland even the beggars have access to drink. Given all the short stories the Doctor of Liquor Studies, Li Yidou, has written, each revolving around liquor, why hasn't he written one about beggars? An alcoholic beggar wants neither money nor food; all he asks for is alcohol, and once he's drunk, he can dance and sing, living the free and easy life of an immortal. Li Yidou, this curious fellow, I wonder what he's like. I have to admit that the stories he sent me have transformed my own novel. I'd planned for Ding Gou'er to be a special agent with almost supernatural abilities, a man of brilliance and extraordinary talent; what he wound up being was a good-for-nothing drunk. I cannot continue the story of Ding Gou'er, and that is why I've come to Liquorland: for inspiration, to devise a better ending for my special investigator than drowning him in an open-air privy.

Mo Yan spotted Li Yidou, Doctor of Liquor Studies and amateur short-story writer, as he approached the exit, a conclusion he reached instinctively when he saw a tall, skinny man with a triangular face. He headed straight for the slightly menacing eyes.

The man stuck his long, bony hand over the railing and said, 'If I'm not mistaken, you must be Mo Yan.'

Mo Yan took the icy-cold hand in his and said, 'Sorry to put you to all this trouble, Li Yidou!'

The duty ticket-taker pressed Mo Yan to show her his ticket.

334

'Show his what?' Li Yidou all but shouted. 'Do you know who this is? He's Mo Yan, the man who wrote the movie *Red Sorghum*, that's who. He's an honored guest of our Municipal Party Committee and government, that's who!'

Momentarily taken aback, she stared wordlessly at Mo Yan, which he found embarrassing. He quickly produced his ticket, but Li Yidou dragged him past the railing. 'Don't mind her,' he said.

Li Yidou took Mo Yan's bag and threw it over his own shoulder. He must have been at least five-feet-ten, a head taller than Mo Yan, who took some comfort in noting that Li Yidou was at least fifty pounds lighter than he.

'Sir,' Li Yidou said spiritedly, 'as soon as I received your letter, I passed the good news to Municipal Party Committee Secretary Hu, who said, "Welcome, welcome, a hearty welcome." I was here once already – last night – with a car.'

'But I made it clear in my letter that I'd arrive in the early morning of the 29th.'

'I was afraid that if you arrived ahead of schedule,' Li Yidou replied, 'you'd be all alone in a strange city. I preferred making an extra trip to having you wait for me all that time.'

'I really have put you to a lot of trouble,' Mo Yan said with a smile.

'At first the municipal authorities wanted Deputy Head Diamond Jin to meet you, but I said I'm Mo Yan's close friend, and since he and I don't have to stand on ceremony, I'm the best person for the job.'

We walked toward a fancy sedan parked in a square illuminated by a ring of streetlights. The rain made the sedan look even fancier than it was. 'General Manager Yu is waiting in the car,' Li Yidou said. 'The car belongs to his tavern.'

'Which General Manager Yu would that be?'

'Yu Yichi, of course!'

Mo Yan tensed, as a host of depictions of Yu Yichi slogged through his mind. If things had reached the point where the dwarf, who was unrelated to the investigator, could still wind up dead of a bullet in the investigator's dream, then ghosts and goblins were running the show. I might as well use my *Tales of Investigator Ding Gou'er* as kindling for the oven, he mused.

'General Manager Yu Yichi insisted on coming,' Li Yidou commented. 'He wanted the pleasure of being first on the scene for your arrival. He knows what it means to be a real pal. Sir, don't – please don't – judge him solely by his appearance. If you give him one measure of respect, he'll repay you a hundred times over.'

The words still hung in the air when the car door opened and out jumped a pocket-sized man less than three feet tall ('twelve-inch' [Yichi] was an exaggeration of his smallness). Small but sturdy, he was neatly dressed, looking very much like a well-bred member of the gentry.

'Mo Yan, you little scamp, so you finally made it!' he shouted with an infectious hoarseness as soon as he was out of the car. He ran up to Mo Yan, grabbed his hand, and shook it hard, as if they were old friends who hadn't seen each other for years.

As Mo Yan grasped the tense, nervous hand, he couldn't suppress feelings of remorse over thoughts of how Ding Gou'er had killed this man. Why had it been necessary for him to die? An intriguing little fellow like this, cute as a little wind-up mechanical toy, so what if he'd made love with the lady trucker? He shouldn't have died; he and Ding Gou'er should have become friends, and together they could have broken the case of the child-eaters.

Yu Yichi opened the car door for Mo Yan. Once he'd climbed in next to his guest, he said, releasing a mouthful of boozy breath, 'The doctor talks about you every day. I tell you, this guy worships you. But now that I see you face-to-face, you're not as handsome as he made you out to be. In fact, you look like a run-of-the-mill purveyor of cheap booze.'

Stung by the criticism, Mo Yan replied with noticeable sarcasm, 'Which is why General Manager Yu and I might someday become good friends.'

Yu Yichi giggled like a little boy. 'That's terrific!' he said after the giggles passed. 'A man whose face would stop a clock and a dwarf, friends at last. Let's go, driver!'

The woman behind the wheel, who was not a dwarf, sat silently. Aided by murky light from the square, Mo Yan noticed that she had a pretty face and a lovely long neck.

The car's headlights snapped on and the woman drove skillfully out of the square, spraying water behind her. The smell of opulence hung in the interior. A fuzzy toy tiger on the dashboard jiggled and danced. The music was dreamy; the car seemed to sway to the music like drifting on water. Not even a stray cat appeared on the broad, smoothly paved avenue. Liquorland seemed to be a large city. New-style buildings lined the avenue; the Doctor of Liquor Studies wasn't exaggerating when he called Liquorland a bustling metropolis.

Mo Yan followed Yu Yichi into the Yichi Tavern, with Li Yidou, the travel bag still over his shoulder, right on his heels. The inside of the tavern looked as inviting as he'd expected, with its marble floor waxed to a high sheen. A bespectacled woman sat behind the registration desk; she was not a dwarf. Yu Yichi told her to put their guest in room 310. Keys in hand, she led the party to the elevator and pushed the button before anyone else could get to it. When the elevator door opened, Yu Yichi jumped in and pulled Mo Yan in after him. Mo Yan tried to appear reluctant. Li Yidou stepped in next, followed by the bespectacled woman, after which the door closed. As the elevator climbed to the third floor, an ugly, exhausted face was reflected in the metallic facing. Mo Yan found it hard to believe he could be so mean-looking. In a few short years, he discovered, he had aged considerably. Seeing the reflection of the sleepy-eyed bespectacled young woman beside him, he quickly turned to stare at the numbers on the elevator panel. He was thinking . . . The exhausted investigator was face to face with his romantic rival Yu Yichi in the narrow confines of an elevator. When enemies meet, eyes glow with the fires of jealousy . . . I, on the other hand, am concentrating on the patch of fair skin poking out from under the bespectacled young woman's collar, thoughts of what lay below releasing fantasies that streak across the sky like a heavenly stallion, and that bring memories of the past flooding into my mind. Once, when I was fourteen, I let my hand stray to a girl's breast. With a giggle she said, So you know all about touching those, even at your age, hm? Want to see what they look like? Yes, I replied. OK, she said. I felt cold all over. And so that great purple door to puberty swung open with a roar as the girl began undoing her blouse. I rushed through that door without a thought for the consequences, leaving my youth, a time of running with the animals and raising birds, behind, once and for all . . . The elevator noiselessly came to a stop and the door opened. The bespectacled young woman led us to room 310, opened the door and stood aside to let us in. Mo Yan, who had never enjoyed such top-of-the-line accommodations, nonetheless strode grandly into the luxurious suite and sat on the sofa.

'This is our finest room, I hope you can make do,' Yu Yichi said.

'It's fine,' Mo Yan said. 'As a one-time soldier, I can live almost anywhere.'

'The authorities were going to put you up in the Municipal Party Committee guest house,' Li Yidou said, 'but all the better rooms there have been reserved for honored foreign guests and compatriots from Hong Kong, Macao, and Taiwan who have come for our first annual Ape Liquor Festival.'

'This is better,' Mo Yan assured him. 'I stay clear of officials as much as possible.'

'Mo Yan avoids the limelight, preferring peace and quiet,' Li Yidou remarked.

With a knowing laugh, Yu Yichi said, 'Can a man who wrote *Red Sorghum* really avoid the limelight and opt for peace and quiet? You've only been working at the Department of Propaganda two days, and already you're a veteran ass-kisser.'

An embarrassed Li Yidou said, 'Don't take General Manager Yu's comments to heart, Mo Yan. His caustic tongue is famous here in Liquorland.'

'Not to worry,' Mo Yan replied, 'I can be pretty caustic myself.'

'I forgot to mention, Sir, that I was transferred to the Municipal Party Committee's Department of Propaganda,' Li Yidou said. 'My job is to prepare public announcements.'

'What about your dissertation?' Mo Yan asked. 'Is it finished?'

'That can wait. I'm better suited to this kind of work. News releases are closer to creative work.'

'Sounds OK to me,' Mo Yan said.

'Draw a hot bath for our guest, Miss Ma,' Yu Yichi said. 'Let him wash that sweaty, smelly body of his.'

With a terse acknowledgment, the bespectacled young woman went into the bathroom, from which the sound of running water soon emerged.

Yu Yichi opened the doors of the liquor cabinet, in which dozens of bottled liquors were displayed. 'What'll you have?' he asked Mo Yan.

'None for me, not at this early hour,' Mo Yan replied. 'I'll wait.'

'What do you mean, wait?' Yu Yichi asked. 'Having a drink is a visitor's first responsibility after arriving in Liquorland.'

'I'd prefer a cup of tea.'

'You won't find any tea in Liquorland,' Yu Yichi replied. 'Liquor is our tea.'

'When in Rome, Sir,' Li Yidou urged Mo Yan.

'Well, all right.'

'Come here and choose your poison,' Yu Yichi said.

The array of bottles filled with the finest liquor available nearly made Mo Yan's head swim.

'They tell me you're a class-A drunk,' Yu Yichi commented. 'Is that right?'

'To tell the truth, I'm not that good at holding my liquor, and my knowledge of the subject is severely limited.'

'Modesty does not become you,' Yu Yichi said. 'Besides, I've read all the letters you wrote to Li Yidou.'

Mo Yan flashed an unhappy look at Li Yidou, who rushed to his own defense: 'General Manager Yu is one of us. There's nothing to worry about.'

Yu Yichi took out a bottle of Overlapping Green Ants and said, 'After a night on the train, you'd better try something on the mild side.'

'Overlapping Green Ants is an excellent choice,' Li Yidou said agreeably. 'One of my father-in-law's creations. It's distilled from sorghum and mung beans. To that is added a dozen or more rare, aromatic medicinal herbs. Drinking it is akin to listening to a classical beauty play a zither, a magically conceived rendition that has you pondering things from the remote past.'

'Enough already,' Yu Yichi cut in. 'You and your quack sales methods.'

'Now you know why I was transferred to the Department of Propaganda. Publicity is what we need for our Ape Liquor Festival, and I am, after all, a Doctor of Liquor Studies.'

'Doctoral *candidate*,' Yu Yichi said mockingly.

Yu Yichi took three crystal glasses out of the liquor cabinet and filled them to the brim with a disturbingly green liquor.

Before coming to Liquorland, Mo Yan had read up on the topic of liquor, and knew a thing or two about the rules of tasting. Raising his glass, he touched it with the tip of his nose and sniffed it; then, with his hand, he fanned the aroma that clung to the skin. After that he held the glass directly under his nose and inhaled deeply, then held his breath, closed his eyes, and assumed the look of a man deep in thought. After a while, he opened his eyes and said, 'Not bad, you were right. It has the smell and taste of antiquity, refined and solemn. Not bad at all.'

'Well, I'll be,' Yu Yichi said. 'You do know a thing or two, after all.'

'Mo Yan is a natural-born connoisseur of fine liquor,' Li Yidou chirped.

Mo Yan smiled somewhat smugly.

The bespectacled girl returned just then. 'The bath is ready, General Manager,' she reported.

'Bottoms up,' Yu Yichi said, clinking Mo Yan's glass with his own. 'Take a bath and get some rest. You can sleep for a couple of hours, since breakfast isn't served until seven o'clock. I'll send one of the girls to wake you.'

After tossing down the liquor in his glass, he tapped Li Yidou on the knee and said, 'Time to leave, Doctor.'

'You two can sleep here,' Mo Yan said. 'We can squeeze three into a bed.'

With a wink, Yu Yichi said, 'Rules of the house don't permit men to share a room.'

Li Yidou was about to add his opinion when Yu Yichi gave him a shove. 'I said, let's go!'

Now, finally, I was able to shed my Mo Yan shell. I yawned, spat into the spittoon, and took off my shoes and socks. There was a soft knock at the door. Hurriedly pulling up my trousers, which were down around my knees, and straightening my shirt, I went to open the door. The bespectacled Miss Ma darted past me.

She was smiling broadly, and no longer sleepy-eyed. 'What can I do for you?' Mo Yan asked decorously, his adrenalin rising.

'General Manager Yu sent me up to pour some Overlapping Green Ants into your bathwater,' Miss Ma replied.

'Liquor in my bath water?'

'It's the brainchild of General Manager Yu,' Miss Ma explained. 'He claims that bathing in liquor has positive health benefits. Alcohol kills germs, relaxes the muscles, and stimulates the flow of blood.'

'No wonder the place is called Liquorland.'

Miss Ma picked up the uncorked bottle of liquor and carried it into the bathroom, with Mo Yan close on her heels. The room was still steamy, tendrils of whiteness lending it an air of romance. Miss Ma emptied the bottle into the bathtub, releasing a heavy, rather stimulating cloud of aroma – alcohol, of course.

'There you go, Mo Yan, Sir. Jump in.'

She smiled as she walked out, and Mo Yan detected a vague sense of romance in that smile. His emotions stirred, he nearly reached out to put his arm around her and plant a kiss on her ruddy cheek. But he clenched his teeth to keep his emotions in check and saw Miss Ma out.

After she had left the bathroom, Mo Yan stood for a moment before undressing. The room had a warm, springlike atmosphere. Once he was naked, he rubbed his protruding belly and took a look at himself in the mirror. It was not an encouraging sight. He congratulated himself for not making a huge mistake a moment earlier.

He felt the scalding water and biting alcohol sting as he stepped into the tub and slowly eased his body down until only his head showed, pillowed against the smooth rim. The liquor-enhanced bathwater, with its gentle green cast, prickled his skin, painfully, in a comfortable sort of way. 'That damned dwarf,' he cursed contentedly, 'he sure knows how to live the good life!' In a matter of minutes, the pain was gone. He could feel blood coursing through his veins faster than at any time in his life; his joints felt oiled and soft. A few minutes later, perspiration coated his forehead. His body was relaxed as only a heavy sweat can make it. It's been years since I last sweated, he was thinking. My pores are all stopped up . . . I should let Ding Gou'er soak in a tub with Overlapping Green Ants, then have a young woman walk in on him. That's the sort of detail a thriller needs . . .

His bath finished, Mo Yan stepped out of the tub, threw a robe that smelled of sweet grass over his shoulders, and stretched out lazily on the sofa. Feeling a little thirsty, he took a bottle of white wine from the liquor cabinet and was about to uncork it when Miss Ma walked back into the room, this time without knocking. Tensing at her arrival, Mo Yan hurriedly tied the sash around his waist to cover his legs. Actually, tensing is not the right word; what he felt was much more pleasurable than that.

Miss Ma took the bottle from him, opened it, and poured a glassful of wine. 'Mo Yan, Sir,' she said, 'General Manager Yu sent me up to give you a massage.'

Dots of perspiration reappeared on Mo Yan's face as he stammered, 'There's no need for that, the sun's almost up.'

'Please don't refuse me, General Manager Yu sent me up to do it.'

So Mo Yan lay down on the bed and let Miss Ma give him a massage, all the while concentrating on the image of a pair of icy handcuffs, in order to keep from doing something he shouldn't.

Yu Yichi grinned all through breakfast, causing Mo Yan no end of embarrassment. He knew that anything he said would be superfluous, and that his silence spoke volumes.

Li Yidou ran breathlessly up to the table. Seeing the bags under his eyes and the drawn look on his face, Mo Yan asked sympathetically, 'Didn't you get any sleep?'

'The provincial newspaper was pressing me for a story, so I went back to the office to finish it.'

Mo Yan filled a glass with liquor and handed it to him.

'Mo Yan, Sir,' he said after downing the liquor, 'Party Secretary Hu wants you to tour the city this morning, then join him for lunch.'

'There's no need for that,' Mo Yan said. 'The Party Secretary's a busy man.'

'But you must,' Li Yidou insisted. 'You're an honored guest. Besides, Liquorland is going to rely on your heroic pen to become famous!'

'*My* heroic pen?'

'My dear Mo Yan, eat your breakfast,' Yu Yichi said.

'Yes, Mo Yan, Sir,' Li Yidou agreed, 'please eat.'

So Mo Yan scooted his chair up to the table and laid his elbows and wrists on the snowy white tablecloth. Sunlight pouring in through the tall windows brightened every corner of the small dining room. Soft strains of jazz floated down from the ceiling, as if from far, far away. Muted notes from a trumpet touched the soul. He was thinking of the massage and of the bespectacled Miss Ma.

Breakfast consisted of six modest dishes, an appealing array of greens and reds. They were accompanied by milk, fried eggs, toast, jam, steamed rolls, rice porridge, salted duck eggs, fried fermented bean curd, sesame cakes, little dough twists . . . more choices than he could count. A combination of Chinese and western food.

'A steamed roll and a bowl of porridge is enough for me,' Mo Yan said.

'Eat up,' Yu Yichi said insistently. 'There's no need to be polite, Liquorland has plenty of food.'

'How about liquor?' Li Yidou asked him. 'What would you like?'

'On an empty stomach? Nothing, thanks.'

Yu Yichi said, 'Have a glass, just one. It's the custom.'

'Mo Yan has a touchy stomach,' Li Yidou said. 'A glass of ginger spirits will warm it.'

'Miss Yang,' Yu Yichi shouted, 'come pour for us.'

A waitress appeared, one even lovelier than Miss Ma. She all but took Mo Yan's breath away. 'My dear Mo Yan,' Yu Yichi said, nudging him with his elbow, 'what do you think of the girls of Yichi Tavern?'

'They're like moon goddesses,' he replied.

'Lovely liquor isn't all Liquorland is famous for. Our women are just as lovely,' Li Yidou crowed. 'The mothers of Xi Shi and Wang Zhaojun were both from Liquorland.'

Yu Yichi and Mo Yan laughed.

'Don't laugh,' Li Yidou protested. 'I've got proof.'

'Stop the nonsense,' Yu Yichi said. 'If it's tall tales you want, ask Mo Yan, he's the master.'

Li Yidou laughed. 'You're right. I'm wielding an ax at the door of the greatest ax-man of all.'

They finished breakfast amid more chatter and laughter. Miss Yang walked up and handed Mo Yan a hot, perfumed hand towel, with which he wiped his face and hands. He couldn't recall ever having such a sense of well-being. When he rubbed his cheeks, the skin was soft and silky. He felt absolutely wonderful and relaxed.

'Proprietor Yu,' Li Yidou said, 'we're relying on you for a fine lunch today.'

'I need *you* to tell me that? I wouldn't dare offer anything but the best to Mo Yan, our honored guest from afar.'

'I've ordered a car, Mo Yan, Sir,' Li Yidou said. 'We can walk if you're up to it. If not, we can ride.'

'Have the driver go on about his business,' Mo Yan said. 'We'll just stroll where our feet take us.'

'Fine with me,' Li Yidou said.

III

Mo Yan and Li Yidou are walking down Donkey Avenue.

Donkey Avenue is in fact paved with ancient cobblestones, which have been washed clean by an overnight rainfall. A crisp, chilled, acrid smell rises from the cracks between stones, reminding Mo Yan of one of Li Yidou's stories. 'Is there really a ghostly black donkey that haunts this street?'

'That's a legend,' Li Yidou says. 'No one has actually seen it.'

'There must be countless donkey ghosts that wander this street,' Mo Yan says.

'That's a fact. The street's history goes back at least two hundred years, and the number of donkeys that have been slaughtered here is incalculable.'

'How many a day?' Mo Yan asks.

'Twenty, at least,' Li Yidou replies.

'How could there be so many donkeys?'

'Would anyone open a slaughterhouse if there were no donkeys to slaughter?' Li Yidou assures him.

'Are there enough customers?'

'Sometimes they go away empty-handed.'

While they're discussing the situation, a man dressed like a peasant walks up with two fat black donkeys. Mo Yan goes up to him. 'Say, old villager, you selling those?'

The man gives Mo Yan a cold stare without answering, then continues on his way. 'Want to watch them slaughter a donkey?' Li Yidou asks.

'Yes,' Mo Yan replies. 'Of course I do.'

So they turn back and fall in behind the man leading the donkeys down the street. When they reach the Sun Family Butcher Shop, the man shouts, 'Here are the donkeys, Boss.'

A bald middle-aged man comes rushing out of the shop. 'What took you so long, Old Jin?'

'I got hung up at the ferry landing,' Old Jin tells him.

Baldy opens a gate next to the shop. 'Bring them on in,' he says.

'Hey there, Old Sun,' Li Yidou steps up and greets the man.

'My my,' a surprised Baldy says. 'A little early for a stroll, isn't it, old friend?'

Li Yidou points to Mo Yan. 'This is an important writer from Beijing,' he says. 'Mo Yan, the fellow who wrote the movie *Red Sorghum*.'

'Don't get carried away, Yidou,' Mo Yan says.

'Red Sorghum?' Baldy says, looking at Mo Yan. 'Isn't that the stuff they use to make good liquor?'

'Mo Yan would like to see how you slaughter a donkey.'

Baldy, uncomfortable with the idea, stammers, 'I . . . um . . . there's blood flying everywhere, you don't want all that bad luck settling over you . . .'

'No stalling,' Li Yidou says. 'Mo Yan is a guest of Secretary Hu of the Municipal Party Committee. He's going to do some publicity for Liquorland.'

'Oh!' Baldy says. 'He's a *reporter*. Come on, come see for yourself. This little shop of mine can use the publicity.'

Mo Yan and Li Yidou follow the black donkeys out to the back, where Baldy circles the animals to look them over. The donkeys, apparently afraid, shy away from him.

'For donkeys, this guy is the butcher from Hell,' Li Yidou comments.

'I've seen better, Old Jin,' Baldy says finally.

'Tender meat, shiny black coats, fattened up on bean cakes. What else do you want?'

'You want to know?' Baldy says. 'These donkeys have been fed hormones. They won't taste good!'

'Where the hell am I going to get my hands on hormones?' Old Jin says. 'Give it to me straight, do you want them or don't you? If not, I'll take them away. You're not the only butcher shop on this street!'

'Calm down, my friend,' Baldy says. 'We've known each other for years, and even if you brought me a pair of donkeys made of cardboard, I'd buy them and burn them in offering to the Kitchen God.'

Old Jin sticks out his hand. 'How much?'

Baldy reaches out to clasp the other man's hand, both concealed by their sleeves.

'That's how it's done around here,' Li Yidou whispers to an obviously puzzled Mo Yan. 'The price for livestock is always given by the number of fingers.'

The expressions on the faces of Baldy and the man selling the donkeys speak volumes. They look like actors in a mime drama.

Mo Yan's imagination is piqued by the expressions on their faces.

Baldy's arm twitches. 'That's my final offer,' he says. 'I can't go any higher, not a penny!'

The arm of the man selling the donkey also twitches. 'I want this much!'

Baldy pulls his hand back. 'I told you,' he says, 'I can't go any higher. Take it or take your donkeys away!'

The other man sighs. 'Baldy Sun,' he says loudly, 'Baldy Sun, you son of a bitch, you can go straight to Hell, where all the donkeys will chew you up and spit you out!'

'They'll chew you up first, you damned donkey peddler!' Baldy fires back.

The man unties the ropes. The deal is made.

'Mother of our little daughter, give Old Jin here a bowl of the hard stuff.'

A grease-spattered middle-aged woman emerges with a large white bowl filled with liquor and hands it to Old Jin.

346

Old Jin takes the bowl but doesn't drink. Instead he looks at the woman and says, 'Sister-in-law, I've brought you a couple of black males today. Two big donkey dicks should be enough for you to gnaw on for a while.'

With spittle flying, the woman says, 'I'll never get my hands on one of those trinkets, no matter how many there are. But your old lady ought to be content with the one she has at home.'

With a loud guffaw, Old Jin gulps down the liquor and hands her the bowl. Then, after tying the ropes around his waist, he says loudly, 'I'll be back later for the money, Baldy.'

'Go on about your business,' Baldy replies. 'But don't forget to buy a "meaty offering" to pay your respects to the Widow Cui.'

'She's already got someone,' Old Jin says, 'so I won't have the good fortune to pay my respects anymore.' With that, he strides through the shop, past the counter, and out onto Donkey Avenue.

By this time Baldy has his mallet in hand and is ready to begin the slaughter. Turning to Li Yidou, he says, 'You and the reporter stand over there, old friend. You don't want to ruin your clothes.'

Mo Yan notices that the two donkeys are meekly huddling together in a corner, neither trying to run away nor braying unhappily. They are, however, trembling.

'No matter how feisty a donkey might be,' Li Yidou comments, 'when it sees him, all it can do is tremble.'

Baldy walks up behind one of the donkeys, raises the blood-spattered mallet in his hand, and brings it down hard in the space between the animal's leg and its hoof. The donkey's hindquarters crash to the ground. The next blow lands on the donkey's forehead, laying the animal out flat, its legs spread out in front like wooden clubs. Instead of trying to run away, the other donkey presses its head hard against the wall, as if trying to push all the way through.

Baldy then drags a basin over and places it under the collapsed donkey's neck, picks up his butcher knife, and severs the animal's carotid artery, sending a torrent of purplish blood into the basin . . .

After witnessing the donkey slaughter, Mo Yan and Li Yidou are back out on Donkey Avenue. 'That was damned cruel,' Mo Yan says.

'A lot more humane than the old days,' Li Yidou says.

'What was it like then?'

'Back in the last years of the Qing dynasty, there was a butcher shop here on Donkey Avenue known for its delicious donkey meat. Here's the way they did it: They dug a hole in the ground and covered it with thick boards with holes drilled in the four corners for the donkey's legs. That way it couldn't put up a fight. Then they drenched the donkey with scalding water and scraped every inch of the hide. The customers would choose the part they felt like eating, and the butcher would cut it out for them then and there. Sometimes all the meat would be sold off, and you could still hear the animal's pitiful wheezing. Would you call that cruel?'

'You bet I would,' Mo Yan says, clicking his tongue.

'The Xue Family Butcher Shop reintroduced this method not long ago, and did a land-office business until the city fathers put a stop to it.'

'Good for them!'

'If you want the truth,' Li Yidou says, 'the meat wasn't very good at all.'

'Your mother-in-law says that the quality of meat is affected by the fear an animal feels just before it's killed. That was in one of your stories.'

'You've got a good memory.'

'I've eaten braised live fish,' Mo Yan says. 'Even when its body is steaming under that gravy, its mouth keeps opening and closing, like it's trying to say something.'

'There's no paucity of examples of cruel eating practices,' Li Yidou says. 'My mother-in-law is an expert in that area.'

'Are there many differences between the parents-in-law in your stories and your real-life in-laws?'

'Night and day,' Li Yidou says, blushing.

'I admire your nerve,' Mo Yan says. 'If your stories actually get published one day, your wife and your father-in-law will have you braised, that's for sure.'

'I wouldn't mind. They could even steam or deep-fry me, as long as the stories got published.'

'I don't think it'd be worth it.'

'I do.'

'Let's talk about it some more tonight,' Mo Yan says. 'You're

OK in my book. There's no doubt that you're more talented than
I am.'

'You flatter me, Sir.'

IV

The luncheon is held at the Yichi Tavern.

Mo Yan occupies the seat of honor, Secretary Hu is the host.
Seven or eight other people are seated around the table, all city
fathers. Yu Yichi and Li Yidou fill out the guest list. With all his
experience, Yu Yichi cuts a dashing figure. Li Yidou, on the other
hand, is very uncomfortable, and doesn't know what to do with
himself.

Secretary Hu, who looks to be in his mid-thirties, has a square
face, big eyes, hair combed straight back, and an oily, shiny face;
poised and dignified, and extremely well spoken, he wears his
authority like a cloak.

After three rounds of toasts, Secretary Hu stands up, saying he's
expected at several more luncheons, and leaves. Deputy Head Jin
of the Propaganda Department picks up the decanter to host the
next round. A half-hour later, Mo Yan's head is spinning, his lips
like pieces of wood.

'Deputy Head Jin,' Mo Yan declares, 'I never thought you'd
turn out to be such a fine individual . . . I figured you to be a . . .
child-eating demon . . .'

Mo Yan does not notice the beads of cold sweat that suddenly
appears on Li Yidou's face.

'Our Deputy Head is an accomplished musician – he plays a
number of instruments and sings as well,' one of the dignitaries
says. 'You should hear him sing the part of the legendary Magistrate
Bao. His stentorian voice is as good as the great Qiu Shengxu!'

'Let's hear some, Deputy Head Jin,' Mo Yan proposes.

'If you don't mind my making a fool of myself,' Deputy Head
Jin says.

He gets to his feet, clears his throat, and, in a thunderous voice
with a series of crescendos and diminuendos, sings a long aria

without turning red in the face or gasping for air. When it is over, he clasps his hands and announces, 'Please don't laugh!'

Mo Yan shouts his appreciation.

'May I be permitted a question, Mo Yan, Sir?' Deputy Head Jin asks. 'What's the reason for pissing into the liquor vat?'

His face reddening, Mo Yan replies, 'The rantings of a novelist. Don't take them seriously.'

Deputy Head Jin says, 'I'll drink three glasses if Mo Yan will sing a bit of "Little Sister Strides Boldly Forward."'

'I'm not much of a drinker,' Mo Yan demurs, 'and a very bad singer.'

'A son of Han, a man among men, never drinks without a song. Come come come, I'll drink first.'

Deputy Head Jin lines up three glasses and fills them. Then he bends his head down and takes a deep breath; when he raises his head, he is holding all three glasses in his mouth. He tips his head back until the glasses are bottoms up, then lowers his head once more, placing the glasses exactly where they were.

'Bravo!' one of the guests shouts. 'Plum Blossoms Playing Thrice!'

'Mo Yan, Sir, that's Deputy Head Jin's *pièce de résistance*,' Li Yidou explains.

'It's superb!' Mo Yan says.

'Your turn, Mo Yan, Sir,' Deputy Head Jin says.

Three glasses are lined up in front of Mo Yan and filled to the brim.

'Don't expect any Plum Blossoms Playing Thrice from me,' Mo Yan says.

'One glass at a time, that's all we ask,' Deputy Head Jin says generously. 'We're not out to embarrass you.'

With three more glasses down the hatch, Mo Yan's head is really spinning.

The other guests are urging him to sing.

Mo Yan realizes that his mouth will no longer do his bidding, now that his lips and tongue are out of sync.

'Writer Mo Yan,' Deputy Head Jin says, 'if you'll sing something, anything, I'll drink the "submarine" for you.'

So Mo Yan sings for them, a ghastly sound, as it turns out.

Still everyone shouts his approval.

'All right,' Deputy Head Jin says, 'now I'll drink the "submarine."'

He pours a glass of beer, then a glass of hard liquor, which he lets sink in the taller glass. Picking up the beer glass, he tips his head back and drinks them both together, every last drop.

Just then a woman enters the dining room, laughing loudly – Ha ha. 'Where's the writer?' she asks loudly. 'I'd like to toast him with three glasses.'

Li Yidou leans over to Mo Yan. 'Mayor Wang,' he whispers. 'No one holds her liquor like she does.'

Mo Yan gazes at the Mayor as she approaches: large, square face, fair and delicate, bedroom eyes, moist as an autumn shower, elegantly dressed, looking like a stately woman of ancient times.

Intending to stand up, instead he slides indecorously under the table.

V

. . . Mo Yan Sir Mo Yan Sir what's wrong please wake up This guy wrote *Red Sorghum* but he's a fledgling with alcohol can't hold his liquor but comes to Liquorland to stir up trouble take him to the hospital bring a car over first give him some carp broth to sober him up carp promotes lactation don't tell me he just had a baby a meat boy set it in a big gilded platter with nice leafy celery and big mouth-watering cherries from the US golden juices nice and sticky like honey that doesn't drip get on the phone and have the municipal hospital send an ambulance if something happens to him we'll be in hot water the ambulance lights red as blood like the eyes of a wolf are getting closer this is a big case an important case an unsettled case lawyers and journalists will stand shoulder to shoulder Ding Gou'er Ding Gou'er you disappointing son of a bitch A shortage of grain beat back the Rightist Reversal Movement oppose Bourgeois Liberalization lots and lots of three-legged red-backed frogs showing up in ponds the first human sperm bank Kurosawa's new movie *Akira Kurosawa's Dreams* peach blossoms everywhere demonic ghosts howling Mount Fuji on fire thawing melting dripping like a piece of meat taken out of the fridge and exposed to the sun the flavor of the nineties absolutely delicious sonic waves beeping in an oven I asked Third Uncle Where's Third Aunt Third Uncle said nonchalantly I braised and ate her the views of a Rightist *Pow* countless white shards of mercury explode leaving only an empty shell First memories of the Great Leap Forward how can people eat people why can't people eat people Yi Ya cooked his son and offered him to Duke Huan of Qi and Liu Bei ate the wife of a hunter and Black Whirlwind Li Kui ate the leg of the highwayman Li Gui roasting it first Lu Xun opened the *Diary of a Madman* and found the words Eat People written all over the ancient ledgers First Elder Brother was eaten Second Elder Sister was eaten little boys were eaten too *Exposés of the Corrupt Official World* a novel exposing dark secrets A real loser give him a shot an IV injection with medicine to protect the liver The Eight Immortals of Liquor a big gulp if the feelings are deep a little sip if the feelings are shallow This novel must arouse passion avoid sarcasm and satire the cadres have to be portrayed as real people not caricatures intended as serious literature not schemes and intrigues Lin Biao's broken spear sank into the sand was a missile involved When Mao's Sixteen Points were promulgated I shouted myself hoarse I saw the whiteness of Nuan's breasts couldn't help myself I said Let me have a look just one look it was terrifying Ponies and lambs whinny and bleat rams' bellies are wrapped with cloth to prevent mating birth control China's knotty problem and major contradiction the engineers of human souls cannot avoid it She was the best chef of her generation she heard the agonizing chirps of swallows when she prepared the swallows' nests Li Yidou you're an ass-kisser yourself you led my novel down the wrong path Fan Xiaotian the editor of *Zhongshan* treated me to stuffed buns at the Vegetarian Gourmet and bought me some beer When I was having a drink with Yu Hua he said Ding Gou'er you stop right there I can't believe you're so worthless your hands are covered with the blood of the masses I love you I didn't know I was so deeply in love until I was drunk There's no escape a rope dragging a long long tail At that time I was walking in the field the earth was frozen covered with snow wild rabbits frozen to death hedgehogs too

Liquorland is a fictional place but also a synthesis of many real cities Ding Gou'er is an abominable person who tries to be dashing and refined but cannot All liquors are about the same they make you slobbering drunk Luan Ping investigated the hero Yang Zirong I racked my brain in order to serve in the military For many years the struggle between sex and morality has been a tangle causing much suffering split personality Faulkner learned from Joyce's *Ulysses* can't I also learn from you This is the only way it can be done originally this text was intended to explore the relationship between liquor and women liquor decreases a man's libido but increases a woman's this is the fundamental conflict between Li Yidou's father-in-law and mother-in-law Never tire of the refined in food always strive for delicacy in cooking running out of words and searching for expressions a reality in writing Where did the scaly youth run off to the Ape Liquor Festival is coming soon How to write this chapter it is so depressing the more I write the more impatient I become the woes of Dionysus The liquor was laced with pesticide a bastard of a doctor transfused a woman's blood from childbirth to someone else and caused Spiritual Pollution the more developed the technique of wine drinking the more elaborate the wine glasses become a trap within a trap the country cadre was a boorish uncivilized drinker who forced liquor down County Chief Song and caused his death the wife of the County Chief was my elementary school teacher the court threw out the case saying he deserved to die he shouldn't have drunk so much it was his own fault my teacher said Mo Yan you're well known write an article for the newspaper to report the incident expose the injustice for me officials always protect each other this case will never have its day in court besides he's dead anyway Ding Gou'er nearly died from being drunk vomited all over the place wah wah wah prohibition cannot be enforced Cao Cao tried to prohibit liquor Kong Rong a descendant of Confucius famous for the filial act of giving a larger pear to his older brother mocked Cao Cao by saying the Shang dynasty came to ruin because of a woman but we didn't see King Wen of the Zhou prohibit women Cao Cao was enraged and killed him Cao Cao ate plums and warmed a pot of liquor while talking about heroes Seeing the Mayor off to his new position in the provincial government banquets were held for forty days liquor flowed like rivers raging over the land like the Yangtze drinking is the road to glory the more one drinks the more glorious one becomes Let me tell you why I'm writing this novel I read in a short article where someone was promoted and became rich because of his capacity for liquor which inspired me page after page of drunken gibberish and nonsense froth filling the mouth the vomit made our puppy drunk it died the dog ate it Developing a child's capacity for liquor a man and a woman vie to see who is the bigger drinker they are clearly equals they fall in love they get married on their wedding night the woman says Ow it hurts did you fucking ejaculate liquor inside me you lousy hooligan The cadre's urine is also very pungent a high alcoholic content a baby was born he drank neither milk nor water only liquor and was called Liquor Boy startling the world of liquor great drinkers are worshiped. After a memorial held for a man who drank himself to death everyone got drunk with a sip of liquor comes a string of witty sayings but not for me my mind a raging sea and roaring river inundated with flashing fragments of words and phrases like shards of broken glass a potent sobering-up tonic lets you drink to your heart's content without getting drunk even after a thousand glasses the highest the finest the fairest state of happiness She saw emerald teardrops spill out of the boy's eyes and licked them off with her tongue they tasted like strong liquor a low-grade liquor is a woman whose hair is brittle and yellow whose black eyes are crossed whose head is squeezed flat whose teeth are big and yellow whose freckled face is covered with a thick layer of cheap powder yet still smiles coquettishly and flirtatiously at men why do you want to drink this kind of liquor you should drink fine liquor like a young Russian girl whose skin is smooth and silky overflowing with the natural flavor of wildflowers and grass Mo Yan Sir Mo Yan Sir how are you feeling dead yet The pink serving girl Little Sun has a fine layer of peach fuzz on her upper lip when I touch her she mysteriously looks at the door and waves her hands pregnant with meaning but a subtle smile on her face I say You're wonderful I wish we'd met before you married in exchange for her smile my lips brush her smooth forehead which feels like a gourd it reeks what a drunken cat what a drunken dog what a lush waving her hands to fan the air beneath her nose she turns and runs off followed by a loud bang from the spring door I run into the bathroom and scream at the toilet when I look up at the mirror with its peeling mercury I come face to face with the image of myself aging and ugly my disgusting image shames me how dare I fantasize touching a beautiful young girl Damn some will say I'm obviously imitating the style of *Ulysses* in this section Who cares I'm drunk when you get drunk you're out for three days Little Sun falsely reported that the writer from Beijing drank himself to death Mumbling something the Mayor came to visit you but you couldn't even open your eyes the table the corners of the room the bed littered with tin cans and fruit pears bananas oranges melons tomatoes and a bottle with a black-tailed snake coiled inside What do you feel like eating aren't you going to eat something the black-tailed snake squirms in my throat its sharp scales scrape the inside of my throat wah wah I vomit Li Yidou says from my experience you should drink some liquor the best cure for alcohol poisoning is two glasses of liquor what we call fighting poison with poison No more no more the mere mention of liquor makes me sick gives me a headache Li Yidou I've fallen into your evil trap he ignores my protest a sinister smile he fills a big glass with a pink and emerald green liquid Red-Maned Stallion like a sex-crazed wanton woman laughing hideously inside the glass teasing me horrifying me No no I've had enough Mother help me pinching my ears didn't help so he pinches my nose pries open my clenched teeth and forces the glass of Red-Maned Stallion down that organ of mine called a mouth like a baby with its mother's nipple in its mouth I gurgle but can't spit it out a burning flame licks down my corrupt throat and into my stinking stomach and dissolves I feel gutted by a knife my eyes are closed I want to stand up but can't find my legs where are my legs hanging from the ceiling swinging back and forth like hams from Jinhua hanging in a butcher shop look even more like prosthetic legs hanging from hooks in a specialty store for the disabled Punch the con man the evil-doer Li Yidou but my arms are gone too there's nothing left so much evil cannot go unpunished it's just a matter of time the day of atonement has arrived time for you to die like a phoenix bathing in the fire of self-immolation I'm soaking in an emerald green flame turning this way and that way I didn't think I'd drink myself to death in Liquorland didn't think I'd end up like Ding Gou'er Ding Gou'er is my shadow he has become skinny as a monkey with a game leg his body covered in shit and a drunk's vomit millions of fat white maggots crawling in his hair standing before me he looks me in the eye and gives me a knowing smile which makes me look to the ground where his shadow and mine overlap intertwined impossible to tell who's who He pulls out Ding Gou'er's handgun I recall there's one bullet left for an emergency Go ahead no need to hesitate he says as he whips out the shit-covered handgun with a long-tailed maggot crawling out of its barrel he releases the safety flicks the vomit out of the barrel spits out something like baby's hair he says I'm really going to shoot no more mister nice guy I'm going to fire it at the cannibalistic beasts at the Fascists don't flinch pull yourself up like a black donkey dick OK faster than it takes to tell he aims at our layered shadows on the ground and fires the last bullet a stinking smelly bullet exploding out of the barrel followed by the smell of rotten meat combined with the most terrifying stench in the world a puff of dripping wet green smoke We both feel our hearts pierced with unbearable pain we jump up like carp on dry land with all hope gone it seems our flesh was shot but what springs up from the ground are our shadows then we fall down face to face smiling like true brothers reunited after a long separation . . .